Z

A Crimson Frost

Center Point
Large Print

Also by Marcia Lynn McClure and available from Center Point Large Print:

Dusty Britches
Weathered Too Young
The Visions of Ransom Lake
The Heavenly Surrender
The Light of the Lovers' Moon
Beneath the Honeysuckle Vine
The Whispered Kiss
The Stone-Cold Heart of Valentine Brisco
The Highwayman of Tanglewood
A Cowboy for Christmas
A Bargained-For Bride

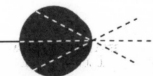

**This Large Print Book carries the
Seal of Approval of N.A.V.H.**

A
Crimson
Frost

Marcia Lynn McClure

CENTER POINT LARGE PRINT
THORNDIKE, MAINE

This Center Point Large Print edition
is published in the year 2019 by arrangement with
Distractions Ink.

The text of this Large Print edition is unabridged.
In other aspects, this book may vary
from the original edition.
Printed in the United States of America
on permanent paper.
Set in 16-point Times New Roman type.

ISBN: 978-1-64358-435-5

The Library of Congress has cataloged this record under
Library of Congress Control Number: 2019948905

To
Lord Alfred Tennyson,
Alfred Noyes,
and Brian Crain . . .
For gifting the world such resplendent and
unparalleled beauty!

To my husband, Kevin . . .
My heart's desire,
My every dream come true,
The love even *I* could never have imagined!

A Crimson Frost

An Inquiry of Favour

"And yet no knight has ever carried Monet's favour," Anais began, "not even in one of her own father's tournaments."

"Perhaps she simply does not fancy any knight in particular and, in owning no partiality, does not wish to proffer her favour," Portia spoke in defense of Monet.

Hidden behind one of the heavy tapestries hanging in the Hall of Ancestors at Ivar Castle, Monet smiled, grateful for at least one ally in Portia. She stood motionless—continued to eavesdrop on the conversation taking place in the room beyond the great hanging drapery.

"Every living creature owns a partiality where knights are concerned. Some simply offer no declaration," Anais said. "I hold no fear of declaring my partiality. Thus, my favour has been carried in many a grand tournament."

Though she could not see her face for the tapestry, Monet noted the thick vanity in Anais's voice. It was true: many a renowned knight had carried Anais's favour of color in tournaments past. Greatly sought after was the favour, and hand, of Anais of Alvar. It seemed a familiar length of lavender silk or satin—her preferred color of ribbon, veil, or ornament—adorned some strong arm at each tournament—ever the arm of a celebrated or distinguished knight of a king's round table.

However, Monet's favour, a scarlet veil or length of silk worn as embellishment to her gowns, had never known the joust—never ridden into battle— for she did not hold favours with lighthearted dalliance the way Anais of Alvar did. Thus, Monet had never lent her scarlet favour to any knight, nor had she requested any knight carry it.

Nevertheless, on this day, the whispered gossip of the young royals beyond the tapestry vexed her exceedingly. She knew the speculation concerning her father and his kingdom—the hushed inferences regarding his only daughter and only heir. Many were they in whose opinion the widower King Dacian—reigning monarch of the Kingdom of Karvana—should again take a wife in attempt to produce a male heir. Many were they who worried King Dacian's daughter, Monet, would not prove a strong enough monarch to hold at bay King James of the neighboring King-dom of Rothbain. James was Dacian's distant cousin, and it was truth James coveted Karvana to near madness. Many were they who whis-pered Monet—as one day queen—could not stay Karvana from falling to James.

Moreover—and further vexing to Monet—was the gossip concerning her troth. King Dacian refused to proclaim her intended—even to Monet herself. Her marriage would be arranged, there was no doubt. Still, Dacian would not name the man to whom he intended to wed his daughter—the man who would one day rule beside her. This caused a great unrest in Dacian's kingdom and to other kingdoms whose rulers sensed James of Rothbain's thirst for conquering—fearing one weak kingdom would find theirs also vulnerable.

"And who has asked to carry your favour in King Ivan's tournament, Anais?" It was Lenore's voice questioning now. "Who will you choose to bear it tomorrow?"

"Oh, many have begged a token of me . . . I assure you that," Anais answered. Monet's teeth clenched as Anais giggled with triumph. "Nevertheless, I will not grant my favour to any of those brave knights who have thus far requested it."

"What?" went up the common exclamation among the young women beyond the tapestry.

"You are in jest . . . surely," Lenore offered.

"Nay," Anais said, giggling once again.

"Then your favour will not be represented in the tournament?" Portia inquired.

"Unquestionably it shall be!" There was a pause. In a lowered voice, Anais spoke, "For I intend to appeal to one knight in particular.

I intend to ask the Crimson Knight to bear my favour in tomorrow's tournament."

As Monet's hand covered her mouth, she was grateful for the harmonious gasps of the young women in the Hall of Ancestors—a chorus of quickly inhaled breaths, which masked her own. Thus, she was not found to be hiding.

"You cannot be in earnest, Anais!" Portia exclaimed. "The Crimson Knight? Sir Broderick Dougray? He has never borne any woman's favour in tournament or battle."

"Perhaps merely for the fact no woman has ever mustered the courage to request it of him," Anais said.

"He is King Dacian's first knight," Lenore began, "celebrated beyond any other knight in the five kingdoms!"

"Yes," Anais said. "And he shall bear my favour in the tournament tomorrow."

"What if he declines, Anais?" Portia asked.

"He will not," Anais answered, her vanity secure. "I assure you, Sir Broderick will bear my favour . . . and I have no doubt he will be crowned champion."

"If only I had been born with a thread of your daring countenance, Anais," Lenore sighed. "Then I might have the courage to beg Sir Broderick to bear my favour in some future tournament . . . for he is the handsomest of any knight living!"

"Oh, but you are not daring, Lenore," Anais sighed, feigning compassion. "Still, take heart . . . for there are many good knights who would be honored to carry your favour tomorrow. Sir Terrence, for example."

"He is near as old as my father, Anais!" Lenore exclaimed.

"He is a valiant man," Portia said, "and my father's first knight."

"I meant no offense, Portia," Lenore said, "only that I wish to have a younger knight carry my favour tomorrow."

"A younger knight might not have such a superior chance of besting the others," Portia offered. "Sir Terrence, with his experience and tried strength, is the only knight entered tomorrow who may well best them all . . . including Sir Broderick Dougray."

"If it is a champion you seek to bear your favour, Lenore," Anais began, "you may as well not lend your favour to any knight . . . for Sir Broderick will be champion. And he will bear a length of my lavender ribbon."

"Perhaps he will bear Monet's favour," Portia suggested.

Monet frowned and clenched her teeth tightly as she heard Anais's amused laughter echo through the room.

"Monet? Now who is in jest, Portia?" Anais asked.

"He is her father's first knight, Anais," Portia reminded. "Further, it would serve King Dacian well to have his first knight crowned champion tomorrow . . . and it would serve the people of Karvana."

"Serve King Dacian and Karvana it may . . . but if the Crimson Knight is named champion, it will be my favour he bears when he is presented," Anais said.

Monet placed one dainty hand to her bosom. Her heart was mad with pounding—mad with angst and apprehension! She could not endure to see her father's first knight carry Anais of Alvar's favour in the tournament. She could not! If Sir Broderick Dougray did win the tournament, the glory should be showered over King Dacian, not over Anais of Alvar—nor her father, King Rudolph. The Crimson Knight's triumph would be the triumph of Karvana as well—Karvana's strength displayed before all, including King James. Nothing must distract from King Dacian's first knight—from Karvana's first knight. A lavender favour at Sir Broderick's arm would distract, drawing attention to Alvar and its king—and away from Karvana and her king.

Monet closed her eyes and silently prayed Sir Broderick would refuse Anais's request to bear her lavender favour. There was more, of course—more to Monet's sudden sense of desperation, her loathing of the thought of Sir Broderick bearing

Anais's favour—more than merely her father's triumph and her kingdom's approval. Yet she would not whisper of it. She would endeavor even not to think of it—her jealousy—her own secreted partiality toward Sir Broderick Dougray. Shaking her head to dispel all thoughts other than those of her father and her kingdom, Monet held her breath and listened as the sound of hastening footsteps met her ears.

"When will you ask Sir Broderick, Anais?" Lenore asked.

"Eventide . . . after King Ivan's feast."

They were gone. Monet stepped from behind the tapestry into the now empty Hall of Ancestors. Her eyes were moist with emotion. Sir Broderick could not bear Anais's favour! She must find the courage to approach the Crimson Knight—the courage to ask him to refuse a princess, the daughter of one of the most powerful kings of the five kingdoms. She must!

The sun hung exactly overhead, round and bright as a golden coin resting against a swath of sky-blue silk. Monet pulled the hood of her cloak over her head as she made her way through the knight encampment. The black cloak well hid her gown and face. Nevertheless, she worried it was yet too fine a garment—that its black velvet sheen might lure attention. And Monet did not want to lure attention on such an errand.

Monet worried Sir Broderick would be away from his pavilion. Nevertheless, she would endeavor to find him—to ask for his loyalty to her father and Karvana. She already knew the profound depth of his loyalty to both. Yet she must be certain—and so she would solicit.

She saw it then—just ahead—the refuge of the Crimson Knight, the white pavilion with crimson flag unfurled atop its center. The crimson flag—its black dragon reared on hind legs, flaming eyes boring through her—threatened Monet with immediate intimidation. Monet paused, wary of being recognized, frightened of facing Sir Broderick Dougray. She clasped her hands together, attempting to steady their sudden trembling. She drew a calming breath, for she was Karvana's princess, and the royals of Karvana were known for their courage. Were they not?

The two front flaps of the pavilion were tied back, allowing Monet to see within. A lone man lay stretched out on the ground. His hands tucked beneath his head, he appeared to be resting. It was Sir Broderick—she knew it was. Even though he lay in repose facing away from her, his form was unmistakable. The Crimson Knight was known as a man satisfied in his isolation. Save for his squire and the men he commanded in battle, he squandered little of his time in casual mingling with others. Thus, Monet's emotions alternated between fear, uncertainty, and determination.

Straightening her posture in an effort to appear more courageous than she felt, Monet glanced about. Where was Sir Broderick's squire? She surely could not approach without some manner of chaperone, could she? Yet time was waning; Anais of Alvar was well known for her impatience. Monet knew Anais would not wait until after King Ivan's feast to approach the Crimson Knight. If she wished to ensure her father's first knight would compete only for his king and kingdom, Monet knew she must act without hesitation.

She approached the pavilion—looked within. Sir Broderick's eyes were closed. It seemed he slept. Still, time was too valuable to stand on propriety.

"May I beg audience with you, Sir Broderick?" Monet asked. She stood just without the pavilion and was pleased when the great knight did not startle—did not even open his eyes.

Simply he asked, "Who is begging audience, young woman?" The deep intonation of his voice sent gooseflesh prickling over Monet's arms.

"Monet, Sir Broderick," she answered. Lowering her voice, she added, "King Dacian's daughter."

At this, the Crimson Knight's eyes opened, his brow furrowing with an inquisitive scowl.

He looked up, and Monet was rendered

breathless. Ever the appearance of Sir Broderick Dougray, the Crimson Knight, had flustered her. Even as a young girl, the acute blue of his eyes had discomposed her nature. There was such a manner of brooding in their remarkable blue, of daring, and of something akin to danger. The Crimson Knight was renowned for his steel gaze—his piercing, dominate gaze—a gaze to set fear into the hearts of men one moment, to infuse desire to the hearts of women the next.

"Princess?" he mumbled. He raised himself and stood. His bewitching gaze caused Monet to tremble further. Sir Broderick glanced beyond her a moment—to one side of the knight encampment and then to the other. "You are not escorted?" he asked.

The Crimson Knight was of great height, and Monet held her cloak hood near her cheek to ensure it would not slip from her head as she looked up at him.

"I am not," Monet answered.

Sir Broderick's scowl changed to a frown of inquisition. "Princess, you should not be here . . . without escort . . . without—" he began.

"I know, sir," Monet stammered. "However, I must beg audience with you, Sir Broderick . . . for I own a request . . . a request of a personal nature . . . a request I wish to remain unheard by any but you."

"Are you threatened in some way?" he asked,

one powerful hand grasping the hilt of the sword sheathed at his hip. "Is your father well?"

"My father is well," Monet answered, "as am I." Monet swallowed, flustered by the odd warmth bathing her limbs as she looked at him.

Sir Broderick's raven hair gave prominence to the severe blue of his eyes, the perfect angles of his face. Her attention rested for a moment on the small cleft marking his squared chin. Indeed, his features of face were far beyond merely remarkable, as was the breadth of his chest and shoulders. The length of his muscular limbs also lent to his exceptional appearance.

"Then why came you here without escort, Princess?" Sir Broderick inquired.

"To beg your benevolence, sir," Monet answered.

She watched as the handsome knight's piercing eyes narrowed. "My benevolence?" he asked. "What benevolence could a princess beg of me?"

Monet glanced away, his striking appearance yet disturbing her. She fixed her gaze to his broad chest before her—to the white tunic with red shield and black dragon coat of arms emblazoned upon it.

"I would have your honor shared with my father . . . with our kingdom . . . with these and none other. This I would beg you, though temptation would endeavor to lead you otherwise," she confessed.

"My honor?" he asked. "My honor already belongs to your father . . . and our kingdom."

"It is tomorrow's honor I speak of," she began, venturing to raise her gaze to meet his once more. "It is said you will easily win King Ivan's tournament, and I would beg you . . . please share the honor with my father and all of Karvana."

Still he frowned; still the severe blue of his eyes lingered on her.

"Your appeal near confounds me, Princess," he said. "Do I not ever bring honor to my king and kingdom? Should I *live* through the trials of the tournament—let alone prevail as champion—what thing could possibly divert the honor from resting on my king and Karvana?"

Monet glanced away—cast her gaze to the ground. Oh, why did he disquiet her so? It seemed she was ever out of countenance in his presence.

"Anais intends to beg you bear her favour in the tournament," she explained.

"Anais?" he asked. "Who is Anais?"

Monet looked back to him, delighted to see the sincere, unknowing expression on his face.

"Anais of Alvar." Sir Broderick's frown deepened. Thus Monet offered, "Alvar's princess? King Rudolph's daughter?"

His frown softened, yet disdain seemed to flame in his eyes. "I never beg tokens or carry favour," he grumbled.

"Yes . . . I know," Monet said. "But how will you refuse without offending?"

"I will simply decline." The loathing in his eyes was growing, yet Monet knew the depth of consequence should her father's first knight provoke a wounded countenance in Anais of Alvar. Anais's father, King Rudolph, saw no fault in his daughter—no matter her behavior or another's testimony. King Rudolph would demand recompense for his daughter's spurned request.

"But you must not simply decline," Monet began, "not a request of Anais of Alvar. I am certain you have heard of King Rudolph's prejudicial concerns for his daughter's sake. Your refusal would not bode well for you or my father. No doubt King Rudolph would demand compensation . . . of some sort."

Sir Broderick inhaled a deep breath, his massive chest rising with indignation and near-spent patience.

"Again you confound me, Princess," he said. "You ask that I share the honor of triumph with only your father and our kingdom . . . yet inform me I may not refuse this princess her request. I beg you then, Princess Monet . . . offer me a path of safe conduct wherein I can remain honorable in your eyes, loyal to my king and kingdom, and yet avoid provoking King Rudolph."

Monet shook her head. "I-I know none. It is

why I have sought you out. To refuse Anais's request would certainly bring discomfort to my father. But to accept it . . . for were King Dacian's first knight to wear—"

"Hush!" he interrupted. He closed his eyes a moment—seemed to strain his hearing. He looked to Monet then, demanding, "Step into the pavilion, Princess."

"What? I cannot!" Monet argued. She wondered why her voice had instantly dropped to a whisper.

"I hear an approach," he said. "A company . . . and not of knights. Therefore, unless you wish to be found out—"

Monet stepped into the pavilion as the Crimson Knight demanded. He, however, immediately stepped without, quickly unleashing the ties of the two front flaps, concealing her within.

"Sir Broderick?"

It was Anais! Monet held her breath, fearful both of being found out and of the Crimson Knight's response to Anais's request.

"Yes?" Sir Broderick's deep voice boomed.

"I am Anais . . . Princess of Alvar," Anais said.

"I am your servant, Princess," Sir Broderick greeted.

Of a sudden, feelings of vexation leapt in Monet's bosom. She loathed Anais of Alvar! Ever she had loathed her—even as a child. She wondered what manner of assembly accompanied Anais. Ladies-in-waiting? Servants?

Curiosity triumphed, and Monet knelt, pressing a hand to the ground in the endeavor of peering through the small opening at the bottom of the pavilion. She could discern the hems of three gowns—ladies-in-waiting—and further the boots of two guards.

"I have come to offer a great honor to you, Sir Broderick," Anais said. "I believe you are one who is worthy of such an honor."

"I am worthy of nothing, your highness," Sir Broderick began, "let alone the honor of basking in your lovely presence."

Anais and her ladies giggled with vain delight.

"You are humble . . . as well as handsome, Sir Broderick!"

Monet frowned, jealousy, resentment, and anger coursing through her limbs. She watched as Anais's hem moved toward Sir Broderick—advanced upon the Crimson Knight.

"And I believe you are he—the only knight at King Ivan's tournament worthy of this honor," Anais said.

"Pray, Princess . . . may I ask what honor you intend to bestow?"

"I would have you bear my favour in this tournament, Sir Broderick," Anais stated. "I do wish you to know that it would be my honor as well as yours . . . for I have heard you have never carried favour into a tournament or battle."

"None visible, your highness," Sir Broderick said.

Monet frowned. None visible? Had Sir Broderick Dougray carried a hidden favour? Again jealousy rose within her bosom—a diverse jealousy—a competitor to the jealousy Anais wrought.

"Do you accept my offer, Sir Broderick?" Anais asked. "Do you accept the honor I am willing to bestow upon you?"

Monet could not breathe! How would he answer? Would King Dacian's first knight prove himself wholly loyal? Furthermore, would he prove to be clever—clever enough to circumvent offense to Alvar, its princess, and its king?

"I fear it is with heavy heart that I must decline, Princess," Sir Broderick said. Monet still did not draw breath. Instead, she waited—waited for Anais's emotional eruption—the eruption of angry indignation Monet knew was forthcoming.

"You refuse?" Anais asked, anger rising in her voice.

"No, your highness," Sir Broderick answered. "Rather, I must decline . . . wretchedly decline."

"Decline? And why?" Anais demanded. "When I offer such an honor to you, Sir Broderick . . . what reason would you have of declination?"

Monet still did not breathe—waited for his response.

"I already carry favour, your highness," Sir Broderick said. "Only this morning I begged a token of another . . . and she has only just granted me the honor to bear *her* favour in King Ivan's tournament."

At last Monet drew breath, sighing reprieve. Sir Broderick Dougray had declined! The Crimson Knight had gallantly offered declination and without contributing malicious offense. He had proffered a lie, it was true, yet in protection of his king. Who would not allow it? For a moment, Monet frowned. *Had* Sir Broderick offered a lie to Anais? Or had he hidden the truth from Monet? Perhaps he had begged token from another— before she had entered his pavilion, before Anais had sought him out. She closed her eyes, shaking her head slightly to dispel the unhappy thought. No. The Crimson Knight was known for his loyalty. Monet was certain he would have informed her had he already begged a token or accepted favour.

There was silence for a moment. Monet knew Anais well; the Princess of Alvar was reigning in her temper. Anais was infuriated—there could be no doubt of it. Nevertheless, even Anais, daughter of Alvar's King Rudolph, could not find fault with a knight who would honor his own word and previous commitment.

"Your loyalty and honor are praiseworthy, Sir Broderick." Anais began, "To keep your pledge and bear another's favour when Anais of Alvar has offered hers? Noble, indeed."

Monet clenched her teeth. It seemed Anais's vanity knew no bounds. Of what greater worth was Anais's favour than that of any other maiden upon the earth?

Monet rose from her knees, frowning with the familiar inflammation of temper provoked by Anais.

"I bid you good day, Sir Broderick," Anais said. "May you fare well in the tournament tomorrow."

"Thank you, your highness," Sir Broderick said.

Monet heard Anais's amused giggle. "Pray not as well as whichever knight bears my favour, however."

"Yes, your highness." Monet noted Sir Broderick's response sounded somewhat forced—thick with impatience.

The sound of retreating footsteps was soon followed by a low, angry growl.

Monet gasped as the pavilion flaps burst apart to reveal the infuriated countenance of the Crimson Knight. The enraged expression of indignation on Sir Broderick's face indeed caused Monet to step back and away from him.

"I have done your bidding, Princess, and declined Anais of Alvar's offer . . . and without striking great offense," he grumbled, his frown deepening still.

"I-I thank you, Sir Broderick," Monet stammered. As the Crimson Knight advanced into his pavilion and toward her, Monet took another step in retreat. "I am in your debt."

"You owe no debt to me, Princess," he said, glaring at her as if she were some threat or enemy he would at any moment strike from existence.

Monet shook her head as despair began to overtake her then. "Yet tomorrow, when Anais sees you bear no favour . . . what then?"

The Crimson Knight's frown softened from that of fury to one of inquisitiveness.

"Are you in earnest, Princess?" he asked.

"Concerning what, sir?" Monet asked in return.

"Do you truly think I would claim to bear a lady's favour and then appear in the tournament without one?" he asked.

Of a sudden, comprehension pierced Monet's awareness.

"Y-you would bear *my* favour, Sir Broderick?" she asked in an astonished whisper. "You would carry my scarlet into tournament?" Surely he was in jest! Yet the thought of the Crimson Knight entering the jousting arena, the scarlet veil of Princess Monet of Karvana knotted at his arm, sent gooseflesh rippling over Monet's limbs.

"Is not your father my king?" he asked. "Is not your kingdom the same I defend? And are not you also representative of Karvana and King Dacian?"

"Yes, sir," Monet answered.

"Then what more appropriate favour could I carry?"

"B-but the Crimson Knight of Karvana never carries favour . . . in tournament or battle."

"Then you have charged a maneuver against me no other foe ever has, Princess," he said, "and triumphed."

"I do not act against you, Sir Broderick," Monet defended. "I only sought to gain you as my ally."

He exhaled a heavy breath, shaking his head.

"I am your father's first knight, Princess," he said. The intenseness of his narrowed eyes increased. "I have ever been your ally . . . from the moment I pledged allegiance to Karvana and its king."

"And it is the reason I came to you," Monet said. "Imagine the people of Karvana—imagine their faces—had their first knight, their most beloved protector . . . imagine had he ridden into tournament with the Princess of Alvar's favour at his arm."

"I would not have accepted her favour, Princess," Sir Broderick nearly growled, his frown deep across his handsome brow.

"And King Rudolph's fury would have—"

"It is done, Princess," he interrupted, raking strong fingers through raven hair. "Whether or not you trusted my loyalty to my king and kingdom . . . I did decline, and I will bring honor to your father and all of Karvana . . . by carrying the favour of their princess into tournament."

"Please do not be angry with me, Sir Broderick," Monet ventured. She did not wish to own his vexation. In truth, she wished to own . . .

"I am not angry, Princess . . . not with you," he mumbled. "Believe what I tell you. I do understand the concerns that drove you to approach me . . . no matter my appearance of fickle temperament."

He did. She knew he did. For all his frowns and menacing glaring, Monet knew Sir Broderick Dougray understood why she had come.

His eyes narrowed as he studied her for a moment. "Do you know the prize King Ivan has named for the tournament champion, Princess?"

"Of course," Monet answered. In truth, she did not know precisely what prize King Ivan had named. Nevertheless, she did not wish to appear ignorant before one so seasoned in battle and tournament. Therefore, having attended many tournaments, Monet assumed the prize would be a golden statue, a finely crafted sword, a high-bred charger, or a thing of worth the like. No doubt a heavy purse would accompany whatever symbol of victory was bestowed as well.

Monet experienced a slight unsettling of her stomach as the Crimson Knight's frown vanished, something akin to a mischievous grin owning his lips.

"And do you still wish to grant me the honor of bearing your favour in the tournament?" he asked.

"Yes," she said, still attempting to appear to own knowledge she did not.

She forced herself to a facade of calm when Sir Broderick's dark brows arched with seeming slight surprise.

"Good. Then you further know the tournament will begin with the Ceremony of Colors . . . each lady presenting her chosen knight with her favour—a length of silk, a ribbon, or the like in the color significant to only her," he explained.

"Yes. An . . . an extraordinary beginning, indeed," Monet stammered. In truth, she had never witnessed such a ceremony. In all other tournaments to which she was in attendance, the competing knights were already in possession of their lady's color when they entered the arena. Monet felt her innards churn at having now twice misled the Crimson Knight concerning her knowledge of King Ivan's tournament.

"Indeed," Sir Broderick mumbled, his eyes narrowing with suspicion as he studied her face.

Monet sensed the heated blush of vermillion at her cheeks yet attempted to appear composed.

"And an unusual end, as well," he added.

"Indeed," she said, wondering if perhaps the champion's prize were something other than the customary honors presented.

"Then you will present me with your favour in the morning . . . at the Ceremony of Colors," he began, "and I will win this tournament for our kingdom, for your father—my king—and for you, your highness."

Monet could not stop a delighted smile from donning her lips. Her heart leapt within her bosom. The Crimson Knight would bear her favour! Sir Broderick Dougray would—for all common appearances—compete in King Ivan's tournament for Princess Monet of Karvana! In truth, Monet had dreamt of just such an occurrence many times. Still, she would not dwell on dreams.

"And you will *accept* my favour when I offer it on the morrow?" she asked, doubt suddenly besting her confidence.

"As eagerly as you will bestow my prize when I am named tournament champion," he said, his grin of mischief broadening. She returned his smile, basking in his pure masculinity, his ethereal comeliness. She wanted to touch him—simply know her hand had pressed to him—to know he was real and not some dream. She was a princess, was she not? Did not princesses own special allowances? Of course they did!

Reaching up, Monet gently placed a dainty hand against one broad shoulder belonging to Sir Broderick Dougray.

"I thank you, Sir Broderick," she said, "for

your loyalty to your kingdom . . . and its king."

"I am—as ever—your servant, Princess," he said, lowering his head in a gesture of respect and compliance.

Monet smiled, her hand warmed by having touched him. She drew the hood of her cloak over her head once more. "I think I am not so afraid of you as I was before coming," she whispered.

Sir Broderick frowned. "What did you have to fear of me?" he asked.

Tilting her head to one side, Monet studied him for a moment—his powerful and handsome countenance causing her heart to flutter.

"Have you forgotten, Sir Broderick?" she asked, stepping from the pavilion. With a breath of light laughter, she pronounced, "There is reason Father christened you the Crimson Knight."

An Enemy Revealed

"Father," Monet began, seating herself next to the King of Karvana.

"Yes, my dove?" King Dacian asked.

"Considering the rare Ceremony of Colors King Ivan has arranged to commence his tournament," Monet ventured, "is there anything else different concerning it? His tournament, I mean?"

King Dacian chuckled, smiling at his lovely daughter. How proud he was of Monet's compassionate soul, humility, and beauty! Her heart was pure, kind, and caring, yet strong as a lion's. He studied the features of her face—the warm violet of her eyes, the pure ruby of her lips, her angular and high-swept cheekbones. Her ebony hair—the exact color her mother's had been—was drawn away from her face, upswept as befit a young woman. How he missed the tender cascade of a little girl's tresses, the bobbing curls Monet had worn so often in her childhood. Yet she was a woman now—ever as beautiful as her mother had been, as slender, as graceful. Oh, how he loved her! His greatest treasure—this was his Monet.

● ● ●

"Anything else different you ask, my lily?" Dacian asked. "Why, yes. Ivan always attempts to make his tournaments . . . distinctive—thus the Ceremony of Colors. There are other alterations as well."

"Such as?" Monet asked. She had not slept well through all the night. Something Sir Broderick had said the day before gnawed at her mind as a mouse to cheese—his reference to the tournament champion's prize, as if it were different from the customary prizes awarded. Furthermore, she had wielded deceit—twice lied to mask her own ignorance. Vain lies were these. She had spent much of the darkest hours of the night in scolding herself for such sins.

King Dacian frowned, tilted his head, and considered Monet for a moment. Monet felt a cherried blush rise to her cheeks.

"Why do you ask?" her father inquired.

"Father . . . I," she stammered. "It is all quite a long and drawn-out tale, you understand."

"*What* is a long and drawn-out tale?"

Monet swallowed the thick discomfort in her throat.

"I-I have asked Sir Broderick to carry my favour in the tournament, Father," she confessed. "Please do not be angry. I—"

Her father's familiar laughter gave her a measure of comfort, his smile warming her heart.

"Why should such a thing anger me, Monet?" he asked. "Sir Broderick is a noble and valiant man. His loyalty to me and his kingdom is unrivaled."

"Then you are not angry with me?" she asked. She had been so fearful—so worried her father may find fault with her favour being displayed in tournament, even by his first knight.

"No, my dove," he said. His smile broadened, a glint of amusement in his eye. "Still, I now have a question of my own."

"Anything, Father," Monet said, relieved to be yet in his good graces.

"There is conduct . . . events, if you will . . . about this tournament of King Ivan's that is unusual. I would ask you now what *you* know of these differences."

Monet shrugged. "The Ceremony of Colors. I have never attended a tournament wherein such a ceremony is performed. And I must confess to being greatly unsettled at being part of it . . . of having to appear before so many spectators."

Again her father offered a chuckle. "Oh, I well believe that by the end of the tournament *that* appearance will be the least of your worries, my dove."

Monet felt her heart begin to hammer within her bosom. She was not at all certain if it hammered for the excitement of the sudden eruptive roar of the crowd as the knights began to enter the jousting arena or from the sense her father and Sir Broderick owned knowledge she did not.

"What do you mean to say, Father?"

Yet her father only laughed, his smile broadening as he nodded to the lead knight to ride past the stands.

"Here rides our knight now, Monet," King Dacian said, "the Crimson Knight of Karvana."

Monet looked to the direction her father nodded. The sight of the Crimson Knight caused her breath to catch for a moment.

Astride a high-marching black charger robed in white, crimson, and black, the Crimson Knight entered the arena. His chain mail and armor shone bright, as did the armored chanfron of his charger—glinting in the morning sun as if each piece had been polished to its highest possible sheen.

The Crimson Knight paused before the stands, where Monet and her Father sat with the other royals. He nodded, the piercing steel of his eyes barely visible through the slit in his helmet. He spurred his horse, and it reared, its white robes, adorned with Sir Broderick's crimson shield and black dragon coat of arms, rippling in the breeze. The Crimson Knight raised his lance in respectful recognition of his king.

The crowd—both common and noble—cheered and applauded as the Crimson Knight's charger stomped and snorted.

King Dacian nodded to his first knight—smiled as Sir Broderick rode on and the procession of knights continued.

"Thus your hero has entered the tournament, Monet," King Dacian said.

"Your Crimson Knight seems lacking in humility," King Rudolph said, taking his seat next to Dacian and nodding as his own first knight approached.

"He only displays his unconditional allegiance," King Dacian said. Monet glanced to where Anais stood next to her father, her expression that of caching some great secret.

"I beg your pardon, Father," Anais said, "but I must away to prepare for the Ceremony of Colors."

"And which knight bears your favour this tournament, Anais?" Monet's father inquired.

"If you will forgive me, your majesty . . . I have promised to keep that secret until the ceremony," Anais said.

"Such wisdom in one so youthful, Rudolph," Monet heard her father force. "You have done well in raising her." Monet knew her father was loathing of propriety—at the necessity of having to offer insincere compliments. King Dacian held no respect for Rudolph, King of Alvar. Yet propriety demanded civility in such circumstance.

"Thank you, Dacian," King Rudolph said, smiling with unwarranted pride.

"Anais," King Dacian said as Anais turned to take her leave, "pray . . . would you allow Monet to accompany you to the ceremony platform?"

Monet tried not to smile—tried not to feel triumphant as the pink plainly drained from Anais's pretty face.

"Monet, your majesty?" Anais asked.

"Yes," King Dacian answered. "She has granted favour in this tournament and is a novice to the Ceremony of Colors. I would be indebted if you were to escort her down."

"Of-of course, your majesty," Anais said—nearly growled—her eyes narrowing with indignation.

"Monet," King Dacian said, gesturing she should follow Anais. Monet smiled when her father offered a nod of understanding.

"Yes, Father," she said, rising.

"Come along, Monet," Anais said—any remnant of a smile fading from her beautiful face.

Four and ten young ladies of royal or noble birth stood shoulder to shoulder on the platform erected for the Ceremony of Colors. Monet held her posture straight—though she considered lifting her skirts and running. All eyes would be upon her when Sir Broderick approached to receive her favour; all eyes in the stands would fall to her. She loathed the thought—abhorred the attention often heaped on her as Karvana's princess.

She ventured a glance at Anais. Head held high, smile soft and laced with vanity, Anais of Alvar shone conceit—delight in knowing all eyes would fall to her. Auburn-haired and green-eyed, Anais of Alvar was nearly as opposing in appearance to Monet of Karvana as she was in nature.

"You have granted favour, Monet?" Portia asked from her place next to Monet on the stage. Portia's golden hair and blue eyes seemed to imprison the sunlight and sky—hold them captive to radiate her lovely countenance.

"I have," Monet said. She could not help but smile, delighted with what she knew the reaction among the other royals and nobles would be when she presented her scarlet favour to the Crimson Knight: astonishment—astonishment and envy!

"But you never grant favour!" Lenore exclaimed in a whisper. Lenore's brown eyes were bright with excitement as well, her acorn hair hanging long down her back, nearly to her ankles.

"This day I do," Monet said.

"To whom?" Lenore asked.

"To the champion of King Ivan's tournament, perhaps," Monet answered.

Portia and Lenore smiled, pleased with Monet's

courageous answer. Anais, however, did not smile—did not look to Monet, nor to any other lady present.

"King Ivan's herald approaches," Portia whispered as a man robed in King Ivan's signature blue and yellow stepped to the front of the platform. "He will herald each knight to come forth and claim our favours."

The crowd in the stands fell silent as King Ivan's herald raised one hand.

"My kings and queens . . . my lords and ladies . . . King Ivan of Avaron welcomes you to his tournament of knights!" the herald announced.

Applause and cheering were allowed for a moment, and then King Ivan's herald raised a hand once more, restoring silence.

"You are well aware of the great event that is one of King Ivan's tournaments," the herald began. "Feasting, music, and dance at sunset . . . brave men in battle at day!" More cheering—a raised herald's hand. "And what manner of unusual prizes has King Ivan collected for his tournament champions? Gold!" Cheering. "Jeweled swords and daggers!" Cheering. "Further, to the tournament champion goes the greatest of all prizes! Not only will he who is named tournament champion choose and name the tournament's Queen of Love and Beauty—"

Monet ventured a glance to Anais when she

heard Alvar's princess lightly laugh—a laugh of conquest.

"—but also a prize above all prizes! A prize worth more than gold or jeweled swords," the herald continued. "King Ivan has granted that whichever gallant knight triumphs as champion in this tournament . . . said knight may claim the lips of his lady . . . a kiss bestowed by she whose favour he bears in this tournament!"

Monet gasped, rendered breathless by the herald's revelation as the crowd roared with approval. She glanced across the arena to her father's seat in the stand. He was applauding, smiling, and nodding his sanction.

"A kiss?" Portia exclaimed. "A kiss? Did you know of this, Anais?"

"Of course," Anais of Alvar answered. Anais looked to Portia. "Do not tell me you chose to give your favour to your father's ancient Sir Terrence, Portia."

"I did!" Portia said. "For he is the best of men."

"Then you will not concern yourself over bestowing a kiss," Anais said. "For is he not worthy of it?"

"Did you know of the promised prize to the champion?" Lenore asked of Monet.

"If he triumphs, I will gladly bestow such a prize to he who bears my favour," Monet said. Nevertheless, of a sudden she feared fainting! The knowledge of the champion's prize was near to overwhelming her. A kiss? Lips? To bestow a kiss, to press lips with, Sir Broderick Dougray— the Crimson Knight? In truth, Monet could imagine nothing more desirable! Yet to bestow a kiss in front of so many—and to a man who no doubt counted kisses as mundane trivialities compared with knightly duties and battle.

"Knights of the tournament . . . approach!" Ivan's herald commanded.

There came upon the air the sound of armor marching in unison.

"As I herald you . . . each one . . . come forth and claim favour from your lady!" the herald instructed. The crowd roared, and the herald raised his hand to hush them.

"Sir Terrence Langford," the herald began, drawing out each word with dramatic result. "Son of Dimitrie Dumitru . . . Earl of Luestin . . . First Knight of Norvola . . . Defender of Queens . . . Rescuer of the Ninth Legion . . . come forth and bear color!"

Monet watched as Portia stepped forward. A knight in dark armor approached, his coat of arms a sapphire shield and roaring bear.

"Present your favour, Princess Portia of Norvola!" the herald called.

Portia nodded to Sir Terrence. Drawing the ribbon from around her throat, she reached out, tying the length of white adornment around Sir Terrence's right armored arm.

The crowd cheered, and Portia smiled, offering a nod to Sir Terrence as he bowed for a moment.

"Prince Martin of Avaron . . . Second Son of King Ivan . . . Prince of Avaron . . . Defender of Innocence and Destroyer of Malice . . . come forth and bear color!"

A knight in a helmet adorned with a gold crown stepped onto the platform. Monet smiled, pleased to see Lenore step forward. Lenore smiled at Prince Martin as she secured her own yellow ribbon to his arm. The crowd cheered, and Monet did not miss the expression of elation on Lenore's countenance. It was clear she favored Prince Martin—more even than Monet had suspected.

King Ivan's herald raised a hand to silence the stands once more.

"Sir Fredrick Esmund . . . Son of Esmund Tudor . . . First Knight of Rothbain's Round Table . . . King James's Favored One . . . Commander of the Fifth Legion . . . Commander of the Third Legion . . . Conqueror of Kingdoms . . . Vanquisher of Weakness . . . come forth and bear color!"

Monet's eyes narrowed as Anais of Alvar stepped forward. Somehow Monet was not surprised Anais should ask one of King James's knights to carry her favour—Sir Fredrick, a man infamous, known for his arrogance and cruelty. Sir Fredrick was branded by his thirst for blood in battle, for his ungallant behavior in

43

tournament. No doubt when Sir Broderick had declined to carry Anais's favour, she had sought out the knight most likely to wound any other in the tournament—including, and most of all, Sir Broderick. Anais secured a length of lavender silk to Sir Fredrick's arm, nodding at him as he bowed to her.

Monet gazed across the arena to her father. King Dacian nodded—a nod of encouragement. Monet let her attention linger on her father, concentrating on his goodness to the people of their kingdom—and the honor the Crimson Knight would bring to them all by venue of the tournament.

Seven more knights were heralded to the platform before Monet's attention was again full on King Ivan's herald.

"Sir Broderick Dougray . . . Son of Kendrick Nathair . . . First Knight of Karvana . . . Favored Warrior of King Dacian . . . Commander of the First Legion . . . Commander of the Second Legion . . . Slayer of a Thousand Enemies . . . Blood Warrior of Ballist . . . Protector of the Kingdom . . . the Crimson Knight . . . come forth and bear color!"

The roar of the crowd was near deafening as Sir Broderick Dougray stepped onto the platform.

"Princess Monet," Sir Broderick spoke, the deep intonation of his voice far more intimidating as it sounded from within his helmet, "pray grant me the honor of bearing your favour."

Monet paused. No other knight had spoken to his chosen lady when heralded to the platform. She was momentarily struck silent—uncertain as to response.

"Accept me, Princess," Sir Broderick demanded. "I am the Crimson Knight of Karvana . . . your servant." The crowd erupted into approving shouts and deafening applause as Karvana's Crimson Knight took to one knee before his princess.

"Pray rise, Sir Broderick," Monet begged, "for the honor would be mine."

The Crimson Knight nodded and stood erect once more. Monet pulled the scarlet silk from around her shoulders. Reaching out, she watched her trembling hands begin to tie the favour to the Crimson Knight's right armored arm.

"If you please, Princess," the Crimson Knight said, "pray tie it at my throat . . . that I may better bear and shield your precious favour."

As Monet reached up, securing her veil around the neck of the Crimson Knight, the crowd roared with approval.

"I will win this tournament for you, Princess," Sir Broderick said. Monet looked up—gazed through the slit in Sir Broderick's helmet— breathless as the severe blue of his eyes captured her own. For a moment, Monet was certain her heart would cease in its beating—certain she may faint from Sir Broderick's nearness, from his gestures and words of respect to her. No other knight had knelt before his lady. No other knight had spoken to his lady—begged his lady's favour be worn at the throat—let alone promised aloud to win King Ivan's tournament in her name.

"Pray take care against any wound or injury, Sir Broderick," Monet said as Sir Broderick bowed. How she worried for him suddenly! As the memory of tournaments past washed over her—of blood and broken bones—she feared for his well-being, as ever she had.

Sir Broderick raised his head, and through the slit in his helmet, she saw his blue eyes narrow.

"Yes, your highness," he said. He turned then, and the crowd roared with a delight.

The Crimson Knight stepped down from the platform, and Monet stepped back to her place between Portia and Lenore.

"Sir Broderick agreed to carry your favour?" Lenore asked in a whisper as the herald called for the next knight.

Remembering the moments she had been secreted in the Crimson Knight's pavilion—the conversation between Sir Broderick and Anais—Monet said, "In truth, he asked a token before I had the opportunity to request it of him."

"Then for your sake, Monet," Portia began, "I hope he wins the tournament for you! To press one's lips to those of the Crimson Knight . . . do you not suppose it would be worth near any price?" Monet looked to Portia to see her eyes bright with merriment and anticipation.

"I do suppose it would be," Monet said, smiling.

"Sadly, you will not know such an honor, Monet . . . for Sir Fredrick will triumph. There is no doubt," Anais said.

"The Crimson Knight has promised to win the tournament in the name of his princess, Anais," Portia said through clenched teeth. "His reputation in tournament manifests he would die before breaking promise."

Anais glared at Portia, then Monet. "Then he may well die . . . for Sir Fredrick told me he would kill any foe barring his way to my kiss."

"It is well my father knows Sir Fredrick, Anais," Portia said. "If Sir Fredrick would kill to clear a path to you . . . then he would expect far more than a simple kiss when he arrived."

Monet heard Lenore gasp—felt her own cheeks grow pink at Portia's assurance to Anais.

"Portia!" Lenore scolded. "Such an implication!"

"It is the truth," Portia said. "And I suspect Anais knows it is the truth."

Monet looked to Anais. The haughty Princess of Alvar simply smiled and returned her attention to the knights in the arena.

Monet—still stunned by Portia's revelation

concerning Sir Fredrick and Anais—looked to the knights aligned in the arena before her. Her attention was instantly drawn to Sir Broderick. He offered her a slight nod, and she returned his acknowledgement by bowing her own head for a moment. As she studied him—his massive form, the polish of his heavy armor, his great height— she was certain the scarlet veil at his throat was merely a dream.

Monet held her breath and allowed her hands to fist where they lay in her lap. The sound of the horses charging—of powerful hooves beating upon the ground—of leather straining and armor braced for battle echoed—thundered as a violent storm. The Crimson Knight's lance struck, splintering into a thousand pieces just above its base. As Sir Ostler fell back—tumbled from his charger and to the ground—Monet closed her eyes and offered a thankful prayer for Sir Broderick's victory and thus his safety.

"He has unhorsed Sir Ostler with one lance!" King Dacian shouted, applauding his Crimson Knight.

The crowd in the stands roared with approval as the Crimson Knight turned his horse. Monet watched as the black charger carrying Sir Broderick Dougray paused before the place where she and her father were seated. The charger reared, and Sir Broderick raised his splintered lance as tribute to his king. Monet bit her lip but could not keep a delighted smile from spreading across her face.

"Well done, Sir Broderick!" King Dacian shouted. "Well done, lad!"

The Crimson Knight nodded as the banner bearing his crimson shield and black dragon coat of arms replaced that of Sir Ostler's on the tournament scoring wall.

"He has yet to face Sir Terrence of Norvola," King Rudolph reminded.

"As well as Sir Fredrick, your majesty," Anais added.

King Dacian was undaunted, however.

"He will face them," he said, "and triumph, no doubt."

Monet smiled, pleased by her father's faith in his first knight.

Yet she next sighed, for the tournament was weighing heavy on her mind. This third day of tournament seemed all the more brutal than the two previous. Monet's father had explained the manner in which a lengthy tournament wore down those knights competing. Three days of mock battling—of sword fight, mace play, wrestling, archery, and jousting—wrought havoc on a man's body. By the third day and the final jousts, most knights were bruised, broken, and worn to the bone with fatigue.

Monet worried for Sir Broderick. He had

battled hard. His victories were the talk of Avaron! Having bested every knight in swords and maces, he had bested all but Sir Terrence in archery. Gossip was his loss to Sir Fredrick in wrestling was to be blamed on the deep wound at his right arm. Sir Fredrick—owning little or no chivalry or sense of fair play—had intentionally plunged his fingers into Sir Broderick's wound during their wrestling, inflicting great pain to the Crimson Knight, thus managing to best him—but only just.

Now the crowd roared as but three banners remained on the scoring wall of the jousting arena. If the Crimson Knight managed to best Sir Terrence and Sir Fredrick, he would, no doubt, be named tournament champion. However, he was wounded, and Sir Fredrick and Sir Terrence were not.

Still, enough strength was left in him to have unhorsed Sir Ostler. Thus Monet hoped the tournament would end with no further injury to Sir Broderick—whether or not he were crowned champion.

Monet had hardly eaten in near three days, her appetite cast off for worry over Sir Broderick and the other knights. It was why she was not in regular attendance at tournaments. She found them brutal, frightening, and difficult to endure. Nevertheless, she knew a weary knight often drew strength from the presence of those he protected or competed for. Therefore, she had attended every event in which Sir Broderick Dougray had competed.

"Let us partake refreshment, Anais," King Rudolph said, rising from his seat. "Sir Broderick will accept his earned respite before facing Sir Terrence."

"Sir Broderick will face Sir Terrence at once," Monet's father said. She watched as her father folded strong arms across his chest.

"Surely not," King Rudolph argued. "He will want rest . . . restoration of his strength before facing another joust."

"He fell Ostler with one lance," King Dacian said. "He will not be worn yet and will face Sir Terrence at once."

"My kings and queens . . . lords and ladies . . . and to all others within the sound of my voice . . . I present to you Sir Terrence Langford!" Sir Terrence's herald began. Sir Terrence's sapphire and roaring bear coat of arms blazoned on his gold tunic, the herald continued, "Son of Dimitrie Dumitru . . . Earl of Luestin . . . First Knight of Norvola . . . Defender of Queens . . . Rescuer of the Ninth Legion!"

Sir Terrence appeared at the far end of the arena, bearing lance, his dark armor ominous beneath the clouded sky.

"As I said," King Dacian began, "Sir Broderick will joust once more before taking his respite."

"You hold too much faith in this man . . . own too much intimate knowledge of this Crimson Knight, Dacian," King Rudolph grumbled. "It can come to no good . . . to trust a soldier so entirely."

Dacian's smile faded. Monet watched as her father's eyes narrowed with suspicion.

"Who then would you have me trust, Rudolph?" he asked. "James of Rothbain? Ah . . . there is a man worthy of trust indeed."

King Rudolph straightened his posture.

"Do *you* place your trust in James, Rudolph? Your allegiance?"

King Rudolph said nothing—only took his seat once more as the Crimson Knight's herald entered the arena.

Monet's heart was pounding, both with angst borne of the conversation between her father and King Rudolph and for worry over the Crimson Knight.

A youngish man was the Crimson Knight's herald. Robed in white, the familiar crimson shield and rearing dragon coat of arms on his tunic, he raised a hand, and the crowd fell silent.

"To all those royal, noble, and common in attendance . . . and in special respect to King Ivan, our host . . . I present to you Sir Broderick Dougray . . . Son of Kendrick Nathair . . . First Knight of Karvana . . . Favored Warrior of King Dacian . . . Commander of the First Legion . . . Commander of the Second Legion . . . Slayer of a Thousand Enemies . . . Blood Warrior of Ballist . . . Protector of the Kingdom . . . Guardian of the Scarlet Princess . . . the Crimson Knight!"

As the crowd cheered, Monet looked to her father.

"Father!" she breathed.

"Guardian of the Scarlet Princess?" King Rudolph asked. "You hold too fast to the dramatic, Dacian."

Nevertheless, Monet saw the smile of pure contentment in triumph on her father's face.

"Father?" she asked.

"Do you not think Sir Broderick has warriored well at this tournament, Monet?" he asked.

"Of course, Father . . . but—" she began.

"Further," her father interrupted, "with my cousin James's veiled threats against myself and Karvana . . . I thought it appropriate he understood the depth of my regard for your safety. Thus, Sir Broderick has accepted this title of honor—Guardian of the Scarlet Princess—at my bidding."

"They are dropping the banner!" Anais exclaimed.

Monet looked to the arena. The Crimson Knight allowed his horse to rear a moment before charging Sir Terrence. Wood splintered, and the crowd erupted.

"Well done! Well done!" King Dacian shouted.

"Broderick shatters his lance against the tip of

Sir Terrence's," Monet heard King Rudolph tell Anais. "Skilled . . . a masterful trick and highly scored."

Monet watched as Sir Broderick turned his horse. She felt a frown pucker her brow as his squire offered him another lance. It seemed he did not accept it as comfortably as he might have. She could see the blood on his right hand—blood draining from a wound at his upper arm.

"He is too wounded, Father!" Monet whispered. "He should not continue."

"He will continue, Monet," King Dacian said. "This is battle to our Sir Broderick."

Monet again clenched her hands into fists—held her breath as the bearer raised the banner. She was paralyzed, unable to draw breath, as she watched the banner drop—watched the Crimson Knight's lance level as his horse charged forward—watched Sir Terrence's charger lurch.

The splintering shards of lances breaking erupted into the air.

"Sir Terrence is given point!" King Rudolph exclaimed, applauding and showing obvious delight in the Crimson Knight's failure to gain point.

Monet looked to her father. Her brow puckered as she saw he only smiled—as if owning some secret delight.

"Father?" she whispered. "He was bested, was he not? Why then do you smile?"

King Dacian offered a quiet chuckle. "You have not attended as many tournaments as I, Monet," he answered in a whisper. "Nor have you watched our Sir Broderick in battle or competition as I have." Winking at her, he added, "What manner of excitement would there be to all these who look on . . . if the Crimson Knight did not cause their hearts to hammer with the possibility of his not triumphing?"

"Your man is worn, Dacian," King Rudolph noted.

"And he must yet face Sir Fredrick Esmund," Anais added. "See the blood at the Crimson Knight's arm?" she asked. "He is wounded and weakened . . . and Sir Fredrick is not."

"He would not be titled the Crimson Knight if there were not someone's blood about him— either from his own wounds . . . or those of his enemies," King Dacian said. "He will triumph, Princess Anais. He may not unhorse Sir Terrence . . . for he owns great respect for the man. Yet on this third opportunity, Sir Broderick will triumph."

King Rudolph laughed. "Such faith in one man . . . it will serve to condemn you, Dacian."

"A wager then, Rudolph," King Dacian said. "My Crimson Knight against Sir Terrence *and* Sir Fredrick. He will best them both today . . . or my white charger is yours."

"Surely you jest, Dacian," Rudolph chuckled.

"You would wager your infamous white charger in this?"

"Of course," Dacian said.

Monet watched King Rudolph's eyes narrow. She looked to the arena—saw the banner bearer raising the banner.

"Done," King Rudolph said. "For if Sir Terrence does not prevail, Sir Fredrick will . . . undoubtedly."

"And when the Crimson Knight is named champion of the joust . . . I will accept the two best chargers in your stables as compensation." King Dacian smiled as King Rudolph frowned, "as a reward to my Crimson Knight for so honoring me."

"Agreed," King Rudolph said.

"The banner, Father," Monet whispered as the banner dropped.

Charging hooves beat the ground. Sir Broderick's lance leveled—as did the lance of Sir Terrence. Monet gasped as the lance of the Crimson Knight broke across the armored breastplate of Sir Terrence. Sir Terrence's lance fell, his body arching over his charger's back. Sir Terrence was not unhorsed, but he was bested. The crowd cheered and applauded as the Crimson Knight's banner was placed over that of Sir Terrence's on the scoring walls.

Monet looked to her father, smiling as he winked at her.

"Sir Terrence is old. It was not unexpected he should be bested by Sir Broderick," Anais said.

"Sir Terrence is a powerful knight, Princess Anais," King Dacian said. "He would not have triumphed thus far in the tournament if he were otherwise."

As her father stood, Monet rose as well.

"And now, pardon us, if you will, Rudolph—Anais," King Dacian said, "for Monet and I must seek refreshment while the Crimson Knight takes his respite before facing Sir Fredrick."

Anais glared at Monet as she followed her father down the stairs leading from the stands. Monet could not keep from smiling at Anais in return. The Crimson Knight would triumph—she knew he would—and she could not help but to revel in the prideful feelings batting about in her bosom. Pride was not a virtue, this she knew. Yet how could she deny it? For Anais's spiteful nature did nothing if not provoke.

"He will triumph, Father, will he not?" Monet asked as she followed her father to the refreshment pavilion.

King Dacian of Karvana chuckled. "He will, my love. And you will lend him your lips for doing so."

Monet stopped midstep. The truth of it—the fact she must bestow a kiss to the Crimson Knight if he prevailed—had ever lingered in her mind. Yet the brutality of the tournament, the near constant pricking of King Rudolph to her father, had served well in distracting her from the fact.

"Oh, Father!" she breathed.

King Dacian paused, turned, and looked at his daughter. A worried frown puckered his noble brow.

"Monet?" he whispered. "Are you indeed well? You look quite pallid of a sudden."

Dacian was indeed momentarily anxious over his daughter. Her face was ashen, her violet eyes glowing amethyst with what appeared as fear. Tiny beads of perspiration lingered on her forehead.

"Monet?" he asked, reaching forth and taking one of her hands in his own. "What is it, my angel?"

Monet's hand rested at her throat, clutching her neck as if she were choking. Dacian could see the fabric of her scarlet dress quivering as her slight form trembled beneath it.

"T-to kiss the Crimson Knight," she breathed, "to press lips with Sir Broderick Dougray . . . I do not think . . . how will I find the courage, Father?"

"The courage?" Dacian asked. "What courage must it take, Monet? You have known Broderick near to six years . . . since he was squire to Sir

Alum." Monet continued to tremble as he smiled with sudden understanding. "It is simple enough, Monet. You must kiss him with the thankfulness of your heart—as a thankful princess, one who knows the glory her father's first knight has brought to the kingdom."

"Yet it is not so simple for me as you say, Father," Monet whispered.

"Do you fear bestowing the kiss in front of so many? Is that what finds you trembling in your slippers?"

"He is the Crimson Knight, Father!" Monet exclaimed, still whispering. "Blood Warrior of Ballist! What need has such a man of a platonic kiss from an insipid princess? He has none. He will simply endure it as another consequence to tournament . . . no different than the wound at his arm."

Dacian smiled. He knew well the tender feelings Monet secreted in regard to Sir Broderick.

"Blood Warrior of Ballist he is," Dacian said. Taking both of Monet's hands in his, he smiled at her—the loving smile of an understanding father. "And far too few are the moments of respite and beauty in his life. To taste the sweet kiss of his princess—to own the first sweet kiss she has ever bestowed to a man's lips—there is no greater prize could be gifted him. Even for the Crimson Knight, Slayer of a Thousand Enemies . . . even for the Blood Warrior." He shook his head, still smiling at her. "No . . . not even the heavy purse Ivan will bestow him can measure against the lingering touch of your tender lips to his, Monet."

"Lingering?" Monet exclaimed. "What mean you in *lingering,* Father?"

King Dacian laughed. "He has fought and bled and bruised his body in winning this tournament for us, Monet . . . for Karvana. He deserves no less than that." Dacian placed a loving kiss on his daughter's brow. "Now, yon approach your comrades, my darling—those young ladies whose knights did not best Sir Broderick. Well you should honor him by addressing their excitement for you."

Monet glanced over one shoulder to see Portia and Lenore fast approaching, two timid ladies-in-waiting at their heels.

Frantic, she looked back to her father. "What women have known his lips before, Father? Yet I . . . an untried . . . an obviously inexpert princess . . . how can I hope to—"

"And *that,* my darling, is exactly why your kiss will taste so sweet to him," her father said. "Now . . . away to your silly little friends. They have, no doubt, much to twitter over." He released her hands and leveled his broad shoulders, smiling. "And I will away to prepare someone to collect Rudolph's best two chargers."

• • •

"Monet!" Portia exclaimed.

"Hush, Portia!" Lenore scolded. "We are about secret business, and you draw too much attention."

Swallowing the fear hanging thick in her throat, Monet turned to face Portia and Lenore.

Upon seeing them, she frowned. They were so marked with excitement they appeared near to apoplexy.

"You must accompany us, Monet," Portia said in a whisper. She reached out and took hold of Monet's hand, tugging at it in gesture she should go with them. Monet looked to Lenore, who nodded, as did the two ladies-in-waiting.

"What? Accompany you where?" Monet asked. Her body yet trembled with the uncertain anticipation of what she must do when the Crimson Knight triumphed.

"It is Anais! She is making for Sir Fredrick's pavilion!" Lenore whispered.

"Why?" Monet asked.

"Why would you suppose, Monet?" Portia said, leading Monet by one hand, forcing her to follow.

"She intends to lend further encouragement to him . . . further incentive that he should be more driven to win the joust against Sir Broderick," Lenore explained.

"What further incentive could she possibly offer?" Monet asked. "Already he would win a large purse, possessions, and her kiss. What more could she promise to him that would—" Monet felt her mouth fall agape as understanding washed over her.

"What more indeed?" Portia whispered.

"It is often I wonder she is not King James's daughter, instead of King Rudolph's," Lenore said.

"Even so, I have little wish to see Anais prove herself less virtuous than I already know her to be," Monet said. Still, she followed as Portia and Lenore hurried toward the knight encampment. A part of her could not believe Anais would so lower herself as to attempt to spur a man to greater feats by bestowing favors of affection upon him. Yet her curiosity was far too ignited to deny. "Still, I admit to being too weak to refuse the opportunity to have my own eyes witness my long-held suspicions of Anais's true character."

Portia smiled. "I too know I should not lower myself. Yet temptation has beguiled me."

"How came you by this knowledge?" Monet asked as they approached the outer pavilions of the encampment.

"Hush! We must be quiet," Lenore whispered. "This way."

Monet followed as Lenore turned, heading in the direction of a small grove of trees aside the encampment.

"My ladies-in-waiting, Dianth and Matild—you know them both," Portia whispered, nodding to the two ladies-in-waiting at her heels. "They were told of the tryst by one of Anais's own ladies," she said. Indeed, Monet was familiar with Portia's ladies. Monet glanced back to see the younger, Matild, blush with obvious guilt. "She informed her ladies of her intention . . . in case she should be missed by her father."

Lenore glanced back, frowning. "You have no lady to accompany you, Monet?"

"I did not wish to burden them with the demands of the tournament," Monet said. "Father is company enough for me."

"Hush, ladies!" Lenore exclaimed. "We are near."

"Surely we will be seen . . . discovered!" Monet whispered. Yet the pounding of her heart—the odd thrill of facing danger rising in her bosom—spurred her onward.

"We will simply say we were taking a turn about the encampment together," Portia said.

"There, your highness!" Dianth exclaimed. "Princess Portia! There . . . just beyond that first tree!"

"Yes, I see them—two figures . . . just there!" Portia said.

Monet's eyes narrowed, straining to see into the grove of trees. She felt her eyebrows arch in surprise, a quiet gasp filling her lungs as she saw Anais and Sir Fredrick. Sir Fredrick's arms bound Anais tightly against his body.

"H-he is terribly bare," Lenore whispered.

"He has removed his armor and shirt in order to cool his flesh before the next joust," Portia explained.

"Hush! Their lips are meet!" Matild exclaimed in a whisper.

Monet glanced back to the woman, smiling in the knowledge that no princess took offense at Matild's disrespect, their attention entirely enraptured by the display before them.

Monet gasped soft as she looked to see Anais and Sir Fredrick indeed involved in an indiscreet exchange of affection.

Portia shook her head. "How easily she gives over her allegiance."

"As well as her innocence," Lenore said.

"And for what?" Portia asked, of a sudden quite vexed. She turned from the scene. "For what, I ask you?"

"Triumph," Monet answered. She turned from the sight as well. It did her no good to be witness to the great lengths Anais had taken to ensure her knight's victory.

"Triumph?" Lenore asked.

"Yes. Her father has struck a wager with mine—his two best chargers against my father's great white one," Monet explained. "Should Sir

Broderick triumph, not only will Anais's pride be bested . . . but also that of her father."

Portia shook her head. "It is not worth the price she is paying. Sir Fredrick is a monster! A heinous, merciless monster! To align herself with him to such a degree . . ."

"And he is King James's knight," Lenore reminded. "See how easily Anais chooses the side in opposition to your father, Monet."

Monet frowned. It was true! Always she had known Anais despised her—though she knew not why. She did know, however, that any royal willing to set themselves so low in the hopes of a tournament victory—how much easier would it be for the same to set themselves against her father and all of Karvana? Had Anais held some affection toward Sir Fredrick—had she cared for him in the least—then perhaps Monet could not fault her for her indiscretions. Yet Monet was certain Anais did not secret any tender feelings toward the brutal Sir Fredrick. Her alliance with King James's first knight was purely for gain—Monet was certain of it.

A deep, throbbing fear began to knot Monet's innards, for it seemed here was another enemy to her father—another ally to King James and his threats against Karvana. Anais of Alvar had joined the enemy's ranks.

A Champion Proved

"I can linger here no longer," Monet said. Lifting the hem of her dress, she hurried away from the grove of trees—away from those who would see the Crimson Knight conquered—away from those who would endeavor against her father and her kingdom in any manner.

"I know your thoughts, Monet," Portia said, hurrying to match stride with Monet. "Yet I remind you that your Crimson Knight will prevail . . . and thus vanquish any endeavor against your father Anais or Sir Fredrick may conceive."

Fighting to restrain tears of fear and vexation, Monet nodded.

"He will prevail . . . I know he will," she said. "For I believe Sir Broderick understands there is far more to be gained by his triumph at this tournament than merely a heavy purse." Silently she prayed—prayed for Sir Broderick's triumph—that the sovereigns of the five kingdoms and beyond would see her father's strength manifest in the strength of his favored knight.

"Look!" Matild gasped. "It is he! The Crimson

Knight! Just there . . . between those yon pavilions."

"Where, Matild?" Lenore asked.

"Just there," Dianth said, pointing. Monet looked in the direction her gesture indicated.

Instantly her heart swelled. She felt breathless at the sight of him! Save his helmet and gauntlets, he yet wore full armor. Blood from the wound at his right arm had dried on the vambrace covering his forearm.

"He is magnificent to look upon!" Portia said. She smiled at Monet. "What woman would not covet his winning the tournament, simply that she may press her lips to his?"

Monet watched as his squire approached. It was well Monet knew Sir Broderick's squire, Eann. He had been squire to Sir Broderick for near two years. Whispers among those laboring in her father's castle were that Sir Broderick would soon ask King Dacian to knight Eann.

"Sir Broderick," Eann began.

"Listen," Lenore whispered. "Perhaps the squire has seen Sir Fredrick and Anais and comes to tell his master."

"You must take respite," Eann said. "I beg you, remove your armor and cool your flesh. Allow me to fetch fresh pads and shine the blood from your vambrace."

"I will cool my flesh when the deed is done, Eann," the Crimson Knight grumbled. "And let the blood remain. It will lend itself to finding Sir Fredrick overconfident, into thinking I am battle-weary and bled . . . too wounded to best him."

"Can it be Sir Fredrick really believes he will be able to best you at the joust, Sir Broderick?" Eann asked.

"He has the promise of a princess . . . the promise she will share his bed if he does, Eann," Sir Broderick said. "And for that, he believes he can joust against me and win. It is a powerful reason to triumph. Such a reason has mustered triumph in many a man."

Monet looked to see Portia's face drain of its blush entirely. Lenore as well was pallid.

"Your highness!" Dianth exclaimed in a whisper.

"Hush, Dianth," Portia scolded.

"Sh-she would not go to such an extreme . . . simply to see her knight as champion," Lenore whispered, shaking her head. "Surely she would not."

Monet shook her head, certain she had not understood the true meaning of Sir Broderick's words.

"W-will Sir Broderick triumph, Monet?" Portia asked. "When Sir Fredrick's prize . . . when Sir Fredrick's promised prize is of such . . . such magnitude?"

"You mean to ask if my kiss as prize is as spurring to the Crimson Knight as Anais's sacrificed virtue is to Sir Fredrick?" Monet said.

"Yes," Portia breathed.

"I am certain it is not, Portia," Monet whispered. "As certain as I am that the loyalty of my father's first knight to his king and kingdom is far more spurring."

"He has seen us!" Dianth exclaimed.

Monet looked to the Crimson Knight and his squire. Sir Broderick's gaze held hers a moment. As she stepped backward, he advanced.

"Sh-should we run?" Lenore asked.

"Run?" Portia asked. "From one such as he? We are simply out in the fresh air. That is all."

As Sir Broderick and his squire advanced upon them, Monet thought her heart might cease in its rhythm, so rapidly did it pound. The mere sight of him in advance—his raven hair caught in the breeze, the piercing indigo of his eyes as his powerful body moved toward her—left her breathless and fearful somehow.

"Princess Monet," Sir Broderick said, stopping just before her. He glared down at her, and she trembled under his smoldering gaze. "It is not wise for you and your companions to be near the encampments."

"We were just walking, Sir Broderick," Portia explained. "The seats in the arena are so very hard and uncomfortable. Our limbs were simply aching for reprieve."

"Yes," Monet added as he continued to glare at

69

her. "We've been walking . . . near that wooded grove."

Sir Broderick glanced toward the grove of trees only a short distance off.

"As I said, your highness . . . it is not wise for you to walk too near here . . . nor is it wise for you to venture near to that grove."

He knew! He must know! Monet was certain the Crimson Knight knew of Anais's tryst with Sir Fredrick. Something about the smoldering state of his gaze told her he was aware of what was transpiring.

"Thank you for your good judgment on our behalf, Sir Broderick," Monet said. "We will linger closer to the arena henceforth."

He nodded, his searing gaze still holding her uncertain one.

"You jousted bravely today, Sir Broderick," Portia said. "Please know that our hearts are with you as you soon meet Sir Fredrick."

"Thank you, Princess," Sir Broderick said. He bowed his head, a gesture of respect to Portia's title. As he did so, a gentle breeze breathed, lifting a length of the scarlet veil Sir Broderick wore around his neck.

Some strange and delicious thrill traveled through Monet's being at the sight of the embellishment. It was hers! Her own veil that he wore! The reminded knowledge caused renewed hope to rise in her. He would triumph! The Crimson

Knight of Karvana would best Sir Fredrick. He would win the tournament, and in doing so, not only would he heap honor upon her father and his kingdom, he would likewise heave intimidation into the bosom of any who dared to ponder any action against a king whose first knight was so thoroughly dominating.

"Eann," Sir Broderick said, rattling Monet from her reverie, "pray accompany Princess Monet in returning to the arena. See that she is delivered to her father forthwith."

"Of course, Sir Broderick," Eann said. He smiled and nodded at Monet. "Princess?"

"Sir Broderick," Monet said, offering a thankful nod.

The Crimson Knight nodded and then turned and strode back into the encampment, Monet's scarlet veil billowing from beneath his armor— trailing after him as a scarlet banner.

"Is it a great wound he suffers, Eann?" Monet asked as they walked. "The wound at his arm?"

"It is a deep laceration, at his upper arm . . . beneath his rerebrace," Eann answered. "It is in serious need of stitching, but he will not allow it to be attended to until he has finished the tournament."

Monet struggled to keep the tears filling her eyes from escaping. The thought of Sir Broderick's wound caused a stabbing pain to pierce her heart.

"But what of infection?" Portia asked.

"I have washed it well—scrubbed torn flesh and rinsed away the dirt. It yet bleeds, and that should keep it fresh enough until he will allow the surgeon to attend him," Eann answered. As Monet's stomach churned at the thought, she glanced at Eann. He seemed entirely unaffected, as if scrubbing wounded flesh and rinsing blood were the most natural of tasks.

"Will he best Sir Fredrick, do you think, squire?" Lenore asked.

"Of course, your highness!" Eann answered. He frowned at Lenore, as if her question were the most foolish his ears had ever heard. "The Crimson Knight will be champion of King Ivan's tournament. There is no doubt."

"Eann!" King Dacian greeted. "Eann, my lad! What brings you to the stands?"

"Sir Broderick bid I see her highness safely delivered to you, your majesty," Eann answered.

"Sir Broderick?" King Dacian asked. He arched an inquisitive brow as he looked to Monet. "And where have you been that Sir Broderick would have cause to see you escorted here? I thought you were in company with Portia and Lenore."

"I was indeed, Father," Monet said, taking a seat beside her father. She was grateful few had returned to the stands—especially King Rudolph and Anais. "Yet we drew too near the knight encampment, and Sir Broderick wished to see our return escorted."

Portia and Lenore had chosen to return to the refreshment pavilions. Yet Eann had insisted upon finding Monet's father, as he had agreed to do. Monet's hands began to wring where they lay in her lap.

"I see," King Dacian said. Monet knew he sensed her unrest. She knew he would inquire concerning it.

Dacian's eyes narrowed as he studied his daughter. He should have insisted she bring one of her attendants with her to Ivan's tournament. He silently scolded himself for not insisting she do so. Yet Monet was of strong character, and she had convinced him otherwise. Dacian determined, in that moment, however, he must not bow to her convictions of independence and self-protection any longer—not with circumstances building the way they were.

"Thank you, Eann," he said, still studying Monet. "Tell Sir Broderick I thank him for his wisdom in sending you as escort."

"Of course, your majesty," Eann said.

When Eann had gone, Dacian placed a protective hand over his daughter's trembling ones.

"What has happened to put you ill at ease, Monet?" he asked.

Monet shook her head. He could see the tears moist in her eyes.

"You would not believe me if I told it to you, Father," she whispered, "for had I not seen it myself . . . I would not believe me."

"I will ever believe anything you confide in me, daughter," Dacian said. He was truly concerned. She seemed so entirely distressed.

"W-we were walking . . . we went to the wooded grove near the knight encampment," she began. Dacian determined not to inquire as to why the young women had ventured so far in the first of it. He would not interrupt, for he would hear her tale—discover the source of her restlessness.

"There we saw Anais . . . Anais and Sir Fredrick. They . . . they were embracing . . . among other things."

Dacian's eyes narrowed. "Go on," he urged.

"It-it is said she has promised far more than her kiss to Sir Fredrick if he would but defeat Sir Broderick," Monet whispered. She looked to him then, fear and trepidation full in her lovely eyes. "I overhead Sir Broderick himself say that such a thing can muster triumph in many a man."

"And he is right, Monet," Dacian said. "However, the defense of a woman's virtue has been the cause of far more triumphs than has the sacrifice of it." He sighed, a slight grin of compassion donning his lips. Gathering his daughter into his arms, he chuckled. "You worry for your Crimson Knight," he said.

"Yes," Monet confessed. Tears escaped her eyes, traveling over her lovely cheeks.

"Well, fear not, my dove," Dacian said. "Fear not. He will rule this day, as champion of the tournament . . . and of virtue."

"But he is wounded, Father!" Monet exclaimed. "A terrible wound at his arm! It yet bleeds and weakens him, I am certain!"

Dacian smiled. Never had he seen such a look of fear and worry in his daughter's countenance. Her eyes—her lovely violet eyes—were the mark, the mark of assurance he needed. Yes. He was assured then. The entire tale assured him, even so far as Broderick sending Eann to see Monet delivered safely. War was coming, and Dacian of Karvana knew what must be done.

"He will strike Fredrick down, Monet," her father said. "If you wish it . . . I will instruct Sir Broderick to waste not a moment in doing so."

Monet frowned. "What do you mean, Father?"

"I will not watch you suffer through witnessing another brutal round of jousting when it is not necessary," he said. He smiled and chuckled. "Quiet your fears, my darling. Sir Broderick will triumph! Within the hour, your fears for his safety will be put to bed . . . and Anais of Alvar will not."

Monet gasped, "Father!" She could not believe his bold remarks.

"The Crimson Knight will champion you both. I give you my solemn promise of that," he said.

"But, Father—" Monet began.

"Here," he interrupted, "we have yet half the hour before the joust. And I saw the most delicious-looking tarts at the refreshment pavilion. Shall we have some brought to us?"

Monet smiled, brushing the tears from her cheeks with the back of one dainty hand. Her heart yet hammered with fear for Sir Broderick's safety—with disquiet over what she had witnessed of Anais near the knight encampment. Yet her father's assurance rallied her hope. Sir Broderick would triumph! He would triumph, and the surgeon would mend his wounded arm. All would be well.

"Yes, Father," she said. "You've always said a good tart makes for a good day."

"Precisely!" King Dacian laughed.

As her father pressed a gold coin into the hand of a young peasant boy, Monet smiled. She knew the boy would receive not only the coin for his errand to retrieve tarts from the refreshment pavilion but also a sweet, delicious tart to enjoy. It was well Monet knew her father—knew his tender heart.

She closed her eyes a moment, trying to dispel the vision in her mind of Anais wrapped in Sir Fredrick's arms. Instead she allowed the vision of the Crimson Knight to wash over her—his appearance outside the knight encampment, her own scarlet veil billowing behind him. She swallowed the excess moisture filling her mouth. Was it the anticipation of delicious tarts to taste causing her to thirst? Or was it the vision of the Crimson Knight—armor glinting in the sun, the sapphire of his eyes piercing her soul?

Monet opened her eyes, gazing out at the arena. In less than one hour's time, Ivan's tournament would be ended. In less than one hour's time, two fates would be decided—her own and Anais's. One conclusion would find Sir Broderick Dougray named tournament champion, Monet's lips pressed to his in grateful thanks. The other would find Anais in ruination. Oh, how she hoped—nay, prayed—for Sir Broderick's triumph.

Inhaling a deep breath of resolve, Monet rallied her courage and faith. He would win. Indeed, the Crimson Knight would prevail. For he had promised to win, and was not the Crimson Knight of Karvana renowned for honoring his promise?

The horns sounded, heralding that the final joust of King Ivan's tournament would begin forthwith. A breeze ruffled the two banners yet hanging on the scoring wall. One belonged to the Crimson Knight of Karvana, the other to Sir Fredrick Esmund of Rothbain.

King Rudolph and Anais had returned to their seats in the stands. Yet though her father was cordial in allowing some conversation betwixt him and King Rudolph, Monet could not bring herself to look at Anais. She knew the spite that would burn in her eyes—the triumphant, knowing smile that would don her lovely lips. Monet would wait—wait until the Crimson Knight had defeated Sir Fredrick. Only then would she look to Anais.

The crowd cheered as Sir Fredrick entered the arena. He spurred his charger to ride fast past the stands. Turning his mount, he approached slowly, halting before King Rudolph and Anais. Lifting his helmet visor, Sir Fredrick gazed at Anais.

"I will bear your favour to victory, Princess," he said.

Monet did not look to Anais. Still, she could well imagine the expression of pride—of arrogance and triumph—plain on her face.

"Thank you, Sir Fredrick," Anais said. "Do so and the reward promised to the tournament champion shall be yours!"

Monet felt her stomach churn at Anais's meaningful assurance.

The crowed cheered as Sir Fredrick's herald

stepped up onto the heralding stage. Sir Fredrick was heralded, and Monet's body began to quiver with trepidation—nervous apprehension.

Following Sir Fredrick's introduction, Sir Broderick's herald took the stage. The crowd in the stands roared with delight. A slight smile found its way to Monet's lips, for it was obvious the people favored Sir Broderick.

"To all those in attendance!" Sir Broderick's herald began. The crowd was silent, and the herald continued, "Good people! My lord, my ladies! Kings and queens! Sir Broderick Dougray . . . Son of Kendrick Nathair . . . First Knight of Karvana . . . Favored Warrior of King Dacian . . . Commander of the First Legion . . . Commander of the Second Legion . . . Slayer of a Thousand Enemies . . . Blood Warrior of Ballist . . . Protector of the Kingdom . . . Guardian of the Scarlet Princess. For your favor I offer . . . the Crimson Knight!"

Monet's heart leapt as Sir Broderick's charger pranced into the arena. The charger reared thrice, powerful hooves beating the ground with each stance. Monet watched as the charger performed a side-stepping prance toward the stands, the crowd roaring with approval as it did so.

She could not help but smile, for it was in that moment she realized the profound wisdom of Sir Broderick. In entering the arena in such a dramatic manner, he not only won the love of the crowd but likewise used the fact to heap intimidation on his opponents.

His black charger reared once more as he paused before the stands—before Monet and her father.

"Your Majesty," came the low echo of Sir Broderick Dougray's voice as he addressed Monet's father.

"Sir Broderick?" King Dacian asked.

"I beg permission to address Princess Monet," Sir Broderick said. The low intonation of his voice sent gooseflesh rippling over Monet's arms and legs.

"Of course, sir," King Dacian said.

Monet felt her bosom might burst, so breathless was she as he raised his visor—his blue eyes boring through her.

"How would you have me conquer this opponent, Princess?" the Crimson Knight asked.

Monet was immediately out of countenance!

He seemed to sense her uncertainty as to how to answer. Thus he added, "Three lances? Two?" His eyes narrowed, and though she knew not how, somehow she read his thoughts—knew what answer he required of her.

"One," she stated. The crowd roared as the Crimson Knight nodded.

"One?" King Rudolph exclaimed. "Your arrogance is matched only by your absurdity, Sir Broderick! It must needs be you unhorse Sir

Fredrick to win with one lance! Unhorse him or kill him. Ha! He has never been unhorsed. It cannot be done!"

"I will unhorse him or kill him," Sir Broderick growled. "And though your daughter may have cause to thank me for doing so, it is not for her, nor in defense of her virtue, that I will do this . . . but for my king, for the Kingdom of Karvana . . . and for the Scarlet Princess Monet."

"My daughter's virtue?" King Rudolph growled. King Rudolph's eyes narrowed as he studied the Crimson Knight for a moment. King Rudolph's chest rose as he drew a deep breath. It seemed, for a moment, he would unleash his tongue at the Crimson Knight. Instead, he slowly looked to Anais.

As King Rudolph glared at his daughter, Monet could not keep herself from looking to Anais.

"Anais?" King Rudolph inquired.

Yet Anais only straightened her posture, looking away from her father and to Sir Fredrick waiting at one end of the arena.

"One lance," King Dacian said.

Monet looked to the Crimson Knight. His eyes narrowed a moment before he reached up, pulling his visor down over his face.

"Unhorse him or kill him. I leave the choice to you, Crimson Knight," King Dacian said.

The Crimson Knight nodded. His charger

reared, beating the ground several times with powerful hooves. The Crimson Knight rode to the far end of the arena, and the banner bearer stepped to the center of it.

The crowd was silent. It seemed no person drew breath, apprehension hanging thick as porridge.

Monet watched the bearer drop the banner. The Crimson Knight charged forward, leveling his lance. The thunder of hooves coupled the strain of leather. As the two knights bore down in assured devastation, Monet did not draw breath. Sir Fredrick's lance was leveled and steady—as was the Crimson Knight's. And then, the brutal crash as the Crimson Knight's lance struck armor—shattered—echoed through the arena. Monet gasped, awed as Sir Fredrick Esmund reeled back at the blow—reeled and fell— entirely unhorsed.

The roar of the crowd was deafening! Monet collapsed onto her seat, struggling for breath, her entire body trembling—tears escaping her eyes to trickle in great abundance over her heated cheeks.

"Well done, Dacian," King Rudolph said.

Monet looked up to King Rudolph, then to Anais. Arrogant irritation in being bested owned King Rudolph's expression, yet Anais's countenance shone only fury and loathing as she glared at Monet.

"You may thank your Crimson Knight for my

two best chargers joining your stables, Dacian," King Rudolph said.

"And you may thank him for the assurance of your daughter's virtue!" Monet cried.

Monet was somewhat surprised when her father did not scold her. Rather he simply placed a comforting hand at her shoulder.

King Rudolph offered no immediate response either—simply stood, eyes wide, mouth open, as if someone had delivered a slap to his bearded jaw.

"King James will conquer Karvana, Monet!" Anais growled.

"Anais!" King Rudolph scolded, rattled from his silence by his daughter's traitorous threat.

Anais was undaunted, however. "He will conquer it . . . and you will be left no better than a pitiful peasant in the field!" Anais added, hatefully.

Taking the hand of one of her ladies-in-waiting, Anais stormed away, even as her father called after her.

"Anais!" King Rudolph roared. When his daughter did not cease in her retreat, he turned to Monet.

"What goes on here?" he growled.

"The Crimson Knight has won the tournament, Rudolph," King Dacian said. He offered a hand to Monet, and she took it. He helped her to rise. "And my daughter must away . . . for the ceremony to honor him will begin shortly. A man named Damon will ride to Alvar to collect your two best chargers and bring them to Karvana."

Monet's father linked her arm with his own—an offer of strength and support. He paused, however, looking to Rudolph once more.

"I wish you well, Rudolph. When next we meet, I hope it is to know a wiser, less arrogant King of Alvar."

King Rudolph said nothing, though his eyes narrowed with indignation.

Monet yet trembled. Dacian could feel her weakness, her lingering fear. It yet held her captive.

"You must recover quickly, Monet," he said. "I know the strength is bled from you . . . too much empathy spent in Sir Broderick's behalf. Yet you must find courage, for he is victorious. And victorious though he may be . . . he is yet bruised, bloodied, and broken for it. You must meet him. Gift him his prize, that he may know he has triumphed in our hearts as well as in tournament."

"Yes, Father," Monet whispered. She yet wept, overcome with emotion, worn through with empathy for the Crimson Knight's weariness and pain—frightened by Anais's horrid behavior and declaration.

"King James will not cease in endeavoring to

capture Karvana . . . will he, Father?" she asked.

"I fear not, Monet," her father said. He had never been one to hide the truth from her for long—no matter how terrifying it may be. "Yet we have right on our side, dove," he continued, "and many good soldiers who love their kingdom."

"And will their king lead them into battle, Father?" Monet asked, though she already knew the answer to her question. King Dacian of Karvana was renowned for accompanying his soldiers into battle. He would send no man into territory he himself was not willing to go.

"Yes, dove. Their king will lead them."

Monet fought to withhold the tears welling in her eyes.

"But, Father—" she began, terror striking her tender heart.

"Their king will lead them . . . with the Crimson Knight of Karvana at his side," her father interrupted. He paused, taking Monet's shoulders between strong hands. His brow furrowed, his voice low and commanding as he spoke next. "Listen to me now, Monet," he said. "I will see you stand strong before Sir Broderick as he takes the champion's stage. I would have you thank him for his sacrifice and tribute to Karvana— to me . . . and to you. There is no doubt in my mind of this tournament being the least of his battles and sacrifices where our kingdom is concerned, Monet. He will yet continue to prove himself only further heroic. Therefore, meet him with strength in your carriage even if it is feigned . . . for I know well your fears. Meet him with gratitude in your whole countenance, and let your lips meet his with the lingering kiss of a humble and indebted princess . . . one deserving of his continued allegiance and protection."

Monet brushed the tears from her cheeks. The brutal pounding of her heart was madness!

"But, Father," she cried in a whisper, "so many eyes upon me. Every set of eyes in the arena will . . . and . . . and I have never before kissed a man . . . let alone one the like of Sir Broderick Dougray! What if I cannot find the courage to . . . to . . ."

"You will find it, Monet," King Dacian interrupted. "You will find it."

"Yet how, Father? How?" Monet could feel her entire being quaking. Her limbs felt heavy; her innards churned near to retching.

"You will find it because you must. You have no choice but to find it."

Monet shook her head, brushing tears from her cheeks. "Father . . . I . . . I do not think—"

"He bore favour, Monet," King Dacian interrupted. "Though I have heard him vow many times never to bear favour in tournament, he bore yours . . . and triumphed. He well knew he would triumph, as he well knew of Ivan's promised prize to the tournament champion . . . as I suspect you did not at first."

Monet blushed. Her father laughed and drew her into his arms.

"What valiant knight would not battle in hope of a tender kiss bestowed by a pretty princess, eh? Such a thing is so rarely obtainable."

Monet lingered in her father's loving embrace. She smiled—laughed a little. "Even the Blood Warrior of Ballist? Even the Crimson Knight?" she asked.

"Even he, Monet," King Dacian said. "Thus, kiss him well . . . for he much deserves to be well kissed. Does he not?"

"Kissed well? Then perhaps he should've borne favour given him by one of cook's kitchen maids," Monet giggled. She felt her terror beginning to subside.

King Dacian chuckled. "The one with the flaming red hair? The one cook caught indiscreetly trifling with Sir March's squire?"

"The very one, Father," Monet said. "Perhaps she would know best of kissing well."

"Perhaps." Another low laugh. "Though I do not think Sir Broderick Dougray would have been willing to ride into tournament to battle against so many worthy opponents for the sake of cook's red-haired maid, do you?"

Monet smiled, gently pushing herself from her

father's protective arms. Brushing tears from her cheeks, she gazed up at him. How she loved him! At times she could not believe she had been so blessed in him as a father. What had she done to deserve such a loving and noble parent?

"I will meet him with strength in carriage," she began, "though it will, indeed, be feigned."

Her smile broadened as her father lovingly caressed her cheek with the back of one strong hand.

"And I will meet him with gratitude in my whole countenance . . . for I owe him more gratitude than even you are aware, Father."

"And?" he prodded.

Monet inhaled a deep breath of courage.

"And I will kiss him . . . the kiss of a grateful, indebted princess, humbled by his gallant sacrifice and service . . . endeavoring to be one deserving of his continued allegiance and protection."

King Dacian smiled. The unreserved love warm in his eyes caused hope and courage to rise in Monet.

"Kiss him for the sake of the handsome and virile man that he is, as well, daughter."

"Father!" Monet exclaimed, a crimson blush rising to her cheeks. "Think you now that I am cook's red-haired maid?"

Monet giggled as her father shrugged. "It is said the Crimson Knight can make conquest of any woman by the mere bestowing of his glance," he said.

"And there are those who believe you were bred of fairies, Father," Monet reminded.

Monet startled as the horns sounded.

"Thus the festivities begin," King Dacian said. "We must hurry to the stage. They will begin by presenting prizes for champions in individual events—maces, swords, and the like. Your Sir Broderick has won much wealth in these alone."

"Do I yet own the appearance of having been weeping, Father?" Monet asked.

King Dacian grinned. "You have the look and beauty of your mother," he answered. "The Crimson Knight will be utterly bewitched by you."

Monet smiled. Oh, how desperately she wished it were true! To bewitch the Crimson Knight— to own the smallest part of his heart—what could measure its worth?

The Champion's Prize

Monet sat, her back aching with faultless posture, her trembling hands folded with deceptive calm in her lap. As she watched Sir Terrence Langford accept his prize as archery champion of King Ivan's tournament, she tried to appear composed. Yet with each twittered whisper—with each pointed finger in her direction—she feared her courage would fail her. Every person present, every soul gathered in Ivan's arena, was waiting—waiting for the moment the Scarlet Princess of Karvana would bless the lips of the tournament champion with his champion's prize—a kiss.

"In wrestling . . . Sir Fredrick Esmund," the herald announced.

The crowd cheered as Anais presented Sir Fredrick with an ornate dagger embellished with gold and emeralds. Such was the tradition at tournaments—for she who had bestowed favour to present the prize to her champion. Monet had presented a similar ruby-jeweled dagger to the Crimson Knight for his triumph at maces and a small golden statue of a peacock for his victory in swords. Monet's legs trembled with such nervous violence upon twice presenting Sir Broderick with prizes, she feared she might simply drop at his feet. Furthermore, the cool blue of his gaze each time their eyes met robbed her of breath, weakening her further.

Now, as she sat watching Sir Fredrick accept his prize from Anais's calm, graceful hands, she wondered whether she would yet find the courage to bestow the kiss promised the tournament champion. She nearly ventured a glance at Sir Broderick. He stood no more than a measure from her. Yet she could not bring herself to look at him, fearing that if she found his eyes already upon her, she might fade—no matter how strong her resolve to remain courageous.

Sir Fredrick nodded to King Ivan in acceptance of the dagger—though Monet noted he glared at Anais before bowing and taking his leave.

The crowd applauded, and King Ivan's herald raised a hand to silence.

"And now, good people . . . I present King Ivan's champion! Sir Broderick Dougray . . . son of Kendrick Nathair . . . First Knight of Karvana . . . Favored Warrior of King Dacian . . . Commander of the First Legion . . . Commander of the Second Legion . . . Slayer of a Thousand Enemies . . . Blood Warrior of Ballist . . . Protector of the Kingdom . . . Guardian of the Scarlet Princess . . . the Crimson Knight . . .

Champion of the Tournament of King Ivan of Avaron!"

The crowd roared with cheering and applause as Sir Broderick again approached the stage platform. He removed his helmet, turned, and bowed to the crowd, displaying gratitude for such profound approval.

Monet's legs somehow managed to find their strength. As Sir Broderick bowed to King Ivan, she stood.

"Bravo!" King Ivan called, applauding as he nodded to the Crimson Knight. "Well done, Sir Broderick! A well-fought battle indeed!" Monet held her breath as King Ivan added, "Now away to collect your prize, sir! And collect it well, my man!"

Monet wondered if every man, woman, and child present could determine the state of her nerves simply by the quiver of her gown as she trembled beneath it. In that moment, she wished she were not swathed in scarlet. How less seen she would feel dressed in black or copper.

She heard his footsteps, his boots heavy on the platform, yet she could not raise her gaze to face him. He stood directly before her—Sir Broderick Dougray—the Crimson Knight.

Knowing it would not be acceptable to continue to stare at his breastplate, Monet slowly lifted her eyes to meet his. He was there—just before her—the bewitching blue of his gaze full upon her. The noise of the crowd cheering was near deafening and only served to further frighten Monet.

"I am . . . your champion, Princess," Sir Broderick said, offering a respectful nod.

Monet swallowed—prayed that when she spoke, her voice would indeed sound.

"You have battled well, Sir Broderick," she said, thankful she had been able to speak. "You have brought great honor to Karvana, to its king . . . and to me."

"Thank you, your highness," he said. The deep, alluring sound of his voice caused Monet's trembling to increase, and again she wondered if the crowd—if Sir Broderick Dougray—were aware of her fearful condition.

"A kiss, Princess!" King Ivan called. "To your champion, a kiss!"

The crowd roared, and Monet looked up into the handsome face of the Crimson Knight. She felt her brow pucker as, of a sudden, her nerves gave way to intense empathy. The Crimson Knight was indeed worn! Great fatigue lingered about his beautiful eyes; his handsome face was streaked where perspiration had cut through the dust and dirt accumulated of battle.

It besieged her then—the desire to comfort, soothe, and offer gratitude to such a champion, to such a heroic man. At that moment, the roar of the crowd fell silent to Monet's ears, the many sets of eyes upon her forgotten as she gazed at her beloved Crimson Knight.

"Thank you, Sir Broderick," she whispered, her hands going to his face. The warmth of his flesh—the sense of his roughly shaven face against her palms—somehow caused a great heated moisture to collect in her mouth. She gazed at his lips—raised herself on toe, pulling his face toward her own. She saw his eyes narrow, as if he doubted she could muster the courage necessary to award him his champion's prize.

"You are most welcome," he mumbled. Once he had again fallen silent, his lips remained ever so slightly parted.

Parted lips? Monet thought. Her mind had only a breath of a moment to determine her course. If his lips were thus parted, then so must her lips be similarly parted if she wished the kiss she bestowed to be in measure.

"Lingering," she breathed. Her father's instruction echoed through her mind a moment before every other thought was banished by the ethereal sense of pressing her lips to those of Sir Broderick Dougray.

His lips were softer than she had imagined they would be—warm and moist. Of a sudden, a new and delicious trembling owned her body, for she realized she was no longer simply bestowing a kiss to Sir Broderick; rather, he was kissing her in return! Somehow their lips were not simply pressed: they were meet—a shared kiss born! The pressure of his kiss lessened just long enough for Monet to gasp against his lips a moment before he kissed her once more—his lips further parted—her own matching their parting. She was rendered breathless by the sudden awareness that the Crimson Knight was kissing her! In that instant, she thought she might literally expire from the rapture his kiss evoked within her.

She swayed backward, her knees having weakened beneath her. The Crimson Knight broke the seal of their lips, his vise grip taking hold of her arm to ensure she did not crumple to the platform.

As the crowd roared with approval, the Crimson Knight's gaze captured Monet's. A slight grin donned his lips—his delicious, masterful lips—and Monet was entirely bewitched. It was true! She knew then the very legends of the Crimson Knight's power over women must indeed be nothing if not pure truth—for she was entirely undone!

Monet struggled to straighten her posture—to subdue the violent trembling of her body borne of his intoxicating kiss.

"Well done, Princess Monet! Well done, indeed!" King Ivan cheered.

"Indeed," the Crimson Knight mumbled, releasing his hold of her arm. Monet fancied that, as he released her, an odd chill of vulnerability washed over her. She suddenly wished he would not have released her—that he would hold her or, at the very least, touch her somehow—forever.

"My good people!" King Ivan called. "I give you your tournament champion . . . Sir Broderick Dougray . . . the Crimson Knight!"

Sir Broderick turned, bowing to King Ivan.

"And now, Sir Broderick," King Ivan began, "who shall reign as the Queen of Love and Beauty of my tournament?"

Still trembling, Monet stepped back, away from the Crimson Knight, that he may endeavor to collect his final champion's prize—the crowning of the tournament's Queen of Love and Beauty.

She watched as King Ivan handed Sir Broderick a delicate golden crown. Adorned with flowers and trailing ribbons, Monet smiled as the Crimson Knight accepted the offered crown from King Ivan. The contrast of the pretty crown against his battered armor and bloodied hand was profound.

"What ties bind me, your majesty?" the Crimson Knight asked. It was a wise inquiry. Many a battle had begun with a tournament champion paying honor or displaying courtly love to the wrong woman—the wife or intended of some royal or noble. Perhaps King Ivan would prefer his own queen be crowned. The Crimson Knight would not risk offense by choosing without direction.

"None!" King Ivan chuckled. "The choice is

yours . . . as champion, Sir Broderick. Thus name the queen."

"Then I name the Scarlet Princess, Monet of Karvana, as tournament queen, your majesty."

Again Monet was rendered unable to draw breath. As the cheering rose to a deafening roar, she watched the Crimson Knight turn and advance upon her. She could not move—could only watch, gaze at him, as he reached forth, placing the crown on her head.

"The Scarlet Princess . . . Monet of Karvana!" King Ivan called. "Our Queen of Love and Beauty!"

"Pray smile, Princess," Sir Broderick said in a lowered voice, "else the people and their king will think you are not grateful for the honor bestowed you."

Instantly, Monet smiled, forced an accepting nod to King Ivan, and offered a grateful wave to the crowd.

King Ivan approached, taking Monet's arm and placing it on his own. Monet sighed with aching disappointment as she watched the Crimson Knight bow to King Ivan once more, turn, and take his leave.

"He will away to a much-needed respite, Princess," King Ivan said. Instantly, Monet forced her gaze from the retreating Crimson Knight to King Ivan. He laughed in his throat and said, "You will sit next to me at the banquet tonight,

Monet. And though I know your Crimson Knight does not often appear at banquet, I will beg him to do so this time . . . that he may offer his strength to your delightfully humble countenance." He laughed again. "Queen of Love and Beauty . . . at such a tender age as yours. You must feel greatly honored, Princess . . . for Karvana's Crimson Knight is not one to relinquish an opportunity to dominate in every regard, is he?"

"Apparently not, your majesty," Monet said.

"That . . . or your lips are far sweeter even than they appear, and with one kiss, you have managed to entirely bewitch him," King Ivan said.

Monet sensed her cheeks blush vermilion.

"I assure you it is his skill in dominance of any circumstance . . . not my kiss," Monet said.

"Either thing is a joy to me! I have never seen the people so thoroughly amused," King Ivan said. "You and your Crimson Knight have won the day!"

Yet as King Ivan escorted her back to her father, Monet sighed. This day, this triumph, belonged to one man—to Sir Broderick Dougray, the Crimson Knight. It struck her then how entirely iniquitous it was that Sir Broderick should battle with such brutal valiance, only to have the glory heaped on those who little deserved the glory. What glory should Monet own for his sacrifices? What glory should her father or her kingdom own? She wondered then from whence such a man drew his reason for such an undertaking as was King Ivan's tournament. For the glory and honor of others? It seemed incomprehensible, and yet did not *she* love her king and kingdom so well as to sacrifice her own well-being for their sakes? Yes—indeed—she did.

"Bravo, my dove! Bravo!" Dacian called as Monet approached, escorted by Ivan himself.

Dacian fancied the roses were still too abloom on his daughter's cheeks—the lingering result of Broderick Dougray's attentions—and it well pleased him. How lovely Monet appeared then, face bright with delight, her lovely head adorned with a crown of flowers and ribbon. Mirth rained over him, knowing the depth of courage it had taken for her to bestow the champion's prize in front of such a gathering.

"Your daughter has proven herself worthy of this crown, Dacian . . . and of her own," King Ivan said.

Dacian nodded, understanding Ivan's veiled implication. His gaze lingered on his daughter—his lovely daughter—so entirely unaware of the strength she and the Crimson Knight of Karvana had lent its king. Ivan's tournament would be the subject of much talk and speculation. Tales of the Crimson Knight's victory would spread as a wild flame, fanned by the account of Karvana's Scarlet Princess and the kiss bestowed her champion. A tale of chivalry and triumph would reach King James's arrogant ears, perhaps plant doubt in his mind—doubt of any easy victory over Dacian, King of Karvana. Further, Karvana's people would hear of the strength and bravery of their princess—their princess, who would one day be their queen.

"Yes, Ivan," Dacian said as Monet embraced him. "She has indeed."

Still trembling from the Crimson Knight's kiss—the sense of it still warm upon her lips—Monet continued to bathe in the security of her father's embrace. Her knees seemed weak, her arms prickled with gooseflesh, at the memory of Sir Broderick's lips pressed to her own.

Closing her eyes, his face appeared in her mind—awash with great fatigue, dust-streaked, and battered. Monet wondered in that moment, if the look of battle was so obvious on his face, what must the body beneath the armor have endured?

"He will be well, Father . . . will he not?" she asked.

Her father offered a quiet chuckle as he lovingly stroked her hair. "He will be well, pigeon," he said. "He will be well."

"I would speak to you privately, Dacian," King Ivan said. "If you please."

"Of course," Dacian said.

Taking Monet's face between strong hands, King Dacian said, "I would speak to Ivan a moment, Monet. Pray settle the enthusiasm and curiosity threatening to tear your friends to shreds while I do, eh?"

Monet smiled, heard giggling, and saw Portia and Lenore approaching.

"Of course, Father," she said.

"Thank you," Dacian said, releasing his daughter.

His attention turned at once to Ivan, and Monet could not help but giggle at the delight emblazoned on the faces of Lenore and Portia.

"You must tell us!" Lenore exclaimed in a whisper.

Taking hold of Monet's arm, Portia added, "Yes! We must know everything of his kiss! Everything!"

The tournament was over. The Crimson Knight had prevailed, showering honor and strength over Karvana and its king. Thus, Monet felt a sudden giddiness well within her. It seemed her concerns—her heretofore serious nature—had all but dissolved! Monet enjoyed a sense of liberation of sorts—a freedom—a venue allowing lightheartedness.

Glancing behind her to ensure her father and King Ivan were at a distance, she said, "I was certain I would faint, consumed by bliss and ecstasy!"

Portia and Lenore sighed and smiled, delighted with her answer.

"Tell us all of it, Monet! Do tell!" Lenore giggled.

"What was it like?" Portia asked.

Monet smiled. "Moist and warm . . . intoxicating as to weaken the whole of my body!"

Monet smiled as Portia and Lenore sighed in perfect unison.

"To press lips with the Crimson Knight!" Portia whispered. "What ever else can measure it?"

Monet expired her own sigh. "I think . . . nothing," she said.

Near an hour had waned since the tournament had ended. Near three hours remained before King Ivan's celebratory banquet would begin. It seemed to Monet enough time following and an adequate time before—and he must be told. She must ease her conscience; he must understand the depth of her gratitude.

The knight encampment was quiet. No doubt all the knights and squires were well steeped in much-deserved and needed respite. Still, Monet was wary as she made for the pavilion of the Crimson Knight of Karvana.

Quickly, the thought of her father—his perpetual warnings of taking care—tickled her mind. Yet Monet did not enjoy constant escort. Further, what true harm could befall her there? Thus, she hurried on, her black cloak clutched tightly about her, its black hood concealing her features of face.

The sight of the white pavilion of the Crimson Knight—crimson flag with black rearing dragon unfurled atop—caused Monet's heart to leap. He must be thanked. She would not rest until he knew her profound gratefulness. Yet the thought of facing him—the memory of his kiss still lingering on her lips—gave her pause.

Monet closed her eyes—struggled to muster courage. Inhaling deeply, she reminded herself she was Princess Monet of Karvana, whose father and kingdom and self owed a great debt to their Crimson Knight.

Quickly, before her courage could fail her again, Monet pulled back one flap of the Crimson Knight's pavilion and stepped within. Instantly, she bit her lip, stifling an astonished gasp, for the Crimson Knight stood before her—bare from the waist up—binding the ties of a pair of trousers at his waist.

The astonishment and discomfiture of having intruded to find him so inappropriately attired vanished as Monet's attention was drawn to the deep purple bruising across his chest, at his stomach, and over his arms. Blood still trickled from a large lesion at his upper right arm. Monet felt tears welling in her eyes at such a vision of brutality and pain.

"Your highness!" Eann exclaimed as Monet brushed the hood back to reveal her face.

"What means this?" Monet demanded. The Crimson Knight frowned as she advanced upon him. Eann handed him a length of leather attached to a small leather pouch, and he drew it over his head as a necklace, the pouch resting just above his navel.

"It means I am only just finished bathing and have not yet fully clothed myself once again," Sir Broderick grumbled.

"I meant this," she said. Monet pressed her fingers near the wound at his arm to see that, although well-cleaned, it still had not been stitched. "You're bleeding, Sir Broderick!"

"Usually . . . yes," he mumbled.

"Why has a physician not attended you?"

"There are others in the encampment with far worse wounds than mine, Princess," Sir Broderick said. He was scowling at her, yet she cared not—for the wound was far more serious than she had imagined.

"You bore this wound yesterday, and it has been bleeding all of today! Infection will settle here," Monet said.

"Eann has well cared for me, Princess," the Crimson Knight said. "He will acquire the necessaries to stitch it himself, and it will be of no consequence."

"Stitch it himself?" Monet gasped.

"It is many times I have stitched him, your highness," Eann said. "He is strong as a horse and vastly more resilient when wounded than most men."

"Even so—" Monet began.

"Eann will stitch it, Princess," Sir Broderick interrupted. She looked up to find his steel gaze boring through her.

"Then I pray you send him for the necessaries, Sir Broderick . . . before your arm rots off."

The Crimson Knight's brows arched in astonishment. A slight grin softened his lips, and he said, "Pray fetch the necessaries, Eann . . . before her highness has at me with the surgeon's dismembering saw."

"At once, Sir Broderick," Eann said. Monet blushed at the expression of amusement plain on the squire's face.

"You mock my concern for your well-being," Monet said as Eann left the pavilion. She was angry, humiliated, and yet entirely frightened that the Crimson Knight might yet suffer pain and infection.

"No, your highness," he said. He placed a hand at his chest and bowed his head. "I am touched and honored by your distress on my account." He was in earnest—it was obvious—and Monet settled her indignation.

Sir Broderick straightened, glanced beyond

her a moment, and frowned. "Are you again unaccompanied, Princess?" he asked.

"Yes," she admitted.

The Crimson Knight's brow furrowed once more. "It is not wise . . . not safe for you to wander about—"

"I loathe being in constant escort," Monet interrupted. "And I wanted to offer my thanks to you . . . in private . . . where I may say what I mean to say without unwanted ears to intrude."

"Very well," he said.

Monet turned from him, wringing her hands as her mind struggled to recall what she had meant to tell him. His appearance, his lack of attire, and his yet-bleeding wound had sent all organized thought scattering to the wind.

"There is no manner in which to repay you, Sir Broderick," she began, "no thing of value that will offer recompense for what you have achieved today . . . for the honor and strength you lend to Karvana, its king . . . and me."

"I have received recompense aplenty, Princess," he said, "a far better prize than many a knight has received for besting more men than I in tournament."

Monet blushed. Though she knew his flattery was but obligatory, it caused her body to bathe in honeyed warmth all the same.

"I am in earnest, Sir Broderick!" she said, at last turning to look at him. "Pray do not condescend." His eyes narrowed as she continued. "I suppose . . . I suppose that I did hope to realize the value of your triumph when I came to you, begging you not carry Anais's favour . . . yet I wonder that I did not comprehend its full worth, in truth."

"Your highness?" he asked.

"Your triumph, shared with my father and Karvana, has strengthened the kingdom and the power of the monarchy," she explained. "King James did not attend King Ivan's tournament. In his arrogance . . . in his desire to prove himself above the other kings of the five kingdoms . . . as ever, he lingers in Rothbain. Tales of your triumph will resound in his court, and it may lend doubt to his ambitions. I know you are formidably aware of this, yet I wish you to know that I am also conscious of these things. I do not wish you to think I am ignorant or light-minded in this. Further, I wish to comfort myself that you are in reassurance of my gratitude." She looked up into the lucent indigo of his eyes—let her gaze linger on the whole of his countenance and striking appearance. She wondered for a moment what marvelous sensation his soft, raven hair woven between her fingers would awaken.

"You, and only you, have fought the harsh battle of this tournament. You and none other . . . not my father . . . nor any citizen of our kingdom . . . and undoubtedly not I. I wish you to know that, in my mind and heart, the glory of this victory belongs to none but you . . . and I am in your debt that you should so willingly share your triumph with king and kingdom."

He was silent for a moment. Monet frowned as a slight smile curved his lips.

"Are you thinking I am not sincere in my gratitude?" she asked.

"I am thinking you are more your father's daughter than anyone yet realizes," he said, "for Karvana's king said near as much to me only moments after the final joust. Such humility in a king is rare . . . and profoundly honorable. It is why I own such abiding respect and loyalty to your father. He is a great man among others who only claim greatness."

Monet smiled, delighted by her father's humility in thanking the Crimson Knight—appreciative of being his daughter.

"My father is the best of men, Sir Broderick," she said. "As are you." She studied him for a moment, wincing as empathy for his obvious pain washed over her. "How may I show my thanks, Sir Broderick?" she asked. "How may I prove the depth of my gratitude to you?"

Monet felt gooseflesh prickling her arms as his eyes narrowed—as he studied her from slipper to brow. For a moment, a vision of Sir Fredrick and Anais visited her imagination. Was the Crimson Knight in thought of such a prize as

Sir Fredrick would have demanded? Surely not!

"You have already proved it, Princess," he said, his gaze resting on her face once more. "The champion's prize . . . I know it was difficult for you to bestow."

"I was glad to offer it," Monet said. She was irritated at the warm blush she felt pink her cheeks of a sudden. "Yet I would now offer a token of *real* value . . . something you might truly feel is a worthy prize. I would have you name this thing . . . whether a heavy purse, horses— for I know you delight in horses—or some other valuable item I may bestow as further witness of my gratitude."

Again his brow puckered. "You do not think your kiss is of great enough worth to suffice?" he asked.

Monet smiled. "To the Crimson Knight of Karvana?" She shook her head. "I told you, sir . . . I am no fool. Ask me a thing you truly crave, and I will endeavor to bestow it."

"I tell you, Princess—for a knight to receive the lips of his princess . . . is a far greater reward than you imagine," he said. Monet blushed—shook her head in knowing he was skilled at flattery. "Yet if you are to offer another prize . . . who am I to deny it?"

"What then?" she prompted. "What token may I bestow as thanks to you, Sir Broderick?"

"I beg only . . . a truthful answer," he said.

"A truthful answer?" she asked. "To what question?"

"To a question of my choosing. Any question," he said. "If I ask it of you . . . will you answer . . . truthfully?"

"Of course," Monet said.

"I have your vow . . . that you will answer my question in earnest truth?"

She straightened her posture. What question could he possibly ask that she would be tempted not to answer truthfully?

"Yes. You have my word," she said.

She trembled slightly as the piercing blue of his eyes lingered on her. Moisture flooded her mouth as he advanced closer to her. She could well feel the heat of his flesh as he stood before her.

"When first I asked you if you knew the champion's prize for this tournament," he began.

Monet swallowed—attempted to appear unaffected. He knew! He knew she had lied.

"Yes?" she urged.

He grinned, and it was near her undoing! He was so handsome; something about him so entirely disconcerted her.

"You did not know the champion's prize was a kiss . . . did you, Princess?" He arched one eyebrow and added, "You've vowed to tell the truth of it . . . remember."

Monet swallowed again, tightly clasping her hands at her waist.

"No," she admitted. "I did not know it."

The Crimson Knight chuckled, and the sound sent a swarm of butterflies to flight in Monet's stomach.

"I thought as much," he said, "else you would not have agreed to bestow your favour on me."

"That is not true!" Monet exclaimed. Of a sudden, a sort of strange desperation welled within her. Karvana and her father—both shared in the Crimson Knight's honor, whether deserving or not. Therefore, even had she known the champion's prize was a kiss, still she would have begged Sir Broderick's allegiance. She felt her cheeks warm as she thought that, had she known the champion's prize was a kiss, she may have begged his allegiance with even more vigor. "I would still have come to you. I would still have begged your loyalty for my father's sake . . . and for the sake of our people and kingdom."

He grinned, shook his head, and glanced down at the wound of his arm. He did not believe her.

"I vowed to give you the truth, Sir Broderick," she exclaimed, "and I have! Do not dishonor me with the implication I did not answer your question truthfully . . . please!"

"Of course I will not," he said. But she knew. Monet knew he did not believe her. Such was the nature of deceit—once wielded against another, it was not but anticipated. He must believe her! He must!

"Sir Broderick, you say for a knight to receive the lips of his princess . . . you tell me it is a far greater reward than I imagine. Is that not what your flattery endeavors to make me believe?" she asked.

"It is . . . and it was not with vain flattery that I spoke it," he rather growled.

"Then a kiss from your princess—offered here—without witnesses to lessen its value to that of a mere champion's prize . . . if it is such a great and rare reward, then I insist you allow me to prove myself . . . to prove I speak the truth of it . . . that I would have had you bear my favour even knowing the nature of the champion's prize." Monet could not believe her own utterance! Yet she must evidence herself to him— atone for having lied once and prove she had not lied again.

"You need prove nothing, Princess," he said.

"Yes! I do need to prove it! For I will not have you thinking me a constant liar . . . an invariable deceiver! And I would have you know my thanks, Sir Broderick. I would have you *know* it! Further, I would know for myself that you know it," she cried in a whisper.

Monet stepped forward. Raising trembling hands to his face, she was rendered breathless at the feel of his roughly shaven face.

"Princess Monet, do not lower yourself to—" he began.

"I thank you, Sir Broderick," she whispered. "I thank you for your valiant efforts . . . for your hard-fought battle and triumph in behalf of our king, our people, and our kingdom. I am ever in your debt for doing this thing for me . . . for refusing the favour of Anais of Alvar . . . and for bearing mine."

Her hands burned warm with touching him, the heat of his body warming hers. Of a sudden, his great height and the broad expanse of his shoulders intimidated her. Yet she was bound to prove herself to him—to prove she was honest and not a liar.

Monet swallowed, raised herself on toe, and pressed her parted lips to his. Would he spurn her? Would he put her away from himself, revolted by her lack of skill in kissing him—by the fact she was not a woman he wished to kiss?

Her heart leapt in her bosom. She gasped as she felt his strong hand at the small of her back—felt his lips part further as he pressed her kiss once, twice, thrice—each kiss more firmly applied, the moisture of his lips blending with her own—each warm, thrilling coupling lingering a moment longer than the one before. She could not keep her hands from slipping from his face to rest on the breadth of his strong shoulders. The sense of his smooth flesh against her palms caused heat to flood her limbs and body.

Of a sudden, frightened by the sensations

his touch and kiss inflamed in her, she drew away from him—however unwillingly. As her knees struggled to keep the strength necessary to support her, Monet knew: the ability of the Crimson Knight to dominate any circumstance was far more powerful than any man could realize.

"Forgive me my weakness, Princess," Sir Broderick said. His voice was low, its intonation no less than entirely seductive. "You find me in a weakened condition . . . somewhat out of countenance. Forgive me if I gave offense. I should not have—"

"I will not forgive you," Monet interrupted, unable to meet his bewitching gaze. "There is nothing to forgive. And to offer forgiveness . . . for you to ask it of me . . . it is only to say that were you in perfect condition and countenance, you would not have wished me to . . . to prove my earnest words, nor to offer my sincere thanks."

"No, please, your highness," he began. "You mistake me."

Monet looked to him, fearful the moisture in her eyes would betray her heartache at his kissing her being only a matter of weakness of the mind and body—not because he wished to do so.

"I would have begged your help in besting Anais . . . even knowing the nature of the champion's prize, Sir Broderick," she said. "Know you now the truth of this?"

The sapphire eyes of the Crimson Knight narrowed. "Yes," he said.

"And know you now the depth of my gratitude, Sir Broderick Dougray?"

"Yes."

Slowly Monet let her hands slip from the Crimson Knight's broad shoulders and over his massive chest. The soft caress caused Monet to tremble with a pleasing bliss she had never known. Stepping back from him—for she feared she would throw herself against the strength of his body and beg for another press of his lips—she said, "Then I leave you to Eann's stitching."

As Monet pulled the hood of her cloak over her head, the Crimson Knight asked, "King Ivan has requested I attend his banquet this evening. I do not commonly attend banquet. However, in support of my princess, whose favour I carried in this tournament . . . I will attend . . . if you wish it."

Monet studied him for long moments. He was battle-worn—bruised, bloodied, and undoubtedly fatigued beyond anything she could imagine.

"I will leave that decision to you, Sir Broderick . . . for it must be as you wish," she said.

"Will you have escort if I do not attend?" he asked, his beautiful eyes suddenly shadowed with profound weariness. "You are so in habit of appearing unescorted . . . it oft concerns me."

Monet smiled. "I will have my father . . . and King Ivan. And though I admit to owning no fondness for the attentions I must no doubt endure as Queen of Love and Beauty . . . I am not, perhaps, so weak as you think, Sir Broderick. Having twice mustered the courage to kiss the Blood Warrior of Ballist—the Crimson Knight— can I not muster enough courage to endure one evening of banquet?"

"I have no doubt that you can, your highness," he said, a tired grin curving his perfect mouth.

Monet forced a smile, inwardly overwhelmed with disappointment that he would not be seated next to her at banquet. She hoped her hood cached her awe as she allowed her gaze to travel the length of him—from the dark raven of his hair, over the powerful breadth of his shoulders, to the small leather pouch hanging from the thin leather strap around his neck, to the doeskin trousers he wore.

"Good-bye, Sir Broderick," she said.

"Your highness," he said. He nodded and bowed, and Monet stepped from the Crimson Knight's pavilion.

"Thank you, sire," Monet said as King Ivan himself held her chair for her. The whispers concerning the kiss Karvana's Scarlet Princess had bestowed upon the tournament champion hissed from every corner of the banquet hall. Some said the kiss was not adequate—that it did not honor the Crimson Knight as he deserved. Others said it was immoral—too lingering, lips too parted to be virtuous.

Though Monet's resolve to hold strong and steadfast in the tide of gossip had once been resolute, it was waning at being so thoroughly tried.

"Yet your champion does not appear," Anais said from her place across the table from Monet.

"I offered him respite from this evening's demands," Monet said. "Tournament is wearing beyond comprehension. Is it not enough he battled for three days? Must he now be expected to endure the demands of banquet?"

"Indeed," King Ivan agreed. "I too offered our champion reprieve."

"Still, he should attend, Ivan," Rudolph said. "After all the wealth heaped upon him at your hand."

"Wealth he well earned, Rudolph," King Ivan reminded.

Monet glanced to her father sitting next to the empty chair at her left—the chair meant for the Crimson Knight.

"Well earned," King Dacian said. "As well earned as peaceful respite."

Monet smiled as her father winked at her with understanding.

A sudden and distinct hush fell on the room,

followed by a resounding meeting of hands in clapping.

Monet's heart leapt where it lay in her bosom as she looked up to see the Crimson Knight striding toward the king's banquet table.

"Ah! And yet he musters!" King Ivan exclaimed. "A true champion indeed!"

"Forgive my tardiness, your majesty," the Crimson Knight said, taking his seat between Monet and her father. "It was needs be I had a bit of stitching rendered . . . to keep my arm from . . ." He paused, glancing to Monet. "How did you speak it, your highness?"

"To keep your arm from rotting off," Monet giggled.

"Yes, that's it," Sir Broderick said, grinning at Monet.

He had come! He had come to the banquet, though Monet knew he was loath to do so. In her heart, she determined to pretend he had done it for her—that he had forced himself to attendance for her own sake.

"A noble cause for a belated arrival, Sir Broderick. Indeed!" King Ivan chuckled.

Monet felt moisture rise to her eyes, for he yet looked weary, the bruises and cuts causing a notable stiffness in his hands as he raised his goblet for King Ivan's toast.

"To the Crimson Knight of Karvana, our champion of tournament!" King Ivan roared. "And to

Monet . . . the Scarlet Princess . . . our Queen of Love and Beauty!"

The banquet guests cheered, and Monet forced a smile. The Crimson Knight's arm brushed her own for a moment, and she quivered with delight at his nearness.

"It is bad of me, I know," Sir Broderick began in a lowered voice, "but I neglected to return your veil . . . the favour you gifted me for the tournament." He reached into his tunic, but Monet's hand on his forearm stalled him.

"I would bid you keep it, Sir Broderick," Monet whispered. "W-would you keep it? As a memento of your victory today?"

"With pleasure, your highness," he said. He smiled at her, and Monet's breath caught in her throat at the pure magnificence of it.

Attempting to slow the sudden mad pounding of her heart, Monet looked across the table to Lenore and Portia. Each princess was seated to the right of her father, their eyes twinkling with a resplendent, romantic admiration as they gazed at the Crimson Knight.

Monet smiled and ventured a glance back to Sir Broderick. He was in conversation with her father, and she sighed—content to be in the company of the two men she loved most in all the world.

A Call to Battle

War. It was unavoidable—so King Dacian had counseled with his knights the previous day—so he had informed the court and then the people of Karvana that morning. If Karvana were to remain a free and blissful kingdom, it could not fall to James of Rothbain—James of Rothbain, who at that moment was amassing troops at Karvana's northern border.

Monet attempted to appear calm—strong in the face of battle, death, and the threat of Karvana's fall. Yet as she stood before her father—his dark armor and golden-crowned helmet glinting in the morning sun—calm was not what bound her soul. Had it truly been only six months since King Ivan's tournament? She glanced past her father to the Crimson Knight standing just behind him and to his right. Her gaze fell to his lips—not to his armor or chain mail, not to the weapons he bore, but to his face, his handsome countenance, and his lips. She knew his lips—knew his kiss—and never had she ceased in considering it. Not for one moment since King Ivan's tournament, not once since she had kissed him in the arena, in his

120

pavilion—not once had her mind wandered from the memory of his hand at her arm to steady her, of his hand pressed to her back as his parted lips met with her own.

"I must lead the men into battle, Monet," King Dacian said. Her attention was thus torn from the Crimson Knight at her father's side—back to impending battle. "If I am lost—"

"Father, please do not—" Monet began.

"If I am lost . . . you will be queen," Dacian growled. A deep frown furrowed his brow as he near glared at his daughter. "I have left instruction for you . . . you know where."

Monet nodded. How could she ever forget where? The secret compartment in her mother's tomb.

"Yes, Father."

Fury and rage owned Broderick Dougray—Karvana's Crimson Knight. As he watched his good King Dacian strike terror into the tender heart of his noble daughter, Monet, a hatred as he had never known rose within him—a desire to vanquish James of Rothbain with his own hand.

He could see her trembling. By the manner in which her scarlet gown quivered, Broderick knew the princess was awash with fear. He fisted one hand beneath its gauntlet, resisting the compulsion to reach out and touch her—to reassure her he would protect her father. He would defend

King Dacian and Karvana with his life. He wondered if she knew this of him. For a moment, the violet of her eyes lingered on him—seemed to plead with him—beg him for a thing. Yet he knew not what, in truth. To protect her father? To save her kingdom? He was uncertain as to what her frightened gaze wished to convey, but he nodded all the same. Karvana would not fall while Broderick Dougray yet drew breath. This was his silent oath. Nor would King Dacian.

The Crimson Knight felt his eyes narrow as he watched his king give instruction to she who would one day be queen. She would rule well. This he knew, for he had seen the strength in her, the compassion for the people, and great wisdom—even in one so young. Further, he would serve her as he had served her father. If he lived to do so, he would serve her. He felt his jaw tighten as he thought of a new king—Monet's one-day husband. It angered and sickened him to think of any man taking Dacian's throne—of any man taking the Princess Monet to his bed. Yet he would serve the monarchy of Karvana to the death. For good kings and queens were a rarity, as were good knights—and he was a good knight.

Monet could not stop the tears from escaping her eyes. As they trickled over her cheeks, she began, "Father . . . I—"

"Bless them . . . each one as he passes, Monet,"

King Dacian said. "They require your approval."

Monet nodded, and her father pressed a firm kiss to her forehead.

"Knights of Karvana!" he shouted as he turned to face the knights lining the hall behind him. "We go! We fight! We fight for Karvana! For her people! For freedom!"

Monet closed her eyes for a moment as the roar of the knights echoed through the castle.

"To battle!" King Dacian shouted.

Monet's trembling increased as her father brushed past her.

"God be with you, Princess," Sir Alum said. Monet opened her eyes. The eldest of her father's round table, Sir Alum Willham, knelt before her.

Remembering her father's instruction, Monet placed her hand on the top of Sir Alum's helmet.

"God protect you, Sir Alum," she said. The knight, Sir Alum Willham, stood, nodded, and followed his king from the gathering hall.

"God be with you, Princess," the next knight greeted, taking a knee.

"God protect you, Sir Blevin," Monet said, placing her hand atop the helmet of Sir Blevin Jonstone.

Eleven more knights knelt before Monet— eleven more of King Dacian's round table, commanders of legions, heroes of Karvana.

King Dacian's first knight—Sir Broderick Dougray, the Crimson Knight—approached last.

Monet thought her heart might tear itself from her breast, so brutally did it hammer. To send Sir Broderick to war! The thought caused terror the like Monet had never known to seize her in its painful grip.

As tears flooded Monet's cheeks anew, the Crimson Knight took a knee before her.

"God be with you, Princess." The low, powerful intonation of his voice as he addressed her caused her to tremble. "God watch over and protect you, your highness," he added.

Monet placed both her hands on Sir Broderick's bowed helmet.

"God go with you, Sir Broderick," she breathed. "God watch over you. May He wield your sword with you . . . and count you preserved."

The Crimson Knight rose to take his leave. Yet he paused. Monet resisted, barely restrained herself, from reaching out, from throwing her arms around him and begging him not to go—to stay out of harm's way that he may be assuredly preserved.

"I will not let Death claim your father, Princess," he said, his eyes narrowed with determination. "I will give my life to—"

She could not hear him speak it; thus her fingers pressed his lips to silence him. She would not hear him speak of giving up his life—not for anyone, nor anything! Not even for her father or Karvana!

"God . . . protect our Crimson Knight," she whispered.

She turned and fled—ran up the winding stairs leading to the crest of the castle's keep.

Her body wracked with sobbing, she stepped out onto the keep's crest. Far below she could see them—her father astride his white charger, the Crimson Knight of Karvana at his side, thirteen remaining knights of the table behind them. Beyond the walls of the castle kingdom, she could see the glinting in the sunlight—three legions of soldiers ready to be commanded, waiting to be led into battle by her father and the Crimson Knight.

War had come, and the people—the land—Karvana must be protected.

The horns sounded, and the inner gates were lifted, the inner drawbridge lowered. A sudden breeze freshened the air. It caught the gossamer scarlet veil draped over Monet's shoulders, whisking it away—carrying it out over the parapets. The rumble of horses shook the earth as the knights and their king charged toward their legions in await.

Squires followed, cooks, blacksmiths—and Monet trembled.

She could see her father's white charger in the distance. She could see Sir Broderick's armor glinting in the morning sun.

"God protect you, Father," she whispered.

"God love and preserve you, Sir Broderick," she breathed.

She could hear it then—the lute of a minstrel and a familiar tune. Glancing over, she saw him, there in one corner of the keep—the Minstrel Marius. She well knew Marius and the melody he plucked.

"At your bidding, your highness," Marius said with a nod.

Monet nodded. Brushing the tears from her cheeks, she returned her attention to Karvana's soldiers amassing to the north as the minstrel began his ballad—the ballad of "A Crimson Frost."

> Once Ballist was a battle stage
> Where soldiers fought and war was wage
> To keep Karvana for an age,
> And poets yet put ink to page
> Of a Crimson Frost upon him.
>
> As blade met blade 'mid winter snow
> And legions battled row on row,
> The North Wind did begin to blow
> And bid the Reaper then to sow
> With a Crimson Frost behind him.
>
> Up-mounted on his demon stud
> The Reaper reaped amidst the flood
> Of dying men strewn in the mud

As Ballist's field ran red with blood
With a Crimson Frost beside him.

As Winter and the North Wind roared
Ten men would fall to cold and sword.
Ten more and then the Dark Death Lord
Would reap them up into his hoard
With a Crimson Frost to aid him.

Then midst the brutal, bloody fight
The Reaper spied a comely knight,
His hilt and sword a flame of light,
Battling for his kingdom's might
And no Crimson Frost upon him.

This knight so comely, brave, and strong,
Who fought for right instead of wrong
Amidst the battle's bloodied throng
Pure vexed the Reaper's reaping song,
For no Crimson Frost adorned him.

And this, the Reaper's fury fanned—
To see this knight stay Lord Death's hand
And triumph at the battle stand
When Death should rule the blood-stained
    land
And a Crimson Frost consume him.

"What Knight is this?" the Reaper
    growled.

His sickle stilled—his death brow
    scowled.
The Reaper saw his reaping fouled.
"Sir Broderick!" the North Wind howled,
"With no Crimson Frost upon him."

Thus, on the battlefield that day
Broderick was the Reaper's prey
Beneath the clouds of winter's gray
Lord Death, this knight, would surely slay
And cast Crimson Frost upon him.

Then drew the Reaper his death blade,
For Broderick's life must be paid
To see Karvana's glory fade
And spur the Reaper's bloody trade
With a Crimson Frost to aid him.

With sickle and a blade for ware,
The Reaper rode his stud to where
The battle raged, that he may bear
The comely knight to Lord Death's
    lair
With a Crimson Frost upon him.

Yet Broderick, of noble heart,
Knew well the Reaper's ghastly art
And would not let his soul depart
Upon the Reaper's black death cart
With a Crimson Frost upon him.

Thus for his people and their crown,
Broderick turned to face Death down
And with his sword and skill renown
Feared not of Death's dark heinous frown
And the Crimson Frost beside him.

The comely knight met Death each stride.
They battled raw till eventide,
Till Death was weary from the ride
And with his sickle reaping wide
Cast a Crimson Frost upon him.

Sir Broderick then knew the cost
Of fighting Death, though Death had lost,
As, of a sudden, he was crossed
And lay in darkness in the frost
With a Crimson Frost upon him.

Red blood caressed his raven hair.
Red blood was at his brow so fair.
Red blood adorned his breastplate there.
Red blood did stain the very air,
And a Crimson Frost entombed him.

Still, worth he more than measured gold,
Broderick, bound by winter's cold,
Was brave and strong and ever bold,
Drew breath and fought the red frost's
    hold.
Thus the Crimson Frost released him.

This knight, with Death, in battle brushed,
Yet battle-bruised and broken—crushed
Broderick rose and forward rushed
And, with his blade, an army hushed
With a Crimson Frost behind him.

Thus Ballist fell, and bells did ring
For Broderick had spurned Death's sting
And warriored well for his great king.
Hence poets pen and minstrels sing
Of a Crimson Frost upon him.

A lion's heart beats in his breast
Beneath his rearing dragon crest,
This knight, the one who battled best,
Who from his task did not take rest,
Nor let Crimson Frost o'ercome him.

Monet watched her father, the knights, and
the soldiers as the Minstrel Marius sang of "A
Crimson Frost." She thought of the battle of
Ballist three years previous, of the enemies slain
at Sir Broderick Dougray's hand, of his own
wounds—wounds that caused him to suffer in
unconscious darkness long enough for winter's
frost to form over his blood-drenched armor and
blade. Yet he awoke—struggled to his feet to
defeat ten more foes before the renewed warmth
of his body had melted the crimson frost from his
armor.

Sir Broderick and his legion had defeated a common enemy of the five kingdoms. He had battled hard—kept evil and harm from finding its way to Karvana's door. Bruised, broken, and bloodied, Sir Broderick Dougray had returned from Ballist triumphant. Monet would never forget the fear that stabbed her soul as she saw him ride over the drawbridge following the Battle of Ballist, covered in not only the blood of his enemies but in his own as well.

For his triumph at Ballist, King Dacian had bestowed upon Sir Broderick Dougray the title of Blood Warrior of Ballist. Soon thereafter, the people of the Kingdom of Karvana began telling stories of the Blood Warrior of Ballist—the "Crimson Knight," they had christened him. Thus, Monet's father had likewise christened Sir Broderick the Crimson Knight.

Lost in her reverie, it was Marius's voice—the final verse of "A Crimson Frost"—that whispered hope to her mind.

Thus, ever can Karvana trust
No enemy will ever thrust
His blood or bones of flesh to dust
For her first knight is strong and just
And no Crimson Frost will bind him.

Monet turned to Marius and smiled. Hope had returned to her—somehow. The war would be won, Karvana would be saved, and the Crimson Knight would return—as would her father.

Monet stood atop the keep, long after her father's white charger and the Crimson Knight's flag had disappeared over the horizon—long after the legions and knights were gone to battle.

"God protect you," she whispered on the wind. Monet, the Scarlet Princess of Karvana, turned and made her way into the castle keep.

The Gates of Karvana

One month passed; two more followed. Summer was spent—breathed out as a weary sigh—and without a king at Karvana Castle. No knights sat at King Dacian's round table of conferring, and the only soldiers to return to Karvana were either dreadfully wounded—or dead. Autumn was yet youthful, but the air owned a change—a cooling of the breezes whispering of harvest nigh and the impending misery of soldiers battling in bitter weather.

As the days continued to wane—the days of war, of not knowing which man had survived battle and which had not—sleep did not come easy nor linger long for Monet of Karvana. Each morning, weary and worn with worry, Monet would hasten to the castle gate. There she would wait for the messenger—for whatever wounded soldier, yet well enough to ride, to arrive with news of the battle. Each day brought sorrow mingled with sinful relief, for with each herald that King Dacian and the Crimson Knight yet lived and lived well, Monet knew a measure of consolation. Heartbroken though she was for the dead soldiers who would soon follow in the death cart—for their families—the sweet balm of knowing the Crimson Knight and her father were well renewed her hope and fortitude of enduring.

Hope and endurance were cached precious to Monet. As she stood on the castle parapet each midday to address the people of Karvana—to herald tidings of the measure of the war with Rothbain—she drew her own courage from the hope given her at her father's survival, at the formidable stamina and strength of the Crimson Knight. Karvana would be victorious! This she told the people; this she whispered to herself again and again and again. Karvana would be victorious—and soon! The king would return, to rule with wisdom and compassion as he ever had—and with him the Crimson Knight.

Yet eventide thinned Monet's resolve, for this was when Monet visited the families of whatever soldiers had returned to Karvana in the death cart. As the sun began its setting, veiling the earth in the solicitude borne of dusk, Monet would make her way to the homes of the fallen soldiers of Karvana. Ever her father's counselors would beg she not go out among the people— beg she dare not venture beyond the castle walls. Still, go she did, for she was driven to them, that the wives and children of Karvana's fallen heroes might know her heart ached for, and with, their own. Still, the dark heartache of loss—the tears of each wife and child whose beloved protector would no longer hold them warm and safe in his arms—caused a great fear and crushing sorrow to seize Monet's mind, body, and heart. Thus, sleep did not come easy—nor linger—for Monet of Karvana.

There was no breeze the morning the king was returned. As Monet stood atop the parapet, gazing out toward the north, the flags of Karvana Castle hung listless and still. They would have traveled under the cover of night, as ever they did—the wounded and the dead, and those who carried them.

The sun had risen, a great orange orb bathing the earth in the warmth of early autumn, and Monet had witnessed its waking. Reapers were already harvesting in the fields beyond the village. Monet watched them—and waited. She wondered why the death cart and messengers seemed to tarry, for it was their established habit to break the horizon in the brief moments following the first apricot blush of sunrise. Yet the sun had begun its ascension near an hour before. Thus Monet was discomfited and worrisome.

Yet, of a sudden, in the distance she saw then the approach—a messenger mounted and carrying Karvana's emerald flag. Her heart was next pierced with anguish as she saw not one but two carts crest the hill north of the village. One cart bore Karvana's battle banner—an emerald flag with a white wolf bearing teeth. Yet the other cart bore not only Karvana's flag but also another: the banner of the king, white with King Dacian's amethyst shield and white stag rearing.

"Father!" Monet gasped as understanding speared her heart.

Monet fled down the steps leading from the parapet. The shouts of her father's counselors did not slow her, and she ordered the guards at the gate to bid her pass. The outer drawbridge had been lowered in anticipation of the arrival of the death cart and wounded. As Monet rushed its length and ran through the village, even the astonished gasps and exclamations of the people did not diminish her advance.

Breathless and worn, she met the caravan of wounded and dead, tears already streaming plentiful over her cheeks.

"Father!" she cried. "Father!"

"He lives, Princess," a wounded yet mounted soldier told her as she reached the first cart. "The king lives. He is wounded . . . but not mortally."

A whisper of thankful prayer escaped her lips as she reached the second cart to see her father sitting upright—and alive.

"Father!" she sobbed as he smiled at her. He was weary—disturbingly disheveled in appearance. His face, arms, and armor were well marked with the soil and blood of battle, his left leg wrapped with blood-sodden wound dressings.

Careless of propriety or harm to herself, Monet clambered into the wagon. Wary of her father's wounded leg, she yet threw herself into his welcoming embrace.

"Oh, Father!" she sobbed. "Are you well? Are you indeed well?"

His arms were strong about her, his loving embrace warm and comforting.

"I am well, my dove," King Dacian said, chuckling, "though somewhat humiliated to have found myself mortal and subject to such a wound as to keep me from battle."

"I feared Death had claimed you, Father!" Monet cried against her father's broad shoulder. "I saw the death carts approaching . . . one with your banner, and I . . . I thought . . ." She could not speak for a moment, besieged with relief in her father's return—his living return.

"I am sorry to have frightened you, Monet," Dacian said, caressing her tender cheeks. "Yet I am well. I am well."

Monet shook her head, however. The wound at his leg appeared severe, and she yet feared for his health.

"This looks to be no brier scrape, Father," she said.

"No. No indeed. Still, it has been well tended. Sir Broderick himself scrubbed the dirt and blood away . . . stitched the flesh."

Of a sudden, Monet's heart swelled. "Sir Broderick is well then?"

King Dacian smiled. "Sir Broderick is well. And I am well for his efforts. Nay . . . I am alive for his efforts."

Monet's lovely brow puckered with inquisition.

"If not for Broderick's sword . . . I would surely have returned to you heaped upon the death cart with those who gave their last breath for Karvana," he said, gesturing to the death cart afore them.

"Then I am thankful your Crimson Knight is so skilled with wounds and stitching."

King Dacian shook his head. "No. Skilled in seaming flesh though he may be . . . it was his skill in battle, his master's wield of a blade, that first delivered my life."

I will not let Death claim your father, Princess. The Crimson Knight's promise echoed through Monet's mind. Her heart beat mad in her bosom at the very thought of him—at knowing he had kept his promise.

"Tell me of it, Father," Monet whispered. "Tell me."

Dacian smiled. The bright resplendence in his daughter's eyes spoke to his heart, and he caressed her cheek with the back of one hand.

"We were midst battle," he began. "So many of James's soldiers were there—seemed to rise from the very mists of morning—and we battled. An enemy fell my horse and I beneath him. One never understands the true measure and weight of a horse till one lies beneath his flank." He smiled as Monet nodded. "The enemy was upon me—three soldiers of Rothbain . . . and me trapped beneath my horse. It was certain I was that I would be lost . . . that I would never again lay eyes on my daughter—the beautiful Scarlet Princess of Karvana."

Monet took her father's hand, desperate to feel its warm, to know that life was yet in it—in him.

"And then?" she prompted, for she must hear the whole of it.

"And then he was there—Sir Broderick Dougray . . . the Crimson Knight of Karvana," her father continued. "He drew his sword . . . drew even a second sword from a fallen soldier near where my horse and I were fell. And there he battled o'er me . . . defending my life . . . keeping Death at bay. Three Rothbainians he slay there. Wielding two swords, he slay them with seeming ease. Thus I was preserved."

I will not let Death claim your father, Princess. Sir Broderick's words lingered in her heart. She could well see him. In her mind she could see him battling to protect her father's life—a true and valiant First Knight of Karvana.

"The wound at my leg . . . as my men

endeavored to pull me from beneath my dead mount, another enemy fell upon us, striking hard his blade into my flesh before Sir Broderick fell him beside the others he had slain," King Dacian explained. "Broderick's guilt was severe . . . and it was only my constant assurance he had *not* failed me that eased his mind somewhat at long last. He then scrubbed my wound, stitched and dressed it. I felt able enough . . . and I did not want to return to Karvana, Monet."

"You did not wish to leave your men," Monet said, for it was well she knew her father's heart.

King Dacian nodded. "To leave them to battle alone . . . it is not meet with my nature or conscience. Yet my knights were in agreement. James may well think the kingdom weak without a king in the castle. We are battling hard . . . yet we are not pronouncing victory, Monet. Neither is James. Thus in counsel with the knights of Karvana . . . it seems sure James of Rothbain will look to more deceitful methods of battle. He may well look to lay siege to Karvana itself. Thus, it is wise to have her king at hand to wage battle for her on her own lands if needs be."

"You think King James will endeavor to beset the heart of Karvana, Father?" Monet whispered, a wicked fear rising within her.

"James is as low as the serpent slithering through the grasses. He is cowardly. He owns no honor . . . and he will slink from the battlefields if he cannot easily prove himself victor there. He will endeavor to keep our attention thus fixed upon soldiers crashing blades to the north . . . while he conjures methods of destruction poised above Karvana's core. Thus I have returned . . . to prepare . . . to send watchmen . . . to protect our kingdom, Monet."

Monet frowned. "But if this is true, Father . . . should not the Crimson—should not the knights of Karvana return? Would not he know more shelter . . . would not they be needed here?"

Monet was trembling now—trembling at the thought of enemies at Karvana's gate, at the thought of the villagers being subject to harm. It was sufficiently heinous to have soldiers battling and dying to protect Karvana, but if its people too were to die . . .

Dacian felt his eyes narrow. He wondered then—was his daughter conscious of her deep reverencing of Sir Broderick? He thought she was not. He thought she was not fully aware that, in each message she had sent to him at the battle encampment, she had inquired after the Crimson Knight's well-being. He smiled, gratified in the knowledge Karvana's princess—Karvana's subsequent queen—would own such respect for a warrior of the kingdom. In this he knew she would rule Karvana well, with esteem for her protectors, wisdom and strength in her decisions, and infinite love and compassion for her citizens.

Dacian, King of Karvana, was assured—assured the demon James of Rothbain would attempt to strike at Karvana's heart. Further was his assurance strong that the documents of instruction concerning Monet's ascension to Karvana's throne—the documents cached to his breast and likewise in the secret compartment in his queen's tomb—would serve his Karvana well were James to succeed in killing him.

"There are yet legions here, Monet," her father began, "strong men . . . strong leaders to lead them. The knights and their legions must defend our northern border, lest a wave of battle far greater spill into Karvana. We must have time to prepare Karvana for battle . . . or siege."

Fear filled Monet as it never had before. Battle? Siege? Would King James truly battle against Karvana herself? Was he truly so evil as to lay siege to such a great and good kingdom, to cause its people to die of injury, starvation, or disease? What then would be left to rule?

Monet brushed the tears from her cheeks, glancing past her father to the death cart before them.

"How many brave men traveled home in the death cart this day, Father?" she asked.

"One would be too many," King Dacian said. "And yet today there are ten."

"I must have the list," Monet said. "Rider!"

The mounted soldier accompanying the death cart turned his horse—rode to the cart bearing the king.

"Yes, Princess?" he said.

"Pray entrust me with the list of the fallen," she bade him.

The mounted soldier reached into his tunic and retrieved a parchment. He nodded as he handed it to Monet, and she said, "I thank you, sir."

"I know you are in habit of consoling the families of the fallen," King Dacian said. "But you must no longer venture from the safety of the castle, Monet."

"We cannot let the families of these good men linger in thinking we do not share their pain, Father," Monet said.

"Of course not. Thus we will send a penned message to each family."

"A penned message?" Monet exclaimed. "Father! A penned message will not suffice! They must be meet with us . . . see that we share in their loss. Though we cannot begin to measure their pain, we must offer our gratitude and—"

"Heretoforth you will not venture from the castle, Monet!"

Monet was confounded by the commanding tone of her father's voice. His imperial demeanor was not foreign to her, for it was often as ruling

King of Karvana he had displayed such strength and impenetrable fortitude. Yet to be the subject of his warrant—it was discomposing.

"Yes, Father," Monet said.

They had reached the village, and the people were come out to see the king returned. Monet watched as the king smiled, hailed his people, and assured them of his health.

"It is but a scratch," he told them.

Monet watched as the death cart ambled through the village behind the king's cart. All who looked upon it grew silent. Though but ten soldiers lay beneath the heavy canvas covering the cart, the faces of near sixty citizens of Karvana were ashen—bled out of color for wondering who would be told their husband, father, brother, or son had returned to Karvana, never to draw breath again.

Monet brushed more tears from her cheeks. She would mourn with her people! She would! King James was not at Karvana's gates yet, and she would not let her people conceive she did not weep for the fallen with them.

It had been no simple task to leave the castle unseen. The bridges had been drawn once the king was safely within the castle walls. Thus Monet had been driven to the secret passage leading underground from the castle to the royal mausoleum, some distance beyond the outer castle walls. Indeed, the main door to the mausoleum was guarded from without, yet the smaller side doors were not. Once she had slipped through one of the smaller doors, Monet found a stone and tossed it into the brier patch some distance away. The guard at the main entrance to her mother's place of rest was distracted and set off toward the briers.

Robed in a black cloak and hood, Monet made her way around the castle walls and to the village beyond. The families of the fallen soldiers of Karvana, returned to their kingdom in the death cart that morning, must know her gratitude. She would see their wives and children, mothers and fathers. As she hastened across the small wooden bridge spanning the brook, a wave of foreboding washed over her. Perhaps her father had been right to demand she stay within the shelter of the castle. Yet the majority of the citizens of Karvana were not sheltered there. Thus, Monet continued on her way.

"Yes?" came a voice from within the cottage.

As an elderly woman opened the door, Monet swept her cloak hood back.

"I have come in mourning, good mother," Monet greeted as the elder woman's eyes widened. "I have come to offer my heart to those who have lost so much this day. Is this the family of Richard Tailor?"

"The Scarlet Princess!" the old woman gasped. "Princess Monet? At this very door?"

"Yes, good lady," Monet said. "Are . . . are you kin to Richard Tailor?"

"I am no kin . . . though I am pledged to care for his son, now that the father has . . . has gone," the woman said.

"I see," Monet whispered. Orphaned! Another child of Karvana orphaned at King James's wicked hand. "Is . . . is his son within . . . that I may offer my heart at his father's loss . . . that I may express my king's gratitude for such a sacrifice as this?"

The old woman smiled. "You are a good and kind princess, your highness," she said. "But young Richard has gone to the inn—to the Emerald Crown—to find solace in the company of friends. Yet I will tell him of your visit, Princess. It will mean more to him than you can know."

Monet smiled and shook her head. "No. I will meet him myself to offer him my heart at his great loss. I thank you, good mother."

"Pray . . . is it . . . is it wise, Princess? Is it safe for you to be about on such business alone . . . and at night?"

Monet smiled. "Far safer than wielding a blade with our brave men to the north."

The woman smiled and nodded. "God bless and keep you, Princess."

"God bless and keep you, good mother," Monet said, drawing her cloak hood over her head once more.

Monet sighed. Though the Emerald Crown was one of the more respected and tamed establishments in Karvana, dusk was descending. Thus the Emerald Crown would be filled with more men than women. Still, Monet would thank young Richard Tailor, son of Karvana's fallen soldier.

The Minstrel Marius sat amid a table in the center of the room. The melody of his lute was familiar to Monet, yet she lingered not on naming it. She must find young Richard Tailor, offer her heart at his great loss, and visit the family of the next fallen soldier whose name was penned on the parchment tucked inside her corselet.

Marius caught sight of her and offered a respectful nod. Monet nodded in return and crossed the room to him.

"Good minstrel," she began in a quiet voice, "I am come to see a boy . . . young Richard Tailor. Do you know him?"

"Has his father fallen to the battle in the north?" Marius asked.

"He has," Monet whispered.

"A good man was Richard Tailor," the minstrel said. "It was well I knew him."

"And do you well know his son?"

"I do." The minstrel pointed to a fair-haired young man seated at a table nearby. "The young one there." Marius shook his head. "He is a good lad."

"Thank you, minstrel," Monet said.

Monet inhaled a breath of courage. It near broke her heart to gaze into the faces of those enduring loss such as young Richard Tailor surely was. Yet she felt it was the blessing, and curse, of owning empathy—and she was glad she did own it. She thought a moment of Anais: Anais of Alvar owned no empathy. Better it was to suffer with those who suffered than know nothing of their suffering as Anais.

"I beg audience, sir," Monet said to the fair-haired young man seated before her.

The young man looked up and frowned as he studied her cloaked form head to foot. Monet fancied the young man was not so much less in age than she. He was handsome—strong in appearance.

"Who are you?" he growled. The young man's comely countenance was marred with the reddened eyes of weeping.

"One who would speak to you concerning your father," Monet said.

It seemed understanding washed over the youth, for his eyes widened, and he stood to meet Monet.

"I have come to offer my heart's aching to join with yours, Richard Tailor," Monet whispered.

"I have heard you come to visit the families

of the fallen," Richard whispered. "Yet I did not think you would come to me."

"Your father gave his life in protection of me, of my king, of you, and of our kingdom," Monet whispered. "I stand before you humbled . . . honored to know the son of such a great warrior . . . such a selfless man of valor as was Richard Tailor the elder."

Monet reached within her corselet once more, withdrew a small kerchief, and offered it to young Richard Tailor.

"I can offer you no solace, Richard Tailor . . . son of Richard Tailor, fallen soldier of Karvana. Yet I would bid you accept this token—the kerchief bearing tears I shed as I saw your father taken from the death cart and prepared for his burial of honor." Monet trembled slightly—a trembling of shared grief as the young man accepted her token. "His dagger will rest in Karvana Castle's Hall of Valor . . . with tokens of remembrance paying tribute to all those who have fallen to defend our lands and people. His name will be carved into one of the castle stones. Your father, and his sacrifice, will not be forgotten, Richard Tailor."

Monet brushed a tear from her cheek as she watched Richard Tailor draw the kerchief to his face, seeming to inhale its scent.

"We are blessed in our king . . . and our princess," he said. Monet thought the sadness in his blue eyes lessened just a little. "Yet you should not be here, Princess," he said, a frown puckering his brow of a sudden.

Monet shook her head, took his hand between hers, and smiled. "Nor should you," she said, "for we are both of us too young for such sadness and loss."

"It is different for me than for you, your highness," the young man said, lowering his voice. Something about the sudden look of fearfulness in Richard Tailor's countenance caused Monet to shiver with sudden trepidation. "For no one means me harm here."

"What do you mean?" Monet asked in a whisper. "Who of Karvana would mean me harm?"

"No one, your highness," he said. "Yet my father was certain that King James made plans well before this war . . . that a number of men appearing to be Karvanians are indeed in King James's service."

An odd chill pricked the back of Monet's neck. Surely any of the villagers would have recognized a stranger to Karvana—especially in time of war.

"Are there strangers among us?" she asked. "Strangers the village and castle guards are not aware of?"

"Not since months before the battles began," he said. "Yet there are several men who came to

Karvana more than half the year past. My father was always suspect of them."

"Does my father know of this?" Monet asked.

"It is certain he does. It is why there are guards in the village." Richard Tailor paused, seeming to glance at something behind Monet.

"What is it?" she asked.

"There is a man in the corner beyond you, your highness," he answered. "He is cloaked and hooded . . . and it seems he has been watching us since your approach."

"And you . . . you do not recognize him?" Monet stammered.

"I cannot clearly see his face, Princess," he said. "It may be he is merely a farmer . . . sitting in silent pondering. Yet I feel this is not why he watches you in such absolute observation."

Fear gripped her of a sudden. She had been foolish! Her father had forbidden her to leave the castle this night, and yet she had disobeyed him. Just cause or no, she had disobeyed him. Only now did she wonder at the consequence. Was the man behind her a servant of King James? Were there enemies among the villagers—unseen adversaries lying in wait for just such an opportunity to strike?

"He advances, your highness!" Richard growled. "He has risen from his chair and strides this way. Make haste and flee!"

Yet time was not an ally of Monet in that

moment, for no sooner had she turned to flee than she felt powerful hands take hold of her arms.

"You should not be here, Princess!"

Monet nearly fainted at the familiar growl forthcoming from within the black hood before her. Sir Broderick!

"You will not take our Scarlet Princess!" Richard shouted.

Sir Broderick released Monet, sweeping the hood from his head.

"I *will* take her!" he growled. "And I will return her to the castle where she can be protected."

"The Crimson Knight!" Richard Tailor breathed in astonishment.

"Cover!" Sir Broderick shouted of a sudden. Monet gasped as the Crimson Knight released her—drew a dagger from a sheath at his waist, hurling it past her head. Several women cried out, and Monet heard a low moan exhale from someone behind her.

Shouting, screams, and confusion followed as Sir Broderick pushed her to the floor, drawing his sword. Stricken with terror, Monet covered her head as the brutal crash of blade meeting blade rang through the inn. Yet the clamor of battle ceased near as quick as it began. Monet felt the powerful grasp of the Crimson Knight at the back of her neck—as he clutched the fabric of her cloak in a strong fist, pulling her to her feet.

"Bind these men and bring them to the castle gates," he ordered.

Monet glanced about, aghast as Richard Tailor—son of a fallen soldier of Karvana—drew the Crimson Knight's dagger from the forehead of a man lying across a nearby table. Bowing with respect, he offered the weapon to Sir Broderick, who accepted it, sheathing it at his waist.

Richard nodded to Monet—a nodding of gratitude and renewed strength. "Thank you, Princess," he said—though no sound escaped his mouth.

"The boy was right. You should not be here, Princess," the Crimson Knight growled. Monet looked up into the infuriated scowl of Sir Broderick Dougray. His handsome face was dirt-streaked and weary, yet as comely as ever it had been. Her heart beat mad within her bosom as she stared at him in astonished disbelief.

"Long live Rothbain!" a man lying at her feet shouted. Monet looked to him—to the enemy of Karvana there in her midst. The villain grimaced and pressed a hand to a wound at his side—a wound running blood out upon the floor. "Long live King James and—"

The miscreant's cry was silenced by the Crimson Knight's boot crushing his villainous breast—by the tip of Sir Broderick's sword at his traitorous throat.

"I would as soon carve out your gullet as see

you brought to Karvana Castle!" the Crimson Knight growled. "Yet King Dacian will want to face the man who dared threaten his daughter's safety."

Taking Monet by the arm, Sir Broderick began fairly dragging her toward the door leading from the inn.

Monet glanced back—to the villagers of Karvana surrounding the dead man and the wounded one, to Richard Tailor, who nodded his assurance. The Crimson Knight's demand that the men be brought to the castle gates would be obeyed. It had not been necessary for him to have chosen one or two particular men to carry out the deed; his commanding voice had called every man in the inn to hasten to his order.

Monet wondered at Sir Broderick's presence in the inn. How long had he been returned to Karvana? Had he simply been lingering at the Emerald Crown? Or had he known she would find her way there?

As Sir Broderick conducted her toward the door, a man stepped into their path, barring their way. Yet the Crimson Knight did not pause. Monet stood confounded as, releasing his grip on her arm, the Crimson Knight drove one powerful fist to the man's face—then another. Again his fist met with the man's jaw, rendering him benumbed. Like a felled tree, the man crashed to the inn floor senseless and bleeding.

"Bind this one as well and bring him to the gates with the others!" Sir Broderick growled. Taking hold of Monet's arm once more, he pulled her through the door and out into the lavender of eventide.

Monet did not speak—did not dare to offer any utterance. The Crimson Knight pushed her forward, placed his hands at her waist, and lifted her onto the back of a horse bearing no saddle. At once he was mounted behind her, wrapped one powerful hand in the horse's mane, and spurred the animal into a wild gallop. Certain she would slide from the slick beast's back, Monet leaned back against the strong, brawny body of the Crimson Knight, desperately clutching at the soft leather of his trouser thighs in an effort to steady herself.

She closed her eyes—an effort to fortify her courage and strength. Yet her mind began to present a procession of memories, a gallery of images past—of King Ivan's tournament, of the Crimson Knight's victory in swords, maces, and the joust! What mild events were tournaments and banquets when weighed against battles in the fields and spies lying in wait in Karvana's inns?

He spoke not a word to her as they rode, yet Monet could feel his anger. It exhaled from his body as perceivably as the heat of his breath breathed into her hair. He spurred their mount to leap a farmer's fence, his arm tight about her waist to keep her steady as the horse surged upward into the air, coming to earth able, but with jarring force.

Monet wondered at their wild pace. The Crimson Knight rode as if Lord Death himself were at their heels. And then—then she knew. As a rider robed entirely in black suddenly matched the stride of the Crimson Knight's mount to their right, Monet was certain the Reaper himself was upon them. She gasped as another rider robed in midnight met their stride to the left.

"Hold here!" Sir Broderick growled, taking Monet's hand and burying it in the horse's mane. Monet leaned forward, fisting her small hands in the coarse hair.

The rider to the right drew a blade. Monet screamed as Sir Broderick's dagger found its target—the villain's throat. The rider reeled backward, tumbling from his mount to the grassy field slight of Karvana's first drawbridge.

Monet screamed once more as the rider to the left took hold of her arm. Yet his grip was loosed as the Crimson Knight's rowel spur met with the black rider's leg. The rider cried out but was not vanquished.

"Lower the bridge! Archers, take aim!" Sir Broderick shouted, drawing his sword. Grasping its hilt in backguard stance, the Crimson Knight plunged his blade through the breast of the black rider. He did not pause as the enemy's horse reared, felling its rider, but sheathed his bloodied blade and tugged at the ties of Monet's cloak at her throat. Monet felt his hand fist the cloth of her cloak at her back—felt it stripped from her shoulders—heard the flapping of velvet tossed to the wind.

"The Scarlet Princess approaches!" the Crimson Knight shouted as the drawbridge began to lower. "Archers at the ready! The enemy is upon us!"

Monet heard the Crimson Knight's cloak meet the air as well. She turned, looking behind them to see three more black-robed riders at their backs. Breathless with fear, Monet looked ahead—up to the archers of Karvana poised on the parapets. The bridge was lowered, and again Sir Broderick's arm was at her waist to ensure she did not slip from the horse's back.

"Fell the enemy! Fire!" Sir Broderick shouted as the sound and jarring of hooves on bridge planking wracked Monet's tender body. Karvanian soldiers on horseback rode past, the thundering of their horses' hooves near deafening as they crossed the bridge to meet whatever remained of the enemy riders who had advanced.

Once across the inner drawbridge, the Crimson Knight pulled their mount to a halt. He slid from the horse's back, took Monet's waist between strong hands, and lifted her down. Yet the brutal ride had weakened Monet's body and mind more than she had at first conceived. Wavering for lingering fear and bodily strain, Monet clutched at the Crimson Knight's tunic, endeavoring to right herself.

"Are you injured?" Sir Broderick asked, his strong hands gripping Monet at the pit of each arm to support her.

"No, sir," she breathed, yet unable somehow to stand of her own accord.

"You are but winded, Princess," he rather mumbled as, of a sudden, he swept her into the cradle of his arms. "Summon the king to Princess Monet's bower!" he shouted as several guards approached. "The Scarlet Princess is returned and would audience him."

As the Crimson Knight began to carry Monet up the stairway leading to her bower, she could not keep her arms from going 'round his neck. Somehow one thumb slipped beneath his tunic at the back of his neck, entangled with a leather strap there. Monet closed her eyes as the sudden vision of the Crimson Knight in his pavilion at King Ivan's tournament leapt to her mind. She could see him—as clearly as if the moment had only passed a breath before—standing in his pavilion after having bathed following the tournament. She witnessed in her vision the moment he had placed the length of leather around his neck—the length of leather owning the small leather pouch to hang over his sculpted chest and stomach. In that moment, her mind brief wondered what treasure the small leather pouch cached that he would wear it into battle.

She opened her eyes once more as she felt her body lay upon her own bed. Gazing up into the face of the Crimson Knight, Monet felt tears brim in her eyes. The deep scowling frown he wore well brandished his anger—his loathing.

"I-I am sorry to have—" she began.

"The enemy is upon us, Princess," he interrupted. "We must, each of us, be wary."

"I only wanted to offer my thanks . . . my heart to the families of those soldiers who returned in the death cart today," she said. Reaching into her corselet, she withdrew the nine remaining kerchiefs cached there, the small strips of parchment, each bearing the name of a fallen soldier of Karvana. "I wept bitterly for them today," she whispered. She felt overcome with fatigue—defeated. "Each . . . each kerchief bears my tears of sorrow for a soldier. It . . . it is a small token, I know. Yet it is a token, and I only wished to—"

He yet frowned. Still, Monet fancied the look of loathing had left him.

"Pray do not own hatred of me, Sir Broderick," she cried in a whisper as tears flowed over her cheeks. "I did not know the danger was already among us here. I only meant to comfort those who have sacrificed so much."

"It was wise to put off your cloaks, Sir Broderick! Otherwise the archers and guards may not have known it was the Crimson Knight barking orders to them!" Monet wept anew as her father limped into her bower. She watched as her father put a hand at Sir Broderick's neck, pulling him into a thankful embrace. "I thank you for my daughter's life, Crimson Knight. And it seems you were right in your estimations. The enemy is already among us."

"Yes, my king," Sir Broderick said.

Monet winced as her father looked to her then. "Guardian of the Scarlet Princess, indeed," he mumbled. "I assume you have thanked your savior-knight . . . thanked him for his risk of life and limb for your sake."

"Father, I—" Monet began.

"I warned you, Monet," King Dacian said, taking seat on the bed next to her. "I told you we were suspect of James's bleeding his evil into our midst. Did you not believe me? To creep out of the safety of the castle . . . to—"

"I am sorry, Father!" Monet cried. "Truly! Had I known . . . had I known . . ."

"Yet still you would have ventured it . . . would you have not?" he asked. He sighed, a slight smile quirking his lips.

"What manner of princess would I be if I owned no compassion and empathy for our people?" she whispered.

"I understand, Monet," King Dacian admitted. "And it is a rare goodness in you, dove. Yet you must own comprehension of this: the people are strong in their king, their queen, their prince or princess. Were James of Rothbain to endeavor to destroy you or me and succeed . . . the people would be hearts-lost. Their own courage and strength would fail them in feeling the loss of righteous sovereigns . . . thus hope. In this, he would prevail and conquer. He would conquer, or the people would succumb to a defeat they could not battle alone."

Monet could not speak, overcome with humility, fear, and conflict of emotion.

"Thus, thank your brave rescuer, and promise us both that from this moment forth, you will not leave the castle without my bidding. Not while we are at war with James of Rothbain."

"Th-thank you, Sir Broderick," Monet said, though she could not meet his piercing gaze for long. "And I am sorry to have imposed such danger upon you."

"Your heart was well placed, Princess," the Crimson Knight said, "as ever it has been." Of a sudden, he reached out, taking the kerchiefs and parchments from her hand. "I go now to offer these tokens in your stay," he said.

"Pray bathe and take respite first, Sir Broderick," King Dacian said.

"I will, my king," he said, "only after the dead have been properly reverenced . . . as our princess wishes."

The Crimson Knight wore weary. It was evident by the shadows of fatigue surrounding his alluring blue eyes, by the disheveled condition and uncommon length of his raven hair. His tunic was soiled and tattered, and even the breadth of his shoulders did not seem as straight and commanding as was natural.

"Very well," King Dacian said. "Go about your errand, lad. But know this—when first the sun rises on the morrow . . . I would have your audience in the west mezzanine. Preparations must begin . . . all preparations. And your part in these preparations is consummate."

The Crimson Knight turned to take his leave. Yet Monet's voice stalled him.

"I thank you, Sir Broderick," she said. "For my life . . . and my errand."

He looked over his shoulder, nodded, and was gone.

"How . . . how did he know where to find me?" Monet asked. "I think he thwarted Lord Death on my behalf this night."

"He is the Guardian of the Scarlet Princess, Monet," King Dacian said. "Further, we all of us know your heart. He knew you would disobey me in this . . . at least once . . . though I argued with him otherwise. Thus he followed you into the night. As a phantom he was ever at your back without your knowledge."

"I would be dead—or at the very least taken— were it not for him," Monet whispered, brushing fresh tears from her cheeks.

Her father laughed lightly and brushed a tear from her chin. "And to think, last spring at Ivan's tournament, you thought me mad for giving him title . . . for heralding our Crimson Knight as Guardian of the Scarlet Princess. What think ye now, daughter?"

Monet smiled, though she yet wept. "I think you are far wiser than I shall ever be . . . and that I should not endeavor to question your commands again."

Again low laughter. "Do I have your word then . . . that you will trust in my commands henceforth?"

"Yes, Father," Monet said as her father gathered her into his strong embrace.

King Dacian sighed. Perhaps this night was not all for naught. He had been fearful of Monet's counterpoise of certain preparations to come. Yet if this night had apt struck fear into her heart, perhaps she would not oppose his forthcoming demands as she might well have without such a night to her experience.

As Dacian held his precious daughter to his breast, he prayed—prayed for the strength and safety of Karvana's soldiers—prayed for the good people of his kingdom—prayed his daughter would accept her role as heir to Karvana's throne and act as she must to preserve it.

It was the sound of her dreams that awoke her—as much as the vision of them. The mad pounding of hooves upon the ground, the horse's rhythmic breathing as they fled, the Crimson Knight calling the archers of Karvana to arms. Monet awoke trembling and awash with perspiration.

Had it not been for the Crimson Knight, she would have been taken—or dead. Had he not thwarted three men in the inn, two more while astride his mount, what would have become of her? She owed him her life; the valiant knight who had championed her, her father, and Karvana at King Ivan's tournament months before had far greater championed her that night.

War was coming to Karvana. Something whispered the truth of it to her as she stood before the hearth in her bower. War had come to Karvana months before, yet to the great lands beyond, not to the villages and castle itself. Death would be brought to the village and the castle gate. Whether by battle or siege, Lord Death would wander among the people now.

Monet wondered—were there kerchiefs enough to absorb the river of tears she would cry for her people when King James battered the very gates of Karvana?

The Heart of Karvana

"You cannot be in earnest, my king," Sir Broderick near growled. There was no disrespect in his manner—merely the frustration of a soldier eager to return to the defense of his kingdom.

"You know I am in full earnest, Broderick," Dacian said.

Broderick's broad chest rose and fell with the labored breathing of indignation.

"You would ask me to hide? As a coward runs from battle . . . or a jester from consequence?" he asked.

The Crimson Knight was pure vexed. In truth, Dacian fought to keep a smile from his lips. How entirely disconcerted Broderick was! A tiny spark of mirth rose in Dacian's bosom—even for the fear and worry threatening to consume him as a king who must preserve his people and kingdom.

"Nay, my friend," Dacian said. "But I would ask you to protect . . . to serve with a strength untried to one even so strong as you. You see the reason. I know you do. There is wisdom in this . . . broad wisdom. In the end, it may be you alone who preserves Karvana. May it not? I know you see it . . . though you are vexed in having to leave your men to battle in the north without you. Still, I remind you, Broderick . . . this battle may be the greatest and most difficult you may ever know, for it will tax your mind to madness . . . as it will tax your body in a manner you cannot fathom."

Sir Broderick Dougray inhaled slowly. An even deeper frown creased his strong brow. "Oh, it is well I am able to fathom it . . . and this, near more than any other reason given, is why I doubt your choice in me. You put too much confidence in my strength."

"No," Dacian said. "I do not, and it can only be you, Broderick. Only you. There is none other . . . none who can win *this* battle in this war we wage against James of Rothbain." Dacian shook his head, smiling. "Was not this strategy of defense *your* suggestion? At the round table of conferring? Was it not Sir Broderick Dougray who first thought to defend Karvana's heart?"

"Of course," Broderick mumbled. "But I did not fathom such an implement as this."

Dacian paused—felt his eyes narrow as he studied the great Crimson Knight standing before him. "Yet you see the vast wisdom in it . . . its clever conception, do you not? Can you name a better battle strategy, a finer way of besting James, if it comes to the very end?"

"In my current state of wear and fatigue . . . no," Broderick admitted.

"I stand that, were you not already worn with battle and worry, you would have conceived this plan yourself, Broderick," Dacian said. "Perhaps you would not have appointed the task to yourself, for you see yourself as capable of wielding blades only in battle . . . when it has long been the strategy of your mind, the strength of your soul, that I most admire. You will triumph in this, Broderick. You will not fail, nor even falter. Therefore, even if James and Rothbain lay siege to Karvana, the heart of our kingdom . . . the hope of our people will survive. Will you do this thing I ask of you, Broderick? Will you battle where others cannot . . . where I dare not send a weaker man?"

Dacian was silent—watched as doubt and the unfamiliar expression of uncertainty crossed Sir Broderick's countenance. Such compassion Dacian felt. His bosom ached for his friend—for the adversity stretching before him were he to accept the charge asked of him.

At last he spoke. Sir Broderick Dougray answered, "I will. I am a knight of Karvana . . . first knight of Dacian's round table of conferring. What honor would I own if I refused? Far better to try . . . to fight and to fail . . . than to take the weak coward's road and deny such a charge as this." He paused, drew a deep breath, and exhaled it slowly. "Still, it would go easier on my mind if I owned a knowledge of it all, sire."

"Faith, Broderick," Dacian began, "another of your merits. Your faith in God will have to serve for now . . . and your faith in me—faith in my wisdom and judgment." Dacian turned, retrieving a gathering of parchment. He studied the gathering for a moment, gazing upon his own seal. He looked to the signet ring on his index finger—the rearing stag—looked upon its likeness in the wax sealing the parchment. It would be indisputable. When the seal was broken and the content instructions followed, Karvana would be forever changed.

Turning, he offered the gathering of parchment to Broderick.

"Accept this charge I give you, Broderick Dougray. Honor me in this battle . . . and Karvana's heart may be saved," he said. He nodded with approval when the Crimson Knight accepted the gathering without pause. "I will further instruct you now—for thus far you imagine yourself to be held tortured for all your long remaining years, do you not?"

Dacian smiled when Broderick glanced away, a slight blush of crimson rising to his cheeks a moment.

"I have accepted this charge, my king," he began, "and all consequences fixed with it."

"Very well," Dacian said. "Then sit, Sir

Broderick . . . for there is much, much more to fighting this battle before you. Your mind must be as sharp as your weapons."

Broderick nodded, and Dacian began, "The minstrels will be the messengers. Always listen to the minstrels. Their tales and ballads will inform and guide you when I cannot. You will be utterly cut off; thus, mind the minstrels."

Sir Broderick Dougray stood without the king's chamber. Gazing down at the gathering of parchments in his hands—in his trembling hands—he could not fathom his king would charge him with such a strategy. Who was he to fulfill a charge the like? Sir Broderick Dougray? The Crimson Knight? He felt no more worthy of such a charge than a pig boy called to service from slopping swine only moments before. Furthermore, what manner of consummate strength did King Dacian imagine his Crimson Knight to own? What manner of constitution in virtue?

Broderick sat—nearly collapsed—into a chair just without the king's chamber. He fisted one strong hand and drew it to his forehead and then to his mouth as he struggled for strength of endurance. Two days had been given him—two days in which to prepare. He must rise—rise and go forth in preparation. Still, his hands yet trembled. He would pause a moment more—gather his conviction and courage.

He breathed a sigh. In the least Eann would be pleased. When King Dacian had inquired as to whether there were any favor the king might grant the Crimson Knight as pitiful payment for his willingness to serve, Broderick had named two. First, his squire Eann would be knighted. Broderick knew that owning a knighthood was Eann's greatest wish. Further, Broderick had asked the king that young Richard Tailor might enter into service as Eann's squire, that young Richard himself might one day be knighted. It was all he could fathom in those moments when the king had promised him anything— knighthoods for Eann and young Richard.

"Good morning, Sir Broderick."

The melodic lilt of her voice near caused him to tumble from his chair, so unexpected was it.

"Princess," Broderick greeted, forcing himself to rise and bow to Monet. She smiled at him, so innocent to the true demands and destruction of war.

"H-have you been in counsel with my father?" she asked.

"I have," he said. She frowned a little, and he knew she thought him vexed with her.

"Oh, I see," she whispered. Her countenance seemed to change, fear and worry arresting her features. "Is it hopeless, Sir Broderick?" she asked. "The war to keep King James from

171

conquering Karvana? Is it so very hopeless? I beg the truth from you . . . please."

With purpose he allowed his gaze to narrow to a glare. He must strengthen himself for battle. No soft or tender emotions must caress his heart or mind. If King James were to be bested—if Karvana's heart were to be protected—then it must be a soldier, a knight of Karvana, who protected it—not a weakened, fearful boy!

"No," he said. "It is not hopeless. But if Karvana is to survive . . . if she is to be victorious and James of Rothbain vanquished, great sacrifices are yet to be made . . . by all who love and defend her."

"I am one willing to make any sacrifice for her, Sir Broderick," the princess told him. He almost smiled at the sudden straightening of her posture—the indignant rise of her pretty chin.

"Good," he growled, "for it may needs be you sacrifice near all you know . . . as others of us have covenanted to do."

He watched as her lovely amethyst eyes narrowed with suspicion.

"Have I vexed you somehow, Sir Broderick?" she asked. "Have I done something to offend you? Or perhaps you are still angry with me for . . . for disobeying my father . . . for the incident last evening that began at the Emerald Crown."

Broderick studied her for a moment and

wondered—would the Princess Monet appear so becoming if she stood before him in a peasant girl's frock and not the fine scarlet gown she wore? If her ebony hair were windblown instead of perfectly braided, if a smudge of dirt marred her face, would she be as beautiful? She would—he knew it. Further, he feared she would be more so.

"I am only weary, Princess," he said. "Forgive me."

"I would forgive you anything, Sir Broderick," she said, smiling at him.

"Would you?" he mumbled. Her soft brow puckered with perplexity, yet he offered her no time to inquire further. "I am certain your father is desirous of your company this morning," he said. "I therefore take my leave. Good day, Princess."

He did not look at her again, nor wait for her to bid him farewell. Two days—it was all the time allotted him to prepare, and he must prepare—as best he could.

"God help me," he breathed as he strode down the corridor.

"Good day, Sir Broderick," Monet whispered. The great Crimson Knight was quite out of countenance. In truth, Monet had never seen Sir Broderick so out of countenance. Nor had she missed seeing the gathering of parchment he held fisted in one powerful hand. Her father's seal was upon it: charges—battle strategies. Monet swallowed the thick fear in her throat as she watched the Crimson Knight stride away. Her father was sending him back into battle! The thought near tore her tender heart.

Thus Monet did not beg audience by knocking on the great door to her father's chambers. Simply she burst in upon him—so startling him he gasped.

"Monet!" he exclaimed. "You fair caused the Reaper to ghost me! What are you about, rupturing the privacy of an old man?"

"You are not an old man, Father," Monet scolded. "By far you are not. But what task have you set upon the Crimson Knight? I thought he would behead me as soon as speak to me just now?"

Her father sighed. This only increased her concern.

"He was in possession of parchments, Father," she began, "parchments with your seal. What strategies are you sending to the legions in the north? Or have you sent him on a singular errand?" The pounding in her bosom increased— the deep fear for Sir Broderick's safety. Three months she had worried for the Crimson Knight in battle—each sunrise wondered if he would be among the dead returned to Karvana in the death carts. Yet since the night before, since the moment he had revealed himself at the inn, she had known a measure of comfort. Even for the Rothbainians who had attempted to capture or murder her, even for the mad ride to the castle, the archers poised above, even for all of it she had been blessed with the knowledge that Sir Broderick Dougray was well—that he lingered in safety at Karvana Castle.

Further, Monet yet wondered why the Crimson Knight had questioned her when she had told him she would forgive him anything. Was he sent on such an errand of horror as to strip him of his honor somehow? Had he been sent as assassin, to cut off the enemy's head?

"Perhaps you have sent him to behead King James," she said, speaking her thoughts aloud.

Monet frowned when her father chuckled, drawing her from her reverie. "No. I have not. Yet it is a valid suggestion. And I have no doubt Sir Broderick Dougray could accomplish such an incomprehensible task were it given him. But, no, I have not sent him to execute King James . . . as much as the thought tempts me now."

"In any regard, he seemed pure vexed . . . with me, I am sure," Monet said.

"You are thinking he is vexed over the events of last evening . . . the events begun at the Emerald Crown and ended in your bower."

"What else could put him in such state of discountenance toward me?"

"War, my dove. Vexation, frustration, foul temperament . . . these are what war heaps upon a soldier," her father said. "In truth, I thought he might not be quite so vexed still . . . for I have agreed to knight Eann on the morrow at his request."

"Father! That is wonderful!" Monet exclaimed, still wondering what charge her father had given Sir Broderick. "Eann has labored hard to prove himself worthy."

"That he has, and though he is young, I believe he is deserving . . . and ready," King Dacian said. "Young Richard Tailor is to be Eann's squire. This was also Broderick's request."

Monet thought it odd—the manner in which her heart fluttered with delight and pride in the knowledge Sir Broderick would be so thoughtful of his squire and others.

"It is so very admirable that he would request this of you, Father . . . of all the things you must have offered as honor for whatever charge you gave him. Eann will be a great knight . . . and someday so may Richard Tailor be," she said. "Yet what could you have asked of him that he would endeavor to secure Eann's knighthood?"

"Curiosity is well a part of war, Monet," he said. "Yet secrecy is the larger part."

"Forgive me, Father," Monet said, humbled. "I would not endanger Sir Broderick by pressing you to reveal strategies you should not."

"That is wise, Monet. Very wise."

"There. In the least I have made one wise decision these past days . . . though it is painfully difficult not to wonder over such things."

Her father chuckled and gathered Monet into a warm embrace.

"I-I am so glad to see you, Father," she whispered as tears escaped her eyes and trickled over her cheeks, "though I find somehow that I am weaker with you near . . . weaker even than I felt when you were away."

King Dacian kissed Monet's cheek and said, "When I was away, it was needs be you were strong for the people. You could not let them see you frightened or hopeless . . . and your princess's spirit knew this. Now that I am returned, I can help bear this weight with you . . . full take it from you in this moment or that. And there is no shame or weakness in sharing a burden. This you must remember always. Hardship is better endured when shared, my dove."

Monet smiled—sighed with momentary contentment.

"You will never know how glad my heart is in your presence, Father," she said. "These past months, when you were at battle . . . I feel I have not slept sound since you first rode from the castle with your knights and legions about you."

"War does not bode well for sound sleeping . . . that is certain," King Dacian chuckled.

"Perhaps it too is as simple as that," Monet said, moving from her father's embrace to better gaze into his smiling face.

"Perhaps what is so simple, dove?"

"The Crimson Knight's pure vexed appearance. Perhaps he is only weary from battle . . . war-worried and fatigued."

"Perhaps," Dacian said—though he well knew Broderick's countenance bore far deeper concerns. He forced a smile, lovingly caressing Monet's cheek with the back of his hand. How desperately he loved her! How sweetly her people loved her! As he continued to gaze at her, Dacian knew—once again he knew he had acted with wisdom. Karvana's hope must be protected—spirited away to preservation. How he would miss her, his beloved Monet, the beautiful Scarlet Princess—the Heart of Karvana.

"How handsome you are in your fine wine-colored tunic, Sir Eann!" Monet exclaimed. She smiled as a soft vermilion blush rose to the cheeks of young knight, Sir Eann Beacher. Indeed, Eann did look magnificent in his new finery. His sanguine tunic with golden shield and fierce-tusked boar seemed perfectly befitting—a distinct contrast to his fair hair and brown eyes.

"Thank you, Princess," Eann said. "And does not Richard look quite dashing as well?"

Monet nodded, placing a hand on Richard's shoulder. "And do you think you will enjoy being squire to Sir Eann, Richard Tailor?" she asked.

Young Richard smiled. "Yes, your highness."

Monet giggled. She was purely delighted—momentarily overcome with the obvious joy displayed on the faces of the young men she attended.

She thought of the day before. The ceremony of Eann's knighting had been quite affecting! Her father had knighted Eann with great dignity and respect, heralding a speech to all in attendance as to the profound honor and expectations of knighthood. The ceremony had given the people renewed hope—to see a young knight so willing to serve Karvana and its people.

Furthermore, all had cheered with pride and joy when Sir Broderick Dougray, the Crimson Knight, presented Eann a sword. The Crimson Knight's presentation of such a valuable weapon, its hilt bejeweled of rubies, displayed his faith and trust in his once squire, now fellow protector of the kingdom. Eann bore the entirety of the ceremony humbly and well, with demeanor befitting a true knight of Karvana.

Young Richard Tailor had been quite overjoyed to learn he had been selected as squire to Karvana's newest knight. Squiring was difficult, yes, but also very lucrative. Likewise it held the potential of knighthood. With a simple request of favor, the Crimson Knight's generosity had enriched two lives—pure given hope to one who had owned little before.

"Yet what will Sir Broderick do without you, Eann?" Monet asked.

Sir Eann's broad shoulders lifted in an unknowing shrug. "I do not know. He has not told me who he intends to take as his squire now."

"Your father begs audience, Princess Monet."

Monet turned to see one of her father's pages standing just behind her.

"Thank you, Channing," she told the small, dark-haired messenger.

Yet Channing gave no nod—made no move to depart. "He asked me to escort you to your bower at once, Princess," he said instead.

"Very well," Monet said. She felt a slight frown pucker her brow. Her father must own severe news or instruction indeed.

She nodded to Sir Eann—to Richard. "Forgive me my leaving you so abruptly, gentlemen."

"Good day, Princess," Sir Eann said. Richard bowed, and Monet took her leave.

As she followed Channing into the castle, a strange and discomforting warmth began to bathe her limbs. She could not remember a time her father had commanded a page to escort her to him. Had something occurred with the battle to the north? Was King James gathering troops nearer to Karvana?

Somehow, in those moments, as fear began to overtake her, Monet was soothed by the knowledge that the Crimson Knight had not yet returned to the battles of the north. He was yet well, as was her father. Still, she wondered if her father summoned her to inform her they would be returning to the northern battles. Perhaps he had altered his consideration that Karvana's king should linger at the castle. Perhaps he planned to return to the battle with the Crimson Knight.

This thought did not comfort her, and though she knew it pointless, she inquired of Channing, "Does Sir Broderick mean to take his leave, Channing? Do you know . . . is he planning to return to battle? Will my father accompany him?"

Channing merely shrugged his slight shoulders. "I know nothing of why you are being summoned, Princess," he said. He paused then, turning to look at Monet. Glancing about as to ensure their privacy, he whispered, "Yet I do know he has been in counsel with Sir Broderick all this long morning!"

"Truly?" Monet asked in a whisper.

Channing nodded. "I even heard raised voices . . . often . . . especially Sir Broderick's . . . though I could not discern the subject of their conversation."

"Sir Broderick? Raise his voice to the king?" Monet was astonished!

Channing nodded. "And Friar Fleming was with your father this morning . . . as was the Minstrel Marius."

"Friar Fleming? From the village?"

Channing nodded. "Yet I heard no music when Marius was in audience, Princess."

"We must be failing in the north, Channing," Monet whispered. "Father has, no doubt, asked the friar to accompany him on his return. Too many men are dying. Friar Fleming will give their spirits hope." She paused and frowned, pensive. "Perhaps he has asked Marius to join them as well . . . that they may be entertained or—"

"We must hurry, Princess," Channing said, taking her hand, thus leading her on toward her bower.

Channing must be unsettled indeed to take such liberties as to touch her. Monet smiled, delighted by his lack of propriety. Yet the feeling of imminent doom advanced upon her all the more—for what need would her father have to meet with these men in her bower chambers? Was King James's reach so near to Karvana that her father felt no shield to danger—even in his own throne room?

As they approached her bower door, Monet was rendered breathless, for the Crimson Knight stood conversing with the Minstrel Marius and Friar Fleming. The three men looked to her as she approached. Marius nodded a greeting and bowed. Monet nodded to him—to Friar Fleming—to the Crimson Knight.

Dressed in full armor, save his helmet, the Crimson Knight was fierce to look upon. His raven hair was swept back, save one dark strand rebelling to caress his forehead, and his eyes smoldered with indistinct emotion.

"You are to wait here, Channing," Sir Broderick said, yet glaring at Monet all the while.

"Yes, Sir Broderick," Channing said. The boy glanced at Monet—forced a smile of friendly reassurance.

"Your father would speak to you, Princess," Sir Broderick said. Monet watched as he placed his hand on the latch of her bower door. He seemed to pause—drew a deep breath. At last he pushed at the latch and stepped into the room, standing aside that she may pass.

Her father sat upon her bed, his head bowed, his shoulders drooped in a like manner of defeat. In his hand he held parchments—soiled and bloodied. Monet knew that it was a list of the dead. She had seen the death cart approach at sunrise and knew that seven soldiers of Karvana had been returned to their kingdom, never to draw breath again.

Monet startled as she heard the door close and latch behind her. Turning, she saw the Crimson Knight take stance, feet apart, armored arms folded across his broad chest. It was odd he should remain while she would be in counsel with her father.

"Father?" Monet whispered. "What has happened?"

She watched as her father paused a moment before rising.

"It is many hours I have spent in contemplation of how you would be told of this, Monet," he said. He tried to force a smile but could not. At once, Monet began to tremble. Something had transpired. Had James of Rothbain truly won victory in the north?

"It is best to simply say what must be said, Father," Monet said, though the sense of dread welling in her bosom near overwhelmed her.

"Yes," he agreed. He turned to her, his eyes narrowed, a deep frown puckering his brow. "Then let it be said. King James's men—the few that were brought to the castle still breathing, after having endeavored to overtake you at the Emerald Crown—cowards that they are, they have confirmed what we have long suspected. They have revealed James's intentions where you are concerned, Monet."

"Where I am concerned?" Monet whispered.

"King James would have you brought to Rothbain . . . held for ransom or forced to his marriage bed . . . that my resolve to defend Karvana against him might be weakened."

"But, Father—" Monet began as terror swept over her anew.

"We knew this would be his strategy, of course," her father interrupted. "Even I have spoken of it to you. Yet I tell you now . . . this will not be. Karvana must not live in constant fear that its heart may be taken from it."

"Father . . . I am sorry for my disobedience of two nights past," Monet began. He did not yet trust her. Her disobedience on the night Sir Broderick had rescued her had not left his mind— nor his heart. Of a sudden, desperate to own his trust, she pleaded, "I will not go out among the people. This I have promised you, Father. I have sworn my obedience. What fear of King James have I if I remain—"

"Swear it now, Monet," King Dacian growled. "Swear your obedience to your father and king . . . here . . . now . . . that James of Rothbain may be thwarted in one evil strategy in the least."

"I swear it, Father!" Monet cried. She thought of Sir Broderick—of his sworn allegiance and loyalty to her father and the kingdom. "I swear no less obedience than one of your knights! Think you I less obedient than they?"

She watched as her father inhaled—expelled the breath slowly.

"You are Karvana's very heart, Monet," he began, "the true hope of her people. In me, their king, they see power . . . battle . . . protection.

In you they see hope. In you they look to their future. For this reason, and others, you must be preserved. Certainly I would have you preserved simply because I love you more than any thing or person in this world. Yet the people must know you are safe as well. They must know that Karvana will live on in you. Even if James of Rothbain should conquer Karvana's body . . . the people will live with hope in knowing their royal line survives."

A comprehension nearly painful to endure wove through her mind and body. Monet knew then: her father feared siege of Karvana Castle—defeat. The enemy was at the very gate, and King Dacian knew it.

"You are sending me into exile," she said, her understanding complete.

"Yes," King Dacian answered. "And you will go. You will go . . . for you have promised obedience."

Of a sudden, Monet's strength abandoned her. As tears left her eyes to travel in profusion over her cheeks, she said, "You would put me away from you and my people . . . ask me to do nothing in defense or to lend comfort to the kingdom?"

"In this you will defend and comfort her, Monet. Defend and comfort her with hope."

Monet brushed moisture from her cheeks. How weak he must think her—Sir Broderick, the Crimson Knight who stood behind her barring the door, the Crimson Knight who stood ever at the ready to lay down his life for Karvana—as she stood before him bathing her face in tears of fear and doubt.

She had given her father, her king, sworn obedience. She would not let the Crimson Knight think her weak, nor her father.

"Where then do you send me, Father?" she asked.

"I know not," he answered.

"What?" Monet exclaimed in a whisper. How could he not know where she was to be sent?

"You will hear the strategy now . . . and you will obey your part in it, Monet."

"But where—"

"You will be taken . . . and I will not know where you dwell. Nor will any other who remains in Karvana or the castle."

"Taken? By whom? And why will you not know where I am?" Panic was fast rising in her. To be taken from Karvana was loathsome enough. Yet to dwell alone, in a strange place?

"I must not know, Monet. I, nor anyone else," her father said. "For if I am captured . . ." He paused, seeming to consider his words. "I know not what means of torture the enemy employs . . . and though I am myself certain I would never succumb and reveal . . . there are alchemists known to brew such herbs and plants as to turn a man's thoughts to gruel. Therefore, I must own no knowledge of where you will be concealed."

"Father . . . I cannot . . . I cannot . . ." Monet quivered, trembling with fear and panic.

"Listen to me, Monet," her father said, taking hold of her shoulders. "You will leave Karvana. You will dwell safely from it, in secret exile . . . until such time as King James's attack on this kingdom is at an end. If Karvana triumphs and I survive with her . . . you will return. Annulment will then be granted, and I will continue to rule."

"Annulment?" Monet asked. Her mind was a soup of confusion and perplexity.

Yet the king did not pause—only continued, "However, if I am taken or killed . . . there will be no annulment, and you will continue to battle James as Karvana's queen . . . with your then true husband ruling beside you as king."

"Husband? You're speaking in riddles, Father!"

"Pray listen, Monet . . . for little time is given us," he continued. "There will likewise be no annulment if Karvana falls to James. Thus, also in this will Broderick become your true husband, and you and he will live out your days unknown and in an unknown land. Even if the enemy draws too near the gate might this be your fate, Monet . . . for I cannot abide the risk of your being found. In all this manner will Karvana's heart be shielded. In all this manner, Monet . . . you, Karvana's heart, will be preserved."

Monet frowned—trembled with near apoplexy.

Her mind whirled as sudden understanding washed over her.

"You . . . you are forcing Sir Broderick to take me to wife," she whispered.

"I have given him the charge of preserving you, Monet . . . and he has accepted. He will wed you in name only, that you may travel with him, dwell with him for a time in utter propriety . . . until James is vanquished and you can return," her father explained. "It would serve no right purpose to send you off in singular companionship with him were you not wed. Yet the marriage will not be consummated—thus, neither your freedoms nor his are full sacrificed—unless I am taken or killed or Karvana's gates are too pressed . . . or she falls. Only then will he take you to true wife."

"This is madness, Father!" Monet whispered.

"This is battle strategy, Monet," the king said. "If you are removed . . . the enemy is weakened. He cannot capture you and thereby use you as a pawn against me and this kingdom."

"Thus, the Crimson Knight becomes a pawn instead," Monet said. "For the sake of my safety . . . he must—"

"If Karvana falls to James . . . if he triumphs . . . he would use you to soften the pain to the people of Karvana. Imagine . . . if he should vanquish me—our legions—yet stand at Karvana's eaves with you at his side. The people, though saddened at my loss and loathing King James, would yet love you . . . accept you as the true queen. This would give him such a power over the people as you cannot fathom! Therefore, if you are not within his reach, he is somewhat bested . . . no matter the outcome of this bloody battle."

"I am not a fool, Father!" Monet exclaimed. "I understand the strategy . . . the manner in which my very existence may spur James to victory. I do understand! Yet, Father, to force the Crimson Knight to . . . to carry me into exile . . . to force him to . . . Father, you cannot be in earnest!" Monet cried.

"I am in full earnest, Monet," the king rather growled.

"Father," Monet pleaded in a whisper, tears trailing over her lovely cheeks, "I beg you not to do this thing to him!"

"To *him?*" King Dacian asked. "To *him* and not to yourself?"

"He is a knight, Father!" Monet continued, still whispering, still weeping. "A warrior! To tear him from his men and his cause . . . he will ever loathe me if you force him to this!" A fearful sort of desperation began to overtake her. Nothing—nothing could be more magnificent than belonging to Sir Broderick Dougray! Nothing! Ever even Monet had dreamt of it—of being his—of his belonging to her! Yet to force him to accept her—into marrying her—into a marriage from which he would derive no husbandly rights?

He would indeed grow to loathe her. She thought then of his countenance when last they had met, when he had carried the gathering of parchments, when he had glared at her with such discernable distain.

She gasped a quiet breath of understanding as the words he spoke then to her echoed in her mind. *For it may needs be you sacrifice near all you know . . . as others of us have covenanted to do,* he had said. The Crimson Knight had accepted the King's charge to spirit her away to exile, thereby sacrificing near all he knew. And he would loathe her for it—of this she was certain.

"He will not loathe you, Monet," King Dacian said. But Monet would not be soothed.

"It is different for me, Father . . . and well you know it is different," she began, whispering still, "for there was never to be a choice given me— in marriage. As a princess, I have ever known I would not be given choice—that I must marry whomever you required me to marry. But he—"

"It is true. Ever it has been known your troth would be an election . . . *my* election as king and as your father. And my election is that, in this moment at least, you wed Broderick. I do not know what the future holds for you . . . who will one day reign at your side as King of Karvana. Yet my requirement of you at this moment is to marry Broderick, that he may endeavor to preserve our bloodline through preservation of you . . . for James surely means to kill me, Monet. As surely as I am standing here before you now . . . the day may come that I may not stand."

"Please, Father—" Monet began.

King Dacian took Monet's face between powerful hands.

"James will ever seek after you, Monet. Until this war is won by Karvana, he will seek after you. Whether for advantage in strategy or advantage in ruling . . . he will covet you."

Monet frowned. The severity of her father's gaze confounded her to silence.

"I remind you, he may even endeavor to kill you . . . to simply abolish our line. Or he may plan to mingle his own blood with yours to ensure his right to Karvana's throne . . . should anyone have the courage to challenge him if I am defeated."

"You must think me full witless, for I know all these things, Father," Monet said. "I understand I must go . . . keep myself from King James's reach. But why force Sir Broderick to *marry* me, Father?" she asked. "I will go wherever he leads me, Father! I will do his will! You need not force him to bind himself to me."

"It is needs be," King Dacian said, "for I will not have you inhabit together without it. It would be impossible—unthinkable—to allow this without appropriate lines being met in the eyes of God."

"But—"

"Broderick has accepted this charge, Monet," the king said. "And I might remind . . . he accepted this charge with far less emotion and resistance than have you."

Monet frowned, brushing tears from her cheeks.

"My king," Sir Broderick spoke from behind her, "we must make haste. The time is near upon us."

Monet felt her limbs—her entire body—prickle with gooseflesh. The mere sound of his voice had affected her so. In her desperation to avert her father's plan, she had forgotten he stood just behind her.

"He is right," King Dacian said. "We must move forward."

Monet gazed up into her father's worry-worn face. There was pain in his countenance— overwhelming sadness. It was only then she recognized how very difficult it was for her father to send her away—to be without her.

"Monet?" he asked.

She nodded. "I will do your bidding, Father. Of course I will do what you ask. Forgive me my resistance."

King Dacian inhaled a deep breath—exhaled it with seeming renewed conviction.

"Bid the others enter, Broderick," he said.

Monet did not turn; she could not face Sir Broderick Dougray.

She heard the latch of her bower door loosen—heard the rustle of the friar's robe and of footsteps. She heard her bower door close once more and looked up to her father.

He brushed the tears from her cheeks with his thumbs as he tenderly held her face between strong hands. He forced a smile, yet the love shown in his eyes was pure and true—and threaded through his very soul.

"I love you, my dove," he whispered. "One day . . . one day you will know how truly I love you. Though it does not seem clear to you now, one day your mind and heart will know it is true."

Monet nodded—begged the tears still flowing from her eyes to cease.

"We have devised a plan, Broderick and I . . . a distraction. And it is not far from commencing. Thus, we must make haste, Monet. You will wed Sir Broderick here . . . at this moment."

Monet shook her head as fear washed over her once more. "But, Father . . . I—"

"You will leave at once, Monet," King Dacian said, his voice breaking with emotion. Monet began to protest, but her father's stern expression silenced her. Taking her by the shoulders, he turned her to face Friar Fleming and the others. To Friar Fleming she looked—but not to Sir Broderick. To him she could not look, for she did not wish to see the pure vexation and loathing that would be plain on his face.

"Friar Fleming," the king said, "you have been summoned here . . . and your silence has been covenanted. You will now perform the marriage of Princess Monet to Sir Broderick Dougray."

Had she not been so thoroughly terrified, she might have laughed at the expression of astonishment then apparent in Friar Fleming's countenance. Still, even for his evident astonishment, Friar Fleming said, "Yes, my king."

"Marius, Channing, you too will witness this marriage . . . that it may be proved as needs be. Yet to speak of it to anyone would cost you near your life," King Dacian said.

Monet noted the manner in which young Channing's bright eyes widened—even as he nodded in acceptance of the charge given him. She noted Marius did not appear in any manner awed. Rather, he smiled, as if amused by something he had near foreseen.

"S-Sir Broderick," Friar Fleming said. He gestured toward the Crimson Knight, an indication he should come forward.

Monet looked to the Crimson Knight at last, his smoldering gaze causing her to tremble. He did not pause but stepped forthright to stand before Friar Fleming.

"Princess?" Friar Fleming said, nodding toward Sir Broderick.

Monet moved, stepped forward, and stood next to Sir Broderick, to his right. She could fair hear her gown quivering with the mad trembling of her body. She glanced to her father, and he nodded his assurance.

"Broderick Nathair Dougray," Friar Fleming began, "wilt thou have this woman to thy wedded wife? Wilt thou love and honor her, guard and keep her . . . in health, in wealth . . . in illness and poverty . . . casting off all others for sake of her alone . . . and keep thee unto her, and only her, forever?"

"I will," the Crimson Knight near growled, yet without pause.

Monet could scarce believe she had heard his voice, yet she had, and he had given his marriage promise.

She tried to still her mad trembling as Friar Fleming then looked to her.

"Monet Vanya Dacianatis," the Friar began, "wilt thou have this man to thy wedded husband? Wilt thou love and honor him, guard and keep him . . . in health, in wealth . . . in illness and poverty . . . casting off all others for sake of him alone . . . and keep thee unto him, and only him, forever?"

"I will," she breathed. It was near done. Nearly she was wed to Sir Broderick Dougray; nearly she was in exile from Karvana and her father.

"Clasp hands," Friar Fleming said.

Monet was breathless as she felt Sir Broderick's glove and gauntlet as he took her hand. She could not keep from grasping his in return, for she was near to fainting with fear and would draw strength from whence she could.

"Sir Broderick, repeat my words if they be your wish," Friar Fleming said. "I, Broderick, take thee, Monet . . ."

"I, Broderick, take thee, Monet." Again the sound of his voice caused gooseflesh to prick Monet's body and limbs.

"To my wedded wife," Friar Fleming continued, "to have . . . to hold . . . to own from this day for ever . . . for good or for bad . . . for wealth or for poverty . . . in illness or in health. Thus, hereto I covenant thee my troth."

"To my wedded wife," Broderick spoke. "To have . . . to hold . . . to own from this day for ever . . . for good or for bad . . . for wealth or for poverty . . . in illness or in health. Thus, hereto I covenant thee my troth."

Friar Fleming glanced to the king. "Is there a ring?" he asked.

"There is," Sir Broderick answered. Monet watched, as if wandering in a dream, as Sir Broderick placed a small silver ring on her left ring finger.

"Princess, repeat my words if they be your wish," Friar Fleming said to Monet then. "I,

Monet, take thee, Broderick, to my wedded husband."

Though it near sounded a whisper, Monet spoke. "I, Monet, take thee, Broderick, to my wedded husband."

"To have . . . to hold . . . to own from this day forever . . . for good or for bad . . . for wealth or for poverty . . . in illness or in health. Thus, hereto I covenant thee my troth," the Friar said.

"To have . . . to hold . . . to own from this day forever . . . for good or for bad . . . for wealth or for poverty . . . in illness or in health. Thus, hereto I covenant thee my troth," Monet whispered.

"Man and wife," Friar Fleming pronounced. "Thus, it is done. Let a kiss seal it . . . that ye may go forth into the world as one," the friar said.

Monet was still—certain the Crimson Knight would refuse their wedding kiss. Of a sudden, however, Monet was rendered breathless as Sir Broderick Dougray reached out and, with one powerful hand at the back of her head, drew her face to meet his.

For all her trembling and fear, yet a thrilling, intoxicating ecstasy coursed through Monet's body as the Crimson Knight's mouth fair crushed to her own in a heated, moist, bold, driven kiss. This was a kiss far unlike the soft, careful kisses she had known with him before. This was a kiss of power—of duty that would be met—of a challenge that would be bested—and of laying claim.

"The champion's prize be hanged, it seems," said King Dacian, breathing one burst of a chuckle.

The Crimson Knight released her then, and Monet gasped for breath—near would have toppled had it not been for Channing's steady hand at her back.

Monet ventured a glance at Sir Broderick, yet he had turned and was striding toward Monet's bed.

"Thank you, Friar, Marius . . . and you, young Channing," King Dacian said, affectionately disheveling Channing's perfectly combed hair with one hand. "We will leave them now . . . for we none of us must know where they travel."

"Father?" Monet whispered.

Her father kissed her forehead. His eyes misted with tears as he said, "Until we meet again, my love."

Monet shook her head—stood in confounded disbelief as her father followed Channing, Marius, and Friar Fleming out of the room.

"You will change your fine scarlet for these peasant woman's clothes," the Crimson Knight said, gesturing toward a mound of clothing now lying on Monet's bed.

Monet turned to see Sir Broderick, in process of removing his gauntlets.

"When you have finished, you mean?" she asked.

"No. Now," he commanded. "Time is short. We must be ready when the king's planned distraction commences."

He removed the vambraces from his forearms as Monet stood yet astonished.

"I will undress you myself, Princess," he growled, "if you do not make to do so." As he paused in removing his rerebrace, taking a step toward her, Monet gasped.

"No, no, no! I-I can do it for myself," she said.

The Crimson Knight nodded. "I will give you my back for your privacy," he said. He turned away from her and continued to remove his armor.

Slowly Monet slipped her gown from one shoulder. She endeavored to remain conscious—to fend off the black sleep of a faint as she traded her lovely scarlet frock for the simple brown of a peasant woman's kirtle.

Once her finery had been exchanged for the clothes of a commoner, Monet looked to see the Crimson Knight's appearance had also been altered. As he finished tying the points at the front of a brown doublet, she thought for a moment he seemed all the more handsome dressed in the plain white of a linen shirt and doe-brown doublet.

She felt a blush rise to her cheeks, for his eyes

traveled the length of her—from toe to head and back.

He frowned, and she was assured that any beauty she may have owned theretofore was vanished without her lovely scarlet gown. She watched as the Crimson Knight strode to the hearth. He bent, placing his fingers in the ashes. Rising, he returned to her, and Monet gasped as he touched her cheek, her chin, one temple. Running his sooty fingers along his own jaw, he then reached out and tugged at several strands of her hair, gently coaxing them from her long, loose braid, to hang unruly about her face.

"Are you ready then?" he asked.

"Of course not," Monet said. He frowned with disapproval, and she sighed. "Yes," she breathed.

"Then let us away to exile, Princess," the Crimson Knight said, "for I will not let Karvana's people lose hope."

As she followed the Crimson Knight from the warm safety of her bower, Monet paused—glanced back to see her beautiful scarlet gown abandoned on her bed midst the litter of armor strewn next to it.

Into Exile

The Crimson Knight took hold of Monet's hand, leading her through the most secluded parts of the castle. It was true enough that his very touch—the feel of his bare hand clasping hers—was, in itself, sufficient sense to affect her. Yet coupled with fear birthed of the knowledge she was being led into exile, Monet wondered would her body ever cease its violent trembling.

The Crimson Knight led her into the east mezzanine, through the secreted doorway hidden behind the tapestry there, and down a narrow spiral of stone steps.

"But . . . but I have brought nothing," Monet whispered. And it was true! Only in that moment did she recognize she had nothing about her, save the garments she wore.

"I have prepared every needful thing," Sir Broderick said.

"*Every* needful thing?" Monet asked, endeavoring to match his swift pace.

He halted, turning abruptly and causing that she stumbled into him. Placing a hand on one of the broad shoulders before her, Monet steadied herself to find the Crimson Knight glaring at her with severe indignation.

"The king deems me pure competent, Princess," he said. "And I am." Even for the dark of the corridor, his eyes burned. Monet wondered—was it simply the fire of the torch he carried reflected in the bewitching blue of his eyes? Yet it was not; his eyes held their own flame, and she nodded her submission to the faith her father owned in him.

They continued, the stone steps winding downward to a tunnel. It was well Monet knew this tunnel, for it had been her escape from the castle on occasions before. It would lead to the royal mausoleum.

The length of the Crimson Knight's stride gave cause that Monet near had to run to match it. Yet he hurried onward, through the dark tunnel, his torch lighting their way.

"Hush," he whispered as they stepped out of the tunnel and into the mausoleum. At once, Monet heard it—music, laughter, the sounds of merriment.

"What is it?" she whispered.

The Crimson Knight snuffed the torch flame. "A fair," he whispered, leading her to the front of the mausoleum, toward the door. "A distraction," he explained. "Your father has had minstrels, jugglers, jesters, and the like gather within the castle walls to entertain the people . . . to distract them that we might make our way from Karvana unseen. The people will cheer . . . refresh themselves in knowing their king is ever mindful of them even for war approaching the gates. And we will escape without notice."

Monet nodded. The Crimson Knight raised a finger to his lips, a gesture she should speak no more. Without a sound, he moved to the door leading from the mausoleum. She began to move toward him, but he held up one hand to stay her.

Still trembling with fear and uncertainty, Monet glanced about—to the tombs of her ancestors. Her eyes rested for a long moment on that of her mother's. How bitterly she missed her mother! She was loath to think of her mother entombed in the dark, musty confines of the mausoleum. Yet she knew only her mother's dust rested there; she knew her mother's soul delighted in the flowered meadows of heaven. Tears filled her eyes, for, of a sudden, the renewed ache of loss in her was profound. She thought of the king's instructions—the sealed parchments she knew to be hidden in the secret space in the angel monument of her mother's tomb. At once, a deep curiosity clasped her—a bitter sense to rebel— to take the king's instructions from their hiding place, break her father's seal, and know who her father had set down as her betrothed before King James had brought war to Karvana. With strategies so altered because of the war—for she knew her father's decision to send her to exile with the Crimson Knight to guard her had been of recent planning—her curiosity as to who her father would have required her to wed otherwise or in some future time near caused her to seek out the hidden instructions. Yet she had promised obedience, and breaking her father's seal for curiosity's sake would be far and yon from obedient.

Monet's attention was arrested by voices— one seeming very familiar. Quietly moving to stand behind Sir Broderick, Monet listened. The Minstrel Marius was at the door, speaking to the mausoleum guard.

"Pray, let us assist the young friar yon . . . for he has stumbled into a rabbit's burrow and injured himself."

"I cannot leave sight of my post," the guard said.

"Nay, and you will not . . . for he is just there. See him?" Marius said. "There, writhing upon the ground. His pain must be great indeed."

"I will help him to stand with you . . . but you must bear him away," the guard grumbled.

"Thank you, brave soldier," Marius said.

The Crimson Knight paused a moment. Monet gasped as he reached back, fisting the cloth at the neck of her kirtle in one hand, pulling her from the mausoleum as he stepped through the door.

"Be quick!" he whispered, releasing her dress and taking hold of her arm.

Monet glanced aside—to the mausoleum guard helping Marius to pull Friar Fleming from his position of sitting in the grass. With their backs to the mausoleum, they did not see the Crimson Knight leading Monet across the grassy space between the mausoleum and the outer castle wall.

Monet was breathless by the time they reached the wall—breathless from the mad pounding of her heart. She wondered how often in his life the Crimson Knight had found necessity in skulking about in like manner, for he was as wily and quick as a fox.

"I have a cart and horses waiting just beyond the village," he said, drawing a brown hood up over his head. Reaching over, he pulled Monet's hood over her head as well. In truth, Monet had not noticed her garment had a hood attached— having changed her princess's clothes for those of a common woman in such haste. "It is not a long walk . . . and the people should be well enough distracted by now."

Monet nodded and followed as he strode out across the meadow margin of the castle. The wildflowers of autumn were yet bright on the meadows, and as she walked she allowed her gaze to linger on the fields of tawny grains beyond. She looked to the orchards—smiled at the baskets of apples abandoned beneath trees yet heavy laden. Harvesting had paused, for there was a fair at Karvana Castle, and fairs were rare delights. How wise and cunning her father was! The fair had drawn near everyone to the castle and away from the path she and Sir Broderick now trod.

As they walked, Monet looked all about and around, promising her heart she would never forget the visions her mind owned of Karvana at harvest. She wondered if she would ever see her beloved Karvana again. Or if she did, would it live happily under the same reign?

The comforting scent of wood smoke rising from hearths in the village hung light in the air as Monet followed the Crimson Knight past the cottages and buildings of Karvana. She was full astonished at the manner in which they went on unnoticed. Several children, trailing after their parents on their way to the castle, waved as they passed, and an elderly woman, sitting in repose upon a weathered chair near the Emerald Crown, nodded to them.

"Good day, young lovers," the elderly woman said.

"Good day, kind mother," the Crimson Knight said, bowing to her in slight.

The old woman smiled a toothless smile and laughed.

"Ah! There are much merrier things than fairs

for young lovers to be about on such a fine day . . . are there not?"

"Indeed, there are," the Crimson Knight said.

Monet blushed in spite of her determination not to do so.

"Then you best be about them," the woman said.

"Indeed, we will," he said. Taking Monet's hand, he drew her from just behind him to his side.

"Do not linger in being shy, sweet girl," the old woman called to Monet. "No woman ever died from letting as handsome a lad as that one steal a kiss or two 'neath the willows." Monet felt her blush swell, yet managed to offer the old woman a kind nod as the Crimson Knight led her onward.

Soon they came to a grove of willow trees standing just beyond the village. There stood one horse, another harnessed to a large cart heaped with supplies and other goods.

"How far will we travel?" Monet asked as the Crimson Knight helped her to the cart seat.

"Not far," he said. "The remainder of this day and all of the morrow. It is not so far . . . only slow travel with a cart."

Not far? Near a full day's travel and another? She wondered what great distances the Crimson Knight had traveled in his life that would deem two days' travel as not far.

"Where are we bound?" she asked.

He sat beside her and took hold of the lines. As the Crimson Knight snapped the leather at the back of the cart horse, the cart heaved forward. The second horse, tied to the back of the cart, followed with head hanging, as if disappointed to be merely walking.

When he did not answer her inquiry, Monet said, "I will know it when we arrive, Sir Broderick. Why keep our destination from me now?"

"Ballain," the Crimson Knight answered at last.

"Ballain?" she asked. "Near Ballist?" Of a sudden, Monet's fear increased twofold. Ballain?

Monet had heard of Ballain—in tales of Ballist and Karvana's battle there years before. Ballain had been a wild and willful township near Ballist, ruled by the corrupt Lord Morven. Once a wealthy and respected noble, Lord Morven had altered in his years of maturity. Having served Monet's grandfather, King Seward, as a worthy and honorable knight, Lord Morven had been corrupted by wealth and power. Upon King Seward's death, Lord Morven had begun to conspire against King Dacian in secret, raising two small legions of troops comprising murderers and thieves and banished soldiers from distant kingdoms. When whispers of Lord Morven's treachery had reached King Dacian's ears, he sent the Crimson Knight and a legion of Karvanian cavalry and soldiers to Ballain to prove or disprove the rumors of treason. But the Crimson Knight and his legion did not reach Ballain, for Lord Morven and his treasonous followers lay in wait in Ballist before it. Thus, the bloody Battle of Ballist was fought. Though the Crimson Knight and his men were victorious, a heavy price was paid. Over half the men who had left Karvana for Ballain were lost on Ballist's fields. Lord Morven was vanquished—run through by the Crimson Knight's own blade. Still, the ambush at Ballist was infamous, and Monet wondered if the people of Ballain had truly forsaken their willful and wild ways.

"Yes . . . Ballain," the Crimson Knight mumbled.

"Will they be welcoming to Karvanians?" she asked.

The Crimson Knight looked to her, his eyes narrow, his countenance quite perfectly cheerless.

"We will not know . . . for they will not discern us to be Karvanians."

She remembered then—this was exile in all secret.

"Who will we be?" she asked.

The Crimson Knight drew a deep breath, exhaling slowly.

"We will be Alvarians . . . weary of King Rudolph's arrogance and weak rule," he said.

Even for the fear residing in her bosom, Monet could not keep a pleased smile from her lips.

"Oh, I quite like that," she said. "For I despise Anais of Alvar . . . as well as her father."

Monet quickly glanced to the Crimson Knight when she heard him chuckle. She was fair astonished at the sudden softening of his countenance. The slight smile he wore, the absence of a frown to furrow his brow, together with his peasant's attire caused that he looked very nearly affable.

"I spoke unkindly," she began. "Still . . . am I wrong in thinking you do not fault me for it?"

"You are not wrong," he admitted. "It is only that I am amused at hearing you speak so plain."

Monet inhaled deep, attempting to draw courage that she may speak even more plainly.

"I . . . I am sorry my father condemned you to this charge, Sir Broderick," she said. "I know you are a soldier above all else . . . that you must be loath to abandon your men to play watcher to me. The whole of it is absurd in the least. I am well able to keep from harm."

"Yes," he mumbled, "as you well proved two nights past at the Emerald Crown."

Monet blushed at his intimation she had shown herself quite *unable*.

"Admittedly, I did not realize the true danger the night I left the castle," she said. She dropped her gaze, studying her hands for a moment—the silver band on her left ring finger. "And I thank you for my rescue. Still, I am full aware now."

She sighed. Somehow the desperate fear that had fisted her in its hateful grip only half the hour before was giving way to acceptance—and resolve to endure. "Yet I am sorry it is you who has been yoked with me in exile."

"I am a soldier first," he said. "And I do own a measure of animosity at leaving my men to battle without me. Still, to be charged with the preservation of the heart of the kingdom . . . with secreting the king's only child? I am in constant bethinking of the great honor it is . . . to be so trusted by my king."

Monet sighed once more and looked ahead to the road before them—the lovely willows near its margin. How she loved to see the graceful sway of the leaf-laden branches. Soon the leaves would fall, and the trees would slumber till spring.

"I am only a girl . . . like any other," she said. "My worth is not above that of the other girls in Karvana . . . or the world. In truth, it is not so unlike to chess. My father's chess pieces, all carved from the same marble . . . mix them up in the world, toss them to the ground, and one is worth no more than the other. Yet place them in a fixed position on a chessboard, and they are valued differently. In truth, I do not think it is decent or right—neither for the maid who must labor in the fields . . . nor for the princess who must leave behind the only one who loves her to hide with strangers."

"Yet you might own no proficiency for harvest . . . and she may own none for compassion of the people," the Crimson Knight said. "I battle well, but were I to endeavor to compose a ballad the like Marius is able . . ." He shook his head. "Right or not, it is often our talent and character as much or more than our inherited station that determine where we are led in life . . . as well as what trials we may face."

Monet felt her eyes narrow as she looked at him. She smiled, delighted by both his comely appearance and his wisdom.

"So you are wise as well as battle ready," she said.

"And you are humble as well as selfless," he said. "This is why I have chosen that we should hale from Alvar . . . for its princess is in exact opposition to Karvana's. Therefore, who would think to suspect of two Alvarians in Ballain?"

He smiled at her then, and Monet thought sure her heart would take to flight as a bird and escape her bosom by way of her throat.

"Still, I am sorry for you in this, Sir Broderick," she said.

"Broderick," the Crimson Knight said. "Broderick is a common enough name. You will call me Broderick."

"And I shall be Monet?" she asked.

"No," he said. "Monet is not a common

name . . . and Princess Monet is far too known through all the five kingdoms. I will name you . . . Prissy."

"Prissy?" Monet exclaimed. "You cannot be in earnest!"

Monet did not miss the delicious grin of mischief tugging at the corners of his mouth.

"As the king told me just two days past . . . I am in full earnest," he said.

"But I do not like that name," Monet said. "It is not mine."

"Yet it does put me in mind of you somehow. Prissy you shall be." His eyes fair twinkled with mirth. She imagined for a moment that he was teasing her. Yet this was Sir Broderick Dougray— the Crimson Knight. Surely she was mistaken.

"I will not speak to you if you call me Prissy, Sir Broderick," she said.

"Broderick," he corrected.

Monet shook her head, attempting to dispel the sudden fear rising in her again—the renewed awareness she was being taken into exile, away from her father and all she knew. And she could not even keep own her name.

"I-I cannot name you simply Broderick," she said. "It is far too familiar. It is not appropriate."

"I am your husband," he growled, his temperament altered of a sudden. "How more familiar must I make myself?"

He was vexed with her. It seemed he was easily

vexed when she was near him. She understood then that, no matter his reassurance that he did not feel tortured by her father's charge to take her into exile—to protect her—yet he did.

"Very well," she said. "You will be Broderick, and I will be—"

"Prissy," he finished for her.

"As you wish, Sir Broderick," she mumbled. When he scowled at her, she said, "Broderick."

He spoke no more. Monet sensed he did not wish to converse with her any longer, and so they rode on. For hours and hours they traveled—until Karvana was far behind them and dusk descended.

Monet's eyes opened a little. Her body ached—in particular her neck. She gasped—sat upright as she realized the cart had stopped—that her head had been resting against the Crimson Knight's strong shoulder. When she had fallen asleep she did not know, but darkness was upon them now, and she was chilled.

"Forgive me," she said.

Sir Broderick said nothing as he climbed down from the cart. "We will pause here," he said.

Monet glanced about. The moonlight revealed they were halted in a small recess of rock among a thick grove of trees. She realized then he meant her to sleep in the open. She had never in her life done such a thing.

"Are we to have a fire?" she asked, for the night air was already frightfully chilled.

"No," he said, "for we must not risk discovery."

She opened her mouth to argue. Yet as she watched him pull a fur from the cart, she knew she should not. This was a man well skilled at battle—all manner of battle. If he deemed no fire should light the night as a beacon to their encampment, then no fire should light it.

There was certainly no room in the cart in which to lay down to rest. Thus, Monet assumed they would sleep on the cold ground. Tears filled her eyes at the thought of such cold discomfort, for she was painfully weary of a sudden.

"You will rest here," Sir Broderick said. She watched as he spread the large bearskin on the ground near the rocks. "The rocks should keep the breezes from you."

"And where will you rest?" she asked, for he did not spread another skin on the ground. Rather he returned to the cart, drawing the harness from the cart horse.

"I will stand watch," he said. He led the cart horse and the other to a nearby tree. Tying their bridle reins to a low branch, he patted the soft neck of each animal, speaking in a soothing voice to them as they began to nibble grass.

"Stand watch?" she asked. "Through the entire of the night?"

"Of course," he said, taking her hand and

helping her down from the cart. Of a sudden, she shivered, her body thoroughly chilled in the night air.

"You cannot stand watch all the night," she said. "When will you take your rest?"

"When we reach Ballain," he answered, leading her to the place near the rocks where the bearskin lay upon the ground. "I will rest tomorrow night."

"I will not rest if you are not at rest as well," she told him. "How can I?"

"It is of no consequence, Princess," he said. "It is many a night a soldier does not rest."

A sudden gust of wind blew about them, and Monet shivered, her teeth fair knocking together. Wrapping her arms about her, she trembled with the terrible discomfort of the cold night.

"You are too chilled," Sir Broderick said, a frown of deep concern furrowing his brow. "In falling asleep as we traveled, your body cooled."

"I fear I am not so sturdy in the wind and cold as your comrades of battle might be," she admitted. Her teeth so chattered it was near hurtful.

"Do not worry over it," he said. "A bit of chafing and a heavy fur about your shoulders and you will rest warm enough."

Monet nodded—watched as he returned to the cart and retrieved another fur.

"Come," he said, taking her hand and pulling

her to sit on the bearskin. He sat down before her, taking her hands in his and blowing warm air on them.

The sense of his heated breath on her hands caused her body to rush with gooseflesh. He rubbed her hands between his own—blew breath on them again. His strong hands next rubbed at her shoulders and upper arms as he endeavored to chafe her to warmth. Yet still she trembled with being chilled.

"Forgive me my weakness, Sir Broderick," she began. "I fear I am not as immune to weather as a knight."

"You would not be a princess if you were," he said. He smiled a slight smile, and she knew he was not vexed with her—in the least, not at that moment. "Here," he said, leaning back against the rocks. "I will warm you a moment."

Drawing his legs up, he drew her between his knees, and Monet was breathless with delight as he pulled her back against his body. He spread the fur around them, his arms encircling her body beneath it. She felt his heated breath on her neck as he endeavored to warm her flesh with it.

"Forgive me, Princess," he said. "I did not think to recognize you might be more vulnerable to the elements than I. And the night is not so warm as I hoped."

"D-do not concern yourself, Sir Broderick,"

she said, teeth still clattering in her head. "I must learn not to be so weak."

Again he blew his warm breath on her neck, chafing her arms with strong hands beneath the fur.

"It is not a weak young woman who finds the courage to leave her kingdom . . . her home . . . and those who know her . . . to dwell in exile with only a rough and disagreeable soldier for company," he said.

"You do not need to endeavor to flatter me, Sir Broderick," she said. "I know I am not so strong as you . . . but how could I be? Further, it takes no courage to leave one's kingdom and home when one has been commanded by the king to do so. Further, you are not always rough and disagreeable. You must not be . . . for women fawn after you for far more reason than just your pretty face."

His chafing of her arms ceased at once, as did his breath upon her neck.

"Pretty?" he near growled.

Monet smiled—as warmth and fatigue began to overtake her. "You do not think you are pretty, Sir Broderick?"

"Pretty is termed when describing women, not men . . . and certainly not knights and soldiers," he mumbled.

Monet giggled. His pride was wounded, though she had meant to compliment him. An unfamiliar sense of liberty began to wander through her bosom. Even for the cold of the night—and the fear of the unknown path down which the Crimson Knight was leading her—Monet found that, in the open solitude of the wilderness, her mind and soul—even her body—felt free, unbound by expectation and propriety.

"I think that I am not so thoroughly terrified of you as I was a day ago, Sir Broderick," she said as his strong hands began to chafe her arms once more.

"First you term me pretty . . . and then dub me terrifying in the next breath," he said. "I do not know what to make of it."

"Make of it that you are . . . pretty terrifying, Sir Broderick Dougray," Monet said, smiling at the warmth of his breath in her hair.

She heard him chuckle. "And you possess a wit I was not so thoroughly aware of before this day," he said. "Do you intend to be ever so forthright in speech during this period of exile?" he asked.

"I am only tired, Sir Broderick," she answered. "Therefore, fear not. I am certain that on the morrow I shall be as frightened and as doubtful as ever."

"And I suppose I shall be as terrifying as ever," he mumbled.

"There is no doubt," she whispered—warm—safe held—in the powerful arms of the Crimson

Knight. "And far as pretty," she mumbled to herself, smiling as her eyes then closed.

Broderick sensed Karvana's princess drifting into heavy slumber. It was certain the Princess Monet was more tired than ever in her life she had been. He felt the gooseflesh leave her arms as she warmed—felt her body relax against his as she surrendered to fatigue. He scolded himself for having let her become so thoroughly chilled. He might have known better, for a princess was not as familiar with bodily hardship as was a soldier. What good would there be in spiriting the Scarlet Princess to exile to save Karvana's hope if the Reaper were to steal her instead?

A breeze lifted a strand of her hair to his cheek—the scent of her skin to his nostrils—and he ground his teeth with resistance of desire. His hands ceased in their smooth chafing of her arms—light gripped them instead as he attempted to contain his thoughts—thoughts of her beauty—of their remote isolation and solitude.

As he bent his head, allowing himself the simple pleasure of the warm flesh of her neck so near to his chin, he frowned, pained by the sudden memory of having raised his voice to the king. In the moments that morning before young Channing had been sent to summon Princess Monet, he had spoken harsh to the king. It was true; he had near shouted, demanding to know why King Dacian had chosen him, Broderick Dougray, to carry the Scarlet Princess into exile. He had demanded to know what purpose the king had in the marriage, one that would cause the princess to loathe the Crimson Knight and one that might well find the Crimson Knight reigning as King of Karvana one day—an honor and burden Broderick did not wish to own. He had demanded of the king as to what foul sin Karvana's first knight had committed to deserve being placed in such a torturous circumstance as that of being wed to a woman he could not wholly have as wife.

King Dacian—ever wise and compassionate—had not rebuked, nor even scolded. "I love you as I would love my own son, Broderick," he had said. "And I ask that you know this. I know you are the only man I may entrust with my daughter's care and safety . . . the only man worthy of protecting the heart of this kingdom . . . the only man who loves this kingdom enough to take up this charge and to honor it."

Broderick had knelt before the king near instantly, his anger reined, his mind and heart humbled by the king's incomparable trust and faith—by owning his favor and love.

"Forgive me, my king," Broderick had said. "I am but a soldier, greatly fatigued and worried for my kingdom . . . and in truth . . . again questioning my own strength and resistance."

"You will not falter, Sir Broderick," the king began, "and, in proving your valiance, shall one day be rewarded with such a measure of prize you cannot fathom at this moment."

"I will bear this charge, my king," Broderick said. "I will keep my oath to protect the Scarlet Princess of Karvana . . . though it cost me my life."

"I know the truth of it, Broderick," King Dacian said. "And know that your anger, fear, doubt, and frustration . . . they are not simply cast off by your king."

Broderick grinned, amused by the memory of King Dacian's own smile—the smile of mischief he had worn upon his face in the next moment when King Dacian had said, "Thus, to you, in all this burden of charge you carry . . . I will allot to you a small margin of pleasure in that you may kiss the Scarlet Princess whenever opportunity is ripe . . . on condition that you kiss her well when you do."

Broderick had been astonished to silence. It was not until the king laughed—bade him rise from his knees—that he found his wits about him once more. He thought certain the king was in jest, and he had thought such until the moment Friar Fleming commanded the marriage between Sir Broderick and Princess Monet be sealed with a kiss. He had glanced up at the king to see him nod with absolute assurance. Thus, he had kissed her—the Scarlet Princess, the heart of Karvana, his wife in task only.

Broderick brushed away the silken ebony tresses the breeze had caused to caress his face. He could linger no more. Thus he was careful and lay the princess down upon the bearskin. She did not stir but a little, and he covered her with the second fur.

He paused in leaving her—studied her for a long moment. Here lay the heart of Karvana— the very hope of the people. The king of the most beloved of kingdoms had trusted her preserving to him. He would not fail his king; he would not fail the Princess Monet; he would not fail and lose the respect of the king and the people he had won—the hard-fought honor he owned.

Broderick Dougray determined then, in that moment, to hold the princess as such of what she was—the kingdom's greatest treasure. Each time he looked at her, he would see not the pretty Princess Monet—not the graceful creature that any and all knights of Karvana delighted in seeing. No. He would see only a treasure—a jewel. He would gaze on her as if she were a gemstone—a diamond worth more gold than even a king possessed. He would not see a soft, tender-fleshed young woman—a young woman with lips sweet as berries and a smile like the sun. No. She was, absolute, a treasure—and he was the knight charged with guarding it.

Exhaling a deep breath of great fatigue, Broderick stood and strode to the cart. Tomorrow they would travel to Ballain. He would set himself up as a horseman, for though the king had given him wealth aplenty to live out his entire life without the need of hard labor, it would draw suspicion from the townspeople if he had no manner of living. Further, idleness would drive him to madness. Therefore, he had determined himself to be a horseman in Ballain. Broderick Dougray knew horses—their breeding, their training, their worth. He hoped the man he had paid to bring six of his horses from his estate at Karvana Far to Ballain would make haste about it.

He gazed up into the black of the midnight sky—to the silver half-moon and the twinkling shimmer of the stars. His mind wandered to Princess Monet, for he did own deep compassion for her. To be stript of all she knew—it was a harsh charge indeed.

Of a sudden, however, he frowned. "The Crimson Knight . . . *pretty?*" he growled, as if the word were bitter meat. "Hmmph."

In Ballain

Monet glanced about. The cottages and other buildings of the village of Ballain were well cared for. Autumn flowers yet bloomed in the meadows beyond, and the reapers reaping in tawny fields did not appear so unlike those in Karvana. A delightful array of happy and laughing children played on the road margin. Several older boys were in practice as archers near a sturdy mill whose wheel traveled round and round, carrying water from a lovely pond.

As Broderick drove the horse and cart through the village, many villagers stopped to stare at the unfamiliar faces only just arrived at Ballain. Still, others smiled and waved welcome. Monet met each smile with one of her own—each wave with a nod in grateful greeting. The day was light and bright, and so seemed the people of Ballain.

"They seem friendly," Monet said.

"Yes. They do," Broderick mumbled.

As they neared the smithy, a large man stepped from the shelter of it. Monet felt her brows arch in astonishment. The man was near the largest she had ever seen! He wore only trousers, his arms and chest caked with dust and perspiration. His skin was baked bronze by the sun—even his head, for it was bald and as smooth as marble. He appeared to be near as old as her father, yet bodily more powerful.

"Good eventide, stranger," the enormous man greeted. His voice was deep and booming, reminding Monet of distant thunder. "Welcome to Ballain."

"Thank you, sir," Broderick said. "I am Broderick, and this is Prissy . . . my wife. We are come to Ballain in search of a new life."

"I am Bronson . . . and welcome again," the man said. "Might I ask what drives you from your old life?"

Broderick had warned Monet that the people of Ballain might be suspect of strangers. Karvana was at war, and though Ballain was a distant township in the kingdom, it was part of Karvana still and would be on guard.

"We are come from Alvar . . . pure vexed and weary of King Rudolph's arrogance and weak rule," Broderick explained. "Karvana knows a good king . . . or so we are told."

"A good king indeed," Bronson said, "yet a king and a kingdom threatened by war."

"Indeed," Broderick said. "Yet Karvana is

known for her strength . . . and I would rather a strong kingdom held threatened than a weak one."

"I am a blacksmith," Bronson said. "And what trade do you offer Ballain?"

Monet endeavored to keep from trembling. The blacksmith was deep wary. What if they were not welcomed at Ballain? Where would Sir Broderick take them to exile then?

"I am a horseman," Broderick answered. "Would Ballain have need of a man of horses? The fair best it has ever seen?"

Bronson laughed. He was full amused and nodded approval.

"Indeed! Indeed we do have need of a horseman," he said. "Welcome to Ballain, Broderick . . . and to your lovely young wife."

"Thank you, sir," Monet said.

Bronson approached the cart and offered a hand of welcome to Broderick. Broderick accepted his hand in a firm grip.

"There is a small inn . . . just around the bend there," Bronson said, pointing to the road ahead. "The Sleepy Fox will put you up fine enough 'til you secure a shelter of your own." He paused a moment, pensive. "I myself own a small dwelling close by. It stands empty and has fences sufficient for two horses. I would sell it to you for a good price."

"Is there room for more fence?" Broderick

asked, "for I will have six more horses to shelter in another day or two."

Bronson nodded. "Indeed! Full enough room for more fence."

"Then I shall consider it if you have the time to take me there on the morrow," Broderick said.

"I have the time," the blacksmith said. "Therefore, take your Prissy to the Sleepy Fox for the night. I am certain she is weary with travel . . . are you not, lass?"

"A bit," Monet said. He was a charming man, this Bronson the blacksmith. Monet had favored him near at once. There was something commendable in the manner in which he rather guarded the village—a protective nature she found comforting.

"And might I sway you to joining us for our evening meal on the morrow . . . as a gesture of welcoming?"

Broderick glanced to Monet. She could see the suspect in his eyes—the wariness. It seemed he was awaiting her response.

"How kind," she said.

"We accept," Broderick told the blacksmith then.

"Good! I will tell Sarah and our young lads that we will sup with Broderick the horseman and his beautiful wife Prissy at sunset on the morrow," he said, a broad smile on his weathered face. "I will meet you in the morning, Broderick . . . that you may see the dwelling I offer."

"Thank you, Bronson," Broderick said. "It was good to be welcomed to Ballain in such a friendly manner as this."

Bronson nodded to Broderick. "Good eventide, Prissy," he said to Monet.

"And to you, sir," Monet said, smiling at him as Broderick slapped the lines at the cart horse's back.

As they rounded the bend to see the Sleepy Fox, Monet said, "You truly expect me to answer to Prissy?" She did not like the name. It was silly, and it was not hers.

Sir Broderick smiled. "It is your penance . . . for terming me pretty the night past."

"I did not mean to give offense, Sir Broderick," she told him.

"Broderick," he said. "I am Broderick to you now. And you are Prissy." His smile of pure mirth was so delightful to gaze upon that she could not bring herself to scold him further. Perhaps he would only name her Prissy when in the presence of others. Further, she mused it was a playful sort of name. Though the great Crimson Knight of Karvana was known for his battle strength and oft severe nature, his naming her Prissy had revealed his softer temperament.

She thought then of the night before—of being

held against his body as he endeavored to warm her. By the first rays of sunlight that morning, she awoke to find him readying the cart for their departure. Yet the sense of being in his arms had lingered in her dreams all through the night. She silently scolded herself for finding pleasure in exile—in thinking on dreams when Karvana's walls were being threatened. Still, what woman could keep from dreaming of the handsome, powerful Crimson Knight?

"I will see the blacksmith's property at first light," Broderick said as he closed and bolted the door. The room was small but warm and welcoming. "I would hope it is sufficient, for we should not linger long at the inn. Dwelling at the inn would draw attention . . . mark us as strangers here."

Monet's eyes widened as Broderick removed his doublet and linen shirt.

"I asked the innkeeper to draw a bath," he said, nodding toward the wooden tub filled with steaming water in one corner of the room near the fire. "You may bathe first."

"Bathe? I-in your company?" Monet gasped.

Sir Broderick sighed. He was weary. Indeed Monet knew great weariness owned him, for he had not slept in two days. "I cannot leave you alone, Princess. Not in this unfamiliar place. I will give you my back as privacy . . . and you may trust it. Still, I am in need of rest, and I would have you bathed so that I may do likewise and find respite in sleep." He turned to her, a frown of inquisition furrowing his brow. "Yet if you do not desire to bathe—"

"Oh, no! I greatly desire it, Sir Broderick," she said. It was true! Never could she remember having felt so soiled and in need of bathing.

"Then make haste . . . if you please, Princess," he said. She watched as he took a chair that sat near the bed and turned its back to her. Seating himself in the chair to gaze out through the open shutters into the black of night, he sighed—poor weary.

Monet did make haste and bathed as quickly as her efforts allowed. Wrapping herself in a bathing robe hanging near the hearth, she hastened to the satchel Sir Broderick had informed her held other garments meant for her. Quickly she dressed in a fresh kirtle, for there was no other more comfortable garment in the satchel.

"Shall I summon the innkeeper to draw a fresh bath for you, Sir Broderick?" she said.

He stood, stretching his arms at his sides. "No. Common folk do not afford such luxury," he said. "And we are now common folk." He paused, his eyebrows arched. "May I have the courtesy of your back, Princess?"

"Oh! Of course," Monet exclaimed. At once she turned from him and took his abandoned seat in the chair facing the shutters. There was no breeze, and thus she was not chilled in gazing through the opening in the wall looking out into the night.

Monet combed her long, wet hair with her fingers. How glad she was to feel clean once again. She had not enjoyed the dust and dirt of traveling in the cart. Further, her body ached from the rough and rutted road they had ridden. Such a weariness in body Monet had never known. She wished only to rest—to find respite in sweet slumber. Still, she must wait—wait until Sir Broderick was finished bathing.

"Sir Broderick?" she began.

"Broderick," he mumbled.

"I have heard you are skilled with horses," she said. "Father says your stables at Karvana Far keep the best stock in the five kingdoms. Will not the people here recognize your horses as the sort only the wealthy may afford?"

"The horses being brought are not the finest in my stables. By far they are not," he answered. Monet could hear the soft sounds of the water lapping in the tub as Sir Broderick bathed. "Yet they are of strong stock. Villagers who labor hard are in need of them. They are animals a man will find pride in owning."

Monet continued to comb her hair with her fingers. She was silent of a moment, thoughtful.

"How long before we left Karvana . . . how

long had it been since Father charged you with taking me into exile?" she asked.

"Two days," he said.

Monet shook her head, astonished. "You had but two days given you to plan? All this you devised in but two days?"

"Yes."

"The morning following the night you brought me back to the castle from the Emerald Crown," she began, "Father charged you that morning. Did he not?"

"He did."

"It was why you were pure vexed with me . . . that morning when I met you just without my father's chamber."

"I was not vexed with you, Princess," he said. "Only I was angry with . . . with . . ."

"With having to play watchman to a princess when your men are battling for their lives to the north," she finished.

"It is not all as you imagine," he mumbled. "There are many . . . intricate pieces . . . parts and consequences to this strategy to protect you that you cannot fully understand. And I will confess . . . a certain amount of frustration overcomes me regarding this charge at times. I fear it will yet prick my temperament on occasion. Perhaps I should offer a sequence of apology to you beforehand."

Monet smiled, amused by his honesty.

"What do you make of this man Bronson?" she asked.

"He is watcher for the village . . . protects it with more loyalty than any lord would," he said. "Since Ballist's battlefield and the end of Lord Morven's stewardship, your father has not chosen a steward to oversee Ballain. Thus, it seems the blacksmith is wary—as he should be . . . as all who dwell here should be."

Of a sudden, he appeared at her side, clothed in naught but trousers. She watched as he closed and latched the shutters.

"I would put you to bed now, Princess," he said. Monet felt her eyes widen for a moment, yet he continued. "You will sleep on the upper and I on the truckle." She watched as he reached beneath the bed and pulled out the truckle bed.

"I do not think it will fit you," she said as she studied the small truckle bed. "Far better I should rest there and you in the upper."

"No," he said. Yet as he strode to the door to ensure the bolt was well laid, Monet quickly lay down upon the small truckle bed. It was large enough for her to sleep whole comfortable—yet she did not doubt Sir Broderick would find little comfort on so small a sleeping place.

When he turned and saw what she had done, he frowned. "This is not acceptable, Princess," he said.

"It is full well acceptable . . . for I fit here and

you there," she said, gesturing he should take the larger bed. "I could not sleep otherwise. For you have been without rest for far too long, and I would see you sleep sound."

"I could remove you," he threatened, although wearily.

"Yes. You could . . . but you will not . . . for we are both weary and in need of rest," she said as she quickly plaited her hair. "This is not a battle to win or lose, pretty Crimson Knight. This is only logic and wisdom." Monet did not know why the night always brought with it her silly nature—a deep desire to tease him. Yet it did.

He heaved a sigh of great fatigue and forfeit. "I am well worn . . . far too worn to argue," he said as he stretched out on the upper bed.

"Good night then, Sir Broderick," she sighed.

"Good night, Prissy," he mumbled.

Monet smiled, delighted with the playful nature that arose in him now and again. In her teasing him *pretty* once more, he had countered with the loathsome *Prissy*. Yet in her own state of worn and weary fatigue, she was not vexed—simply amused.

It was only moments till his breath breathed slow and measured—only moments till he sound slept. Monet lifted her head on one hand and elbow, studying him by the light of the dying embers in the hearth. She was not frightened— not in that moment—and she knew it was for the sake of the Crimson Knight at her side. He was ever as handsome in reposed slumber as he was awake, and she shook her head, full admiring the face and form of Sir Broderick Dougray. She wondered then, had her father charged Sir Broderick with the means of her exile because he was the most capable to bear the charge? Or had he charged the Crimson Knight because the king understood it was he in whom his daughter was most confident? Monet knew well her own thoughts and fears. She knew that were it any other knight in the bed next to her in the small room, she would not have slept—would not have trusted so certain that all would be well—as well as it could be when enduring exile.

A wave of deep loneliness washed over her—a wave of missing her father, of sudden fear for the kingdom, and of dread of the unknown path stretched out before her. Yet she endeavored to calm herself. All would be well—of certain it would. She would not think of the requisites of her marriage to Sir Broderick—tried not to think of the truth of it all, of how bitterly woven the web was. It was often following the moments Friar Fleming had pronounced Monet as wife to Sir Broderick Dougray and as she had traveled with Sir Broderick to Ballain that she had considered her father's terms. She could not endure Karvana's fall or the loss of her father. Further, she knew Sir Broderick did not wish to rule as king. Still, to suffer annulment, followed by marriage to an unnamed man—she could not think on it! Her heart began to beat with worry and fearful anticipation. She felt as a fox, desperately fleeing the hunt, all the while owning knowledge that to endeavor further was futile. She could not see Karvana saved and keep the Crimson Knight for herself: she could not own both.

Closing her eyes, Monet struggled to calm her breathing. *All will be well—all will be well,* she thought. She looked again to Sir Broderick in slumber so deep and so near to her. She would think on the future no more. She would live one day and then the next. Further, she would savor being near him. One day he may not be near her—her beloved Crimson Knight—but this day, this night, he was.

"All will be well. All will be well," she whispered—whispered until the soothing words lulled her to slumber.

Monet wiggled her nose—rubbed at it with one dainty finger. The dust in the cottage was profound, having known years of gathering. Monet paused in her efforts to tidy the small dwelling. Glancing out the window, she smiled as she watched Sir Broderick laboring to extend the fences just beyond the path. It was no wonder the blacksmith boasted strong arms and a pleasant nature. Hard work and good company did nurture such good things. It was often in the past Monet had noted the pleasant faces of the villagers of Karvana, in stark contrast to the often severe or frowning brows of the nobles and royals. It had always seemed to Monet that the common folk knew more laughter and mirth than did those of noble or royal birth. Already her arms ached with the unfamiliar work of readying the cottage for comfortable dwelling. Yet she had never known such a sense of satisfaction in tasks accomplished.

As she watched Sir Broderick, perspiration beading on his brow and chest, she knew he must be glad to have a task to set himself to. Having been at battle for three months previous—having been stripped of his comrades and knightly life—it was no doubt he was glad to be no longer idle.

There came a knock upon the cottage door, and Monet startled.

"Who is there?" she asked. Her heart was pounding mad in her bosom, for fear had washed over her of a sudden. Had someone followed? Had someone discovered the place of their exile?

"It is Sarah. I am wife to the blacksmith, Bronson," came the pleasant voice of a woman.

Monet exhaled the breath she had been holding. She opened the door to see a lovely woman and six strapping boys standing at the threshold.

"Hello," the woman said. She smiled a beautiful

smile and nodded a friendly greeting. Monet returned her smile, delighted by her enchanting countenance. She was near in height to Monet, brown-haired, and brown-eyed. "I am Sarah," she said. "And these are our boys."

"I welcome you," Monet said. "I am . . . um . . . Prissy." Naming herself Prissy was far worse even than hearing Sir Broderick so name her. Yet she continued to smile and stepped aside, that Sarah and her sons might enter.

"We have brought chestnuts . . . from the tree near the wood," Sarah said, offering a basket to Monet.

"Thank you," Monet said. "It is very thoughtful of you."

"We are not so kind as you may think," Sarah said, smiling. "In truth, my boys could not wait till the evening to see you . . . their father having told them of your beauty. They were determined to see you at once."

Monet felt her cheeks pink as a tall, broad-shouldered young man with dark hair nodded to her and said, "I am Stroud . . . eldest son of Bronson Blacksmith and Sarah."

"I am glad to meet you, Stroud," Monet said.

"And I am Wallace," a second young man said. He was similar in appearance to the first, yet owned his own countenance of mischief. "The second son."

Monet nodded, and a third boy approached. "I

am Kenley," he said. His manner and appearance were that of his brothers. Monet deemed him to be perhaps fifteen years, Wallace and Stroud perhaps one and two years his elder.

"I am Birch," the fourth son offered. Birch appeared perhaps twelve years, and he stepped aside to reveal two more brothers, appearing to be one and two years younger than he. "These are the youngest of the Blacksmiths," Birch said, "Carver and Dane."

Monet smiled, pure delighted at the sight of Sarah and her six brawny sons.

"You are very pretty," the youngest said. "Father said that you were."

"Thank you, Dane," Monet said. "And thank you for coming to welcome us."

"May we meet your husband?" the eldest, Stroud, inquired.

"Of course. He is out at the fences just now."

All six boys turned and hurried out of the cottage. Monet giggled as she watched them go.

"They are quite headstrong," Sarah said as she too watched the boys approach Sir Broderick, "like their father."

"I thank you for coming," Monet said, "and for the chestnuts. It is so difficult to be in a new place."

"Indeed," Sarah said. "But you will find Ballain to be a good place to dwell. There are good people here."

"It is good to know," Monet said.

Sarah glanced about the cottage. "It is such a sweet home, is it not? I hold such fond memories of the place. I hope it will one day hold such memories for you and your handsome husband."

"I am certain it will." Monet sighed as she gazed for a moment through the open door to where Sir Broderick stood in conversation with Sarah's sons. She thought for a moment that she would like to have six sons that resembled the Crimson Knight in the manner in which the blacksmith's sons resembled him.

"May I help you with your tidying?" Sarah asked.

"Oh, I could not press upon you in such a manner," Monet said.

"It would be my pleasure," Sarah said, smiling. "We are going to be fast friends, Prissy. This I know already. Thus, why not converse as we work? It will seem less taxing in that . . . do you not think?"

Monet smiled. "I am certain you are right."

"Though I cannot say your husband will accomplish his task more quickly with my sons about him. They would endeavor to tempt him into playing with them," Sarah said.

"Playing?" Monet asked.

Sarah nodded and smiled. "Oh, it is always their way with their father. In one moment, he will be at work, laboring at the smithy as he should . . . and in the next he is gone, out in the woods or by the stream, wrestling about with his sons . . . pretending at swords and daggers instead of shoeing the horses needing to be shod."

Monet giggled. "He is a good father then?"

"The very best of fathers," Sarah said. She smiled, and Monet felt comforted. The bright resplendence of Sarah's countenance was testament of her true happiness. This was a woman true in love with her husband, proud and loving of her sons, content in her village life. Monet envied her happiness—her peace and safety. Sarah's cheeks were pink with her joyful countenance; her smile and offer of friendship were earnest.

"And what of your man?" Sarah asked. "He is heavenly handsome and appears to own no fear of labor. Bronson says he is a horseman."

"He is a fine horseman," Monet said, "and a great man . . . a selfless man."

Sarah smiled. "Then he is the best of men. I am glad you are come to Ballain, Prissy. I feel in my heart that you and I will be glad of knowing one another."

"I am certain of it," Monet said—for she was.

The day had passed quickly. Monet found herself grateful in Sarah's company, as well as her help in tidying the cottage. Sir Broderick had accomplished much as well—though not so much as he had hoped, having spent the better part of

243

the afternoon in sparring at wooden swords with Bronson and Sarah's sons.

At eventide, as they supped with the blacksmith and his family, Monet learned much concerning the village of Ballain as she sat in conversation. It seemed the miller and his wife were friendly of Bronson and Sarah. Young Stroud found the miller's daughter to be the most beautiful in the village—both in face and spirit. The tanner had eight daughters—one of whom Wallace fancied—and was a kind widower. The young thatcher had wed a pretty weaver the year before, and their first child was expected to arrive within a fortnight.

As Monet listened to the descriptions of the people of Ballain, she was further assured of Sir Broderick's wisdom. Ballain was remote, yet its people worked well together—seemed to live well together. Further, there seemed to be a sense of privacy, mingled well with good-fellowship. Still, it had not always been so.

"Lord Morven was a beast," Sarah said. "I am not saddened to know he is gone."

"Lord Morven was lord over Ballain . . . steward of the village before his death," Bronson explained. Certainly it was well Monet knew the story of Lord Morven; better still did Sir Broderick know the tale. Yet she was far curious to hear Bronson and Sarah's telling, for they had lived it all.

"He seemed merely greedy at first," Bronson said. "But then King Seward died. Morven was not fond of King Dacian. Morven thought Dacian too tender in heart . . . too loving of the people."

"Too loving of the people?" Monet exclaimed. "What would Lord Morven have a king be of his people?"

She felt Sir Broderick's hand clasp her own beneath the table around which they sat. She had said too much and determined to remain silent for the rest of the evening. Had she threatened their safety in exile already?

"It is as we all thought," Bronson said. "Seward had been no good king for some years. It was glad we all were of Dacian's taking the throne. Yet Morven was not glad . . . for Dacian would see the people happy and the lord stewards less wealthy. Thus, Morven began to gather men."

"We went into hiding for some time," young Kenley said. "I remember being frightened of Lord Morven's taking Father from us to battle against our own king."

"We began to fear Morven would indeed lay some sort of attack to the castle at Karvana," Bronson said, "that he would endeavor to harm Dacian."

Sir Broderick still held Monet's hand in his own beneath the table. She felt his grasp tighten a moment and looked to him. His expression was stern. No doubt the memories of Ballist's battlefields were raining over him. Yet what path could he take? There would be no good reason to ask Bronson to cease in telling of Ballain's trials.

"Still, our king is wise and not so blind as was his father," Stroud said. "You have heard of Ballist's battlefields, have you not? Even in Alvar you would have heard of it."

"We know the story well, yes," Sir Broderick said.

"Then you know . . . if not for King Dacian and his Crimson Knight, Ballain might well have been lost," Wallace said.

"Ballain did not hold with Morven's dislike of Dacian," Bronson said. "Yet we were all of us at the mercy of a corrupt steward. I do not like to think what may have happened to this village and its good people had the Crimson Knight and his legion not battled triumphant in Ballist."

"It is good the battle did not come to Ballain," Sir Broderick said.

Monet thought him suddenly paler than before. She desired to reach up—to smooth the slight frown from his brow with a kind caress. She had moved before even she had realized it, trailing soft fingers over his handsome brow and over his cheek.

He looked at her, his alluring blue eyes saddened somehow, even for the slight smile he offered her.

"You seem weary, Broderick," Sarah said. "No

doubt you labored longer than you needed today for having taken from your task to play with my boys."

"Yes. Travel and fences are wearing, indeed," Bronson said. "Why not retire early and find respite in the arms of your pretty wife, horseman? Tomorrow you may labor again. It is one certainty in life, is it not?"

"Indeed, it is," Sir Broderick said. "I hope it will not offend if I thank you for such a fine meal, Sarah, and you men for such fine conversation, and take my leave. The horses I await may be here on the morrow, and the fence is not ready. I must rise early in that I may complete it."

"Of course, dear," Sarah said. "And Prissy must be greatly fatigued as well. The cottage was in great need of tidying."

Bronson stood, offering his hand to Sir Broderick as he stood as well.

"I will have the thatcher visit you as soon as possible, for I know the cottage thatch is in need of repair," he said as Sir Broderick took his offered hand of friendship.

"Thank you, Bronson," Sir Broderick said. "And to you, Sarah . . . and to you young lads for your youthful vigor today. It has been far too long since I played at swords."

Monet smiled, thinking no doubt it had been long since Sir Broderick Dougray, the Crimson Knight, had *played* at swords.

"Thank you, Sarah," Monet said as she and Sir Broderick passed the threshold. "You have all shown more kindness to us than I could ever have imagined."

Sarah smiled, her eyes bright with gladness. "You may call on us for any needful thing. And at any moment."

"Thank you," Monet said.

Friendly waves were exchanged, and soon Monet was beside Sir Broderick as they walked toward the cottage Sir Broderick had secured from the blacksmith.

"You do not like to linger on memories of Ballist," she said. "It is understandable."

He said nothing, and Monet shivered for the chill in the air.

"I am sorry for speaking without thought," she said. "Do you think I harmed our charge in any way?"

"No," he flatly answered.

"Do you truly think your horses will arrive tomorrow?" she asked. She would not have his thoughts linger on the pain raised in him for the talk of Ballist—at the memories no doubt torturing his mind. "How many did you say the man was bringing?"

"He will bring six," he answered. "We will keep the cart horse . . . and Tripp, of course. Yet I will endeavor to sell the others to any villagers who may have need of them."

"Tripp? He is the horse that followed us so grave in countenance when tied to the cart . . . yes?"

Sir Broderick looked to her, a slight smile touching his lips.

"Grave in countenance?" he asked. "And how did you come by his countenance being grave?"

Monet shrugged. "He seemed in low spirits . . . as if he would rather be put to pulling the cart than led behind it. As if he would rather keep from being idle." She smiled. "In that he reminds me of you somewhat, for you do not meet well with idleness."

"In that you know me . . . I will not deny it," he said. His mood had lightened, his frown softened. Monet smiled, for she had succeeded in turning his thoughts from Ballist.

Again she shivered as the cool autumn breeze chilled her. "I think it is colder here than in Karvana," she said.

Sir Broderick nodded. "It is. We will heat some stones by the fire to warm your bed."

"Do you think there are many, many spiders in the straw we laid in the beds today?" Monet asked. Sarah had helped her to lay new straw beneath the tick in the bed. It had been three spiders Sarah had counted falling from the straw as they worked—and Monet did not delight in spiders.

Sir Broderick chuckled. "Would you have

me test your bed for spiders before you retire?"

"Do not stand in feigning spiders do not worry you, Sir Broderick," she began, "for every person in all the world full loathes them."

"I will test your bed for spiders, Prissy . . . and I will heat several stones for you as well. Yet I beg you to allow me to find my bear's skin soon . . . for I am well worn this night."

Sir Broderick had previously declared his intention to sleep upon the bearskin laid before the door. The windows of the cottage were small; thus, the door would be an intruder's first choice of entering. Monet had offered argument, reminding Sir Broderick that she was smaller, her body not so heavy—thus the bearskin would serve her well. Yet Sir Broderick had stood firm and commanding. She was a woman, and women should have the advantage of comfort. He had allowed her to take the smaller bed in the inn simply because he had been too worn for argument, but he would not hold with her being in more discomfort than he another night. Further, there was the guarding position at the door, and Sir Broderick meant to guard it well.

He had called her Prissy, and she would not bow to his teasing.

"Very well, pretty knight," Monet said as she crossed the threshold into the cottage. "If you will battle my spiders for me . . . I will heat stones and prepare your bearskin."

Sir Broderick smiled and nodded. The great fatigue in his countenance near caused Monet to reach forth and caress his brow again, but she stayed her hand and simply returned his smile.

As she lay upon her bed, no canopy or curtains to help defend her of the cold, she thought of the blacksmith and his lovely wife—of their six brawny sons. She wondered if all those who dwelt in Ballain were as welcoming. She hoped that they were.

Drawing her legs to her chest in an effort to warm herself, she frowned. She could well hear the Crimson Knight's breath, slow and sound. It seemed he slept warm—in the least warm enough to find sleep. Monet, however, wondered if the heated rocks in her bed had already cooled, for she was chiiled and stiff. She touched one of the rocks Sir Broderick had wrapped in cloth and placed in her bed. It was warm on her fingers, but she thought it did not warm her bed so well.

She glanced to the door. The fire yet burned in the hearth, and she could see Sir Broderick stretched out upon his bearskin. His hands were tucked beneath his head; his arms and chest were not covered by the fur spread over him. Yet he appeared to sleep sound. Monet shivered, so thoroughly chilled she feared she would never be warm again. She thought, were she nearer to him, it would warm her—he would warm her.

She thought Sarah was not so cold in her bed, for Bronson would be with her there.

Monet closed her eyes tight. She would not think on it. The Crimson Knight was her protector—with her simply for her father's charge. Further, if he could find respite in sleep with nothing but a bearskin and fur for comfort, then she would find it in her fresh straw bed and heated stones.

She bade memories of Karvana to linger in her mind. Her father's face was there—and oddly, that of young Channing. Tawny fields and tree branches heavy with fruit lingered in her thoughts—as did the Crimson Knight—and King Ivan's tournament. Of a sudden, Monet felt her mouth warm with the memory of pressing lips with the Crimson Knight. She saw him there in his pavilion, having won his final joust, his arm still bleeding from his wound, the leather strap hanging from his neck, the pouch it held. How his eyes had smoldered when she had entered— how soft his raven hair had appeared.

Monet sighed, her shivering having ceased. Sleep would find her. She was at last warm, and she was safe, for the Crimson Knight of Karvana was there at her door—and in her mind.

The Cottage Kiss

The nights in Ballain continued to grow cooler. As the days passed, Sir Broderick labored hard to prepare for winter's coming, as did Monet. It was often Sarah, and one or two of her sons, would help Monet in gathering nuts and late berries while Sir Broderick and Bronson fortified shelters for Bronson's pigs and sheep. Bronson had agreed to give Sir Broderick a share in the meat of any animals he slaughtered—payment for his help in fortifying their pens and for a fine horse of Sir Broderick's he wished to own.

Monet had never known such hard labor. Each night, as she lay in her bed, endeavoring to warm herself with heated stones from the hearth, she would think on the day—on the profound labor required to survive in the village. Though she knew how to wash and beat clothing, cook, mend, build fires, and reap, she had never before performed such tasks at so constant a pace. Still, she was grateful for the great fatigue that would send her to sleep each night, for her bed grew colder and colder, even for the warming stones.

She wondered how Sir Broderick had not

caught his death of the cold and hard labor. Rising well before the sun, he would tend the horses and labor at splitting wood till light broke the horizon. He would then labor with horses or alongside Bronson through near the entire day, pausing only briefly to take nourishment and drink. Monet marveled at his diligence and unmarked endurance. She knew he labored hard to keep his mind and body at the ready. Certainly he played at wooden swords and wrestling with Bronson's sons, but play did not keep a knight fit for battle, and Monet knew his thoughts were ever of battle. Sir Broderick was ever wary. Rarely did he appear to be off guard—neither in body nor mind. As Monet settled somewhat into village life, Sir Broderick did not. Though he lived the life of a horseman of labor in Ballain, yet Monet knew his mind was that of a knight— ever watchful of the enemy's approach.

It was for this reason—his ever readiness—that Sir Broderick had fashioned a hiding place. In the dark of early morning he had indeed split wood for winter fires. Yet Monet knew something of his work that others did not—the false front of the woodpile. Sir Broderick had dug into the side of a small hill near the cottage, burrowing a hole—a space large enough in which both he and Monet could fit. Using iron nails, he then built a false wall of fire logs—a wall that for all eyes, save Monet's, appeared to be nothing more than a neatly stacked pile of wood. Near the false wooden wall lay several piles of split logs, strewn with intention to look as if they stood ready to be added to the larger, neater pile. In truth, the false woodpile was a master work of deception—further proof of Sir Broderick's wit and knowledge.

For all this—for all his taxing labor and preparation in readiness—Sir Broderick still slept on the cottage floor, against the door with not but a bearskin beneath him and one fur with which to cover his body. Monet wondered at his powerful endurance; yet he had, more than once, assured her of his comfort and health. He had explained the life of a soldier—that to sleep beneath a thatched roof surrounded by walls was far more desirable to sleeping mid-autumn and winter in the open.

Thus, three weeks were passed—three weeks in which Monet endeavored not to worry to near madness over her father and her people—three weeks in which Monet grew to know and love the villagers of Ballain. Yet there was more—more to cause the Scarlet Princess of Karvana to oft feel frightened and hopeless in the secret depths of her heart—the Crimson Knight.

It was true. Never had Monet denied to herself the love she secreted for Sir Broderick Dougray, the Crimson Knight. Ever had she known she loved him. She had known she had loved him when she was only a young girl, when he had first been squire to Sir Alum Willham, as when he was knighted. She had loved him at Ivan's tournament and every moment since. Even standing in her bower—as Friar Fleming performed their marriage ceremony—even then she had not denied to her heart and mind that she loved him. Yet with each passing day spent in Ballain at playing his wife, with each moment in his company within the cottage, with each conversation shared, Monet began to fear she could not endure life without him.

The battle raged in her—her desire to see Karvana triumph and be saved from King James was ever warring with her desperation to remain Sir Broderick's wife—to become his true wife and remain so. Before Ballain—before war with Rothbain and her father's charge that the Crimson Knight spirit the Scarlet Princess to exile—Monet had never known reason for hope. Always it was told her—and always she understood—that her marriage would be arranged. In this she had spent many hours—nay, many years—in persuading herself to the knowledge and acceptance of the fact she could never belong to the man she truly loved. Yet as they lingered—as weeks passed with no word from her father—Monet could sense hope and despair battling in her. She could not lose her pretty Crimson Knight! She could not see Karvana fall to James of Rothbain! Yet only one could be, and it oft sickened her that the path she truly wished for in silence was the path that led her and kept her in Ballain with Sir Broderick.

Thus Monet busied herself all the long day—as Sir Broderick did—and the weeks passed with no word from her father.

"Prissy!" Sarah called as she hurried toward Monet. Monet looked up from her place near the stream. Her hands were sore, chilled from washing in the cold water of the stream. Sarah's cheeks were pinked, as ever they were. The resplendent smile upon her lovely face caused Monet to smile as well, even for having no reason.

"What is it?" Monet asked.

"The baby has come!" Sarah exclaimed. "Grayson and Wilona have had their baby!"

Monet giggled as utter delight washed over her. The young thatcher, Grayson, and his lovely young wife, Wilona, had long been awaiting the arrival of their firstborn child. There was much worry in the village, for Wilona was quite young.

"All is well then?" Monet asked, drying her hands on her apron and hurrying to meet Sarah.

"All is well! Though it is near the largest baby I have ever in my life seen," Sarah giggled. "And you will not guess what they have named him!"

"What?"

"Dacian!" Sarah exclaimed. "For the king . . .

for Grayson says King Dacian will not let Karvana fall, and perhaps a babe named for him will give the angels cause to aid the king further."

"And Wilona is well?" Monet asked, honored by the tribute to her father the king.

"Very well . . . yet strong and pleased in her baby!"

"When may I see him?" Of a sudden, Monet longed to see Wilona's baby—to hold him and feel of his tiny fingers and toes.

"There will be a feast tonight. All the village will be there! And then, on the morrow, Wilona will welcome visitors," Sarah explained. "Stroud and Wallace have already begun to build the fire in the village. We must make haste . . . for Bronson will roast a pig, and I must make bread. You should bring your turnip stew, Prissy! It is far the best I have ever tasted!"

"You are only being kind, Sarah," Monet giggled. "Still, I will bring the stew."

"Oh, Prissy!" Sarah sighed, taking Monet's hands in her own. "There is nothing so wonderful as new baby! You will know this one day. I hope it is soon."

"As do I," Monet said. Her heart felt as if it had been pierced by a dagger of a sudden. Would she ever know the joy of bearing children? If she did know such a joy, would her joy be complete if the babes she bore were not Sir Broderick's? Still, she would be happy for Wilona and her

Grayson. She would not linger in misery and pity for herself and what may or may not be.

"Away now, Prissy," Sarah said. "We must prepare."

"Very well," Monet said. "I shall tell Broderick. Surely he will be glad of respite from his labors that he may help Bronson with the pig."

Sarah smiled, brushing a strand of hair from Monet's cheek.

"You are so sweet, Prissy," Sarah said. "How glad I am that Broderick brought you to Ballain."

"And I," Monet said. She smiled as Sarah turned and hastened toward the village.

At once, Monet was nearly overcome with distress. Always Monet had loved the people of the Kingdom of Karvana. Ever she had felt empathy and cared for them. Yet in living among her father's subjects as she now did—to call them friends, to love them as she had begun to love them—she feared it would only heap more pain upon her somehow.

Shaking her head to dispel the foreboding raining over her, Monet set off in search of Sir Broderick. Sir Broderick would calm her worries—without a knowledge he had done so. Yet he would calm her. In Sir Broderick, Monet would find her strength once more.

Monet clapped her hands, laughing as she watched the miller dancing with his wife. The

Miller Aldrich had purchased three horses from Sir Broderick. Sir Broderick had assured Monet that in horse trade the miller was far more skilled than he had expected. The miller's wife was Claire, and she was as plump as she was jolly. Monet laughed as they danced, near as clever and nimble as jesters! Monet giggled as she looked to Stroud—to the way he fawned over the miller's daughter, Winifred.

"He will wait one year more before asking for her hand," Bronson said, having noticed Monet's attention to his son. "For then he will no longer be my apprentice and may away to build his own forge in another place."

"They complement one another in appearance," Monet said. "And it is clear his feelings for her are far beyond merely her beauty."

Bronson chuckled. "Yes! He has favored her since he was a boy and she just a small little thing." He paused and then asked, "And how long did you favor your Broderick before he took you to wife?"

"Near as long as I can remember," Monet said.

"He is a fine man," Bronson said. "A rare man."

Monet nodded. "He keeps me safe," she said.

"And warm through these cold nights," he said, offering a teasing wink.

"Yes," Monet said—for it was true enough. Did not Broderick place the stones by the fire each morning that they would be well warmed for Monet's bed when darkness fell?

Broderick had been in conversation with Grayson, whose eyes twinkled as the stars in the sky for his joy at his son and well wife. He stepped closer to Monet as he watched the miller and his wife. Monet heard him laugh, and goose-flesh covered her arms at the delightful sound.

"I do like Aldrich," he chuckled. "He is such a merry fellow . . . and his wife is clear as merry."

Monet glanced to Sir Broderick, smiling as the sight of him stole her breath.

"Yes," she said. "They are charming."

"I have sent word for more horses," Broderick whispered, leaning to speak into Monet's ear, "for Tripp is in want of more company."

"I have never known such a spoiled horse," Monet whispered. "Would that I knew your favor so well as Tripp." She smiled at him, and his own smile broadened.

"Do you wish me to feed you oats and curry you at eventide?" Sir Broderick asked.

Monet giggled, delighted by his teasing. She reached up, twisting a lock of his hair around her finger. "It seems you are the one in need of currying. Your hair is quite disheveled tonight . . . and nearly as long as my own."

Sir Broderick arched one dark brow and leaned back to study the length of the dark braid trailing down Monet's back—near to her waist.

He reached back, tugging at her braid. "I think not," he said.

The music ceased, and everyone clapped in delighted approval of Aldrich, the miller, and his wife, Claire.

The Crimson Knight raised a hand to his mouth to hide a great yawn of fatigue. Monet could not keep from placing a palm to his cheek.

"You labor too hard, pretty Broderick," she whispered.

"I labor as I should, pretty Prissy," he said. Yet his eyes were dark beneath, his shoulders held not so broad as they were before the feast.

"Let us go," Monet said, "for I cannot endure to see you so worn."

"The longer I linger in fatigue . . . the deeper sleep will I know," he said.

Of a sudden, Monet gasped as several young girls surrounded them, giggling and wrapping all manner of garlands woven of bitter-sweet, grapevine, and leaves about her and Sir Broderick.

Bronson laughed as all those present clapped and cheered.

"What is the meaning of this?" Sir Broderick asked.

Monet smiled, delighted by the manner in which the garlands bound her to Sir Broderick. She pressed her hands to his chest, gazing up at him as the girls continued to wrap them together.

She cared not why it was happening. She cared only that she was drawn close to him—that the warmth of his body warmed her as no hearth-heated stones ever could.

"When one babe is birthed . . . the children of the village wish for another!" Sarah explained. "They would beg the angels that the next babe be born to you and Prissy!"

Instantly, Monet's delight was vanquished. She felt her eyes well with tears, the deep ache in her heart and body so complete she feared she might cry out for the pain of it. He was not her own! His children would not be hers! Of a sudden, the loathsome truth flooded her being, and she was drowned in deep despairing.

Yet, as ever, Sir Broderick stood stalwart and quick-witted.

He said nothing—simply he smiled at her, took hold her chin in one strong hand, and drew her face to his. Monet did breathe as he kissed her light—did not gasp as he kissed her firm. Visions of Ivan's tournament, of the white pavilion of the Crimson Knight, and of Friar Fleming in her bower burst forth in her mind as the crowd of villagers surrounding them cheered with approval.

Of a sudden, Sir Broderick stretched his arms, snapping the garlands that bound them and lifting Monet to bend over one broad shoulder.

"We bid you good night, friends," Sir Broderick

chuckled as he turned and carried Monet from the celebration of Grayson and Wilona's fresh babe.

Once they were far from the center of the celebration, Monet said, "You may put me down on my own feet, Sir Broderick. I am well able to walk."

"Ahh . . . but they yet watch us," he said. "I will carry you to the cottage . . . and there you may find your feet."

"I do not wish to be carried thus!" she exclaimed.

Monet gasped as Sir Broderick took hold of her legs, pulling her body from his shoulder to rest in the cradle of his arms. She could not stop her own arms from encircling his neck as he strode through the dark of the night toward the cottage they shared.

"I am sorry you were put to such grave humiliation," he mumbled. "But they must believe we are in earnest in being wed."

"What grave humiliation was mine?" she asked. Tears yet brimmed in her eyes, though she strove hard to contain them.

"The implication that you should bear a child of me," he said. "You are a princess . . . and to be so offended as to endure the implication of bearing the child of a mere knight—"

"There would be no humiliation in bearing your child!" Monet interrupted. "Princess or not, I would bear your child willing and proud!

264

I would find no shame in . . ." She ceased in her confession.

"You are the Princess of Karvana," he said, his eyes smoldering with raw emotion as he glared at her. "If Karvana triumphs, one day you will sit on her throne as queen. The children you bear will be heirs to the kingdom."

"And if my father falls . . . you will be Karvana's king," Monet whispered. "You would be father to her heirs."

"Your father will not fall . . . nor will Karvana," he mumbled.

"Then you have nothing to fear, Crimson Knight," she said, struggling in his arms. "Karvana and her king will endure. Thus, soon you will be released from your charge and no longer shackled to me!" He let her feet fall to the ground and released her as she said, "Then you may kiss whomever you choose . . . instead of the silly princess you are ordered to protect."

"But I am fond of kissing you, Prissy," he said.

She looked up to him, astonished into silence.

"Thus we have traded confessions. I confess to being fond of kissing you . . . and you confess to owning no shame in bearing the children of a knight."

He was not vexed with her. There was no anger in the sapphire of his eyes—only great fatigue.

Monet reached up, caressing his strong jaw.

"My father would honor you, Sir Broderick. If

he knew the strength of hard labor and wise wit you employ in keeping me secreted, he would set you above all others in the world. And you are ever kind to me . . . though I know you are sore vexed to be so trapped."

"I am fond of kissing you, Prissy," he said as he opened the cottage door and bid her enter. Monet bit her lip—delighted by his confession—though she did doubt the full truth of it. "And you are not so terrified yourself, are you?"

Monet smiled as he bolted the door and removed his doublet and shirt in readying to retire.

He chuckled. "I shall never forget the look of pure dread on your pretty face at Ivan's tournament . . . the moment before you would kiss me as the champion's prize."

Monet felt her cheeks warm with a blush as she watched Sir Broderick light the logs in the hearth. It was true! She had nearly fainted at the platform of Ivan's tournament.

"The Crimson Knight," she began, "not one to approach unwary."

Broderick sat on the floor before the fire—stretched his long legs out before him, resting on one elbow as he considered her. Monet sat down as well, for the fire was already warming.

"I thought I would surely decease!" she confessed. "Imagine! To kiss the great Crimson Knight? To brave kissing him was frightening enough. Yet to kiss him before such a throng of people . . . terrifying!"

"You were quite pale," Sir Broderick chuckled, unable to stifle a yawn, "as if you thought to kiss Lord Death himself."

Monet giggled, delighted in his careless manner of repose. In truth, the bareness of his upper body was somewhat flustering. She wondered that he was not overly chilled. He was so very admirable to look upon—far more than well formed. His anatomy was profound, to say the very least of it. Still, though the sight of him so exceedingly disrobed was wholly unsettling, it likewise provoked a secret delight in Monet as ever it did.

Her gaze lingered a moment on the small pouch hanging from the leather strap around his neck. She had wondered at it before—wondered what small thing such a man would treasure so thoroughly that he would keep it with him always.

"And consider a moment my own feelings," he said, startling her from her contemplation of his anatomy and leather ornament.

"What do you mean?" she asked.

"To kiss the Princess of Karvana," he answered. "To touch one held so profoundly forbidden to touch. Far greater men than I have been brought to death for less than a kiss forced upon one such as you."

"You did not force a kiss upon me. I gave it," she said, smiling at him.

"I accepted it. Rather, I took it," he countered.

"And I was so relieved that you did," she sighed, her heart fluttering at the memory. "For I thought sure you would refuse me . . . or in the very least think me a feeble fool." She shook her head, " 'Kiss him well,' Father told me," she said, mimicking her father's deep, commanding voice. "Kiss him well?" She laughed. "I asked Father if he thought I were cook's red-haired maid, for I had no experience and . . ." She gasped in realizing she had only just confessed her tender rawness in the art of kissing.

"Cook's red-haired maid," Sir Broderick chuckled, however. "I have heard of this one. In truth, I have seen her."

"Seen her? At the castle?" Monet asked, of a sudden overly curious as to where and why Sir Broderick had seen cook's red-haired maid.

His smile broadened. "At the Emerald Crown. It is often she frequents the inn at late night . . . serving wine and ale."

"She does?"

"She does. And you say she is known for kissing a man well?"

Monet frowned a little, the hot sting of jealousy rising in her bosom. "I have only heard such a thing. I have never witnessed it. H-have you? Have you witnessed her kissing a man? Or have you . . . that is to ask . . . do you know of your own experience that she kisses a man well?"

"Of certain I do not," he said with another low laugh. His eyes narrowed—burned with a sort of devilish mischief as he said, "Though I *can* witness the Scarlet Princess may kiss a man well."

Monet smiled—blushed in spite of her determination not to do so. "You only endeavor to soothe my tender pride."

"Not in the least," he said, "for you did kiss me well . . . though I admit to holding the second kiss you gave me as favored of the two. For you gave it freely . . . not because King Ivan commanded it."

Again Monet blushed, feeling as if a swarm of yellow butterflies had taken flight in her stomach.

"Again you endeavor to soothe my pride," she told him.

"No. It is well you kissed me," he said.

"H-have many others kissed you well?" she asked. In truth, she did not want to hear of other women he had kissed. Yet she was driven to know—by some unseen device of self-torture.

"Not so well as you," he said. The smile on his face was entirely that of allurement—the same some mystical creature of enchantment might employ to lure its prey. Monet was briefly too affected by him to respond. Her heart and body wished to believe him, yet her mind whispered that this was the Crimson Knight—a man known for his magnificent allure.

"Thus, you have only just offered to me proof of your wily ways," she said.

"My wily ways?" he asked.

"It is said the Crimson Knight is able to infuse desire to the hearts of women . . . with merely his gaze," she said. "You, my dear Sir Broderick, are gazing at me in such a manner as to . . ."

"Infuse desire to your heart?" he asked, his voice low—provocative in tone.

Monet blushed and felt breathless of a sudden. Still, she endeavored to appear calm. "You, my pretty Crimson Knight . . . are a knave. A rogue of the worst sort," she teased.

He sighed with feigned and false disappointment. "You have found me out then," he said. "Thus, though I endeavored to lure you into once more kissing me well . . . I am bested by your cleverness."

"Lure me into kissing you well?" Monet laughed. "If you want to be well kissed by me, Sir Crimson Knight . . . you have but to ask it." She giggled, delighted by their friendly jesting. Their jesting had increased in their time spent in Ballain. Monet adored not only their moments of solitude in conversation but also their teasing and jest.

One dark eyebrow arched as Sir Broderick asked, "Do you offer challenge to me, Princess?"

Monet smiled, her soul of a sudden far too playful in nature—her mouth far too moist with wanting to kiss him.

"I offer you the chance to prove you are neither liar nor rogue," she said. "If I truly kissed you well at Ivan's tournament so long ago . . . then you would desire that I should—"

"Kiss me now then," he challenged. "And I will prove I am not a liar . . . though there may linger in me the slight soul of a rogue."

"Do you think I am yet too fearful of the Crimson Knight to kiss you, Sir Broderick?" she asked—though in truth her limbs had begun to tremble.

"But I am only Broderick . . . the humble horseman of Ballain," he said. Again his voice was low—alluring—near bewitching in its intoxicating effect. "Then kiss me . . . for you said I had only to ask."

"Very well," Monet whispered. Her heart pounded with such wild madness she thought sure Sir Broderick's own ears could hear it. Yet so wanton was she of his kiss of a sudden, she cared not for propriety—cared not that she would never truly own his heart. Thus, leaning forward—heart mad-pounding—she kissed his lips ever so lightly. The simple sense of his lips to hers caused such a quiver of delight to rush through her body, she thought she might be rendered to fainting.

"Oh, but kiss me *well,* Princess," he mumbled, his eyes smoldering with mischief and bewitching allurement. "Kiss me well . . . and such a kiss I will mingle with your mouth as to keep you bliss-bound for all the hours of the night."

Monet gasped at the gooseflesh rushing over her limbs at the implications of his speech. It was then she realized—if the Crimson Knight's gaze did not infuse the hearts of women with desire, then the words spoken from his alluring mouth most definite would—for she could raise no resistance to his command and promise!

As moisture flooded her mouth, Monet leaned forward, pressing her lips to Sir Broderick's in another yet tentative kiss. Near at once he firmed the press, one hand sliding to the back of her neck. She trembled as his lips persuaded her own to parting. Dizzied by the wild waves of emotion and desire his touch and kiss were weaving about her, Monet pressed one palm to his stomach to steady herself. His flesh was warm beneath her palm; soft-skinned he was, yet solid as stone. Her touch somehow caused that the nature of his kiss should ripen of a sudden, and he pulled her into his arms—against the bareness of his body—as his mouth then drew hers into such kissing as she had never dreamt. Warm, demanding, and thorough was his kiss, and yet she sensed there was more—something in him held reserved. His mouth left her own, trailing kisses over her cheeks to alight on her neck.

"Broderick! I say, Broderick! Man? Are you there?"

Bronson's deep booming voice and violent pounding on the cottage door so startled Monet as to cause her heart to leap in her bosom. Sir Broderick growled as the seal of their lips was broken by the sudden intrusion. He released Monet and clambered to his feet.

Striding through the room, the Crimson Knight opened the door.

"Wolves have attacked the miller's horses," Bronson said. "It is sure some cannot be saved. Yet will you come . . . try to do what you can?"

"Of course," Broderick said.

"Were only horses attacked?" Monet asked as Sir Broderick snatched up the linen shirt he had cast aside a short time before.

"Only horses," Bronson said. "It seems we did not hear them for the merriment of the celebration."

"Draw the bolt until my return," Sir Broderick said. Monet nodded, watching him disappear into the darkness without the cottage.

Drawing the bolt, she sighed. "Wolves," she grumbled. She felt compassion for the Miller Aldrich, for she knew the loss of horses could be to his great detriment. Still, the moments before Bronson had pounded upon the door had been the most blissful of her life!

Monet sat before the fire. The sense of his strong arms about her still warmed her—as did the sense and taste of his kiss. She closed her eyes, remembering the champion's prize at Ivan's tournament—the kiss she offered the Crimson Knight in his pavilion—the furious sealing kiss forced in her bower—the lighthearted kiss in the village a short time before. Yet the cottage kiss—the kiss Sir Broderick had asked of her there before the fire—the kiss he had given and taken—surely nothing could meet the resplendent pleasure the cottage kiss had begat. Nothing!

The Knights Exemplar

It had been far late into the night before Sir Broderick returned. The wolves had killed one of the miller's horses, lamed another, and injured a third. Sir Broderick himself had put down the lame horse, though he was encouraged of the third horse's ability to full heal. Still, it was a great loss—both to the miller, who needed his horses for his trade, and for Sir Broderick, who had seen both horses nurtured at his stables at Karvana Far from foals. Sir Broderick had returned to the cottage sore weary and greatly discomfited. He had said little to Monet upon his return. Simply, he had bolted the door and taken up his place on the bearskin before it.

Monet knew him to be wholly fatigued. Yet as he slept through the sun's rise, she began to worry over him. Ever he had risen before the sun. Even when he had passed days without sleep—as he had as they traveled from Karvana to Ballain—even then he had raced the sun to rising.

Monet's tender brow frowned with deep concern as she stood studying him a moment. He slept sound—more sound than she had ever known him to sleep.

Kneeling beside him, she pressed one palm to his cheek. He startled, his eyes opening at once.

Monet exhaled the breath she had been holding, relieved to see he yet breathed. Somehow she had feared he would not.

"Princess?" he mumbled. He seemed near confused for a moment, as if his mind were not at once certain as to where he was.

"Sir Broderick?" Monet asked. "Are you well?"

He frowned, closing his eyes for a moment. "I am," he said.

He sat up from his bearskin bed, clasped his hands at the back of his head, and stretched away the lingering tethers of sleep. He rubbed his eyes with one strong hand. Monet could not help but to smile at his tousled hair and rather boyish appearance. Without conscious thought, she reached out, combing her fingers through his soft raven hair several times. She thought she could be lost in bathing in such soft raven locks, for his hair was as the silk of heaven between her fingers.

"I have never known you to let Sir Sun defeat you in the race for morning," she said, smiling at him as she brushed a strand of hair from his forehead.

He did not respond—only sat staring at her as if astonished somehow.

"Are you hungry?" she asked. "I have prepared your breakfast. Even some of the ham Bronson brought yesterday." Still he did not make conversation. Still he continued to stare at her—nearly as if he did not know her.

"Sir Broderick?" she asked. "Broderick . . . are you well? Do you hear me?" Panic began to rise in her, for he was never so slow to converse.

He could yet feel the blissful sense of her fingers in his hair. Her touch had quite con-founded him. He hoped she would not notice the gooseflesh her touch had provoked over his arms and chest—hoped that if she had noticed it, she would think he was merely chilled by the morning air.

In those moments the great Crimson Knight of Karvana doubted his own strength of resistance. The kiss he had shared with the Scarlet Princess the night before had near been his undoing. Weary and worn from hard labor and pleased by her teasing, he had not been able to deny himself in partaking of her lips. Had Bronson not summoned him with mad pounding upon the cottage door, Broderick Dougray knew he would well have kept his promise to the Princess Monet—his promise to have kept her bliss-bound for all the hours of the night in kissing her. Yet now, her touch—her sweet fingers combed through his hair—it was near as threatening to his resolve to keep from her as their shared kiss in the night had been.

Further, she had named him Broderick. At long last—after weeks of his assurance she should do so—at long last she had called him Broderick, not Sir Broderick. Though he had come to accept— nay, to find joy in—her terming him her pretty Crimson Knight, it was yet more formal than his given name. He wondered, had she even been aware she had named him Broderick?

"Truly, Broderick," she asked, a frown at her pretty brow, "are you ill in some way?"

"I am well," he said and saw the expression of worry soften upon her lovely face.

He would have her! He would! He would gather her into his arms—there, on the bearskin before the door. He would kiss her—hold her— and beyond!

Yet a vision of King Dacian intruded in his mind—a gathering of sealed parchments, a charge to protect the heart of Karvana from any and all who would dare to harm her. If he knew nothing else of the Princess Monet, it was that she honored her father—would be obedient to his commands above all else. Further, what if she did not truly want the Crimson Knight as husband? Certainly she had spoken the night before— assured Broderick that were Karvana to fall she would find no shame in bearing his children. Still, this was no more than obedience to her father's instructions. It did not mean she would want him as husband, only that she would endure—for she was royal, and royalty did nothing if not endure arranged marriages. He would nest on such thoughts of her no longer.

"I was merely considering on the loss of the miller's horses," he said. "And I am hungry." He forced a smile, and she seemed relieved—if only a little. "Pray allow me to press water to my face, and I will join you for breakfast. Unless you have already had yours."

She smiled, and he thought the sun was not brighter than the smile of the Scarlet Princess. "No," she said. "I waited for you."

He smiled, and Monet thought there was no more delightful thing to see than the handsome smile of Broderick Dougray. Even yet the memory of his kiss was fresh in her mind—the sense of it warm on her lips. He was merely worn. That was the reason for his late rising.

As Broderick—and he was Broderick, for Sir Broderick might never have kissed her in like manner Broderick the horseman of Ballain had before the fire the night before—as Broderick left the cottage to refresh himself, Monet set about placing ham and cooked eggs on a plate for him.

He returned with haste and sat at the small table, across from her.

"Did you sleep well?" he asked. Monet smiled as he began to eat.

"Far better than you, I am sure," she said. "What will the miller do without his horses?"

Broderick sipped from the cup she had placed before him. "I will give him two horses more. When the others I sent for arrive . . . he shall have two."

"But can he pay for them? For if you simply gift them to him . . ."

"He can pay . . . for one now. And he will trade us grains for the other," he said. "It well is a good trade for both our sakes."

"Why did the wolves attack them?" Monet asked. "I did not think they would endeavor to attack stabled animals."

"One of the horses had been injured . . . bore a small cut on its hindquarters. I suspect the wolves sensed the blood," he explained. "Game is also in short supply. Bronson has told me that Lord Morven near hunted the game to gone here before Ballist . . . and not for need of it."

Monet nodded. "Lord Morven was corrupt in every way . . . was he not?"

"He was," Broderick answered. "He was responsible for the cause of much misery and the deaths of many good men . . . many of *my* good men."

"Was there truly a crimson frost, Broderick?" she asked of a sudden.

"There was," Broderick said. "It covered the dead . . . and me for a time. Winter descended upon Ballist as if summoned by the Reaper." He paused to eat for a moment before continuing. "The dew was rare heavy one morning particular. And though it was dew at sunrise, it was frost by eventide . . . frost frozen over blood . . . and thus appeared to be crimson."

"But you vanquished . . . rather your will and strength did," Monet said.

He looked at her, his eyes filled with sad remembrance. He pressed one hand to the pouch hanging from the thin length of leather around his neck. "The Reaper did not take me that day in Ballist . . . for I did not let him. And as my body warmed . . . so the crimson frost about my armor was banished."

Monet smiled. "I know it is a painful memory for you," she said. "Yet you can see why the people love the tale so. It is a tale of strength, of honor . . . of a great knight battling for his kingdom."

"And it is a tale of triumph over threatened death," he said. "Thus, I know why the people talk of it still . . . why Marius and other minstrels sing of it. In truth, it has given even me strength, for I am in constant reminding myself . . . that if I found purpose and strength enough to be victor over Lord Death at Ballist . . . then there is much else of which I am full able."

"You are the greatest knight Karvana has ever

known," Monet said, "perhaps even the world has ever known."

Broderick chuckled and shook his head. "I am glad for your confidence," he said, "or your flattery . . . whichever it is you offer."

Broderick studied Monet for a moment. Should he share his suspicions with her? Her owning him as the greatest knight in Karvana had caused him to wonder if perhaps the time had come. King Dacian had charged him with the princess's protection and preservation. He knew the ways and means of doing so were his choice. Still, they were in exile together—and in marriage together—whether or not either would remain as such. Thus, he felt inspired to tell her—to know her thoughts.

"What do you know of Exemplar Knights?" Broderick asked.

Monet felt her brow furrow with curiosity. "The Knights Exemplar? My grandfather's elite table of knights?" she asked.

"Yes," Sir Broderick mumbled. "What knowledge do you own with concern to them?"

Monet smiled. How curious. What reason could Broderick own for such seeming lighthearted conversation—even at breakfast? Still, she would humor him, for she yet sensed a great unrest about his countenance.

With a careless shrug, she began, "I am certain you know far more than I . . . for though you were not born in Karvana, you were Sir Alum's squire."

"I do know something of them . . . yet Sir Alum was not as forthcoming as you might think. You may own a knowledge that I may not. Thus, tell me what you know of the Knights Exemplar."

"They were . . . exemplary!" Monet smiled and breathed a little giggle. He smiled, amused with her wit. She continued, "I remember them—that is, I have a vague reminiscence of a few of them. I was very small when they were dispersed." She sighed, remembering the green tunics and gleaming blades of the Knights Exemplar of King Seward's reign of Karvana. "They were such knights as were never before seen! Skilled with weapons far beyond any knights in the five kingdoms, and their bravery knew no bounds . . . nor did their loyalty to one another."

When she paused, he encouraged, "And?"

Monet sighed. "And their code of chivalry was extraordinary . . . unparalleled. That is, until . . ."

"Until?" Broderick prodded.

"Until . . . until my grandfather's first knight . . . until he . . . he . . ."

"Until Sir Ackley Carrington seduced the king's daughter," he finished for her.

Monet nodded. "Yes. My aunt . . . the Princess Eden, my father's favorite sister . . . they say she was beguiled by Sir Ackley's charm and . . . and banished."

"They say?"

Again Monet offered a slight shrug. "I do not remember well my Aunt Eden," she said. "For Father, Mother, and I were often at Karvana Far then . . . and I was so young. Still, I have heard the stories my father tells of her . . . and of Sir Ackley . . . and of their being spirited away. And I do not think he seduced her. In the least I do not think it was in the manner my grandfather declared it."

"Why?"

Monet bit her lip—felt a warm blush rise to her cheeks.

"I think they loved one another and that my grandfather, King Seward, did not approve. I think they fled . . . ran away together. My father thinks as I do." She ventured a glance at Sir Broderick—quivered with delight when she saw the pleased grin on his handsome face, his eyes narrow with approval.

"And?" he prodded once more.

"And thus my grandfather, King Seward, had the Knights Exemplar cast out . . . broken apart for Sir Ackley's disloyalty. For the passionate actions of one, the Knights Exemplar were banished. My father has ever carried a great weight of guilt for it. When my grandfather died and my father took the throne, he sent word to the farthest corners of the kingdom . . . word that any Exemplar who would return to Karvana would have his place, prosperities, and wealth restored. Only one Exemplar returned."

"Sir Alum," Broderick said, smiling.

"Yes," Monet sighed. "Sir Alum Willham. He had been my grandfather's youngest knight of the round table of conferring. He was brave in his return . . . did not hold my father responsible for the mistakes of the previous king. Father granted him property and wealth and a seat at his table. He was first knight for many years . . . until . . ."

"Until I was named first knight," he mumbled, an expression of regret and guilt owning his handsome face.

"Yes," she whispered.

"You know the story well," he said. She watched as he leaned back in his chair, studying her with approval. "And what is your opinion of the Knights Exemplar? Would they defend Karvana once more? Would they be counted ally or enemy?"

Monet giggled. "Sir Alum was the youngest, pretty knight . . . and even he now boasts snow-white temples. Yet . . . it is said among the people that the Exemplars were so beloved of Karvana— so loving of Karvana in return—that they would never raise a blade against her. Still, to wage war in defense of her? What loyalty would they own to a kingdom whose king so mistreated them?"

"Yet that king is dead, and another now sits on Karvana's throne . . . one who would vindicate the great Exemplar Knights . . . one who would gladly right the wrong done them. Do not you think then . . . could not one of these lost Knights Exemplar . . . could not he be counted an ally?"

Monet felt an odd quiver travel through her body. As was often the truth, the Crimson Knight owned a knowledge she did not. Of this she was certain.

"You are feeding me fodder of preparation for something else, Broderick. Are you not?" she asked. "Pray tell me what you are thinking."

Broderick paused, inhaling deeply as if in coarse contemplation. "The blacksmith," he began.

"Bronson?" she asked. "What of him?"

"He bears two marks—one beneath each arm . . . just here," he said, motioning to the place under his strong arm—a hand's width above the bend in it. "A circled brand. Do you know this mark?"

Monet felt her own eyes widen. "You have seen this? He bears the mark on each arm . . . on both? Are you certain?"

"I am."

"The mark of the Knights Exemplar! The symbol of their eternal brotherhood!"

"Hush!" Broderick scolded, reaching out and placing a hand over Monet's mouth a moment to quiet her excitement. She wondered if he were in suspect they were not alone in the cottage—though she knew well they were.

Tugging his hand from her lips, she whispered, "An Exemplar Knight! Here in our village? Bronson?"

"I am not sure certain," Broderick said, lowering his voice. "But there is much about him that gives me cause to believe that he is one of them. What man would endure the pain of branding if it were not so? What reason would a man own for playing at being an Exemplar when they are no longer banded?"

"He appears in age to be one who could have been an Exemplar," Monet offered.

"And he is yet strong . . . keeps himself fit for hard work . . . and perhaps battle."

"And you are thinking his sons are far too skilled with a blade," Monet whispered. Broderick frowned with inquisition, and she blushed. "I have watched you play at battle with them on occasion. Stroud and Wallace . . . even Kenley and Birch are wielders well of wooden sparring swords."

"And do you remember, the first night we supped with them . . . young Kenley, when we were speaking of Ballist, he said the family hid . . . for they feared their father being taken by Morven to battle against the king."

Monet nodded; she did remember it.

"Further . . . what need has a blacksmith of so many horses?" he said. "He owns four . . . asks me to sell him two more . . . near one for each son. This is a knight's method, not a blacksmith's."

"You tell me you are not certain . . . yet I can see that you are," Monet said. "Is it only to share curiosity that you tell me this now?"

Broderick paused—seemed to consider. "It would be good to know . . . if a fight came to us here . . . it would be good to know there was one we could trust," Broderick mumbled.

"And we well could trust a true Exemplar Knight!"

"I believe we could," he said.

Monet could feel her own eyes bright with excitement. An ally! One living in exile as she and Broderick lived. Surely he could be trusted. Surely he was still loyal to Karvana and her king.

"Yet which one could he be? His name, I mean?" Monet asked, of a sudden overcome with curiosity of her own.

Broderick shook his head. "How could we know? And what would the need be of knowing which he is?"

Monet smiled. "Among other reasons . . . to satisfy my own curiosity."

Broderick chuckled. "Well, as much as I wish to settle your fevered mind, there is no way of knowing . . . other than his choosing to reveal to us."

She giggled. "I learned a song once, as a child. My grandmother taught it to me before her death. I remember hearing Marius sing it as well—the names of the Knights Exemplar, put to melody."

Broderick smiled. "Then sing it to me, Prissy . . . that we may endeavor to discern the Exemplar here."

"Very well," she said. "Only remember . . . it is a song meant for children. It is very simple."

"As it should be," he said.

Monet patted her cheeks, silently pleading that their blush would fade. Inhaling a breath of courage, she then sang the song of the Knights Exemplar.

> Twelve knights to marvel . . . twelve
>   knights of fame,
> Twelve Knights Exemplar . . . twelve
>   knights of name.
> Thus name them now, each Exemplar
>   bold,
> The Knights Exemplar . . . their legend
>   told!

> Sir Ogden Mather sits at the round,
> With a wild steed and a milk-white hound.

> Sir Hunter Kenley born of Devon,
> With brothers five and sisters seven.

Sir Alum Willham, knight young and
  brave,
Fair of hair and a handsome knave.

The wisest of all Sir Leland Knox,
Strength of a wolf and wit of a fox.

Sir Ackley Carrington, strong and tall,
Will crush the enemy—bones and all.

Sir Garrick Jarvis, with gauntlet strong
And a jeweled blade, saves right from
  wrong.

Sir Stanley Sheppard guards the flock,
With force of iron and might of rock.

Sir Fairfax Ewing, first son of Roan,
Cousin to King of Karvana's throne.

Sir Richard Hamilton, Exemplar nine,
Is partial to game and wench's wine.

Sir Payton Ransley bears one green eye.
Blue is the other—as blue as sky.

Sir Wakefield Denton, with fingers eight,
Lost one in battle and one to fate.

Last, brave First Knight is Sir Elton Kent.
He serves the kingdom—wherever sent.

Twelve are these at King Seward's table,
Twelve with horses in Seward's stable,
Twelve who fight for Karvana's sake,
Twelve knights with trembling in their
    wake.

Monet finished her song and said, "And that, my pretty Crimson Knight . . . is the song of the Knights Exemplar."

Broderick smiled, drawing his hands together in pleased applause. "Well done!" he said, chuckling. "Well done!"

Monet nodded and said, "I thank you for your approval, good sir. And I bid you use it to your aid in our quest to determine which Exemplar our Bronson may once have been."

"Very well," Broderick said, lowering his voice once more. "There *are* pieces of description in it."

Monet smiled. "Pieces I never fathomed as owning consequence before. As a child, it was merely a song to sing in passing the time. Yet in this moment . . . I do see!"

"Thus, we can reason . . . Sir Alum Willham is in your father's service at this moment. In service . . . or dead of battle in the north. Therefore, the blacksmith is not Sir Alum."

"Dead?" Monet breathed. A vision of Sir Alum, kneeling before her as she wished him well in riding to battle, lingered in her mind.

Broderick shook his head, placing one strong hand of comfort over hers where it lay on the table. "No . . . not our Sir Alum. He battles still . . . I am sure of it. Remember . . . I squired . . . he taught me. " He meant to comfort her a little, and he did.

He smiled and asked, "Which Exemplar owned but eight fingers?"

Leaning forward, Monet smiled and whispered, "Sir Wakefield Denton . . . and Bronson owns all ten fingers. Therefore he cannot be Sir Wakefield Denton."

"Precisely." Broderick exclaimed. He reached out and brushed a strand of hair from Monet's cheek. The gesture caused the delicious delight of gooseflesh to swathe her arms.

"And you—you, a woman who regards such things—what color are our blacksmith's eyes?" he asked.

"Brown," Monet breathed. "Then he cannot be Sir Payton Ransley . . . for he had one green eye and one blue."

"Thus we have cast off three of the twelve as possibilities."

Monet felt her own eyes narrow as she studied him. "You have determined, without doubt, that it is so?" She said. "You have determined Bronson the blacksmith is indeed one of the banished and lost Knights Exemplar?"

"There is more than the brands on the under-flesh of his arms that whispers to me," he said. "The swords he fashions with his bellows and hammer—swords of such perfection, with such the detail of a true craftsman—no ordinary black-smith expends his strength forging weapons afforded only by knights and kings."

Monet nodded in agreement.

"And it is true what you say," Broderick continued. "Always I have wondered over Bronson's sons. They are far too skilled in brandishing blades . . . both swords and daggers. It is in my mind they are accomplished with maces and bows as well. These are not mere peasant boys gifted of God with the apt wielding of weapons. These are young men who have been trained to battle. Their skill, their form . . . it is distinct. Sir Alum taught me in like manner. For one who knows the ways of the great Exemplar Knights, it is easy to discern that Bronson's sons have been knightly trained."

"How long have you been suspect of this, Broderick?" Monet asked.

He paused. "You will not be angry with me?"

Monet smiled. "Of course not. Why ever would I be angry with you for being so foxish in your wit and wisdom . . . in your skill of discernment?"

He nodded. "Then I confess to knowing some-thing surrounding him the moment we arrived in Ballain. He is a profound leader. It is pure obvious he has experience in leading men . . . for he leads the village with the wisdom and manner a knight might lead his men. Further, he watched over each person and family . . . as if they were his own kin."

"Perhaps he is then Sir Stanley Sheppard," Monet offered.

"Why say you he is Sir Stanley?"

"For the reason I know the song far better than you," she giggled. "Sir Stanley Sheppard . . . who guards the flock?"

Broderick nodded. "I see the wisdom in that."

"And in the rest of Sir Stanley's verse . . . with the force of iron and might of rock," she said.

"Hmm. It does indeed put one in mind of a blacksmith," he mumbled.

"Yet there is Kenley to consider," Monet said.

"His son?"

Monet nodded. "Is young Kenley so named for his father's true name . . . the Exemplar Sir Hunter Kenley? Or is he named for his father's friend?"

Broderick laughed. The Scarlet Princess was full possessed by curiosity! Her eyes were bright with wonder. She was beautiful!

"Or perhaps," Monet began, "perhaps he is Sir Richard Hamilton . . . the gambling wencher!" Her mouth dropped in wonder as her mind continued to conjure. "Perhaps then Sarah was once a wine wench at the Emerald Crown . . . and Sir

Richard spirited her away into banishment with him!"

Again he laughed, wholly amused by her speculative chatter—wholly delighted by her company.

"Sarah does not seem the wenching sort," Broderick offered.

Monet arched one brow. "Are you so familiar with the wenching sort as to recognize them at first sight?"

"No," he said, smiling. She knew he was amused by her, though she knew not whether it was her appearance, her words, or her ways that amused him. "And though you know even less about the wenching sort . . . you do not truly think Sarah was once a wine wench . . . do you?"

Monet shook her head. "No. She does not seem anything akin to cook's red-haired maid."

Broderick chuckled.

"Oh, you must discover it, Broderick!" she exclaimed. "Else I am gnawed to death with curiosity!"

"I will endeavor to discover if he would, in truth, be counted our ally. Beyond that I cannot promise you, Princess . . . for there is a reason he is named Bronson Blacksmith here. I would not risk revealing his secrets, for they are his for his reason . . . and for the protection of his family, no doubt." He smiled at her, and she nodded.

"You are right . . . as always it seems you

are," Monet said. She leaned forward. "Yet you must promise to share any knowledge you may gain as to which Exemplar Bronson is. Do you promise?"

He smiled and nodded. "I will tell you what I discover." His eyes narrowed, and he leveled a forefinger at her. "But you must not press Sarah. We must remain in secret here, Monet. If she is the wife of one of Karvana's banished Exemplar Knights, she will be wary of too many questions asked . . . as would we."

"I will not press her," Monet said. She leaned forward, till her face was only a breath from his. "But I will press you." Quickly she kissed him on one unshaven cheek. Pushing her chair from the table, she near leapt to her feet. She could not linger so close to him, for his nearness was causing such a flutter in her bosom as she could not breathe calm.

"Tripp is at the fence," she said, opening the shutters to gaze out the cottage window. "You are tardy with feeding him, and he is sore vexed with you."

"Then I best tend him," Broderick said, studying her as she looked through the window at his impatient horse.

He rose from his seat at the table, retrieving his shirt and doublet. She had kissed him sweet upon one cheek—as a wife would kiss her true husband. Of a sudden, Broderick wished he owned more secrets to be shared with her, for the Scarlet Princess was delighted by mystery—and he enjoyed delighting her.

"I will return at midday," Broderick said.

"I will be here," Monet said, smiling at him. How handsome he was! How delicious to look upon, dressed in his brown doublet and peasant's trousers. Further, how wise was he! To have discerned the presence of an Exemplar—the Crimson Knight was as wily as he was handsome!

She watched him leave the cottage—watched him through the window as he tended Tripp and the other horses. It was full sure Broderick favored Tripp, as it was full certain Tripp loved his master. Monet frowned, curious as she watched Broderick stroke Tripp's rather disheveled mane. She could hear the Crimson Knight speaking to the animal in a low, soothing voice, and she wondered why they favored each other so.

At length, Monet busied herself in the cottage. She could not stand at the window and gaze out at Broderick all the day long—though she would savor doing so.

As she tidied, placing the now cold stones from her bed near the hearth to begin warming for the night to come, she first hummed the melody. Yet soon she whispered the song as she labored, singing, "Twelve knights to marvel . . . twelve knights of fame . . . twelve Knights Exemplar . . . twelve knights of name. Thus name them now, each Exemplar bold. The Knights Exemplar . . . their legend told."

Sir Broderick Dougray tied the horse to the post without the smithy. He could feel the heat of the forge—hear the breath of the bellows as Bronson labored within.

Stepping into the darkness, he called, "Bronson." The clatter of the hammer against iron and anvil echoed a moment longer. Bronson turned and nodded to Broderick and gestured his attention would be free soon.

Broderick smiled and nodded. He watched Bronson labor for a moment more. Then he turned to the wall at the back of the smithy. There were the swords of which he had told Monet. He had seen them—discerned their worth and pure master-made quality when first he had entered the smithy when the first six horses had arrived near three weeks past. Hidden in shadow, some sheathed and others not, the swords in Bronson's smithy beckoned to Broderick as a fairy whisper. Row upon row of swords there were—ornate hilts of some, simple hilts of others. Yet to one who knew weapons, these were crafted of a man who not only knew swords but used them well.

"Have you come for trifling or service, Broderick my friend?"

Broderick turned to face the blacksmith—a once-great and respected Knight Exemplar of Karvana.

"Perhaps both," he said, "for Tripp must be shod anew . . . and I am weary of work today."

Bronson's smile broadened. He chuckled. "Weary? You? Yet we were both of us at the Miller Aldrich's till near sunrise . . . were we not?' "

"Indeed," Broderick said. He looked to the swords once more. "You are craftsman as well as blacksmith, it would seem."

"I am," Bronson said, "for iron work is necessary . . . but laborious and dull." His eyes narrowed as he seemed to study Broderick. "Would you like to better know my work?"

"If you can spare the time, yes."

Bronson's smile broadened. "Very well, Broderick. Approach." The blacksmith held out a hand to the wall of swords—a gesture to Broderick that he may look upon the swords more closely. Yet his command of approach stirred Broderick's mind and senses, for it was the same command Sir Alum had used in sparring with Broderick Dougray, his squire—the same Sir Broderick Dougray had used in sparring with his squire, Eann.

"These are fine swords," Broderick said. "At

least . . . they are fine to my horseman's eye."

Bronson chuckled. "Indeed . . . I am a fine crafter of swords. Here is one you will like." Broderick watched as Bronson reached forth, lifting a sword from the wall and handing it to him. As Broderick gripped the hilt, he inhaled deep. The feel of the hilt in his hand stirred him. The weight and balance of the weapon was perfect. Of a sudden, he wished he could spar with the sword he now held instead of with the wooden ones Bronson's sons provided.

"It is called Gauntlet," Bronson said. "I crafted it as tribute to a fallen knight of Karvana . . . one who fell long ago."

Broderick studied the sword—the gleaming blade and ornate hilt. "A fine weapon is this, Bronson . . . and a fine tribute."

Bronson held a hand toward Broderick, and Broderick surrendered the sword to Bronson's hold.

"Here is one of interest," Bronson said. Reaching up to the wall, he pulled a longsword from its sheath. Broderick gripped the hilt of the long, double-edged slashing sword Bronson offered. He smiled, both for the beauty of the weapon and the knowledge it affirmed of Bronson's identity. This was a weapon most difficult to forge—and forged at great expense. No mere blacksmith could afford the forging of such a magnificent weapon—not without commission.

Broderick marveled the pommel's perfect fit to his hand. He nodded approval.

"Magnificent!" he mumbled.

"I am glad you are pleased, Broderick," Bronson said.

Broderick was startled, yet quick in his defense, as the blade Bronson wielded cut the air—met with his own blade wielded.

"My sons say you wield a blade well," Bronson said. "Are you fearful of sparring with steel?"

"What do you think?" Broderick chuckled.

Broderick's heart hammered with the thrill of the sound of the blades crashing—the strength his body so long had held hidden. As Bronson cut and thrust, Broderick countered—knowing he was at spar with one of the great Knights Exemplar.

"You are well trained—exquisitely skilled with a sword—for a horseman," Bronson laughed, strengthening his stance.

Broderick smiled. "And you . . . you are strong and skilled . . . well trained . . . for a blacksmith."

With a roar of laughter, the blacksmith attacked, yet Broderick met his attack with the dexterity and strength of Karvana's great Crimson Knight.

The blacksmith was masterful in his wielding of the blade! Broderick thought even Sir Alum was not so skilled and strong. Blow for blow they sparred—Bronson chuckling, Broderick enthralled and proud of knowing such a worthy challenge.

With one final thrust ably defended, Bronson laughed, his breath rising and falling with the labor of mock battle.

"You would fell me hard and easy, Broderick," Bronson said.

"Nay . . . neither hard nor easy would you be felled, blacksmith," Broderick said. He owned only infinite respect and admiration of the great and nameless knight before him.

"And do you like the blade?" Bronson asked. "Does it meet with your approbation?"

"I am none worthy to approve or otherwise, friend," Broderick said. "But it is a fine weapon . . . a very fine weapon.

Bronson chuckled. "Then read its name, Broderick . . . and know it."

Broderick's brow furrowed with inquisition. Still, he held the sword straight, that the sun may glint on the blade.

Sir Broderick Dougray smiled—chuckled. There, eloquently engravened on the burnished steel, were the words.

"The Crimson Frost," he read aloud.

"This blade I forged in your honor, Sir Broderick Dougray," Bronson said, "when the Crimson Knight confounded both the Reaper and Lord Morven at Ballist." Broderick nodded, and Bronson said, "This . . . swords are my manner of offering tribute to those who protect the kingdom when I am bound and unable to do so."

"Am I so incompetent at disguise?" Broderick asked, yet studying the fine weapon in his hands. Of a sudden, he wondered—if Bronson so easily saw his knighthood, could the villagers discern it as well?

Yet Bronson chuckled, his eyes merry with mirth as he shook his head. "No more than I, it would seem." He paused, still smiling. "I was at Ivan's tournament. I saw the tournament champion battle to victory," Bronson said. "Stroud and Wallace were with me . . . for they do so enjoy witnessing tournament."

Broderick laughed. "Then you knew me. You knew me the moment we struck hands when first we arrived." He felt his smile fade a little. "And if you were at Ivan's tournament . . . then you know Prissy's truth as well."

Bronson nodded. "I do. And yes. The day you arrived in Ballain, when first we struck hands in greeting . . . I knew." He paused, chuckling once more. "Tell me . . . does Karvana's Scarlet Princess wholly approve of being named Prissy?"

Broderick smiled and shook his head. "In truth, she is loath of it. Yet I have named it her penance."

"Penance?" Bronson asked. "Who is a knight to order penance of a princess?"

"A knight she in constant terms *pretty.*"

Bronson scowled, yet laughed. "*Pretty?* Ooo! Then she well deserves such penance."

"Thank you," Broderick said. "It is good to have a comrade near to agree with me."

"Yet . . . you are pretty, I suppose . . . in particular for a knight," Bronson teased.

"No more pretty than you," Broderick countered.

Still, Bronson only laughed—for it seemed laughter was in him always. "Far more pretty than I, Sir Broderick. Far and away more pretty! It is why the ladies and princesses at Ivan's tournament were all so delighted in your presence. It was such at every tournament where you and I were both in attendance."

Broderick smiled. "So it was not just Ivan's tournament that caused me to be familiar to you in Ballain?"

Bronson shook his head. "No. I have seen you compete many times . . . but it was at Ivan's tournament that I was first aware of your passion for the Scarlet Princess . . . and hers for you."

"You speak of the champion's prize," Broderick said.

"I do. She was full frightened near to death to bestow a kiss upon you . . . and all for the fact that she loved you already. And you . . . you were not one to stand rigid and proper whilst she bestowed your prize." Bronson laughed as he said, "No, indeed not! Only the Crimson Knight of Karvana could be brave enough to sip nectar from the lips of a princess with her king father looking on."

"She took pity on me . . . that is all," Broderick said. He endeavored to oppress the racing of his heart. Always thoughts of Monet sent his heart racing—his blood burning. "She was grateful I won Ivan's tournament . . . for the honor of the kingdom."

"Rubbish!" Bronson exclaimed. He returned the sword, Gauntlet, to its place on the wall— took the Crimson Frost when Broderick offered and replaced it as well. He took seat in a chair nearby, tucking his hands behind his head, displaying strong arms—and the brands of a Knight Exemplar.

Broderick frowned a moment. "You say Stroud and Wallace were with you at Ivan's tournament?"

"Yes."

"Then they too own the truth."

"And Sarah . . . for I keep nothing from her," Bronson said.

"And they are as trusted as you?" Broderick asked. He did not wish to offend Bronson, but he wondered at secrets being kept. The past had taught him that very few who walked the earth could pure keep silent when owning a secret.

"They are," Bronson said, smiling. "The secret of your Scarlet Princess lover is safe with us, Broderick."

Broderick nodded. "You are full well observant. I would not doubt you know all there is in the world to know."

"I know that you have led Karvana's princess into hiding . . . and I can well imagine why the king has charged you to do so. Yet one thing I do not know," Bronson began. "Are you indeed wed? Or do you only play at it?"

"You—with the powers of a seer it seems—yet you do not know if we are wed?" Broderick asked.

Bronson's eyes narrowed. "I cannot discern if you are wed, for you have the look of frustration . . . in truth, of anger at times. And she . . . she does not hold confident in your affection for her. Thus, I cannot discern whether you are truly wed . . . or simply play the farce. Yet I cannot believe Dacian would send her into exile with you—a man—and not see you wed first."

"We are wed," Broderick said.

Bronson arched a brow. "Ahh. I see. Wed . . . in name only." He chuckled. "I see now why you labor to such brutal fatigue in fashioning fence and keeping battle-ready."

"I am charged with protecting her . . . with preserving the heart and hope of the kingdom."

"Which would hold no power over you if she were an ugly old crone with a bad temperament," Bronson mumbled. "Yet she is not. And it is full evident she cares for you . . . and you for her.

This charge . . . is it infallible? Or is there hope you may have her yet?"

Broderick shrugged broad shoulders. "If the king is killed, she belongs full to me as wife. Or . . . if Karvana's gates are threatened and the king sends word, in this also will I wholly have her. Yet if Karvana triumphs, as we all pray she will . . . I will not know the princess as wife."

Bronson shook his head. "How good it is you and not I that was given this charge, brother. For were I married to a woman the like . . . I could not resist her."

"She would not esteem me otherwise, and in that I would be thwarted as well. Therefore, even if I were able to betray her father and my kingdom . . . I could not betray her."

Bronson's eyes narrowed; an approving smile spread across his face. "And this is why Dacian has charged *you* with preserving the kingdom, Broderick . . . because you are a man above men . . . a man of true and infinite honor."

"I am that . . . or a fool," Broderick said.

Bronson chuckled. "Well, lad, take heart, for in all of it . . . you are pretty at least!"

"I can see I should hold my tongue with you . . . in some regard at least," Broderick chuckled.

"Let us strike hands once more, Sir Broderick Dougray," Bronson said. He held forth a strong hand, and Broderick accepted. "Brothers in knighthood are we, Crimson Knight. I can be trusted, with your life and that of the Princess Monet. In this, you believe . . . do you not?"

"I do," Broderick said.

Bronson nodded. "Good."

Broderick would not press Bronson to reveal more. He was an Exemplar, cast out by King Seward, one who had forged not only swords but a life as Bronson the blacksmith. In knowing it had been full seventeen years since the Knights Exemplar had been banished, he knew Bronson must ever remain the blacksmith of Ballain.

Warming

Monet was thankful in owning Bronson as ally. Not only did the knowledge of his loyalty and strength lend comfort to her, it seemed to encourage Broderick. In some manner she did not fully understand, Broderick now knew assistance in bearing his burden of protecting her, and she could see it offered a tiny respite to his mind. Monet's pretty Crimson Knight still labored fierce. Yet it was often Broderick and Bronson would retire to the woods just behind the cottage and spar with swords or maces. Monet knew Bronson's friendship and knighthood fed Broderick's hunger to remain battle-ready—assured him that his strength and power had not been lost for having to live common and confined in their exile.

Further, Monet was glad of Sarah's knowledge of their secret, for it offered her friendship and strength as well. Sarah spoke to her as ever she had before—as if Monet truly were just the wife of Ballain's horseman and not the princess of the kingdom. This gave Monet respite. As Broderick found strength in the company of a fellow knight, so Monet found strength in a true friend. Certainly, Sarah was older than Monet—near the age her own mother would have been had she lived. Still, this was trivial, for both women owned youthful hearts—hearts that were kindred in spirit.

"There is a rather large cropping of holly . . . not so far from the village," Sarah said. "It is ever I gather it to adorn the hearth—not just at Christmas, but through the winter full. It is so bright and cheerful in its green and red berries. We will go together and gather some in a few weeks' time."

Monet smiled as Sarah stitched. "Your stitches are so dainty, Sarah . . . so very perfect," Monet said. And it was true. She had seen no finer embellishment on linen, not even in the castle.

"Thank you, Prissy," Sarah said. "I hope it will please Wilona. Young Dacian must have a pretty blanket for his cradle."

"I fear my stitching is not so fine as yours, Sarah," Monet sighed. "Wilona will well know which edge you stitched and which edge did I."

Sarah paused, studying Monet's work as she held it up for her approval. She smiled and patted Monet's knee.

"Your stitching is full as good as ever mine was," she said. "And Wilona will be pleased with our gift . . . no matter if the stitches are mine or yours. She is a sweet girl. I can only hope my own sons settle with such sweet wives as Wilona is to Grayson."

"Does it worry you?" Monet asked. "Their taking wives . . . setting out on their own paths?"

Sarah nodded. "Near constant," she admitted. "Still, I keep busy . . . and faithful in hoping they will all be as happy as ever Bronson and I have been."

Ever Monet had noticed the faithful, true, and consuming love Bronson and Sarah shared—a thing rare and to be admired. Since learning Bronson was indeed one of the banished Knights Exemplar of Karvana, she had often wondered at Sarah's knowledge of it all. Still, she had paused in inquiring—till now.

"Did you know Bronson was exiled when you married him?" Monet asked.

"I did," Sarah answered, continuing to stitch. She smiled. "Yet he was as handsome as any mythical god of legend . . . and quite as strong. Furthermore, never had I known a man more akin to mirth and merriment. Ever he was smiling. Ever he still does smile . . . and laugh. Even with such a burden as banishment—lost wealth and honor—ever he smiles. Ever the sun shines in my Bronson's eyes." Sarah sighed. "I loved him at once, and my love never wavered. It never shall."

"I love that you love him so," Monet said, exhaling her own sigh of delight. "I think it does not matter a man's wealth and title. What matters are his character and spirit."

"Let us pretend Broderick were in truth a mere horseman of Ballain," Sarah said. "Would you full love him as well? Were he not the regarded Crimson Knight of Karvana . . . would you choose him over any other?"

"Of course!" Monet giggled. "And far more easily, for I *could* choose him then . . . and I would know if he would choose me for myself . . . and not because he was charged to."

"You love him quite completely, do you not?" Sarah asked.

Monet shrugged. "It is ever I have loved him . . . since I first saw him, I think. And not simply because he is so handsome, but for the man that he is . . . for his loyalty, his integrity, his wit and wisdom."

"And he loves you for the all that you are," Sarah said.

"He cares for me, I know," Monet said. "But if he loves me, it is because he loves Karvana. He sees me as her hope . . . her heart. All knights love the princesses of their kingdoms for this reason. But it is far different than being loved because you are the woman he would choose to love . . . as Bronson loves you."

Sarah was silent. She studied Monet for a moment—pensive, it seemed.

"Do you truly think he cares for you only

because you belong to the kingdom he protects?" she asked.

Monet shrugged. "I think he . . . in the least I hope he counts me a friend. We converse well. He appears to enjoy my company." Monet smiled, feeling a blush rise to her cheeks. "It is even he kissed me once since we came to Ballain."

"Truly?" Sarah said, her smile broadening with delight. "And still you think he only considers you the kingdom's treasure to guard?"

"Yes. Oh, certainly he is a man owning desires all men own. I am not so foolish as to be blinded to the fact. And sometimes I wonder at my father's cruelty . . . cruel in giving him a charge to have a wife he cannot . . . he cannot . . ."

"Have?" Sarah finished.

"Yes," Monet said, blushing.

"If he did not love you, he would not keep your father's charge so perfect," Sarah said. "It is his love for you that keeps him from you, kitten."

"He would not defy my father," Monet said. "He has too much honor."

"And you would not tempt him to . . . would you?"

Monet shook her head. "He would not esteem me if I could not prove myself capable of respecting his charge. He would loathe me then . . . and I could not have him loathe me. I could not live with such a knowledge."

Sarah giggled, shaking her head.

"Why such mirth, Sarah?" Monet asked, giggling a little herself. "It is the truth I speak."

"It is only I remember when I once thought similar as you do now . . . before my eyes were opened wholly to love and all its grand deceptions, trials, and misunderstandings."

The cottage door opened, and Broderick himself passed over the threshold. At the mere sight of him, Monet's heart began to hammer in her bosom—not so unlike Bronson's hammer against the anvil in the smithy.

"The sun begins to set, ladies," he began, "and yet you strain your vision at stitching."

"We have only just finished, Broderick," Sarah said, gathering the blanket and stitching materials, "and I am certain Bronson is bellowing about in search of means to soothe his appetite."

"Thank you for allowing me to work at the blanket, Sarah," Monet said.

"Thank you for helping me," Sarah said. She smiled. "What do you think Wilona would say were she to know it was the Scarlet Princess of Karvana who stitched her baby's new blanket?"

"My stitching is worth no more than any other woman's in the village," Monet said.

Sarah smiled. "She is humble . . . that one there," she said, looking to Broderick as she cast a nod toward Monet.

"Thankfully, yes," Broderick said.

Sarah reached forth and pinched Broderick's

squared chin. "And such a pretty knight she owns as her guardian!"

Monet laughed as Broderick sighed, shaking his head. "I am in thought of beating the blacksmith when next I lay eyes on him . . . for he amuses himself far too easily with vexing me."

"Bronson amuses himself at teasing everyone," Sarah laughed. "Sleep well, Prissy."

"I will. Thank you, Sarah," Monet said.

When Sarah had gone, Broderick closed the cottage door, drawing the bolt. Shaking his head as he chuckled, he removed his doublet, loosed the points at the front of his shirt, and sighed with great fatigue.

"It is well I should beat you, Prissy," he said.

"Me?" Monet giggled. "Why beat me for Bronson thinking you are pretty?"

"Because it is you who termed me so," he said, smiling.

"But it was not me who told him you were so termed," Monet reminded. "Therefore, you cannot be vexed with me over his teasing you. I am already yoked with the penance you set forth . . . Prissy—indeed I loathe it."

He continued to smile, his eyes bright with pleasure at their jesting.

"Furthermore, you are pretty . . . so why are you so easily vexed when you are told the truth of it?" she asked, mischief pure leaping in her bosom.

He frowned then. "Do you really think I am pretty? Girls are pretty . . . or sometimes young boys could be termed so, I suppose. But not men . . . and surely not knights."

Monet smiled. He was truly discomfited in that moment.

"Oh, you know you are handsome, Sir Crimson Knight," she said. "You know I only term you pretty, for it keeps my heart and mind light where you are concerned."

"What do you mean?" he asked. "What do you mean it keeps your heart and mind light where I am concerned?"

Monet forced a smile, though she felt quite out of countenance at having spoken so unguarded. "I . . . I mean, it amuses us both . . . gives us cause to jest and stay light of heart . . . rather than ever worrying over our circumstances of exile," she lied. In truth, she termed him her "pretty knight" for the fact she liked to think he was hers—her handsome, strong protector and her heart's desire. Further, she found she was more able to resist throwing herself into his arms and begging for his love by so teasing him. Still, she could not confess it. "You call me Prissy . . . and I call you my pretty knight. Laughter is the best way in which to endure hardship. Is it not?"

His frown deepened. "Then you do not think me pretty?"

Monet smiled, giggling with delight. He was next offended? In the first he had been vexed at her terming him pretty, yet now he was vexed for thinking she did not find him handsome.

Monet went to stand just before him. She could not resist reaching up to weave her fingers through his soft coal hair. She would own honesty in speaking to him, even at the cost of her pride—and heart.

"You are the most handsome man I have ever seen, Sir Broderick Dougray," she said. "You are pure evidence of the reason all women dream of belonging to knights . . . and not kings and princes."

"All women?" he asked, a slight smile soothing the frown at his brow.

"All women," she assured him.

"Even princesses?" he asked.

"In particular princesses . . . for they should reap more pity than other women who dream of knights."

"Why? Why should princesses reap the more pity? They want for nothing."

Monet shrugged. "Nothing save true love. Princesses are forced to kings and princes . . . very few of whom are the quality of my father. Arrogant and weak are most that I have known. Thus, though a noble lady or common girl can hope to win a knight's heart and he her hand . . . a princess is imprisoned by duty. Her heart is not so free to choose. Therefore, do you not think a princess should own more pity?"

Broderick's eyes narrowed as he studied the Scarlet Princess. She was clever—he could not deny her that. He was well impressed at the tapestry she had woven in order to settle his wounded pride. Princesses dreaming of knights—rubbish! Still, he could not but admire her wit and skill at flattery. He was certain any other knight may well have believed she was in earnest—claiming knights were more desirable than kings and princes.

As he gazed at her, the brutal and familiar flames of desire began to burn in his limbs. His mouth began to water for want of hers; his hands began to ache with wanting to touch, his arms straining with keeping from taking her in embrace. He could not linger, lest his strength be dissolved.

"Does your father know you are so sinful a liar?" he asked, chuckling and stepping back from her.

"I am not a liar, pretty knight," Monet said. He continued to study her, though he did not move nearer to her again. Thus, she went to the hearth, for there was mutton stew for their meal warming in the kettle there. "But I have prepared our meal."

Her thoughts still lingered on their conversation. Thus, as she stooped to move one of the stones she would use to warm her bed that she may retrieve the stew kettle from the fire, she did not think of the stone's being hot. She cried out as the hot stone touched the tips of her tender fingers.

Instantly fisting her wounded hand—for the hurt was intense upon it—she drew it to her bosom, wincing with unfamiliar pain.

"You are burned!" Broderick exclaimed, striding to her at once. He took her hand, and she shook her head, certain his examining it would cause further discomfort. Yet Broderick slipped his thumb into her fist—pressing hard against her palm so that her hand was forced open.

"I must have cold water!" Monet said. Surely cold water from the stream would cool the burning pain.

"No," Broderick commanded, however. "Cold water will hasten blistering."

Monet gasped, her eyes widening with astonishment as Broderick then placed the end of each tender burned finger in turn to his mouth. The warm moisture of his tongue served to instantly comfort her pain. He was in repeat of this method of soothing her pain several times, his smoldering gaze holding captive her own enamored one.

Monet's heart pounded with such brutal force within her bosom, she thought sure the Crimson Knight could hear it! She swallowed the excess moisture gathering in her mouth as she watched him tend to her wounds. After long moments, he held her hand out that he may study it.

"Better?" he asked, still holding her hand, his thumb still pressing her palm.

Monet could not speak, overcome with astonished awe—and desire.

She nodded, and he asked, "Are you certain?"

"Yes," she managed to whisper. She thought sure she would faint into the blackness of unconsciousness when he nodded, drew her hand to his face, and moved his thumb aside to place a firm kiss in her palm.

She could not draw breath as his mouth then placed a moist kiss to the soft, sensitive flesh at her wrist. Slowly he raised her arm, resting it on his shoulder as his free hand took her other wrist. Yet Monet did not need his unspoken instruction, and she let her arms go around his neck as he gathered her against the strength of his body.

His face was so near to hers she could feel his breath on her lips, and she closed her eyes, blissful in the sense of it.

"My mother ever said . . . a kiss lessens the pain of any wound," he said. His voice was of the warm, alluring tone Monet so loved. He light kissed the corner of her mouth. Monet's hands found their way to caressing the back of his neck to weave his thick raven hair with her fingers.

"Then she was ever wise," Monet whispered.

Monet gasped as Broderick's lips pressed her own in one firm and driven kiss—but only one. Though he did not release her, he did draw his face from hers, an expression akin to anguish furrowing his handsome brow. Monet knew he was in conflict—his charge from her father treading heavy on his conscience. Still, she would not lose the chance of his kiss—she would not! Thus, she drew him to her, pressing his lips in tender, inviting kiss of her own application. Though he indeed returned her kiss—nay, he commanded it—yet she knew he was careful. His powerful hands fisted the cloth of her dress at her back. She could feel the strength in his arms as they bound, yet she sensed he held himself bridled. Though his mouth was warm and moist upon hers—though the kisses they mingled were flavored of desire—still she knew she did not full own his passion. She knew that his desire to remain honorable and obedient to her father was winning him—and she would not fault him for it.

"Enough," he mumbled as he broke the seal of their lips. He placed strong hands at her shoulders, gently pushing her away from him. "I-I am sorry for the burns."

Monet smiled at him. Oh, how desperately she wished to tenderly caress away the furrow at his brow. Still, she would not distress him further.

"It was no fault of yours, Broderick," she said. "However, the scorched flavor of your stew will be mine." He grinned, and she turned toward the hearth. Perhaps supping would ease the guilt she could see plain on his face.

Her body yet trembled with the lingering delight of his kiss—of being held so in his arms. Yet Monet served a plate to Broderick where he sat at the table. She set her own plate across from him and sat as well.

"What was it that so vexed your Tripp today?" she asked. She would ease his mind—converse lightly to distract him.

"It is well you know that horse," he answered, "for he was vexed—sore vexed."

"I thought he would near break down the fence before you rode him at last. Is it he is not used to being fenced as he is here?"

"He is not," Broderick said. "He was calmed by the outing."

Monet smiled. "You favor him . . . though I cannot understand why. He owns such a fiendish temperament."

"It is long I have had him," Broderick said. "I foaled him at my stables . . . and he is well trained."

"He is your piece of Karvana," Monet said. "In him you remember who you truly are . . . where you truly belong."

"Perhaps you are right," Broderick said. "I am sorry you do not have such a thing to bethink of Karvana."

"But I do," she said.

He frowned, inquisitive. "Yet you brought nothing," he said. "It is sure I remember your alarm . . . as we were descending the steps to the mausoleum tunnel. It was then you realized you had nothing about you."

"Oh . . . I have something of Karvana," she said.

"What?"

His curiosity was full awakened; he was distracted from his guilt at having succumbed to kissing her.

"It is a secret . . . and I know you would not press me for a secret," she said. He would not press her; she knew he would not. Furthermore, even if he did, she would not tell him that the thing she had was far better than Tripp—for she had him, the Crimson Knight.

No word had come—no message from Karvana or the king. Monet had not been over worrisome at the fact, not in the first weeks of their exile to Ballain. Still, as more weeks passed with no word, she did begin to suffer in worry for Karvana—for her father and her people.

Oh, certainly the villagers of Ballain gathered word from travelers. Karvana was at war. King Dacian held King James of Rothbain at bay to the north. There also abounded rumor that James endeavored to entice King Rudolph of Alvar to joining him in waging war against Dacian. Thus far no alliance had been struck between James and Rudolph, yet all knew Dacian and Karvana feared such an alliance. Karvana might endure—rise and defeat James and his soldiers. Yet could she defeat Rudolph and his legions as well? Most likely not.

Such conjecture pure discomfited the Crimson Knight—Monet could see it bold in his countenance. She knew it was full the worst torture for him to stand in silence—listen to the threats against his kingdom, unable to defend her. She feared it would vex him to madness. She feared it would worry her to joining him.

"The messengers will be minstrels only?" Bronson asked as he stood watching Broderick curry Tripp. Tripp whinnied, and Monet stroked his mane to calm him. The horse sensed his master's deep unrest.

"Yes," Broderick growled.

Monet glanced to Sarah, who arched eyebrows in concern of Broderick's temperament.

"Then your course is sure," Bronson offered. "There have been no minstrels to Ballain since you arrived. Therefore King Dacian desires you linger as you are . . . in damnable waiting."

"Rudolph cannot join James," Broderick said. "Karvana cannot hold against such numbers."

"Rudolph is a coward," Bronson growled. "He

is far more fearful of vexing Dacian than James."

"Unless he is convinced Dacian will fall."

Monet continued to stroke Tripp's mane.

"If Dacian falls, then you will be King of Karvana and would take up the spear against those who threaten her," Bronson said.

"Dacian cannot fall . . . for I do not wish to be king," Broderick said. Monet frowned—tried not to feel her own pain at his utterance. She did not wish to think on her father's death, nor on Broderick's not wishing to take her full to wife.

"And that is why you would be a good one," Bronson said. "Those who strive for power and dominance are not the great rulers, Broderick. This you know well."

"Come, Prissy," Sarah said. "The sun is setting, and it is far too cold to linger." Monet looked to Broderick—to his deep frown and angry countenance.

"Good night, Bronson," Monet said as she followed Sarah toward the cottage.

"Good night, Prissy," Bronson said.

Bronson watched the women amble toward the cottage. "She misunderstood your vehemence," he said.

"What?" Broderick asked.

"The princess," Bronson explained, "she thinks your opposition to being crowned is proof you do not truly want her."

Broderick breathed a puff of disbelief. "What man would not want her?"

"She is perhaps not so hardy as you perceive her to be, boy," Bronson said. "Women—all women—are creatures of the heart. We are creatures of body, you and I. Of the heart we are forged as well. Still, youthful women of little experience with men . . . do not believe it of us. They do not believe we own the ability to love the way they do. She believes you care for her because she is the king's daughter, the heart of the kingdom. She believes you look upon her as a stone about your neck . . . one who tempts your virility perhaps. Yet still she thinks you care for her because she is your kingdom's hope."

"Surely not," Broderick grumbled.

"It is time you were warming her, Broderick," Bronson said, lowering his voice.

"Warming her?" Broderick asked. "It is not my charge to warm her. My charge is to protect and preserve her . . . and then give her up. What fool would taunt and torture himself with imagining this was not the truth of it? Beyond my charge, my passion for her would pure burn her to ashes if it were unleashed." Broderick shook his head. "I cannot touch her. Thus she cannot be warmed . . . not now . . . not by me."

Bronson's eyes narrowed. "Dacian would not wed her to you if he truly did not intend you to have her in the end, Broderick. This know . . . for it is well I know Dacian."

Broderick was silent—pensive. It was often his own knowledge of the good king Dacian had whispered the same to him as it had Bronson. Still, he knew Dacian did not hope to die in defending Karvana. Further he knew Dacian did not wish to see the enemy at Karvana's gates. Thus, he had confirmed the charge Dacian had given was all that it seemed to be—a charge to protect the kingdom's hope.

"You think Dacian would, with intention, endeavor to see a lowly knight sit as king on Karvana's throne? You think he would wed his daughter to one owning no royal blood." Broderick shook his head. "No. He is King of Karvana. He will think of Karvana's future."

"Exactly," Bronson said.

Broderick ground his teeth—fell an angry fist into the fence before him. "Do not endeavor to play at giving hope of my having her, Bronson!" he growled. "It is slight I hold to my promise to the king. It is in near madness I keep from taking her to wife!"

"Warm her, Broderick!" Bronson growled, placing a strong hand at Broderick's shoulder. "It is why I say to you, warm her! It will keep you from madness . . . and her! You keep too hard from her! I am not telling you take her to your bed and be traitor to the king. I only tell you, neither you nor she will endure this exile without a warming of some sort. In truth . . . did Dacian give you no respite in this charge?"

Broderick endeavored to calm his breath. "He allotted . . . as he spoke it, a small margin of pleasure."

"Indeed?" Bronson chuckled. "And what margin did he grant?"

"Her kiss . . . when opportunity is ripe."

Bronson laughed and slapped Broderick hard on the back. "That is well warming, lad! Well warming!"

"And more dangerous in threatening my honor than any sword I have faced in battle," Broderick mumbled.

"Not for you . . . not for the Crimson Knight," Bronson said. "For you love her and will not fail her in your charge."

Broderick shook his head, exhaling a heavy sigh. "You are a great one to tell another to warm what he cannot have, for you have Sarah—all of her—full and for many years."

Bronson chuckled. "Oh, but I did not always have her full, Broderick Dougray. I did a measure of torture in warming her only . . . a measure even you could not deny proves me strong."

Bronson laughed again, and Broderick cooled his heated temper. He was a good friend, this blacksmith of Ballain. A wise man, as well.

"Now," Bronson began, "Stroud rode to Ballist today. He found what you asked of him."

Broderick smiled. "Did he?"

Bronson nodded. "He did. He has it at the cottage. Let us fetch it that you may gift it tonight."

Broderick nodded. Somehow he was strengthened. He wondered what trials Bronson had faced in winning his Sarah. It was Monet told him Sarah knew Bronson was banished before she wed him. Yet what had the great Exemplar endured before winning his Sarah? He felt again an odd kinship to the man.

"Yes. I will gift it tonight . . . for it looks to be bitter cold," Broderick said.

"Bitter cold indeed," Bronson chuckled.

"Do you know what day tomorrow is, Prissy?" Broderick asked as he removed his doublet and shirt.

Monet set two extra stones by the hearth. Already the night was cold, and she wondered would she ever find sleep in such discomfort of temperature.

"Of course," she said, shivering a little. "The fifth day of the week . . . Thursday. Why do you ask?"

"Do you think I, First Knight of Karvana, would not remember Karvana's greatest holidays?"

Monet smiled. Certainly she had not thought

he would take notice of it. Still, if he meant to wish her good tidings on her birthday, she would welcome them with delight.

"What day do you think it is, pretty knight?" she asked.

He smiled, his eyes bright with mischief. "I think it is a great day for celebration in all the kingdom . . . for I think it is the Scarlet Princess's birthday."

Monet giggled and asked, "Did Father include that in the gathering of parchment that held your charge? Did he tell you never to forget to wish me good tidings of my birthday?"

Oh, how she hoped her father had not included the instructions! How desperately she hoped Broderick himself had remembered the occasion.

He frowned. "You offend me, lady!" he exclaimed, only feigning offense. "Do you think I would not remember one of the greatest events of our kingdom's history . . . the birth of the fair Scarlet Princess?"

She smiled, though she was, of a sudden, made somewhat sad by a then realization. The Crimson Knight ever called her Prissy—ever termed her the Scarlet Princess. It was never did he call her by her true name; never did he utter Monet. Though she had long named him Broderick whenever they spoke, he did not name her her true name. She silently whispered to herself he was only being wary—careful that they not be found out in their exiled state. Still, it caused her heart an odd aching in that moment.

"It is no more important than the birth of any other girl," Monet said.

"It is true that every birth is a gift from God and should be celebrated," he said. "But I do not serve every person ever born . . . nor do I hold every person as favored as I hold you. Thus, glad tidings . . . for tomorrow the kingdom will celebrate your day of birth, Princess!"

It was dark in the cottage. The flame of the hearth fire mirrored in his eyes was fierce and somehow alluring.

"You are very kind," she said. "In truth, I must admit to being astonished you remembered."

He frowned playfully. "What?" Shaking his head, he opened the cottage door—as if with purpose to leave.

"No! I-I did not mean to offend you, Broderick!" she exclaimed.

Broderick smiled and reached without the door.

Monet gasped, her hands going to cover her mouth as awe and delight washed over her. Broderick closed the door and drew the bolt. He held in his hands a warming pan—a brass pan with a long handle meant to hold fire embers and coals from the fire, that it may be placed between the linens of a bed to warm them.

Monet felt tears brimming in her eyes. How had he come by such a luxury in Ballain? Further, a more thoughtful gift she had never known! The pan would warm her bed far better than hard, quick-cooling stones! She stood in disbelief, overcome by his gift.

"It is a brass warming pan," Broderick said.

"I know," Monet whispered, accepting the warming pan as he held it out in offering it to her. She studied the shining brass of the pan—the long, intricately carved handle. Tears renewed in Monet's eyes. Never in her life had she been given anything so attentive! She winced for a moment, her thoughts lingering on the endless near whining Broderick had endured—the near nightly complaints she had offered to him over being forever chilled.

"It is . . . perfect!" she said, smiling at him—silently praying she could restrain her tears of tender joy.

Broderick shrugged broad shoulders. "It was the second best thing I could fathom to keep you warm at night," he chuckled.

"Oh, this is far better than heated stones . . . and you well know it," she giggled. "How can you endeavor to imply stones are still the first best thing to warm me in my bed?"

"You misunderstand my implication," he said, a delicious grin of mischief on his handsome face. "I merely said this was the second best thing to warm you in your bed. I did not say the stones were first."

Monet shook her head, too delighted with his gift to wade through solving one of his riddles.

"How did you come by this, Broderick?" she asked.

"By means of sending Stroud to Ballist . . . for I could not go myself and chance being recognized," he said. "I am sorry you have been so cold in the night, Princess."

Monet placed a hand to her bosom, attempting to still the mad beating of her heart. He knew her! He knew her well! Further, he cared for her comfort.

Monet placed the warming pan on the table nearby. She could not contain her joy! Turning, she threw her arms around the neck of the great Crimson Knight.

"Thank you, Broderick!" she whispered as tears escaped her eyes, running rivulets over her cheeks. "I . . . I cannot believe you have been so thoughtful toward me . . . after all my whining and weak complaints . . . and still you are thoughtful." She paused, giggled, and drew back from him, her arms yet encircling his neck. "Or perhaps you are only weary of hearing me whine and complain. Perhaps your gift is not so kind to me as it is to you."

He shook his head and smiled. As his arms encircled her, Monet felt the wild rush of goose-flesh over her limbs.

"I do not want you to be cold any longer,"

he said. "I know what it is to sleep with heated stones . . . and cannot see you sleep in such discomfort any longer." He frowned. "But I do not understand your tears, Prissy. You are glad of the warming pan . . . are you not?"

Monet glanced away, brushing the tears from her cheeks. "I have had many birthdays . . . many gifts—jewels, horses. Minstrels have written ballads in honor of my birthday; poets have penned sonnets for me." She yet could not look at him. Still she continued, "Yet none of it . . . none of those was ever truly gifted with such . . . such thought to me. No gift I have ever received was as meant for me as was your gift now."

"But . . . but it is only a warming pan," Broderick mumbled, his brow yet furrowed with an inquisitive frown.

"I know," Monet whispered. "You must think me such a silly girl." She looked at him then. "But you do see . . . do you not? You thought of me . . . of me . . . not of the kingdom and how your gift would appear to others . . . not of my father and endeavoring to display your wealth and worth to him. You only thought of me and my discomfort . . . of how you might ease it." He gazed at her, an expression of mild guilt on his countenance of a sudden. Thus she pressed, "And do not say it is your charge to my comfort. It will spoil the gift, and I know you did not think of the warming pan because of your charge."

His guilt softened, and he shook his head. "I confess I did not think of it for reason of my charge . . . though I am of a sudden washed with guilt at not having done so previous."

"No!" Monet laughed, taking his squared jaw between her small hands. "I am glad you did not think of it as per charge. Thank you, Broderick!"

Again she embraced him. She wished to ever embrace him—to be held against him as she was in that moment.

"I-I cannot full express my delight to you, Broderick," she said. "How can I possibly tell you what your gift has meant to me?"

"Could such a gift, perhaps, earn Ballain's horseman a prize like unto that a tournament champion might expect?" he said.

Monet drew back from him, of a sudden shy at having displayed her unguarded affection for him.

He was smiling at her, his eyes bright with the mischief she so loved to see in the blue mirrors.

"Do you endeavor to mock me on the eve of my birthday, pretty knight?" she asked.

"I endeavor to kiss you on the eve of your birthday, Princess," he said, "to discern whether or not your flavor has altered . . . now that you have aged."

"I told you once before," Monet whispered, "I will ever kiss you at your bidding, pretty knight."

"Then kiss me, Princess," he said, smiling. "For

it cost me a horse to Stroud . . . that warming pan there," he said, nodding to the pan on the table.

Monet did not linger—did not allow a breath that a bashful nature may rise in her. Simply she pressed lips with him once—lingering—twice—lingering—thrice—moist, warm, and lingering.

Gooseflesh bathed her body—breathless was her bosom! Rapt in the arms of the Crimson Knight, Monet knew nothing else in the world! There was not Karvana in danger; there were no people who suffered in fear. She did not care that winter approached or that the coming snow may cause her cold misery. Only she cared for Broderick—only cared that he held her—that her heart was unleashed as she kissed him.

His mouth was warm and moist. He tasted a flavor she knew only to be Broderick Dougray. Firm he kissed her—slow and measured he kissed her—and Monet knew bliss.

Yet there was something—something her body whispered—something her heart defined. Slowly, she broke the seal of their lips, holding his handsome face between her hands as she studied him.

"You are being careful with me," she whispered, gazing into the alluring blue of his eyes. "I can sense it."

"I am always careful with you, Princess," he said.

"Do not call me Princess!" she cried in a

whisper of a sudden, her hands going to her forehead, and she winced. Her bliss fled as fear and doubt flooded her being. Even for his gift, was she naught but a piece of Karvana to him? "You call me Princess with purpose at times. I know you do . . . though I know not why, and I would ask you not to. Further, I wish you would cease in *always* being careful with me. I am not an infant."

"Forgive me," he said. Still, she glanced away from him, the pain in her heart near too piercing—the twisting frustration in her body and soul maddening.

Monet sighed. "I forgive you," she muttered, still frowning. She felt her lower lip pulse with a tiny pout. She looked at him then, admiring the intense comeliness of his entire countenance. "For it seems I can never stay angry with you for very long." Pain and fear were still in her, but she would not burden him with her weakness. Shaking her head, she forced her lips to curl in a smile. "Thank you for the warming pan," she said. "It truly does hold more to my heart than you can know." Lifting herself on toe, she placed a tender, lingering kiss on his whiskered jaw.

A slight gasp escaped her lips as his strong arms encircled her body of a sudden. Monet's heart leapt in her bosom as Broderick pulled her body flush with his own, his embrace tightening. Warm moisture flooded her mouth once more as he gazed at her—as she studied the strong lines of his face, the tempting shape of his mouth.

"It is your birthday," he said. The sweet warmth of his breath on her face caused Monet to quiver. "Thus, if you wish me to be intimate in names and careless in kisses . . . then I will be intimate and careless." She was entirely overcome with desire as he whispered, "Or rather careless in names and intimate in kisses . . . Monet."

She felt her lips part, struggling for breath as he held her face between his powerful hands.

He took her then—took her mouth with his own, ravishing her with moist, smoldering kisses! His hands encircled her throat; his thumbs braced beneath her chin as it seemed he endeavored to derive from her mouth some enchanted nectar to quench an insatiable thirst.

Monet found drawing breath near impossible—yet she cared not! The flavor of Broderick's mouth blending with that of her own spurred her to being careless of comfort, propriety, or any other rationale. As his arms bound her against his powerful form, her hands knew pleasure at caressing the breadth of his shoulders, the back of his neck—at being lost in the raven softness of his hair.

He broke the seal of their lips as his mouth sought out the tender flesh of her throat. Again and again he trailed soft, moist kisses over her throat—to her cheek—at her neck just below her ear.

A gasp—a sigh of blissful felicity—escaped Monet's throat as Broderick clutched the edge of her bodice at her neck, tugging at the cloth until her left shoulder was exposed. He placed several moist and lingering kisses at her shoulder before returning his attentions to her mouth. Carelessly driven kisses of near frantic passion burned between them—kisses offered and accepted—shared.

His arms banded 'round her waist. He lifted her—pushed her back against the cottage wall as his mouth bore down against hers.

Monet's mind burned with her unspoken love for Broderick, her whole self aflame with desire. In those moments she wanted nothing—nothing save him—nothing save his passion raining over her—consuming her as the waves of the sea!

Of a sudden, he broke the seal of their lips. His arms released her, and he pressed a fist to the wall on either side of her head.

"Monet," he whispered, hanging his head before her.

"No," she whispered, for she could see lucidity threatening to own his mind once more. Reaching out, she took his handsome face between trembling hands, raising his gaze to her own. His eyes were narrowed, glazed with lingering passion and desire.

She leaned forward and kissed him soundly on the mouth. He seemed to draw nectar from the warm moisture of their kiss once—twice—and then he put her away from him.

He breathed heavy. "It is foolish to want what I cannot have, Monet," he said. "*Princess* Monet."

Monet felt tears brim in her eyes—placed a palm against his cheek as he straightened his posture.

"I am not fool enough to believe that the Crimson Knight would not have something if he *truly* wanted it . . . whether or not consent had been given," she said. "You are ever my protector, are you not? And I am ever the charge given you by your king."

He said nothing—only continued to near glare at her with smoldering sapphires. Thus, she dropped her hand from his face, brushed the tears from her cheeks, and forced a smile and pleasant countenance.

Glancing to the brass warming pan on her bed, she said, "At least I shall sleep warm tonight . . . and with no stones in my bed to disturb me. I thank you, Sir Broderick."

Would that I could warm you in your bed, Monet, Broderick thought. Raking trembling fingers through his hair, he chuckled—a slight chuckle akin to some madness—and smiled, amused by her innocence. She had not understood his implication when he told her the warming pan was the second best thing to warm her through the night. She had not understood that the first best thing would have been the Crimson Knight himself. And it was just as well she did not comprehend it, for he could have endured very little further temptation where the Scarlet Princess was concerned—lest he find himself in breach of his covenant with the king, in forfeit of his honor and virtue as a knight. He well knew bedding her as wife would be worth any sacrifice. Still, he would have her only at her father's will. For though she was not conscious of it, he knew she would not esteem him otherwise—no matter what passion may whisper.

"You are welcome, Princess," he said, offering a single nod.

"It is my favored gift . . . of all the gifts I have ever received," Monet said. As she moved past him, she added, "Save one."

Monet smiled—for she thought she sensed a blush rose to his cheeks at her implication that his kiss was her true favored gift.

The Minstrel's Message

Monet feared Broderick would withdraw—that he would now find necessity in keeping from her company. All through the long dark of night following their shared moments of passionate bliss, she had lain awake in worry over it. He already labored sore for all the hours of the sun. Though she thought he could not labor worse, she worried he would endeavor to do so—that he might avoid her company. Further, she feared he would find reason to be angry with her for being the cause of their exile—of his imprisonment in Ballain.

As she lay awake, gazing into the dark nothing of the cottage at night, she thought she could not endure were he to withdraw from her company. Were Broderick to cease in joining in conversation with her, cease in his playful teasing, cease to be the best of company she could imagine, then she could not endure. She thought of the other knights of Karvana—considered each great man at her father's table round of conferring. Monet knew she could not have lived so content in exile had any other knight been given the charge to protect the heart of the kingdom. She knew her father knew it.

All manner of doubt, uncertainty, worry, and fear began to plague Monet's mind there in the cold dark of night. Would King Rudolph join King James to fight against Karvana? Was her father yet safe? Were the novice knight Sir Eann Beacher and his squire, Richard Tailor, yet well and fighting with the legions battling to the north? Did Sir Alum Willham yet survive? Were many men killed? Would Bronson the blacksmith keep his secret of being one of the banished Knights Exemplar? Would Sarah see her sons well married to sweet wives? Would Stroud win the heart of the miller's daughter? Would the village's new babe, Dacian, be strong and healthy through winter?

For hours did Monet worry and weep, for it was the way of night's darkness—to bring doubt and worry through weary minds and frightened hearts. Still, somehow—in some moment before sunrise—Monet did find sleep. When she at last awoke, it was near midmorning. She rose, and from the window she could see Broderick with the horses—with Tripp—currying the favored animal and speaking low to it as he did so.

She would not call to him through the window. She would not go out and intrude upon his solitude. Yet as she studied him, watching the manner in which he pampered the animal, her

thoughts were whisked back to the night before—
to Broderick's gift of a warming pan—and to
his kiss! As gooseflesh blanketed her limbs, as
her heart swelled with the overwhelming love
it hid for the Crimson Knight, she turned from
the window. She could not allow her thoughts
to linger on love, hope, or passion. She was a
princess in exile—a princess whose kingdom was
threatened—and she must remember it. Though
she wished with all her heart she could be simply
the wife of the horseman of Ballain, she knew she
could not. It was not her lot in life to know the
contentment borne of owning the true desire of
one's heart, and she must renew her acceptance
of the truth.

"Sarah!" she breathed aloud. A visit with
Sarah would divert her frightened and hopeless
thoughts.

Quickly Monet dressed and prepared a simple
breakfast. She did not even pause to eat at the
table—simply placed a piece of linen over a
plate she had prepared for Broderick, took two
bites of ham for herself, and left the cottage.

As she neared the center of the village, she
was curious, for there seemed to be far more
people astir than was common. Monet smiled
as she walked, delighted at seeing several of the
miller's daughters placing garlands of holly and
pine boughs about the shutters of the mill.

"Hello, Prissy!" one of the girls called. It was

Merry, Miller Aldrich's daughter whom Stroud fancied.

"Hello, Merry!" Monet called in return. "Are you girls adorning the mill for winter celebrations already?"

Merry smiled. "Today is the birthday of Princess Monet . . . of the Scarlet Princess of Karvana! Did you not know?"

Monet forced a smile. "Of course! Of course! I had quite forgotten it was come upon us so soon."

"You and your Broderick must come for the fire tonight," Merry said. "There will be singing and dancing and pastry aplenty!"

"We will most assuredly be there," Prissy said. She waved at the girls, who smiled and waved in return. She wondered what it would be like—to be able to join the revelry of a birthday celebration in honor of Karvana's princess without having to smile for near the whole of the day, all the while having to express gratitude for a hundred different gifts given of obligation.

The thought of gifts led Monet's mind to the brass warming pan Broderick had gifted her the night before—of the intimate kisses they had shared. Whether for the cold of midautumn or the delight at the memory, Monet's arms prickled with gooseflesh, and she hastened toward the cottage of Bronson and Sarah.

"We are baking pies for the celebration this evening!" Sarah exclaimed as Monet passed the threshold into the cottage. "All manner of pies . . . any we can concoct."

Monet giggled at the expressions of pure loathing and humiliation blazoned on the faces of Carver and Dane. No doubt they were in deep wishing they were not the youngest of the blacksmith's sons, for then they could be out sparring or splitting wood—instead of baking pies with their mother.

"And it seems you are having a marvelous time of it," Monet said.

"Indeed," Sarah giggled. She bent then, placing a tender, motherly kiss on one cheek of each unhappy boy. "However, if you are willing, Prissy, perhaps you could help me for a time . . . and Carver and Dane could away to the forge to check on their father for me."

Instantly the boys' faces brightened.

"Truly, Mother?" Dane asked.

Sarah nodded. "Yes. Off with you both. I too am a bit weary of baking."

Monet laughed as she watched the boys race from the cottage, as if the Reaper himself were at their heels.

"What a cruel mother you are, Sarah," Monet began, still smiling, "forcing them into baking pies."

"It is true," Sarah said, embracing Monet in a warm greeting. "I have learned well the art of torture." She brushed flour from her apron and asked, "And are you enjoying your birthday, Miss Prissy?"

Monet shrugged. "I did not know the outer villages celebrated my birthday. I thought only Karvana made such a commotion."

"Oh, no!" Sarah exclaimed. "It is a reason for frolic . . . and we commoners love to frolic. It keeps our spirits high, particularly in the colder seasons when oft life does not hold as much natural cheerful merriment." Monet watched as Sarah went to a small wall cupboard nearby and retrieved something from within.

"I have a gift for you," she said.

"Oh, no," Monet whispered, shaking her head. "Please do not tell me you—"

"It is only a small token, kitten," Sarah said, offering a lovely linen kerchief to Monet.

Monet smiled, delighted by the lovely stitching upon it. Tiny scarlet flowers adorned one corner of the kerchief; a white vine of leaves trailed along its outer hems.

"Oh, Sarah!" Monet exclaimed in a whisper. "How lovely! It is purely wonderful! Thank you!" Throwing grateful arms about Sarah, Monet embraced her hard.

"Oh, it is not such much," Sarah said, returning

Monet's embrace. "Only a small token of my affection for you."

Releasing Sarah, Monet studied the kerchief once more. "How lovely it is!" she whispered.

"You are easily pleased . . . in particular for a princess," Sarah said, smiling.

"It is such a lovely gift, Sarah," Monet said. "Anyone would be pleased to own something so beautiful . . . honored that you would take such care in stitching it." Monet tucked the kerchief into the front of her bodice that it may be protected. "I shall treasure it always."

"I wonder what Broderick will gift you as his gift," Sarah said.

Monet giggled. "Oh, do not play at being innocent, Sarah. You well know what Broderick sent Stroud to Ballist to obtain."

Sarah nodded. "Of course! But how came you by the knowledge?"

"He presented it to me last night, and I admit to being entirely delighted in his thoughtfulness!"

"It was thoughtful. I thought as much," Sarah said. "It is ever he has worried over your being cold. Naturally, Bronson suggested that Broderick warm your bed himself . . . but your Crimson Knight is chivalrous to an end."

"He would not fail my father in his charge . . . not for all the world," Monet sighed.

"He would not fail *you,* kitten," Sarah said.

Monet forced a smile. "The miller's daughters

were hanging garland without the mill," she said. She did not wish to linger on speaking of Broderick and his charge to protect her. It was her first reason for seeking Sarah's company—for means of distraction.

Sarah smiled, full understanding. "They are very merry in nature, Aldrich and his wife . . . and their daughters," Sarah said. "If Stroud wins young Merry's heart, he will know a delight in life with her."

"How many pies do you yet plan to bake?"

"In the least four," Sarah said.

Monet smiled. She would help Sarah with her pies. It would keep her thoughts from Broderick—from craving his company as the bee craved honey.

By midday, Sarah's pies were finished and cooling at the table. Sarah had explained that the villagers would soon cease their labors. They would not work the full length of the sun's rule of the sky—for this was a day of celebration! Sarah told Monet that all the villagers would soon meet in the square, gather around a large fire, and dance and sing and make merry late into the night.

"But why is it cause for such celebration?" Monet asked as she sat across the table from Sarah. "My birthday is of no greater meaning than anyone else's."

"Your birth gives the kingdom its future," Sarah said. "A royal family without heir lends itself to causing unrest. Subjects do not feel safe in what is to come . . . for they do not know what is to come. Yet Karvana has a princess—a good, kind, and loving princess—and all Karvana's people know that their happy life will go on in you."

Monet shook her head. "How can they be so certain? With King James threatening the kingdom so . . . how can the people yet make merry? What if my father is killed and James takes Karvana's throne?"

Sarah shook her head. "The people believe their king to be infallible . . . near omnipotent. We know King Dacian cares for us—that he, more than any other king perhaps, will fight for Karvana's people . . . even more desperately than he fights for her lands. Thus, we make merry for the fact his daughter *is* his daughter . . . that she loves her people as her father does. The Scarlet Princess will one day reign as queen of Karvana. Her birth should be celebrated." Sarah smiled, "Furthermore, it is reason to cease in labor—to eat, laugh, and dance! In all of it, what better reason would you ask?"

"I love to laugh and dance," Monet admitted with a sigh. "And to eat as well!"

"Exactly!" Sarah giggled.

Both women startled to gasping as the cottage

door burst open, revealing an angry Crimson Knight.

"Broderick!" Monet exclaimed. He stood before her, eyes smoldering with fury, broad chest rising and falling with labored breathing. "What is it?"

Bronson appeared then, stepping into the cottage as well. "I told you she would be with Sarah, Broderick," Bronson said. He chuckled, patted his friend on one shoulder, and said, "She is well and safe . . . as I told you she would be."

Monet gasped, of a sudden washed with understanding. She had lingered too long with Sarah—had forgotten Broderick's midday meal.

"Oh! I am sorry, Broderick," she said. "Forgive me. I did not think of the time and—"

"You are ever at the cottage at midday," he growled. "When I returned to find you were not there, I thought . . . I thought . . ."

"He thought you had been found out and taken," Bronson finished. "I assured him you were here, but he would not believe me and insisted upon searching for you. You are a naughty girl, Prissy. You have worried your husband most exceeding today."

"I-I am sorry, Broderick," Monet said. "I did not think . . ."

She fell silent as Broderick simply reached forth, taking hold of her hand, thus coaxing her to rise from her seat at the table.

"I am sorry, Sarah," Broderick said. He ran strong fingers through his raven hair, attempting to soothe his temper. "When I did not find her at the cottage . . . it is the celebration in the village. It somewhat unsettles me. I saw several strangers arrive with carts this morning, and I . . . I . . ."

"Jugglers, traveling merchants, and musicians come to Ballain for the celebration, no doubt," Bronson explained.

"Yet they are not known to us . . . and I must be wary for Monet," Broderick said.

Monet felt warmth bathing her, for he had named her Monet—even before Sarah and Bronson.

"And you are right to be wary," Bronson said. "The celebration of the birth of the Scarlet Princess will begin soon. You must attend, lest the villagers know suspicion. Yet you must be careful, lest the travelers are not all what they seem."

Of a sudden, Monet's joy was lessened. Broderick yet held her hand; he had been worried for her, and in this knowledge she knew delight. Yet strangers had come to Ballain, and Broderick was vast unsettled. This knowledge did not delight her. It frightened her, and she moved nearer to the Crimson Knight—felt her hand clasp his more firmly.

Broderick nodded. "We will meet you at the

square for the celebration, Bronson. Yet first I would counsel with Monet for a time."

"All will be well, kitten," Sarah said. The lovely woman forced an encouraging smile. "You are in Broderick's care. All will be well." Sarah tenderly kissed Monet on one cheek, brushing a strand of hair from her cheek.

"Thank you for the gift, Sarah," Monet said, "and for your friendship." A strange and discomfiting sense of foreboding pinched Monet's heart. Surely it was only her imagination. Thus, she endeavored to ignore it—even as it grew within her bosom.

"You are not alone in this, Broderick," Bronson said. He patted Broderick sound on the back as he opened the cottage door. "There are swords here that will aid you in keeping your charge if you need them."

Broderick nodded, placing one grateful hand on Bronson's broad shoulder. "Thank you, my friend."

Monet followed Broderick out of the blacksmith's cottage—followed as he led her not toward their own cottage but toward the woods nearby.

The air was crisp and cool with the scent of burning pine as its breath.

"I thought you were angry with me," Broderick said as they walked. He yet held her hand, and Monet yet savored the bliss of his touch.

"Angry with you?" she asked.

"Yes. I thought perhaps you were angry with me for my weakness last evening . . . that you had set out for Sarah's and been waylaid by one of these travelers."

Monet was washed with guilt. What his worry must have been when he had returned at midday to find the cottage empty, no midday meal prepared. She felt sore responsible for causing him worry.

"I am sorry, Broderick," she said. "I did not think to tell you I meant to visit Sarah."

He stopped then, midst a grove of pines, near a large cropping of wild holly.

"This is where I want you to come," he said. He had never let go of her hand—not since they had left the Blacksmiths'. He now took her other hand, glaring at her with firm command. "If something happens . . . if you are separated from me in some way . . . I want you to come here. We have the false woodpile, yes. But if you cannot go there, I want you to come here. There is a hollowed out space behind the holly. I would have you wait there until Bronson would come for you. Do you understand, Monet?"

Monet began to tremble. "What do you mean? How would we become separated?"

"Just tell me you will come here if we are separated."

"You frighten me, Broderick," she whispered,

for she well understood him, and it entombed her in fear. He was giving her instruction—instruction on what measures to take should he be injured or killed—no longer able to protect her.

"I do not wish to frighten you," he said. "Only to prepare you. Do you understand me?"

Monet nodded. Yet frightened, she would appear strong before him.

He smiled a bit, raising one strong hand to her face. His palm was warm against her cool cheek, and she returned his smile.

"A minstrel lingers with the travelers, Monet," he said.

"Does he bring word to you? Does he bring word of Karvana?" she asked in a whisper.

"We will not know until the celebration . . . for no minstrel will speak a message to us. We must listen to the ballads and songs he gifts the people of Ballain at the celebration," Broderick explained. "Only then will we discern whether he bears a message from the king."

"But there is hope that he will bring a message . . . is there not?" she asked.

He smiled, and Monet near melted at the handsome sight of him.

"Yes," he said. "There is always hope."

Monet smiled—breathed a sigh. "I slept warmer last night," she told him. "The warming pan was far preferred to stones."

"You slept warmer, perhaps," he began, "but not so sound, I think."

Monet frowned a little. "And how would you know how sound I slept . . . or not?"

"You tossed about in your bed as a bucket tossed to the waves of the sea," he chuckled. "I near rose and tied you down . . . for I did not sleep any better for sake of it."

"I am sorry," Monet said. "I was somewhat restless in the night."

"Somewhat?"

Monet smiled. "Very well . . . I was sore restless. I am sorry you did not rest for the sake of me."

"Kiss me here in the wood . . . and I will forgive you my stolen respite," he said.

Monet was breathless at the low and alluring flavor of his voice. Something had changed in him. Where she had feared he would withdraw for guilt of their shared kisses, he had not. Nor had he named her by the loathsome name of Prissy. Not once since he arrived at Bronson and Sarah's cottage had he termed her so.

"With pleasure, my pretty knight," Monet said. "I will glad kiss you here in the wood . . . but I would have you kiss me first."

"Very well," Broderick said.

He did not pause but gathered her into his arms, against the powerful strength and warmth of his body. His mouth knew hers at once—and without timidity. Full he kissed her—full he endeavored to draw from her lips some sweet nectar to sustain him. Her hands lost in the soft bliss of his raven hair, Monet met his wanting—her own craved passion for him ripe and ravenous.

She would linger in kissing him thus forever! For all eternity she would stay in his arms, press lips with him, mouths blending in this delicious exchange of affection! If it could be so—she would!

His whiskers chaffed the tender flesh about her mouth, but she cared not! The strength of his arms so tightly bound her as to near crush the breath from her, but she cared not! In those moments Monet cared for naught else—not the crisp air, not the strange travelers in the village. Held in the powerful arms of her love, Monet did not think of Karvana or her peril. She did not worry for her father or his subjects. In those moments there was no Crimson Knight charged with preserving the Scarlet Princess: there was only Broderick, and she was only Monet who loved him.

For hours they lingered in the wood—now kissing, now conversing, then kissing once more—till the noises of the village celebration traveled upon the wind to the place where they tarried.

"We must away," Broderick said, caressing

Monet's tender cheek with the back of his hand. "We cannot be missed."

"And we cannot miss the minstrel's songs," Monet said, smiling at him.

"No . . . we cannot," he whispered. His eyes narrowed as he gazed at her; a frown slight furrowed his brow. He tender kissed her lips once more and then took her hand and started toward the village.

The village of Ballain fair sang with merriment in celebration. Some of the strange travelers were merchants and had set up market stalls with all manner of wares for purchase. Jugglers and musicians abounded. Even there was a man with a small black bear trained to dance. Monet thought never had a fair or celebration at the castle seemed so merry!

It seemed the face of every villager of Ballain was alight with joy and laughter. Children ran and played in the margins of the square. Couples danced to the music played by three brightly dressed musicians. Hard labor and care were forgotten, as was the approach of cold winter. All in the village seemed to rejoice in hope, and Monet thought perhaps it was not so bad to have the day of her birth remembered, if Ballain's delight were result of it.

At last, the minstrel appeared. Monet had been impatient, even knowing minstrels the like of Marius and others preferred to wait until a celebration was nearly over before appearing with ballads to entertain.

"Do you know him?" Monet asked Broderick. Broderick had insisted upon wandering through the village—seeing each face of each stranger that had come to Ballain—before allowing Monet to join him. He was fearful some might recognize the Scarlet Princess. Yet he saw no face familiar, nor had Monet since joining him. Broderick had not been able to find the minstrel, however. Even he had worried the minstrel had gone. Still, he appeared now, dressed in crimson and black.

"No. He is a stranger to me," Broderick whispered. "Yet do you see the color of his cloak?"

"Crimson," Monet breathed.

"Or scarlet," Broderick said, smiling at her. "And black woolens. Also two scarlet feathers, as well as one black, adorn his hat."

"Does his attire speak to you?" she asked.

"It does. He is come of Marius," he whispered.

Monet's heart began to pound fierce within her bosom. Marius! Perhaps there would be word of her father and Karvana!

"Welcome, minstrel!" Bronson called. All the villagers hushed at the sound of Bronson's voice. "Welcome to Ballain!" Clapping rose forth, and the minstrel bowed.

"I thank you for your welcome, good people of Ballain," the minstrel said. Monet watched as each villager gathered nearer the fire—nearer the minstrel. "I am the Minstrel Reynard, and I come with songs and ballads with which to charm you. Some old, some new . . . but all are true."

Monet smiled as she saw the children of Ballain settle themselves on the ground just before the minstrel. It seemed the excitement of the children bled into her own bosom, and she looked to see Broderick smiling as he watched them as well.

"A song then, minstrel! We beg you!" the Miller Aldrich called.

The minstrel bowed and began to pluck the strings of the lute he carried.

"Good people of Ballain, I give to you the ballad of . . . 'A Crimson Frost'!"

The people of the village of Ballain cheered. Monet well knew how these people would favor a ballad preserving the tale of their own delivery from tyranny. Yet as she clapped and ventured to Broderick, she knew he was somewhat discomposed.

"Does it pain you . . . to hear the tale retold?" she asked in a whisper.

"It does not pain me so much as it discomfits me to hear it sung in my presence," he mumbled.

Monet took his arm, linking her own with it and moving nearer to him where they sat on a fallen tree used as bench in the square.

"You and your men saved these people from oppression and shame, Broderick," she whispered. "You near gave your life in defense of a threat to the kingdom. Do not be discomfited in it tonight . . . for they would thank you if they knew the Crimson Knight lingered among them."

"Once Ballist was a battle stage," sang the Minstrel Reynard, "where soldiers fought and war was wage, to keep Karvana for an age, and poets yet put ink to page . . . of a crimson frost upon him."

The villagers listened to the minstrel—made not a sound—as he wove the ballad of "A Crimson Frost." When he had finished, there was such a noise of cheering, Monet wondered if Broderick thought himself at tournament once more.

"Thank you, Minstrel Reynard!" Bronson called. "Pray . . . another ballad, please!"

The minstrel did perform again—then thrice more—each song or ballad earning him cheers, gifts of cheese, pastry, and even coin. He sang first an aged ballad, of Karvana Far and the young prince Dacian's rise to the throne. He played "The Visitor in Willows," and even Monet's neck prickled with gooseflesh as she imagined the ghost of a long-dead lady wandering in search of her murdered lover. The Minstrel Reynard sang "The Lost Princess of the Realm," and even he sang "Bold Knights of Seward"—a ballad praising the great Exemplar Knights, a ballad

Monet had not heard since she was a very small child.

Following each song or ballad, Monet would look to Broderick. Had the minstrel's tales held a message? Words and meanings only the Crimson Knight could discern? Yet with each ending Broderick would shake his head. Monet began to fear there would be no message from her father— no word of Karvana. Perhaps Reynard was only just a minstrel, traveling the kingdom to earn his living.

"Would the good people of Ballain . . . would all enjoy a new tale in song?" Reynard asked.

Cheers of encouragement were heard. Monet glanced to Broderick—saw his eyes narrow with suspicion and interest. Her own breath quickened as her heart began to pound within her bosom.

"What tale is this?" the Miller Aldrich called.

"Oh, this is a tale most divine," Reynard said. As he began to pluck at his lute, he said, "A tale of romance . . . of secreted love . . . and of lips pressed in bliss." The crowd of villagers clapped—called out their encouragements. "This, good people, is a tale of a princess and her knight lover. I give to you, people of Ballain . . . 'The Champion's Prize' . . . the ballad of the Scarlet Princess and the Crimson Knight."

Monet was rendered breathless! As all of Ballain cheered and clapped, begging Reynard to hasten in commencing his performance, Monet could not draw breath! She looked to Broderick, and he gazed at her for a moment. Monet still clung to his arm, and his hand moved to rest on her leg. Pressing her knee with reassurance, he returned his attention to the minstrel. He would listen—Broderick would listen to the same words sung as Monet would hear. Yet he would hear what Monet knew not how to hear. Thus, she tightened her embrace of his arm—and waited.

In the heavens the gilt sun guarded—as a
    gold piece swathed in blue—
Brave knights mid Ivan's tournament,
    who battled as champions do.
For the Champion's Prize Ivan promised
    could not be measured its cost . . .
Yes, the Champions Prize Ivan promised,
The rare Champion's Prize Ivan promised,
Oh, the Champion's Prize Ivan promised
    was worth more than diamonded frost.

Gold statues and pieces of silver—great
    wealth and honor profound.
The knight who would win Ivan's favor,
    mid riches would he abound.
Yet gold and silver and jewel'd riches did
    not tempt one knight so bold . . .
One knight whose heart longed for one
    lady's,

Great knight whose heart longed for one
    lady's,
Bold knight whose heart longed for one
    lady's . . . meant Ivan's rich prize to
    hold.

A kiss from the lips of a lady . . . or
    maiden of noble birth.
Press lips with a lady or princess was the
    Champion's Prize of worth.
Thus to win King Ivan's tournament
    meant honor never 'fore known.
And the Crimson Knight meant to win it.
    Yes, the Crimson Knight meant to win
    it.
Oh, the Crimson Knight meant to win
    it . . . kiss the heiress of a throne.

For the Crimson Knight loved a princess,
    a maiden of royal birth.
Yet he loved her in painful secret, as the
    heavens love the earth.
Still, before him a chance opportune, for
    one knight to kiss a maid . . .
To press lips with the princess he loved,
    Taste the lips of the princess he
    loved,
From the lips of the princess he loved,
    this knight would not be stayed.

So the Crimson Knight sought his princess—she that unknown owned his
soul,
That he may endeavor to kiss her and at
last count himself as whole.
To the Scarlet Princess he wandered—to
she he so long battled for.
He once battled in Ballist for her.
Yes, he battled in Ballist for her.
He had battled in Ballist for her . . . to bar
evil from her door.

The great Crimson Knight found his lady,
midst nobles and royals crowned,
And he begged her give him a token, that
he may to her be bound
By her favour in Ivan's trials, that he may
have hope to taste
Her sweet lips pressed tender to kiss him,
Oh, sweet lips pressed tender to kiss
him,
Win her lips pressed tender to kiss
him . . . win her kiss soft, nectar-laced.

Her eyes were as amethyst jewels, her
frock a silk scarlet red.
Her hair was as raven as midnight woven
with sapphire thread.
Her face held the grace of an angel; her
lips were wild-berry wine.

Thus the Scarlet Princess of beauty,
    Yes, the Scarlet Princess of beauty,
There the Scarlet Princess of beauty stood
    ripe as the grape of the vine.

As the Crimson Knight strong approached
    her, the Scarlet Princess so fair
Did not speak of her own love for
    him . . . the secret *she* did long bear.
As he knelt on one knee before her,
    begging a token to clasp,
The Scarlet Princess wished fervent,
    The Scarlet Princess hoped fervent,
The Scarlet Princess prayed fervent to be
    in the Crimson Knight's grasp.

He was ever her equal in beauty, this
    raven-haired knight of the realm,
As tall as the oaks in the wild wood, in
    armor and bright burnished helm.
His eyes were the sapphire stream that
    flowed midst her ebony hair.
And he raised his gauntlet to greet her.
    When he raised his gauntlet to greet
    her,
As he raised his gauntlet to greet her, his
    kiss would be hers did she swear.

Then she granted him full a token . . . her
    favour—a scarlet veil.

366

And she begged him that he should
    triumph, through Ivan's fest-battle
    gale.
She asked for their king and their king-
    dom, that her knight would win with
    haste.
She called Crimson Knight to triumph,
    She bid Crimson Knight to triumph,
She begged Crimson Knight to tri-
    umph . . . that her lips to his be placed.

He rose from his knee with the
    token . . . her favour—the scarlet
    veil—
And he gave his princess his promise that
    in battle he would not fail.
Yet his promise had been proved before—
    on Ballist's red battlefields.
Though the princess knew not of it,
    No, the princess knew not of it,
Scarlet Princess knew not of
    it . . . Crimson Knight's secret token-
    shield.

For 'round his neck hung a length of
leather—a rare gift bestowed of the
king—
And it carried a token of favour—a
dark raven woven ring.
The braid of the Scarlet Princess, held

close to his broad, strong breast
Had at Ballist's fields pure saved him,
    Oh, at Ballist's fields it did save
him,
When at Ballist's fields, it had saved
him . . . been the savior of his bleak
quest.

As he strode from his princess he
lingered on thoughts of the tokens he
bore . . .
Of the veil at his throat wove of
scarlet and the secreted locks that he
wore.
He would ride and fight tournament
battle; he would win Ivan's promised
prize.
He would know the sweet lips of his
lady,
    Know the nectar-laced lips of his
lady,
Taste the nectar-laced lips of his
lady . . . own the amethyst of her eyes.

The tournament battle was brutal, as
challengers fell swept aside,
By the Crimson Knight's mace and
lances—by his power and strength in
stride.
He was battle-worn, weary, and

bloodied, but he rose to each
challenger new . . .
For the Scarlet Princess of beauty,
    Yes, the Scarlet Princess of beauty,
His sweet Scarlet Princess of
beauty . . . whom he loved most fierce
and true.

She had seen him best all at maces; she
    had seen his charger rush.
She had heard the crowd rise up roaring
    for the lances he had crushed.
Though his rerebrace was stained with
    bleeding, yet he bore her favour
    smart.
So the Crimson Knight of Karvana,
    The brave Crimson Knight of
    Karvana,
Thus, the Crimson Knight of Karvana
    won the kiss of Karvana's heart.

The Crimson Knight stood before her on
    the platform at Ivan's stands.
The Champion's Prize would be claimed,
    midst the clapping of common hands.
Thus the Scarlet Princess fair trembled as
    she raised to the Crimson Knight,
And he kissed her as even she kissed him,
    Yes, he kissed her as even she kissed
    him,

Oh, he kissed her as even she kissed him
    as the sun flashed its last light.

And such was the love that was blended,
    when their lips pressed in soft bliss,
That a fragrant wind came up on them . . .
    summoned by lovers' first kiss.
And away the wind carried crimson, with
    scarlet bound in its arms.
Crimson Knight held his love—Scarlet
    Princess.
    Crimson Knight kissed his love—
    Scarlet Princess.
Crimson Knight and his love, Scarlet
    Princess, thus spirited by love's
    charms.

Oh, he holds her still in his power—safe
    in love—boundless embraced.
As the fragrant wind whispers to them,
    they blend kisses, sweet nectar-laced.
And she knows he will hold her
    always . . . that he loved before ever
    she knew,
For he carries her braid at his bosom,
He yet carries her braid at his bosom,
Still he carries her braid at his bosom . . .
    o'er his heart . . . his love ever in
    view.

Thus all noble and common of sub-
    jects . . . of Dacian's kingdom proud,
Will fear not when enemies threaten, nor
    shrink from battle's bleak cloud.
For the Heart of Karvana is clasped, safe
    in the grip of true love,
For the Scarlet Princess of beauty,
    Oh, the Scarlet Princess of beauty,
Yes, the Scarlet Princess of beauty is held
    fast in his gauntleted glove.

So break the vast seal of your fearing; go
    forth and conquer your dread,
As the great Crimson Knight begged the
    favor of the princess veiled in red.
As the Scarlet Princess of beauty
    bestowed well her Champion's Prize,
Swift break the seal of forbearance,
    Swift melt the seal of forbearance,
Crack fast the seal of forbearance, and
    claim *your* Champion's Prize!

The crowd of Ballain villagers roared—shouted
and cheered with approval. Monet watched—
astonished into silence, unable to move—as the
Minstrel Reynard bowed low before the people.
Of a sudden, as villagers rushed forth to bestow
gifts to the minstrel for his song of love and hope,
Monet felt the tears on her checks. She brushed
them quickly and gasped when Broderick stood,

leaving her at the bench as he approached the minstrel.

She saw him pull a coin from the pocket of his doublet and offer it to the minstrel. Reynard studied the coin for a moment and then bowed to Broderick.

"I thank you for your generosity," Reynard said.

"And I thank you for your ballad," Broderick said.

Monet rose, walking to the place where Broderick stood in conversation with the minstrel. The ballad had indeed served as fodder for excitement. All in the village were merry, begging Reynard to repeat his offering of the new ballad. He agreed, and the excited villagers began to settle once more.

Yet Broderick did not settle. Taking Monet's arm, he led her to the place where Bronson and Sarah stood, aside of the others.

"The enemy is at her gate," Broderick growled. "Karvana stands threatened." Monet could sense the fury in him, for he gripped her arm tight— near to hurting her.

Bronson nodded. "And in this you have instruction. Your charge is made clear."

The meaning of their words—the conversation between Bronson and Broderick—did not full wash over Monet, for her attention was at something else. The words of the minstrel's song echoed in her mind.

Quiet she whispered, "For 'round his neck hung a length of leather . . ." She quick pressed her hand to Broderick's chest; she could feel the leather strap he ever wore. She moved her hand down, over his body, till she felt the small leather pouch beneath his doublet at his stomach.

She gasped as Broderick's hand covered her own, pushing it from his body. He glared at her; she could see him fair trembling with scarcely restrained fury.

"Karvana will not fall, Broderick. We will not let her fall," Bronson said, placing a firm hand on Broderick's shoulder. "The enemy is at the gate, but the king yet lives . . . and he will not let Karvana fall. In this Dacian has his charge . . . and you have yours."

Broderick did not speak. Simply he started away from the village square and toward the cottage he and Monet shared.

"What does the ballad tell you, Broderick?" she begged him as he hastened to the cottage. "For though my ears heard the same words as yours . . . I know they mean more to you."

Monet gasped as, of a sudden, Broderick lifted her into the cradle of his arms, kicked open the cottage door, and crossed the threshold. He let Monet's feet drop to the floor; he closed the door and drew the bolt.

Raking trembling fingers through his raven hair, he hastened to the hearth and laid a fire.

"You will speak to me of this, Broderick! Please!" Monet begged as tears escaped her eyes to moisten her cheeks.

He stood a moment, gazing into the hearth as the fire kindled and next burned.

"Karvana is threatened. The enemy is at the gate," he mumbled. He turned, his eyes narrow, smoldering sapphires burning through her. "You will have no need of the warming pan in your bed this night, Monet . . . for I must follow my charge . . . and take you to wife."

Swift Break the Seal

Monet brushed the tears from her cheeks. He was angry; her heart ached with pain. In all the world she wanted nothing more than to be the true wife of Sir Broderick Dougray—to be owned by him—to own him in return. Yet in those moments she understood the cost of winning her deepest wish—Karvana.

"Tell me, Broderick," she began in a whisper. "Tell me of the minstrel's message. Please tell me all you understood that I did not." Monet's thoughts had been arrested by the ballad's tale of the secreted love of the Crimson Knight and the Scarlet Princess. The minstrel's song had woven a spell over her, it seemed—one that left only images of Ivan's tournament in her mind and a painful curiosity about the leather strap and pouch around Broderick's neck. Thus, she had not ably discerned many other parts of the message.

Broderick turned from her—exhaled heavy as he gazed into the hearth.

"It was certain it was written of Marius himself," he said.

"How do you know this?" Monet asked. She did not doubt him—only wished to own the knowledge to discern Marius as ballader.

"It is sure Marius's ballad . . . for there are markers," he began. "Marius has placed particular words in the lyric . . . words he agreed to leave for me. In planning your exile, I bade Marius place sequences of particular words in a ballad if it were of him and meant for me. Marius penned a list—ten sequences of words to help me discern if a ballad were a message. There were four of these sequences in this ballad."

"Which were they?"

He remained before the fire—did not turn to face her—yet spoke. "The first refers to the king's state of health—'diamonded frost.' Diamonded frost . . . it tells me your father yet lives, rules, and is in good health." Monet brushed another tear from her face and moved to stand next to him before the fire, for she was chilled.

"I am sore thankful for it," she whispered.

"As am I," Broderick said.

"Is there a sequence Marius will send if Father is not well?" she asked, for she wished to discern future ballads as Broderick was able.

"Crimsoned frost," he mumbled.

"Yes . . . I see," Monet whispered. "And next?"

"The second sequence is 'battle's bleak cloud.' It refers to the enemy . . . tells us James is at

Karvana's gate, as a cloud hovers in threatening a storm. Marius openly referred to James being at the gate, of course. Yet this sequence, combined with the third and fourth, instructs me in my charge. The third sequence is 'sweet nectar-laced' . . . and the fourth, 'swift break the seal of forbearance.' "

"It instructs you to take me to wife . . . for the king fears Karvana may fall," Monet said. "Thus he has doomed you to life as a peasant . . . with me as your shackle." She brushed more tears from her face. Oh, how she loved Broderick—how desperately she wanted to belong to him. Yet he was the great Crimson Knight—the valiant knight who would battle to save his kingdom—the powerful knight now doomed to the simple life of a peasant. How could he truly want her when it would cost him all that he knew and loved?

He was silent for a moment. When he spoke, his voice was low. She sensed a thing akin to fear in him. "Your father sends a message to you, Monet . . . through the ballad. I see his wisdom in it . . . yet I fear he may be mistaken in your feelings."

Monet frowned. "But I own no sequence of words to discern."

"No," he said. "You do not. But you know the tale the ballad spins . . . for you lived it. Your father has revealed something to you. There is revelation—proof of . . . of what he suspects in you . . . and what he knows in me."

Monet felt as if she might simply fall to the floor in a heap of sobbing, heartache, and fear. Yet she was not so weak as she wished to be. Thus she began, "It . . . it is the tale of Ivan's tournament . . . of the champion's prize," she said. "The ballad begins at the tournament, with description of the sun . . . of the prizes the knights who battle may win. It tells of the great champion's prize . . . a kiss from a lady . . . and of the knight who wishes to win his lady's kiss." Monet glanced to Broderick, who studied her with narrowed eyes. Monet shrugged and said, "Naturally, Marius has woven a secret romance through the ballad . . . perhaps to represent our exile together."

"Perhaps," Broderick said.

Monet frowned. "The knight . . . the Crimson Knight . . . asks the princess for a token to bear in tournament that he may win her kiss." She smiled a little and looked to him. "This is where Marius trips a bit . . . for he was not there to know that I asked you to bear my favour. You did not ask me."

"Did I not?" Broderick said, a slight grin at his lips.

"No. You did not," Monet said. "I came to you . . . to beg you not bear Anais's favour."

"But you did not ask me to bear yours," he said.

Monet frowned, for he was indeed correct. She shook her head and said, "In the least you did not beg me on bended knee to carry it. Thus, Marius embellishes there."

"It does not matter. Go on," he said.

Monet nodded, struggling to remember the ballad.

"It goes on with description, embellishing my beauty . . . though I like that he sang my hair was woven with sapphire. That I liked." She smiled, and Broderick chuckled lowly. She frowned again, pensive. "The knight begs her favour, and she grants it. And he is thoughtful as he leaves her, thinking on a token-shield . . . a secret token that had saved him in . . . in . . ." Monet was breathless, her heart pounding mad of a sudden. "A token that saved him in Ballist." She remembered then what she had thought of only moments after the Minstrel Reynard had finished his song. " 'None visible,' you said," she whispered. "In your pavilion, when I came to you before Ivan's tournament began . . . Anais told you it was said you had never before carried favour . . . and you said, 'None visible, your highness.' "

With trembling hands, Monet took hold of the front of Broderick's doublet. The Minstrel Reynard had indeed sung of the leather strap around Broderick's neck—the ballad telling a tale of a token hidden in the pouch, a raven braid woven of the Scarlet Princess's hair.

"It cannot be," she breathed as she began to untie the points at his doublet. "It is not true!" Surely Marius had only embellished, desirous to pen a ballad that enchanted any who were to hear it. A ballad of secreted love and unquenched desire was always preferable to one of mere meadows and trees.

"Monet," Broderick said as she continued to struggle with untying the points of his doublet. He took hold of her hands, but she broke his grasp. She fair tore open his doublet to reveal the pouch hanging from the leather strap around his neck.

"I first saw this at Avaron . . . in your pavilion . . . when I came to you after your final joust," she whispered. "H-how long have you kept this? The minstrel sang you owned this at Ballist. That cannot be true. Surely it cannot!" Tears streamed over Monet's cheeks. Surely it could not be that the great Crimson Knight of Karvana had borne such a token! Surely Broderick had not clasped a lock of her hair to his breast in secret.

"Since first your father charged me seek Lord Morven in Ballain . . . before Ballist," he said.

Breathless, Monet opened the pouch. With trembling fingers, she withdrew the small ebony braid within, woven as a small ringed circle and tied with a tiny scarlet ribbon.

"Three years you have borne this?" she sobbed.

"Near four," he mumbled. "Your father first charged me as Guardian of the Scarlet Princess near four years ago . . . in secret . . . and it did save me in Ballist."

"I do not understand," she whispered, still staring in confounded disbelief at the ebony braid she held. "How . . . how did this save you in Ballist?"

"It woke me from the Reaper's grasp," he said. "I was sore wounded . . . my blood trailing out upon the ground. Darkness had overtaken me . . . as had the crimson frost. I was cold . . . dead cold there on the battlefield. There was no warmth left in me. Thus the crimson frost covered my armor, littered my hair, froze my flesh. Yet of a sudden, something over my heart warmed a little . . . enough to wake me, and I drew breath once more. My eyes were yet closed, and I saw you. In my mind I saw you . . . the Scarlet Princess of Karvana . . . and the token your father had given me whence he charged me as your protector warmed me where it lay on my chest. My heart began to burn with life, and I rose . . . for I would not see Lord Morven lay siege to Karvana Castle and harm you. In those moments, I cared not for Karvana, her king, or her people . . . but I would let no harm near you. Thus, I rose . . . as even the Reaper approached . . . for there before me was Morven, fresh and strong, having stood back in cowardice as his men fought and died. I was battle-weary and worn . . . near dead . . . but as Morven raised his sword to strike me down . . . I felt the token of your hair beneath my armor, and I ran him through."

Monet replaced the token braid—placed it safe in the leather pouch hanging at Broderick's stomach.

"No one knew of this token," Broderick said. "Only your father and I. Not even Eann knew what the leather pouch held. Do you then see how your father speaks to you through Marius's ballad?"

"The ballad tells me you will long guard me . . . as ever you have," Monet whispered. She could not believe more; she would not endeavor to hope that her father spoke to her of Broderick having secreted a love for her.

"The ballad speaks far beyond, Monet," he said. "You know this. In your heart you know this."

Monet knew well then—that Marius and her father had conspired to reveal to Broderick her secreted love for Sir Broderick Dougray, for the ballad spoke plain of it. Yet still she could not believe the Crimson Knight of the ballad true loved the Scarlet Princess—that the Crimson Knight, there in the cottage, loved her.

"In my heart I do know it speaks to you of more than your charge," she whispered. "Yet if you

382

would have me know revelation in it . . . then you must know revelation, as well."

"I would face any legion alone . . . battle the Reaper himself . . . and still I would not be so fearful as I am before you here," he said. She could not look up into his face—simply she stared full at his chest, bare before her, adorned by the leather strap and pouch that hid a token of her own hair.

"What has the Crimson Knight to fear here?" she asked.

"Marius's ballad revealed my heart," he said, his voice low and alluring—the flavor she so delighted in. "I would bed you as wife not for the sake of your father's charge . . . but for my own sake . . . for that of my heart, which you alone hold. Further, I would have you because you wished to have me. Thus, you have made a coward of me . . . for the ballad reveals my long and secreted love for you, Monet. Yet Marius may have well embellished the thoughts and longings of the heart of the Scarlet Princess. In this, I stand before you more fearful than ever I have been in all my life."

Monet brushed tears from her cheeks—smiled as she wept. She placed a tender hand to his chest—felt his heart beating strong beneath her palm.

"I was . . . I was so young when first you came to Karvana with Sir Alum," she whispered. "You were young as well . . . just fourteen years. Yet even then your jaw was square and strong. Your eyes were pure as sapphires. Even Mother said they were more beautiful and bright than the jewels in her crown. Your hair was as raven as midnight . . . and your shoulders far too broad for one so young. One day, I was with Mother, visiting a sick woman in the village. You were there. An old man had stumbled and fallen. Several young men were mocking him. They did not move to help him . . . only stood in cruel taunting." Monet smiled at the memory. Brushing tears from her cheeks, she looked up into the ethereal comeliness of Broderick's face "You bested them . . . all three . . . with naught but your fists for weapons. Then you lifted the old man into your arms and carried him to his family. It was in that moment that I first loved you. I used to lay in my bed at night . . . weeping . . . sobbing . . . for I knew my husband would be chosen for me . . . that I could never own you. Even if you cared for me I could never belong to you. Then Ivan's tournament was upon me . . . and the champion's prize. I determined it would be enough . . . that the memory of your kiss would carry me through life . . . and that . . . and that . . . whomever Father chose as my husband . . . I vowed it would be you. Your kiss I would feel pressed to my lips whenever I must endure . . . the touch of another." She paused—glanced away a moment—shy and blushing. "Marius did not embellish the love I have long secreted for you, Broderick. And I am wicked," she breathed, "for often I have wished that James would pound at Karvana's gate . . . so that I may be your true wife." She looked up, and the smoldering emotion in his eyes caused gooseflesh to race over her limbs. "What use is such a wicked princess to poor Karvana now?"

Broderick smiled, one powerful hand cupping her chin.

"More use than the wicked knight who loves her," he mumbled. His thumb caressed the softness of her lips, and she smiled.

"You would be my wife?" he asked in whisper. "You would give yourself to me?"

Monet let her arms go around his neck—wove her fingers through soft raven hair.

"Only if you love me . . . and not because it is your knightly charge," she whispered.

"I do love you, Monet," he said. "Ever I have loved you."

He gathered her in strong arms, pulling her body flush with his own.

"And I love you . . . my pretty Crimson Knight," she breathed.

His mouth descended to capture her own, in the blending of ambrosial, nectar-laced kisses— the beginning, at last, of true love's blessed consummation.

Monet knew cold no more. In the dark nights of early winter slept she warm in the arms of her lover-husband, Broderick—the horseman of Ballain. One week passed, then two. Three weeks wasted since the Minstrel Reynard had delivered the ballad message to Broderick and Monet.

Certain it was true, Monet knew boundless bliss and happiness in knowing Broderick loved her. Certain it was true, Broderick owned the same in knowing she loved him. Still, for all their long conversations in attempting to convince one another otherwise, they worried for their kingdom, their king, and his subjects.

Early winter had slowed King James's attack. Though his legions camped just without Karvana village, he did not attempt to lay siege to the town and castle. It was a foolish king who endeavored to battle winter as well as conquest a kingdom. James was greed-driven, not foolish.

This Monet discerned as she and Sarah sat in the blacksmith's cottage after supping.

"Rudolph yet pauses," Bronson said. "He is a coward, and it may serve Karvana well."

"He *is* a coward," Broderick began, "and therefore weak . . . pliable of mind. James has but to find a method of convincing, or a means to control him, and Rudolph will falter."

"I am weary of this war talk, Prissy," Sarah sighed. "Let us, you and I, away to the next room . . . where we may speak of happy things."

Sarah rose from the table, as did Monet, but Bronson caught her hand, staying her.

"We will cease this speak of war, Broderick," Bronson laughed, "for we are driving away our wenches . . . and we certain do not want to be without our wenches!"

"Indeed!" Broderick chuckled, taking Monet's waist between his hands and pulling her to sitting on his lap. Monet giggled, took Broderick's handsome face between her palms, and quick kissed him on the mouth.

"You are a bad man, Bronson the blacksmith," Sarah giggled, though she promptly sat on her husband's lap, caressing his smooth-shaved head with one gentle hand.

"I am!" Bronson said. "For I wish to hear a song."

Monet bit her lip with delight, for it was Sarah knew many songs, most of which were mirthful.

"And which song is it you wish to hear, blacksmith of Ballain?" she asked.

"My favorite," Bronson laughed, " 'The Merry Ale Wench'!"

Broderick laughed, and Monet could not help but caress his face. How she loved him! How entirely and wholly, utterly, and deliciously she loved him.

"Very well, Blacksmith," Sarah said.

Monet giggled as Sarah left her comfortable

seat on Bronson's lap, stepping up onto the table.

Broderick smiled, cupped Monet's chin, and drew her lips to his in a moist, warm, and lingering kiss.

" 'The Merry Ale Wench,' " Sarah said, bowing. Monet clapped her hands softly in rhythm as Sarah danced light on the table and sang.

> Oh, there was a merry ale wench . . . with
>> cheeks of rosy pink,
> And she did serve all manner of amber
>> ale drinks!
> Oh, how the patrons loved her . . . the
>> men who met her there,
> For she was young and pretty . . . with
>> ale-amber hair!

Monet laughed, delighted by both Sarah's song and light dance and the look of love and admiration on her blacksmith husband's face as he gazed at her.

> Oh, the ale wench was Fanny . . . her
>> mother's name was too.
> And she bewitched the patrons with the
>> ale her father brewed.
> Yes, many men wished Fanny would
>> bless them with her kiss,
> But they dared not to touch her, for she
>> owned a fatal fist!

Of a sudden, the door to the blacksmith's cottage flew wide—a breathless Stroud at the threshold startling all within.

"Father!" Stroud shouted. He was wild with distress—yet paused, frowning as his gaze fell to his mother. "Mother?" he asked, pure perplexed as he studied her a moment. "Why stand you on the table?"

"Stroud," Bronson said, tearing his son's attention from his mother. "What is it?"

"The minstrel . . . Reynard . . . the one who was here only weeks past," Stroud began, "he has been brought to Ballain . . . bloodied and beaten and arrow-wounded. He yet lives, but he is in a bad way. The miller does not know if he will survive. It seems he has been robbed."

Monet rose from Broderick's lap as he stood.

"Has the minstrel spoken, Stroud?" Broderick asked.

"No, Sir Broderick . . . but he is awake," Stroud answered.

"We must speak with him," Broderick said to Bronson.

"Yes . . . at once," Bronson agreed.

Broderick looked to Monet, gripping tight her hand. "You will come with us. This cannot be mere chance. You will stay close to me."

Monet nodded. "Of course," she said. She trembled as she and Broderick followed Stroud to the mill. Bronson was at their backs—ever wary.

Indeed, the Minstrel Reynard was badly beaten. Monet winced at the sight of him, for her soul whispered it was he found himself harmed for sake of Karvana—for sake of her.

The Miller Aldrich and his wife tended the beaten man.

"Will he live?" Broderick asked.

The miller shrugged, combing strong fingers through silvered hair. "I cannot yet tell you," Aldrich said. "He is badly beaten . . . though I did remove the arrow. It was at him through the back."

"Did you yet have it?" Broderick asked.

"Yes," Aldrich said. He reached beneath the table on which the Minstrel Reynard was laid out, producing an arrow and handing it to Broderick.

As Broderick studied the arrow, so too did Bronson and Aldrich.

"Rothbainian," Bronson mumbled.

The minstrel moaned, and Monet could not keep from placing a comforting hand at his brow.

"Minstrel Reynard?" she whispered.

"Swift break the seal," the minstrel mumbled. "The Crimson Knight must break the seal . . . swift he must break it."

"Where were you attacked?" Broderick asked. "From whence came you to return to Ballain?"

"Ballist," Reynard breathed.

"He is fevered," the miller said. "He is speaking

ballad words of Ballist and the Crimson Knight."

"Yet he . . . he holds brave . . ." the minstrel whispered. "In Ballist he holds brave."

"Who?" Bronson asked.

But Reynard fell unconscious and spoke no more.

"But who would endeavor to beat and kill a minstrel? Why not rob him and cast him aside?" Aldrich asked.

Monet felt tears fill her eyes. She looked to Broderick, fury plain on his face.

"Bronson," Broderick began, "you must set the village at the ready. A Rothbainian arrow though a minstrel's back . . . a minstrel who claims he was at Ballist so near Ballain . . ."

"King James is stretching his arms," Bronson said.

Broderick nodded. He looked from Bronson to Monet.

"Forgive my Prissy, Aldrich," he said. "She is weary and must retire."

"Take her then, Broderick," Sarah said. "Bronson and I will linger to help here."

"I am so sorry," Monet whispered, yet caressing the bruised and bloody brow of the minstrel.

"I know it is frightening, Prissy," the miller said, "but it is no fault of yours."

Monet forced herself to nod at the miller—though she well knew Reynard's condition was full her fault.

"Ballist is too close," Broderick said as they hastened to the cottage. "If there are Rothbainians lurking there . . . then they will soon seek out Ballain."

"Who do you think holds brave in Ballist, Broderick?" Monet asked. Fear was full in her soul. Of whom had the minstrel spoken? Who held brave in Ballist?

Broderick shook his head. "It is not the king. He would not be so easily captured . . . and what reason would James have for taking him to Ballist? If that is what you are thinking . . . that it is somehow your father . . . it is not."

Still, Monet breathed yet with little ease.

"Will we flee Ballain?" she whispered as they entered the cottage.

Broderick closed the door and drew the bolt across it.

"Ballain is one of the farthest townships from Karvana," Broderick said. "If King James's reach finds Ballain . . . it will find any village." His eyes narrowed as he looked at her. "We will be watchful of strangers. We will hide ourselves in the woods." He frowned, his eyes moist with emotion. "But know this. Whatever comes . . . I would die in preserving you, Monet."

"Do not talk of death, Broderick! Please do not speak such things," she said.

At once he gathered her into his arms, warm

against the strength of him. Monet let her arms embrace him tight—wept against his strong chest.

"Very well," he said, his voice low and soothing. "We will linger through the night. On the morrow we must plan. But for now, I will keep you warm in our bed . . . safe in my arms."

Monet pressed to him, desperation coursing through her being. She would hold him—for he was hers! Sir Broderick Dougray—the Crimson Knight—the horseman of Ballain—he belonged to her full body and heart, and she to him.

The noises of the night seemed loud and strange to Broderick. As his beloved lay restless in his arms, he listened. He would not sleep; he had known he would not. Yet there had been no manner other in which to lead Monet into bed and sleeping. His mind told him to run—that they should not linger in Ballain. Yet to flee in winter's cold—without preparation—he was uncertain as to the wisdom in that too. In truth, his heart had surrendered—to his love for Monet. For the weeks past he had bathed in the beauty of her love for him—pushed thoughts of war and knighthood to the far corners of his mind. Yet he remembered now, he was a knight—First Knight of Karvana, Guardian of the Scarlet Princess, Blood Warrior of Ballist—and a fight was coming to him. Of this he was certain.

The Crimson Knight drew his wife tight to his chest—buried his face in the sweet fragrance of her soft hair. Gently, he kissed the back of her neck, tasting her flesh. He well knew he could be killed in preserving her. Yet he cared only for her—her life and love.

Of a sudden, Monet turned in his arms. Though he could not see her eyes for the dark in the cottage, he knew she looked for him, for he felt her soft hand at his cheek.

"My pretty knight is plagued with worry and planning," she whispered.

Her fingers caressed his lips as he said, "Yes." He felt her mouth press warm and inviting to his own, and he returned her kiss once—twice—took her mouth with his own as his passionate love for the Scarlet Princess consumed him.

"Yet why did they choose to beat a minstrel?" Bronson asked. "It is sure they were searching for any who might own information. But a minstrel?"

"Oh, it is true they are often weak of body and light-minded," Broderick said. "When in truth . . . who hears more than a minstrel? Are they not often present in banquet halls, throne rooms, and village squares? Sitting silent, save for when they are plucking lutes and singing ballads . . . who would have better opportunity to hear ill-guarded secrets?"

Monet glanced up to Sarah, who nodded in agreement with her husband.

It was long Broderick and Bronson were conversing in the forge. Broderick was helping Bronson to ready weapons—for the men in the village—and for himself.

Monet rose, for the forge was stifling and the talk of weapons and battle frightening.

"Monet?" Broderick asked, however.

"I only mean to breathe a breath without, Broderick," she said. He had not let her from his sight since the night before, and she was well glad of it. Yet the forge was so dark and close.

"I will go with her," Sarah said. "Just without . . . for only a short time."

Broderick opened his mouth to forbid it, but Bronson's hand on his shoulder calmed him.

"If they keep to smithy wall?" Bronson asked.

Broderick nodded. "Keep to the wall," he said.

"Yes," Monet agreed.

Sarah pulled her cloak tight about her shoulders as they stepped from the smithy into the cool air of winter's morning.

"We shall be needing furs soon," Sarah said.

"It is colder," Monet said. She followed Sarah to the side wall of the smithy, where sat a small bench. The two sat down upon the bench, and Monet laid her head back against the wall.

The village seemed so still. She could hear the distant lapping of the mill wheel still lifting water from the pond. In the distance, children laughed, and a breeze whispered through her hair.

"Princess Monet?"

Was it the whisper of the breeze she heard—a whisper so soft as to own the timidity of a child's voice? Yet when she felt Sarah's hand at her arm, Monet opened her eyes. She could not draw breath—not even gasp. Her lips parted as horror fair entombed her—yet she could not speak—she dared not—for the sharp blade of a dagger pressed the tender flesh of the boy's throat. He was dirty—dried blood at the corner of his mouth, the deep purple of painful bruising at one swollen cheek. His page's cloak was torn, his dark hair matted and disheveled.

"Channing?" Monet whispered as tears left her eyes to rain over her cheeks.

"Do not speak," Sir Fredrick Esmund commanded in a whisper, "lest I slit his throat and bleed him out before you."

The Bravest Page

"Do not cry out, Princess," Channing whispered, tears brimming in his frightened eyes. "All will be well."

"Release the boy," Sarah demanded.

"Hush, woman!" Sir Fredrick growled. Monet did not breathe as Sir Fredrick's dagger blade hard pressed Channing's throat, the tip of it drawing blood just beneath Channing's left ear. "I *will* kill him."

"Sarah," Monet said in a whisper. "Pray do not press Sir Fredrick. Make no sound."

"Come with me, Princess," Sir Fredrick growled. "Come with me. Bring your friend . . . and we will discuss the boy's life."

"You are dead if you go with him," Sarah whispered.

Monet looked to her beloved friend—wept for the tears brimming in Sarah's eyes.

"Channing is dead if I do not," she whispered.

"Make haste," Sir Fredrick breathed. "If you summon the blacksmith in any way, I will open the boy's neck."

Monet rose, as did Sarah.

Oh, how Monet wanted to cry out—call for Broderick! Yet Channing's frightened eyes, the bruising about him, his disheveled appearance— Sir Fredrick would kill Channing if Monet cried out. Of this she was certain.

Monet and Sarah kept to the backs of the cottages, as Sir Fredrick instructed. No one saw them, for the village was yet quiet, the cold of morning still lingering upon it. He led them into the wood—near to the cropping of holly Broderick had once led her to—once kissed her before. Monet wondered then—would she ever know his kiss again? Was her beloved lost to her, as perhaps her own life may be?

"Far enough," Sir Fredrick said. As he paused to look about—to ensure their privacy—Monet acted. Lunging toward him, she drew a second dagger from a sheath at his waist. Holding the dagger firm with two hands, she pressed the tip of the blade to her bosom.

"Release him!" she cried out. "Release the boy and Sarah . . . or King James will have you executed for failing in your charge!"

"Princess!" Channing cried. Sarah gasped but stood firm.

Sir Fredrick's eyes widened. He was unsettled—yet held fast to Channing.

"I will kill the boy," Sir Fredrick growled. "Do you doubt I will do it?"

"I do not," Monet said, "for you are a filthy

coward! Yet kill him . . . and you will not bring me back to King James alive. And he does want me alive . . . does he not? Else you would have killed me at first sight."

In truth, Monet knew she could not plunge the blade into her bosom—she would never and could never take her own life or any others. Yet she hoped Sir Fredrick were not so certain of her incapability.

Sir Fredrick's eyes narrowed. "The boy has told us of your father's forced marriage." Monet looked to Channing. Tears were streaming over his young cheeks, and Monet wondered what abuse he had endured—what harm had come to him that would cause him to reveal her marriage. Yet she did not fault one so young of revealing while being beaten and tortured. Ever she had adored young Channing, just as her father favored him. She felt only love and compassion for Channing—loathing and anger for those who had harmed and pressed him.

"Yes . . . the boy told us of your father's valiant attempt to preserve the royal bloodline of Karvana. If I release the boy, he will no doubt hasten to the village to inform your decrepit old husband that you have been taken. Elderly or not, Lord Shelley is still able enough to raise an alarm that you have been taken."

Monet frowned. She did not speak, though perplexed. She must think. Lord Shelley? Lord

Robert Shelley was an ancient noble of Karvana, steward of the village of Neville beyond Karvana Far. Monet looked to Channing. The frightened blue eyes of her father's favored page seemed to plead with her—and she understood. Though Channing had been captured, beaten, and threatened into revealing King Dacian's charge of exile where Monet was concerned, the young boy had somehow been able to keep the name of Monet's true husband as secret. Channing was Lord Shelley's grandson, and he—knowing Lord Shelley was of a branch of near-extinct royalty—had been sharp of wit—known such a marriage would have seemed plausible enough to King James to be believed.

"Lord Shelley will indeed raise the alarm," Monet said. "Yet the alarm will be raised in like manner when it is discovered I am gone. Thus release the boy to Sarah . . . with instruction to linger . . . and I will go with you. Willing I will go if you release them. If you do not . . . I will die, and King James will be thwarted." Monet brushed tears from her cheek. "Release him! You are causing him pain and fear! If you do not release him, I swear I will not return with you . . . not alive."

"Hush, woman! Lest you raise the alarm yourself and watch the boy bleed out before you!" Sir Fredrick growled.

Monet tried to calm her trembling. Oh, why

had they left the forge? For the sake of fresh air? She was self-loathing at her own weakness. Broderick had not wanted her to leave his side—yet she had pressed him, and he had allowed it. Her mind silently shouted his name—cried out for him—*Broderick!*

Monet inhaled a deep breath of courage—pressed the dagger tip near painful to her bosom.

"You are not alone. I am sure you are not, Sir Fredrick," Monet said. "Then release the boy. Order that he should linger here with this woman until we are well away . . . even there is a small clearing behind the crop of holly . . . there," she said, nodding toward the holly. "Let them shelter there till nightfall. Even leave a man to watch them from afar to ensure they do as you have commanded. They may go to the village after sunset . . . if Lord Shelley does not miss me first. It will be impossible for the villagers to track us at night. Do this . . . or you will not return me living to King James."

Monet watched as Sir Fredrick's eyes narrowed. "You will come of your own accord?"

"You have my word," she said.

"Swear it!" Sir Fredrick growled. "On this boy's life . . . swear you will not struggle . . . that you will accompany me willingly."

"I swear it!" Monet cried. "Now release them, or I will sure pluck out my own heart!"

Sir Fredrick's eyes narrowed. He studied her

for a moment, no doubt uncertain in trusting her word. Trembling, Monet stood firm. He must believe she meant to die before letting him kill Channing. Though she would not take her own life, she would fright Sir Fredrick to her death at his hand before she would see Channing killed.

Channing cried out as Sir Fredrick pushed him forward and into Sarah's arms. Sarah embraced Channing, smoothing his disheveled hair, kissing his tear-stained cheeks.

"Come to me, Princess Monet," Sir Fredrick growled. "I have your word . . . and I may yet throw the dagger through his heart!"

"Princess!" Channing cried.

"Silence!" Sir Fredrick barked.

Monet lowered the dagger she held, offering it to Sir Fredrick as she walked to him.

Instantly, he took her arm—brutal gripped in his hand.

"It is I think King James would see me delivered unharmed . . . as well as alive, Sir Fredrick," she said.

He glared at her, eyes narrowed with loathing.

"You! Woman!" Sir Fredrick barked, looking to Sarah. "Do not speak to this boy. And, boy . . . if you speak one word to this woman before sunset . . . my men will tell me if you do, and it will not bode well for Karvana's princess. Do you understand?"

Channing brushed tears from his cheeks, nodding.

"Woman?"

Sarah nodded as well—held Channing tight and protected against her body.

"Then come, Scarlet Princess of Karvana," Sir Fredrick said. He smiled, a triumphant smile of arrogance. "King James awaits."

Monet looked to Channing. "You are a brave boy, love," she began, "and a very wise friend." She looked then to Sarah. "Tell Lord Shelley of my love for him."

Sarah nodded, brushing at her tears.

Monet brushed more tears from her face—paused, saying, "Do as you are told, Channing . . . Sarah," she said. "Wait until sunset. Then seek out my husband. It is well you know he will care for you. He will come for me. You know that he will. Your quick wit has saved us, love."

"Lord Shelley, indeed," Sir Fredrick chuckled. "Dacian assured knew pure desperation in preserving his line . . . to wed you to a relic the likes of Shelley. Come then, Princess," Sir Fredrick said, tugging her arm, "for you have given your word."

Monet gasped as Sir Fredrick took hold of the back of her dress, pulling her away from the frightened boy—from her beloved friend—from Broderick's protective reach.

"See that they do not speak . . . nor leave the

grove till sunset. If they attempt any conversation or escape, bring them to me," Sir Fredrick ordered as a Rothbainian soldier approached. Monet breathed a quiet sigh. She had hoped Sir Fredrick owned a breath of chivalry. As a knight—even as a knight of Rothbain—he was bound to honor his word.

Sarah and Channing would be well. Further, they would be found—and soon. Monet knew Broderick would miss her. Ever watchful as he was, perhaps he had already missed her. He would find Channing and Sarah, and he would come for Monet. Of a sudden, Monet was not so frightened as she had been a moment before—for she knew Broderick loved her and would come for her.

She looked at Sir Fredrick as he led her through the wood. Even she stared at him.

"Why do you study me so, Princess?" he asked. "Are you wishing your father had wed you to one so handsome as I . . . and not some relic of the kingdom past?" He chuckled.

"I was only just imagining how you will look without your head," she began, "for my husband will surely see you bled out by his own hand if you harm me."

Sir Fredrick sneered. "Lord Shelley bleed me out? And I am the fairy king, Princess."

"I hope the man you left to guard my friend and the boy . . . I hope he did not mean so much to you," Monet said as she yet walked beside him. "For if my husband should come upon him . . . if your man should engage my husband . . . he will not be returning to you. Not alive."

Sir Fredrick laughed. "Do not tell me . . . do not tell me you have found feelings for this man your father wed you to!"

"Do not endeavor in arrogance over my husband, Sir Fredrick. It may well cost you your life," Monet said.

Sir Fredrick continued to chuckle, however. "Ah, Princess," he sighed. "In the least the return to Karvana may be amusing in your company."

Monet said no more. She would keep her secret—the true identity of her husband. And when the Crimson Knight came for her—when he bested Sir Fredrick at war as easily as he had in lances at Ivan's tournament—full she would relish the expression on the villain's face then. Broderick would come for her. She must know patience and keep her wits about her till he did.

"They are not at the cottage," Broderick growled. "The false woodpile has not been touched."

"Sarah would not allow the princess to leave," Bronson said. He ran one trembling hand over the smoothness of his head.

"They have been taken," Broderick said. "My soul tells me it is true."

Bronson hurried to the wall of the smithy.

Quickly, he took down several swords—including the Crimson Frost he had once shown to Broderick.

Handing the Crimson Frost to Broderick, Bronson shouted, "Stroud! Wallace!" A moment later, as Bronson secured his own to his waist, Stroud and Wallace entered.

"Father?" Stroud asked.

Broderick could see by the manner in which the boys stood at the ready—their father had trained them for battle.

"Wallace," Bronson began. "Bring Kenley. Tell Birch to stay with Carver and Dane. Your mother and the princess have been taken."

"Mother?" Wallace exclaimed.

"The Gauntlet is yours, Stroud," Bronson said, handing the longsword to his son. Stroud nodded and strapped the sheathed sword at his waist. "You may choose your weapon, Wallace," Bronson said. "You and Kenley may choose . . . and then you will go to the miller. Tell him the village is in danger. We must arm ourselves . . . all of us."

"Yes, Father," Wallace said, taking his leave at once.

Bronson gathered daggers then, handed two to Broderick, and placed two in his own belt.

"We will find them, my friend," Broderick said. He could feel his knightly strength returned—and with it his rage.

Bronson nodded. "We will."

Broderick had never known such fear. When he had left the smithy in search of Monet—when he had not found her near—he had been fearful near to madness. Calm and rational thinking had been lost to him for a time. Yet he had breathed deep a moment—stood pensive for a time. He knew King James would not order Monet killed—that he would want her delivered to him alive and well, to serve whatever villainous purpose he owned. In his heart Broderick knew his beloved wife lived—though he was not so certain of Bronson's. Still, he thought Sarah might be used as a pawn—a tool of convincing Monet to do as she was commanded. In this, Broderick hoped Bronson's beloved was yet well.

In striding from the cottage back to the smithy, his strength had been renewed. The strength of the First Knight of Karvana had returned—as well as his wisdom and wit.

"We will track them," Broderick said.

Bronson nodded. "Then let us do so."

"There were no tracks near the cottage," Broderick said as they stepped from the smithy into the cold of winter. "And Monet would not have gone far for the breath of air she begged." He shook his head. "I should not have lost sight of her . . . not for even a breath."

"Do not linger on regret, my friend," Bronson said. "Go forward and leave the past where it is."

Broderick looked about the ground outside the smithy. The snow and mud were mingled. There were many footprints. His eyes searched—his mind battled as he studied the markings in the mud and snow.

"Here," he said, squatting low and gesturing to a place nearby. "These are theirs . . . Monet's and Sarah's. Small . . . not so deep as the others."

"Yes," Bronson said. "It is hard to see . . . but they trod here."

Standing, Broderick followed the tracks to the side of the smithy—to the bench against one wall.

"They took respite here," Bronson said.

Broderick continued to frown as he looked about. Of a sudden, he slowly cocked his head to one side. "What is this?" he asked.

Bronson and Stroud gathered near to Broderick.

"A child?" Stroud asked.

Broderick nodded. "And an armored man."

"How know you he was armored, Sir Broderick?" Stroud asked.

"The print is deep . . . and the shape . . ." Broderick said, tracing the print with his finger.

"The shape is that of a sabaton, Stroud," Bronson mumbled.

"Foot armor," Stroud said.

"Yes. And the print is deep enough in the mud that one can make out the rowel spur at the heel." Bronson stood, frowning. "But what child is this?

Surely we would be now alerted if there were a child missing from the village."

Broderick looked at the tracks—studied them carefully.

"Here," he said. "Leading toward the wood. The child was near dragged . . . yet Monet and Sarah led." His heart began to hammer mad in his chest.

"He threatened the child's life, no doubt," Bronson said. "They went for sake of the child."

Broderick nodded as he followed the tracks toward the wood. He thought of the day he had taken Monet into the grove of pines, near the holly cropping. His mouth watered at the remembered kisses they shared. He began to tremble, fear of losing his lover quick gripping him. Inhaling deep, he calmed himself, however. He would be no use to Monet if he allowed fear to own him.

"This knight would not be alone," Bronson said, drawing his sword as they approached the wood. "At the ready, Stroud," he growled.

Broderick heard Stroud draw his sword—drew the Crimson Frost from its sheath as he stepped between the trees.

Near instantly a soldier was upon him. Swift, the Crimson Knight blocked the soldiers down-thrusting sword, running the enemy through in the next moment. Another man appeared— then two more. Blades flashed, the sound of steel against steel echoing through the wood. Broderick fought fierce, as did Bronson and Stroud. It seemed mere moments before he stood, breathing heavy, gazing down at the four dead Rothbainian soldiers littering the ground—bleeding red upon the Ballain snow.

One Rothbainian moaned, and Broderick was quick upon him.

Placing a foot to the man's throat where he lay, the Crimson Knight growled, "Where have they been taken?" The wounded soldier did not answer—simply glared at Broderick with proud defiance. Broderick removed his foot from the soldier's throat, slipping the tip of the Crimson Frost through the space between his helmet and breastplate. "I will take your breath and bleed you slow out if you do not speak!" he shouted. "Where have they been taken?"

"Sir Broderick?"

Broderick looked up when he heard the child's voice. From behind the cropping of holly, a boy emerged—and Sarah.

"Channing?" Broderick breathed as recognition fast struck him. The bruised and disheveled boy ran forward. Sobbing, Channing threw himself against the great Crimson Knight, and Broderick embraced him.

"Mother!" Broderick heard Stroud exclaim. Bronson was fast to his lover, gathering her in his arms and kissing her.

"Channing?" Broderick breathed. He fell to his knees, taking the boy's face between his hands. "Where is Monet?" he asked—for fear gripped him once more. Sarah was well, and so was Channing—however he was brought to Ballain. Yet Monet—Monet was not with them. "Where is the princess?"

"Sir Broderick!" Channing cried. "They have taken her! Crimson Knight! They have taken the princess!"

"Rothbainians?" he asked—though he knew already it was true.

"Sir Fredrick and his men!" the boy sobbed.

"Fredrick," Broderick breathed.

"Tell your knight, boy," Bronson said, kneeling beside Channing. "Tell your great Crimson Knight the tale . . . and he will champion her."

Channing nodded—brushed tears from his cheeks.

"I-I was sent on an errand from the castle. I was sent to the village . . . with information for the Minstrel Marius. The king dressed me as a peasant and bade me find Marius . . . that I might deliver his instructions," Channing said.

"Penned instructions?" Broderick asked.

Channing nodded. "But I dropped them. With purpose I dropped them as I was being carried to King James."

"You are wise far beyond your years, boy," Bronson said.

"Go on, Channing. Tell me the tale," Broderick prodded.

"A soldier came upon me before I reached the Emerald Crown . . . before I reached Marius," Channing said. "He struck me, put me on his horse, and took me to an encampment . . . King James's encampment in the north. He beat me, Sir Broderick. He beat me, and yet I would not tell them of the king's exile of the princess," he cried. "I endeavored to tell them nothing, Sir Broderick," Channing whispered. "I tried not to tell them of the exile . . . and they beat me more . . . so long and so hard did they beat me . . . and then . . . and still I did not tell them. But then . . . then they swore they would kill her!"

"They meant to kill Monet?" Broderick asked. The others had gathered around—listened well. Broderick's breath came labored. Had he been so wrong? Did James truly mean to have Monet murdered instead of simply taken?

Channing shook his head. "No . . . not her . . . the other princess . . . the one they had taken already. They held her before me. They . . . they cut her deep at one shoulder. They . . . they said they would kill her if I did not reveal what I knew. I could not watch a princess bleed out, Sir Broderick! I could not!"

"Of course not, Channing," Broderick said. "Of course not."

"And so . . . I told them the princess had been sent into exile with her husband. This I told them . . . though I did not tell them you are her husband, Crimson Knight," the boy sobbed. "I-I told them the king had wed her to old Lord Shelley . . . my grandfather. I did not tell them the Crimson Knight was the Scarlet Princess's husband."

"That was wise, Channing. Very wise," Broderick whispered.

"What other princess is this they have, boy?" Bronson asked.

"Princess Anais . . . King Rudolph's daughter," Channing said.

Broderick looked to Bronson as full understanding met them both.

"He would use the daughter to own Alvar's legions," Bronson said.

Broderick nodded. He looked back to Channing then.

"This was near Karvana they beat you, Channing . . . yes?" he asked.

Channing nodded. "At the encampment without the village."

"And the other princess . . . and King James . . . they remain near Karvana. Sir Fredrick and his men brought you here . . . but they remain?"

Again Channing nodded. "They did not know where to look for Princess Monet," he explained, "for I did not know where you had taken her. Others were sent to look . . . but Sir Fredrick chose to look in Karvana Far . . . and then Ballist. In Ballist there was a minstrel. He sang for the people . . . the ballad of a 'The Crimson Frost' . . . and then a new ballad . . . one I had not heard before."

" 'The Champion's Prize,' " Broderick mumbled.

Channing nodded. "Sir Fredrick did not so much listen to the ballad as he did watch the minstrel," he said. "I heard him say the minstrel put him much in mind of another . . . of Marius . . . whom he had heard once in Karvana. Sir Fredrick suspected the minstrel of . . . I do not know his thoughts, only that he ordered his men to beat him. And then . . . they let him escape. Sir Fredrick and his men followed the minstrel to Ballain. They brought me . . . for they knew the princess would not see me harmed."

The boy began sobbing then. "It is my fault, Sir Broderick. I have failed the king and the kingdom. I am traitor to the crown for I have caused that my princess is in danger!"

"No, Channing. No," Broderick assured him.

"Somehow they knew I was from the castle. It is my fault Princess Monet is gone!"

"Channing," Broderick began, "do you know why you were there . . . in the princess's bower the day we were wed? Do you know why only you, the friar, Marius, and the king himself knew of the exile?"

Channing shook his head—wiped tears from his cheeks.

"Because I chose you, Channing," Broderick said. "You have ever been the princess's pet . . . have you not? Does not she delight in your friendship? Does not King Dacian trust you with his most important of messages?"

"Yes," Channing said.

"I chose you, for there would be two witnesses to any marriage . . . that it may be sure," Broderick continued. "Marius was one, for he had a part to play in our exile. You were the other, for I never imagined the enemy would suspect you of owning such secrets of war."

"You chose me?" Channing asked.

"I did," Broderick said.

"And I failed you!" the boy sobbed.

"No, Channing. You championed us all. You are the bravest page any kingdom has ever known! You did not reveal all to Sir Fredrick. In causing him to think Monet is wed to your grandfather, you have ensured that he will not expect how wholly he has vexed the Crimson Knight . . . her true husband."

A small smile curled Channing's pale lips. "And the Crimson Knight will lop off Sir Fredrick's head if he harms Karvana's princess," he said.

Broderick smiled as well, tousled the boy's

hair, and added. "Yes. You have proven I choose my allies well, Channing."

"Truly?" Channing asked.

"What other boy in all the world would have the wit and courage to lie when being beaten?" Bronson said, his booming laughter echoing through the forest.

"Indeed," Broderick said.

"Will you go now?" Channing asked. "Will you rescue our princess at once, Sir Broderick?"

"Yes," Broderick said, "though I will first return to the village for my armor and horse."

"Your armor?" Channing asked. "But I saw your armor, Sir Broderick. I was the one who moved it from the princess's bower when you had gone. The king bade me bring it to him."

Broderick smiled. "Do you think a knight would wed a princess wearing his battle armor?" he asked. Channing's young brow furrowed. He was sore perplexed. "It was my armor worn at banquet and celebration you took to the king. My battle armor is here with me. Ever it has been."

"But you have no horse," Channing said.

Broderick was astonished by the change in the boy. For one so young, he mustered courage and hope well.

"Oh, I am not without a horse, Channing," he said. "Though I hold no charger here . . . I brought the fastest horse my stables have ever bred. His name is Tripp."

"And you will ride . . . lop off Sir Fredrick's head, and rescue the princess," Channing said, smiling.

Bronson chuckled, and Broderick looked to see Sarah brush tears from her cheeks.

"She was brave, Broderick," Sarah said. "She held a dagger at her own bosom that the boy and I should be left safe."

Broderick's massive body shuddered as he thought of Monet in the hands of Sir Fredrick Esmund—in the arms of King James.

"She is wise and witty, Broderick," Bronson said. "She will know how best to keep herself safe until we arrive."

Channing turned then. "You are familiar to me," he said, pointing to Stroud.

"I am familiar?" Stroud asked. "How so?"

Channing looked to Sir Bronson. "Even you are in my mind, sir."

"The boy is battle-worn, Broderick," Bronson said. "We must get him warmed . . . fed and rested."

"Come, darling," Sarah said, taking Channing's hand. "You and I have endured much together. Let us keep company the rest of the way.

"I know you now! A likeness of you hangs in my mother's room!" Channing exclaimed, of a sudden. "You are she! The lost princess of Karvana! You are banished Princess Eden!"

"His mother was my greatest friend," Sarah explained to Broderick as she sat stroking Channing's sleepy head where it lay in her lap. Though desperate to begin, to find Monet and strip her from King James's evil grip, Broderick listened well as he armored himself—as the lost princess of Karvana spoke.

"Lord Shelley's youngest daughter, Joy." Sarah sighed, a soft laugh escaping her throat. "How merry we were, we two silly girls . . . endlessly fawning over the handsome knights of the kingdom." Sarah closed her eyes. "It was all so long ago."

Broderick nodded as Stroud secured the Crimson Knight's left gauntlet.

"Dacian was healthy . . . in line for the throne," Sarah said. "Thus, when Ackley and I . . . we went to my father, King Seward . . . told him of our love and our desire to wed . . . my father granted permission. Sir Ackley Carrington was the son of Prince Phillip of Devshire. Though not in line for the throne, yet he was worthy . . . and of royal blood. Father consented . . . and then . . . and then came James of Rothbain. "

"King James?" Broderick asked, pausing in his armoring.

Sarah nodded. "James's father often threatened mine with war. He coveted Karvana the way some men want a woman they cannot have.

My father, weakened by age and arrogance, struck hands with King Nathan, then the king of Rothbain . . . and James's father. No doubt King Nathan thought he could work through me, to throw my father from Karvana's throne and seat himself as king. No doubt my father believed a union between the families would serve to silence any talk of war. Thus, he promised my hand to James of Rothbain. He said I would not marry Ackley . . . that he would banish me if I sought further to even speak with him."

"King Seward was fearful Eden would defy him," Bronson said, tugging his breastplate into place. "And so he sent an assassin to kill me. Me . . . a knight of the table round of conferring of Karvana!"

"Ackley killed the assassin, of course. Still, I knew Father would not cease in his attempts to kill Ackley," Sarah said. "Thus, I begged Ackley to take us from Karvana. I knew my brother, Dacian, would ascend to the throne soon . . . for father was ill and could not live long. Dacian would have granted us permission to wed . . . put off King Nathan and Prince James. But I did not want to wait for another assassin to try to murder my lover at my own father's bidding. And so we fled. My father pronounced we had been banished, of course . . . that Ackley had seduced and ruined me . . . and that he had banished us."

"And James's pride aches still," Broderick mumbled.

"I own no regret . . . save one," Bronson said. His armor shone bright in the cottage, even for the lack of bright light.

"The banishment of your brothers . . . the Knights Exemplar," Broderick said.

Bronson nodded. "Yet even for that—even for the shame unfairly heaped upon them—I have my Eden . . . my life . . . and my sons."

"As I will have my Monet," Broderick growled.

"The horses are ready, Father . . . and Wallace has summoned all the village to the square," Kenley said as he entered the cottage.

Broderick smiled as Kenley's eyes widened. He looked first to Broderick, then to his father—the great Knight Exemplar, Sir Ackley Carrington.

"It is long I have wished to see you full armored, Father," the young man said.

"As have I," Stroud said.

Wallace nodded, and Broderick knew the pride rising in the bosoms of Sir Ackley Carrington's sons.

"Mother says you will one day be our king, Sir Broderick," young Dane said.

Broderick sighed. "It may be," he said, "for the woman I love is your Scarlet Princess, and I would brave any horror for her . . . even if it means I must be king one day."

"You will be a great king, Sir Broderick," Sarah

said, "as great as ever was Dacian. It is why he chose you."

"He chose me to protect Karvana's heart," Broderick began, "and I have failed." He would not weaken—though his heart was fearful, his body angry and aching to slay any who might harm his Monet.

"No!" Sarah said firm. "Her heart is beating still for sake of you. Dacian chose you as successor king, Broderick . . . for he knows Karvana's heart. He knows Monet loves you . . . that you love her more than anything, even life itself. He knows you are the greatest of men and will sit the throne of Karvana as the greatest of rulers. It is well I know my brother . . . even for all the years that have passed. He thought first of his daughter's heart, yes—yet of the kingdom's heart and welfare as well. Who better to preserve the princess and the kingdom than the great Crimson Knight?"

Broderick inhaled. Sarah was wise, and he would not linger on thoughts of failure. He was armored. He bore weapons—even the finest of swords, the Crimson Frost, forged by the great Exemplar Knight, Sir Ackley Carrington. He was the Crimson Knight of Karvana, Sir Broderick Dougray—son of Kendrick Nathair, First Knight of Karvana, Favored Warrior of King Dacian, Commander of the First Legion, Commander of the Second Legion, Slayer of a Thousand

Enemies, Blood Warrior of Ballist, Protector of the Kingdom, Guardian and lover of the Scarlet Princess—and he could not be kept from her. Not Sir Fredrick Esmund nor King James of Rothbain—not the Reaper, Lord Death himself—none would bar him from Monet.

"Come, my friend, Blacksmith . . . my brother knight," Broderick said. "We ride for Karvana's heart!"

Bronson's smile grew to a chuckle—his chuckle to booming laughter. "We ride!" he shouted.

"Stroud . . . Wallace," Bronson began as the Crimson Knight and the great Exemplar Ackley stepped from the cottage. "You will ride as well."

Each young man nodded.

"You will gather the Knights Exemplar. You know how to gather them. They will know where to meet," Bronson said.

Broderick smiled, placing a strong, gauntleted hand on Bronson's shoulder. "The brotherhood of the Exemplars is not broken then?"

"Never!" Bronson said, smiling. "And we . . . all Exemplars yet living . . . will ride for Karvana's heart, Karvana herself, and the good king, Dacian!"

Once mounted, Broderick and Bronson rode to the village square. Sir Broderick Dougray's heart swelled as he heard the familiar ring of his own armor—as he thought of battling the men who dared take his wife. He smiled at Bronson when an armored knight, mounted on a familiar horse, approached from beyond.

"You are nothing if not in secret," Broderick said as the Miller Aldrich raised his helmet shield. "And that is a good horse you sit."

"Sir Elton Kent, Knight Exemplar . . . at your service, Crimson Knight! But give me charge, and I will employ it," the miller laughed. "And by the by . . . the finest horseman of Ballain sold me this horse!"

"The minstrels of generations to come shall sing of Ballain," Broderick laughed. "Land of exiled knights!"

Bronson laughed, as did Aldrich.

"Gather men and arms, Sir Elton," Broderick said, "and meet Sir Ackley and I without Karvana in two days' time."

"It will be done," Sir Elton said.

The people of Ballain approached, and Broderick spurred Tripp to rearing once—twice—thrice.

"Good people!" the Crimson Knight shouted. Dressed in his battle armor and mounted on Tripp, Broderick hailed the people of Ballain gathering in the margin of the square. "I am Sir Broderick Dougray . . . First Knight of Karvana . . . and husband to your Scarlet Princess, Monet. I trust in your understanding of why we have been living among you in secret . . . for you are, each one, loyal Karvanians . . . are you not?"

The people cheered, and Broderick could see

the delight, pride, and loyalty full in their countenances. They were not angry at the necessary deception—only proud to know their princess had lingered among them as friend.

"King James is at Karvana's gate," Broderick near roared. "He threatens siege . . . and he has taken the princess . . . your future queen and my wife! We must not fail our future queen! We must not fail King Dacian! We must not let Karvana fall to James of Rothbain! Thus, I call every able man to arm himself . . . to battle for King Dacian and Karvana! As he who will one day be your king, as he who now endeavors that King Dacian may reign long and well before that day comes, I call you to bravery and force . . . that we may vanquish the enemy before Karvana falls!" Tripp reared, snorted, and beat the ground with strong hooves. "Sir Elton Kent, Knight Exemplar, will lead you . . . for Sir Ackley Carrington, Knight Exemplar and husband of the Karvana's lost Princess Eden, will not linger . . . nor will I. I go to retrieve the priceless jewel stolen from us. I go to save the Princess Monet . . . the heart of Karvana! But you . . . you must protect this life you know . . . lest it be taken from you forever! Are you willing?"

Broderick smiled as the cheers of the people broke the stillness of the winter air. Again Tripp reared, anxious to be gone—to move swift as the north wind.

"Then, men of Ballain, gather your arms . . . for you must march this very day!" Broderick shouted. "We will strike the enemy dead . . . rain a crimson frost upon them!"

The people cheered, and Broderick turned to Sir Elton.

"Sir Elton," he began, "in two days, at sunrise, you must be there . . . at Karvana's back."

"We will be there, Sir Broderick," said the miller, Sir Elton. "The devil himself will not keep us."

Broderick nodded. He glanced beyond the village to the cottage—the place where he and Monet had first spoken of their love for one another. He looked to the smithy. Sarah was there, with young Channing at her side, looking on with Kenley, Birch, Carver, and Dane.

"The Scarlet Princess will be rescued, young Channing . . . and Karvana will triumph. All for your quick wit and impenetrable courage and loyalty," Broderick shouted. "For this, you will one day be well rewarded. Of that, you have my word."

The Crimson Knight drew his sword, forged for sake of the knight who bested the enemy and the Reaper in Ballist. Brandishing high the Crimson Frost, the Crimson Knight spurred Tripp to rearing.

"We ride!" he shouted.

Bronson laughed and spurred his mount.

As Broderick's mouth remembered the taste of Monet's kiss—his body the warm sense of hers held in his arms—the Crimson Knight rode hard, a great Knight Exemplar at his side. The pounding rhythm of strong hooves beating the winter ground, the feel of leather in his hands, caused his heart to hammer. He rode swift— as swift as he would plunge the blade of the Crimson Frost through the heart of Sir Fredrick Esmund and lop off the head of King James for having dared to touch his Scarlet Princess.

The Challenge and Price

"Take heart, Princess," King James began, "for you will yet reign over your beloved Karvana . . . as my queen."

"I fear I must decline, James," Monet said. "Karvana already has a successor king . . . and I already have a husband."

She glared at James of Rothbain, loath to see him, his brown hair swept through with gray, his piercing green eyes, his sharp nose, and his weak chin.

King James laughed. "Ah, yes . . . the aged Lord Shelley. Fredrick should well have killed him when the chance was at hand in Ballain. Nevertheless, Fredrick's mistake can be easily rectified. Though . . . I suppose it was your father's mistake first." King James laughed, shaking his head with amusement. "Lord Shelley? Was Dacian truly so desperate to see his bloodline preserved? He well knows I will defeat him here, for Rudolph will join me . . . and Karvana will fall, as will your father. And I will, at last, own Karvana's throne as well as Rothbain's. It is at it was meant to be . . . for I was to have had Karvana long ago."

"Meant to have Karvana long ago?" Monet said. "James . . . has madness joined ignorance in overtaking you?"

Monet gasped but did not cry out when the back of King James's hand met her cheek with brutal force.

"Seward's daughter, Eden, was promised me!" James growled. "I was to marry her . . . and in this I would have had Karvana's throne in my palm—for your father would not have lived long enough to take it . . . I assure you!" He inhaled deep, glaring at her. "Yet Eden was willful and rebellious. She took flight from Karvana . . . with a lowly knight of Seward's table. A knight! When she would have had a prince and two kingdoms to rule over!"

Monet was astonished at James's story. Her father's sister, Eden, promised to James of Rothbain? It was no wonder she fled with Sir Ackley! Still, she would not let him see she was affected, and though her heart beat fierce and her body trembled with fear, she would not let James be satisfied in it.

"I would warn you, James . . . do not strike me again," she said. "Already your life may be forfeit . . . for my husband will be sore vexed when you stand before him, begging for his mercy. And if evidence is seen that you have mistreated me . . . you will die."

Again James struck her. Monet did not cry out, however—though her entire body felt the sting of the brutal blow.

"Silence!" James shouted. "I will hear no more from your mouth this day!" He leveled a forefinger at her and growled, "I will have Karvana . . . and I will have you." He straightened his posture, still glaring at her as he continued. "I will not make idle threats of killing you. Dacian would not believe it, for he knows I must win the people once he is vanquished . . . and killing you would not win Karvanian hearts to me. Thus, I will take you to wife instead." His eyes narrowed, "I know you are thinking that you are wed already . . . but widows are not so uncommon a thing. Lord Shelley will no doubt seek you here, for his honor demands it. He shall be all too easily killed . . . and I will wed you to me. Oh, it is certain I must wait—ensure you do not already carry Shelley's child—for it would be impiety to risk there be another man's begotten in my castle. Yet as I wait . . . I will convince Rudolph to join me. We will lay siege to Karvana and vanquish her king."

"Rudolph will not join you," Monet said—though James had commanded her to speak no more. Yet his hand tight gripping her throat silenced her once again.

"Oh, he will join me," James growled, "for fathers so love their daughters." He snapped the fingers of his free hand. "Fredrick . . . I am weary of Princess Monet's company. Yet we dare not leave her to her fear and trembling in solitude. Bring her company."

Monet willed her tears to stay at bay; she could not show her weakness to James. He released his hold of her neck, and she glanced to Sir Fredrick. The villain who had brought her from Ballain to King James's battle camp just without Karvana village donned a triumphant grin.

"Guard!" Sir Fredrick shouted.

Monet could not conceal an astonished gasp as Anais of Alvar stepped into King James's pavilion then.

"Anais!" Monet breathed. The Princess of Alvar bore deep bruising on one cheek. Tears brimmed in her eyes, yet she held her posture straight.

"You see, Princess," James said, "Rudolph will join me in defeating Karvana . . . for he would not see his daughter harmed." James chuckled, for he no doubt saw the renewed fear on Monet's face. Karvana may defeat James of Rothbain, yes. But could she defeat Rudolph of Alvar as well?

"Let us leave the ladies to their fearful weeping, Fredrick," James said. "We must prepare . . . for Lord Shelley will no doubt be upon us by morning." He laughed, loud and with triumphant arrogance.

Sir Fredrick followed King James as he left

the pavilion. Two Rothbainian soldiers stepped inside and took up the guarding stance.

"Monet!" Anais cried, throwing trembling arms around Monet's neck. Monet had never owned a favorable thought of Anais of Alvar. Always she had thought Anais arrogant, willful, and deceptive. Yet in that moment, she was glad of a familiar face.

"Anais!" Monet cried, returning Anais frightened embrace. "How came you to be here?"

"Sir Fredrick," Anais whispered. "King James will use me to ensure my father will fight with him to win victory over Karvana!" Anais released Monet, shaking her head. "After Ivan's tournament . . . Sir Fredrick began to pen letters to me," she whispered. "He claimed to have fallen in love with me at the tournament . . . spoke of his unquenchable thirst to win my heart. Oh, such letters he did write, Monet! And I . . . I . . ."

"You believed him," Monet finished.

Anais nodded. "We planned to meet . . . that we may see each other at last," she said. "He killed Elizabeth, my lady in waiting, Monet! He ran his dagger across her throat!"

Monet felt tears at her cheeks.

Anais wept. "Elizabeth knew of the letters . . . and she bade me not to go," she said. "But I was willful—as ever I am willful—and so she said she would accompany me. She said she would linger behind . . . that she only wanted to ensure my safe conduct. But . . . when Sir Fredrick tried to force me to go with him, he took hold of Elizabeth. He said he would kill her if I did not go with him. I did not believe him . . . for he is a knight . . . is he not?"

Monet shook her head. "He is no knight—though titled he may be."

Anais nodded. "I did not believe Sir Fredrick when he said he would kill her. I only thought he was desperate to own me. I did not know he endeavored to bring me to King James in order that James may force my father to fight against King Dacian. I paused when he said he would kill her. I laughed and told him he was speaking nonsense . . . that of course I would not go with him. I was a princess of Alvar! I could not go to live with a knight." Anais buried her face in her hands as she wept. She shook her head, saying, "I did not think he would kill Elizabeth . . . but he did! When he put the dagger next to my throat . . . I knew he would kill me too."

Monet trembled—tried to force the vision of Sir Fredrick's dagger at Channing's throat from her mind. As they had traveled back to Karvana—as Sir Fredrick and his men had pushed her to riding so hard her body ached—ever she had wondered if she should have called out for Broderick when Sir Fredrick had threatened Channing. Monet had wondered—doubted—whether Sir Fredrick would truly have killed Channing if she had not followed his instructions. Yet now she knew—if Sir Fredrick could so easily kill Anais's lady, he could well as easy have killed Channing.

Monet was pure terrified! She knew she would not be killed, for James needed her still. Yet she now understood there was no honor about Sir Fredrick Esmund—nothing to prove he had kept his word where Sarah and Channing were concerned. Sarah and Channing had both been well—frightened but alive—when she had left them in the wood near the holly cropping. Yet now she feared they were not well. Had Sir Fredrick ordered the man he had left behind to watch them—had he in truth ordered that the man kill them? Even had there truly been only one man left in Ballain to guard them? Perhaps there were more! Sarah and Channing might have outwitted one man, but what if there were more than one?

"Broderick!" Monet cried in a whisper. What if Sir Fredrick had left many men behind—many men that may have attacked the village? What if Broderick were caught unprepared?

"What will we do, Monet?" Anais asked. "Surely we will both meet our doom . . . either in death or ruination!"

Closing her eyes, Monet endeavored to breathe steady. In her mind she could see Ballain. She could see Bronson laughing in watching his sons sparring with wooden swords. Sarah was there, stitching as ever she stitched, as was the merry miller, Aldrich, and his wife. Wilona's baby, Dacian, was in her thoughts and the poor minstrel, Reynard, who had sung ballads near as perfectly as did Marius himself. And ever— ever there was Broderick—tall, handsome, and strong! She could near feel his arms about her— near taste his kiss on her lips. Ever there had been Broderick. Ever had he been her mind and heart. He loved her—this she knew. He loved her, and he would come for her. She would believe that Channing and Sarah had somehow returned to Ballain—that they were safe in the arms of the Crimson Knight and a great Knight Exemplar. This she would believe—for her heart told her it was so.

"We will wait," Monet said. "We will wait . . . for my husband loves me, and he will come for me."

"Lord Shelley?" Anais whispered. "I heard the boy tell James your father wed you to Lord Robert Shelley. The young page from Karvana Castle . . . they beat him with little mercy, and he held his tongue. Yet when Sir Fredrick placed his dagger to my throat . . ." Anais clutched her throat with trembling hands, as if fearful she would yet find Sir Fredrick's dagger there. "The boy told them of your marriage to Lord Shelley. But, Monet . . . Lord Shelley cannot save us!"

"Lord Shelley is not my husband," Monet said.

Yet she paused in saying more. Anais was weak. She did not trust her to keep secrets from Sir Fredrick or King James. In truth, she knew she would easily give up any secret if it meant she could protect herself.

"But the boy . . . the page . . . he said Dacian married you to Lord Shelley. He said he was there . . . that he was witness," Anais said.

"We must wait, Anais," Monet said. "We must wait. We must, both of us, live through one more night of terror . . . for on the morrow, he will come for me."

"My father is to meet with King James at first light," Anais said. "James will not pause to lay siege to Karvana once my father has joined the battle."

"My husband will not let me linger here," Monet whispered, "nor will he let Karvana fall."

"Perhaps you are not married to Lord Shelley, Monet," Anais said. "But unless you are married to some king unknown to the five kingdoms who commands legion upon legion to battle James . . . what hope have you in the morrow?"

"I have love, Anais," Monet said. "And he will find me . . . even if he has to slay James's army as well as your father's to do it."

Monet closed her eyes once more. She would endure. She would endure the night—the fear and threat—even she would endure the back of King James's hand to her face if needs be. For on the morrow, he would come. Monet knew that on the morrow the Crimson Knight would come for the heart of Karvana.

Eight there were—eight great Knights Exemplar armored and mounted before Sir Broderick Dougray. It was for a moment Broderick bathed in great humility, awed by the sight of the great Knights Exemplar pledging their allegiance to his command. The moonlight on their armor caused that they appeared to be ghosts—spirit knights returned from the clouds of heaven to defend their good kingdom. It was in this state of musing that Broderick fair expected the three long dead and buried Exemplars, Sir Garrick Jarvis, Sir Stanley Sheppard, and Sir Fairfax Ewing, to appear—to descend from the stars as wraithlike comrades to their knight brothers. Even he wondered if Sir Alum would appear, somehow knowing his brothers were gathering and leaving his charge to the north. Yet Sir Alum was a knight of Karvana. He would not abandon his king's charge, even to fight with his Exemplar brothers.

As the emerald banner of the Exemplar Knights waved, caught in the breath of the breeze, Broderick nodded to Bronson, and Bronson offered a nod in return.

"We have our plan, great knights of Karvana!" Broderick said. "We will employ it and triumph!

In doing so, we will save the lives of many of our people and soldiers from the senseless greed and vain arrogance of King James!"

"We ride! We battle! We win!" the Exemplar Knights shouted.

Smiling, the Crimson Knight raised his helmet shield. Ever he had heard tales of the battle cry of the great Exemplar Knights. Never had he hoped to hear the cry itself!

Stroud and Wallace looked on, as did Bronson's other four sons. Sarah and Channing had accompanied Sir Elton and the men of Ballain and Ballist to the wooded margin behind Karvana Castle.

Broderick turned to Stroud, Wallace, and the others. "Wallace," he said, "Channing will show you the way into the Karvana Castle. You must see him safe to the king that he may tell Dacian of our planning . . . of what must be done."

"Yes, Sir Broderick," Wallace said.

"Channing," Sir Broderick continued, "only you can carry this charge to tell the king of our plan. Take the secret path. You know the one."

"The dead queen will aid me, great Crimson Knight!" Channing said. Broderick smiled, pleased with the boy's wit. In this he knew Channing would sure take the secret tunnel leading from the mausoleum, where the bones of Monet's mother rested, to the castle and King Dacian.

"Yes," Broderick said. "Go then. For the time has come upon us."

"Stroud," Broderick said then to Bronson's eldest son. "You will lead the men of Ballain and Ballist to battle if needs be. Your father has trained you to do this . . . and I know that you can measure up to this charge given you. You are young but able and wise. If we fail in defeating James himself . . . then you must lead these men to strike him unaware."

"I will!" Stroud shouted.

"The sun will break the horizon soon!" Broderick shouted. "We will wait for the sun, and then we will vanquish our enemy!"

"We ride! We battle! We win!" The battle cry of the Exemplar Knights rose to the night air.

As the Crimson Knight sat mounted in waiting for the sun to rise, he thought not of battle and glory. Sir Broderick Dougray—successor king of Karvana, the Crimson Knight—thought of his love.

"Monet," he breathed. He would not be weakened by doubt of her safety or fear he may find her harmed. He would find her, tear her from the clutches of the enemy, hold her safe once more. Further, he had determined King James would pay for his crimes—for laying hands to Monet. James of Rothbain would linger no more in threatening Broderick's kingdom, his king, and the Scarlet Princess. As king successor, Broderick Dougray could claim the right to face James—to battle him alone for Karvana's sake. The Crimson Knight would strike the enemy's crown and end the war for the kingdom.

He heard an approach and turned to see Bronson mounted beside him.

"We will be victorious, Broderick," Bronson said. "Your princess will be in your arms once more, and the kingdom will be championed." He was pensive a moment. "It has been near eighteen years since I have seen Karvana's fields . . . the castle rising up like a great beacon of hope. Yet, here, at her back, as her protector . . . it seems no more than a day."

"Before the sun is midsky . . . I will fell a king," Broderick said. He looked to Bronson. "I will fell him . . . or I fall."

Bronson placed a strong hand on Broderick's armored shoulder. "You will not fall, Broderick. The Crimson Knight does not fall. Karvana's successor king does not fall. Further, Ivan's champion's prize awaits. What could a knight do for sake of such a prize?"

Broderick smiled. He looked to King James's encampment far beyond. He would hold Monet before the moon rose again. He would hold her safe in his arms—drink the nectar of her lips.

"What could a knight do for sake of such a prize?" he asked. "In the least, fell a king."

"I go first to meet your father, Rudolph, Princess Anais," King James said as a squire finished in armoring him. He looked to Monet then and said, "Then next to kill yours."

Monet said nothing. Simply she straightened her posture, silently praying for Broderick to find her—to save her father.

"You stand silent, Scarlet Princess," James chuckled. "Have you nothing to say? No threats to offer? Ah! Yes! I had quite forgotten. Lord Shelley will arrive today to rescue you." King James shrugged. "And that is well . . . at least for you. But what of Alvar's poor princess?"

"What?" Anais asked.

"Had you forgotten, Anais," King James said, "my promise to Sir Fredrick? You sore vexed him at Ivan's tournament last . . . and after he had borne your favour so well. It is sure Sir Fredrick is not one to be vexed and settle. Thus, you are my gift to him . . . for his service in procuring your father's army by way of taking you. Further, he fetched to me the Scarlet Princess of Karvana. I cannot gift him wealth, for he has all he would ever need. Thus, he has asked only for you, Princess Anais . . . as payment for his valiant service to Rothbain and her king. I thought you understood this already."

"My father will not fight against King Dacian if you do not release me," Anais said.

"Your father will fight . . . or you will die," King James said. "This is all he need know."

Of a sudden, Anais turned to Monet. It was well Monet knew the expression on her face—indignant rage.

"You said we need only wait, Monet!" Anais cried. "You said you were not married to Lord Shelley . . . that your true husband would come for you and we would be saved! How are we to be saved? It is the morrow now . . . and yet we linger as prisoners!"

"What is this? What lies do you endeavor to weave?" King James growled. He drew back his gauntleted hand, readying to strike Anais.

"It is not a lie!" Anais cried. "She told me last eventide. She told me her husband is not Lord Shelley. She carries hope her husband will come for her. She said he would slay your army and my father's to savior her."

"Lord Shelley is not your husband?" King James asked.

Monet glared at Anais, thankful she had not told the coward Princess of Alvar who her husband truly was.

"No," Monet said.

King James frowned a moment. Yet Monet's faith in his arrogance was made known, for he smiled next and said, "What matter is it to whom your father wed you? By midday I will have Rudolph of Alvar at my bidding. Nothing will keep me from conquering Dacian and taking his throne."

Of a sudden, a breathless soldier stumbled into the pavilion.

"My king!" the soldier panted. "You must come! Karvana's lost Knights Exemplar crest the hill at our back!"

"What?" King James asked. He shook his head—laughed pure amused. "What ploy is this that Dacian endeavors to make?" He struck the soldier hard across one cheek with the back of his gauntlet. "The Knights Exemplar are extinct! Thus they have been for near twenty years, boy!"

"Their banners herald them the Exemplar Knights—emerald banners, white symbols . . . rearing lion, a hound, a bull, an armored arm. These are the Exemplar Knights, my king. It is Sir Fredrick himself who confirms it!"

"How many?" King James said.

"Eight, my king."

"Eight?" King James laughed. "Sir Fredrick is a fool! If these are the lost Knights Exemplar . . . what are eight knights against two legions of men?"

"There is more," the soldier said. "They have King Rudolph . . . and . . . and . . . they are led by the Crimson Knight of Karvana."

Monet inhaled a deep breath, endeavoring to remain calm. He had come for her! Her pretty knight had come for her!

"Nine knights then . . . and one weak king," James grumbled. "I see no threat here! Sir Fredrick is a fool!"

"The Crimson Knight has sent word by messenger—a challenge to Sir Fredrick . . . individual battle," the soldier said. "He calls out Sir Fredrick for laying hand to the wife of Sir Broderick Dougray, Karvana's successor king . . . husband to the Scarlet Princess Monet."

"The Crimson Knight is your husband?" Anais exclaimed. Monet simply nodded to Anais in response.

King James laughed; boisterous was his laughter.

"The Crimson Knight?" he roared. "Dacian wed his daughter to a glorified soldier?"

"If you own one drop of true royal blood . . . one breath of honor . . . you will have Sir Fredrick accept his challenge," Monet said. "You are not afraid, are you, James? What are nine men . . . when you command legions?"

Broderick would not approach without a plan to employ. This Monet well knew. Thus she would kindle his charge—whatever it may be.

"You endeavor to sway me . . . for you would see your husband vanquish Sir Fredrick for being the hunter who stole you," King James said.

"Yes," Monet said.

King James clapped gauntleted hands. "Very well! I will allow it! For Fredrick will save me effort . . . by killing your husband for me. Thus, I will not have to bloody my hands, nor linger in waiting to wed you."

Monet wished to shout at him, to tell him the Crimson Knight would best Sir Fredrick with ease. But she said nothing—held her tongue. She knew Broderick's thoughts; somehow she knew what was in his mind. To ride to Karvana with only eight knights at his side: Sir Fredrick was not Broderick's only prey. King James thought nine men could do no harm. He would be careless and arrogant. And when King James was at his zenith, the Crimson Knight would rise and fell a wicked king!

The Crimson Frost

"How is it you came to be wife to Sir Broderick Dougray?" Anais asked.

Monet stood breathless, overcome with wonder at seeing the Crimson Knight approach. Her heart pounded so mad within her bosom she feared it might leap from her body. It had been two nights since she had been held warm in his arms—yet it seemed a lifetime!

"In all this, Anais—in all you have endured of late—still you stand envious and self-serving," Monet answered. She looked to Anais. "He loves me. He loves me with a strength that would see him ride into the battle encampment of his enemy . . . alone. He does not trust King James owns any honor . . . does not know if James's archers will let go their bowstrings upon him. Yet he rides to me . . . there. He comes to me, no matter what stands between us. My father knew the Crimson Knight loved me in such a manner. In the same manner do I love him. This also did my father know. And what does your father know, Anais? A child was beaten by King James's men and offered up less information than you have this day! I pity your father with such a daughter to offer his kingdom . . . for you love naught but yourself. You ask how I came to be wife to Sir Broderick. Heaven smiled upon me, Anais. Pray it has forgiveness in its heart . . . that it may one day smile upon you."

Anais said nothing—only turned her eyes to the crest of the hill where lingered the mounted Knights Exemplar.

Monet watched as Broderick neared. The sun flamed and shone bright on his armor, his crimson banner, with rearing black dragon, licking the breeze as he rode.

He dismounted—approached. Monet's heart leapt as his eyes lingered on her for a moment. It was only a moment that he looked at her. His purpose could spare no risk in distraction.

"Sir Broderick Dougray," King James said, "the great Crimson Knight. I am honored you have ridden to Karvana to watch me conquer your king."

"James of Rothbain," Broderick began. The sound of his voice sent gooseflesh racing over Monet's limbs. "I would call out your first knight, Fredrick Esmund. I challenge him . . . for having dared touch my wife . . . the Scarlet Princess Monet."

James inhaled, smiling an arrogant smile of triumph. "I will honor you in allowing this challenge, Crimson Knight," Sir James said, "but at a price."

"What price do you name?" Broderick asked.

Monet frowned. A price? What price would James ask?

"I will allow this challenge . . . but it must be to the death," James said. "There will be no champion without a challenger dead on the field."

"Done," Broderick said without pause.

"Broderick!" Monet exclaimed. It was well she knew Broderick could best Sir Fredrick in honorable battle. Yet of a sudden, the memory of Sir Fredrick's oft-dishonorable devices entered her mind—when he had bested Broderick in wrestling at Ivan's tournament. Though she called to him, he did not look at her. Monet knew he could not, lest his strength be shaken by fear for her.

"Done," King James said. King James laughed, full foolish in his arrogance. "Sir Fredrick!" James shouted.

"And now I will name my price," Broderick said.

"Your price?" James laughed. "Your wife in return, I suppose." James shook his head. "Now, Sir Broderick . . . you know I am at war. You know your wife is my pawn of triumph."

"The price is not my wife," Broderick said.

"Not your wife?" King James asked. "You do not wish to know her again?"

"Oh, I will know her, James," Broderick said. "But my price for triumphing over Sir Fredrick . . . this will I name when he lies dead at your feet."

King James laughed. "You cannot best him, Sir Broderick. He is too strong . . . too full of hate and loathing. You have been softened by your pretty princess. Even now I can see her in your eyes. You will not be champion. You will bleed out on the ground before her, knowing she will be mine when you are dead."

"I will name my price when Fredrick is dead," Broderick said. "Do you accept this?"

King James chuckled. "Done."

"Done," Broderick said. He turned then and drew a sword from its sheath at his hip, brandishing it high, the sun glinting on the steel blade. "Let all here witness this accord," he shouted. "Soldiers of Rothbain . . . your king will know my price and abide by it when Sir Fredrick is dead. To this you have heard King James agree. I will hold him to it, and so must you . . . for if he claims to be a king worthy of your allegiance, then he will not break such a word as he has given here."

The cocksure smile faded from James's face.

Monet held her breath. It was she feared King James would set his soldiers to Broderick. She knew he was considering doing so, for Broderick had played well at war. If King James ordered his men to kill such an honorable knight as the Crimson Knight of Karvana—if he ordered that they kill a man of such bravery as to ride amidst them for the honor of his wife—then the Rothbainian soldiers would know the true coward their king was. This he could not risk, for dissent and rebellion might nurture in men already fighting to conquer a king for mere sake of the vanity and greed of another. Yet James may yet command it, and well his soldiers might yet follow his orders—even for their uncertainty.

King James's eyes narrowed. He had made his choice, and Monet did not breathe.

"Sir Fredrick!" King James shouted. Monet exhaled—King James would not risk his men failing him.

Sir Fredrick appeared from a gathering of soldiers nearby. He strode to King James and drew his own sword from its sheath.

"Kill him," King James said.

"Of course, my king," Sir Fredrick growled.

Monet's eyes filled with tears. Broderick did not look at her; she knew he could not. She knew there was more unspoken—that Broderick and the great Exemplar Knights on the hill meant more than simple revenge for Sir Fredrick's having taken her. Yet she could not fathom their plan and thus was overcome with sudden fear.

Broderick raised his sword before his face and bent his head to one side, light kissing the blade before dropping his helmet shield with a tap of one gauntlet.

"Such a pretty sword, Sir Broderick," Sir Fredrick laughed, drawing his own helmet shield over his face.

"A pretty sword made for a pretty knight," Broderick said. "It is the Crimson Frost, forged for the Crimson Knight. And it will live famed eternal . . . as the sword that fell Sir Fredrick Esmund."

"You have forgotten Ivan's tournament," Sir Fredrick said. The two men took stance. "Do you remember the pain I put upon you there?"

"I remember only the charger I won when I unhorsed you in the joust," Broderick began, "unhorsed you at first lances."

Of a sudden, Sir Fredrick raised his helmet shield. "Light armored! Or are you a coward, Crimson Knight?"

"Light armored," Broderick said.

"No!" Monet breathed. She shook her head, letting tears spill from her eyes.

"You see, Sir Fredrick is sure of victory, Princess," King James said to her. "He calls Sir Broderick to light armor."

Monet watched as two squires approached, one at Sir Fredrick's armor, one at Broderick's. Quickly the squires removed Broderick's and Sir Fredrick's armor, till not but vambraces, greaves, and sabatons remained. Light armor left a knight's body full vulnerable, save his forearms and lower legs. Monet knew Broderick was the better knight—the stronger knight—yet for weeks and weeks he had known only sparring. She feared Sir Fredrick's hatred and blood-lust would spur him—that Broderick's love for her, his exile, and no doubt his fatigue might find him ill-prepared.

Again the two took stance. Broderick's raven hair, dark yet in the sun, gave him the appearance of strength. There was no sound, save that of the banners in the breeze.

Monet gasped as the Crimson Knight attacked first. Charging at Sir Fredrick, Broderick struck. Sir Fredrick's blade crashed against Broderick's, the sound ringing through the air as a battle bell. Monet covered her mouth with her hands to keep from crying. This was not tournament: this was battle to the death!

Sir Fredrick raised his sword to strike. Blades crashed once more as Broderick defended the blow. Blow for blow they battled, and Monet could not but watch in horror! Each time Sir Fredrick wielded his blade, she feared it would meet with Broderick's flesh. Metal crashing echoed. There was no respite—simply battle—battle that would end in death.

There was a pause then as Broderick and Sir Fredrick circled as two lions stalking prey.

"Are you weary, Crimson Knight?" Sir

Fredrick asked. He was short of breath. Monet thought Sir Fredrick's breathing more labored than Broderick's. Further, Broderick did not seem in the least weakened, and this renewed her hope.

"Of playing at swords with you? Yes," Broderick said.

"Playing at swords?" Sir Fredrick chuckled a light laugh. "I will kill you, Crimson Knight . . . and King James will take your wife to his bed."

"You should not have laid hands on her, Fredrick," Broderick growled. "And I *am* weary of playing at swords."

Broderick quickly took stance. Grasping the blade of the Crimson Frost in one hand, the pommel in the other, he drove the hilt into Sir Fredrick's face. Sir Fredrick reeled back with the force of the blow. He did not fall but raised his sword two-fisted, held high over his head in preparation to strike. Sir Fredrick did not strike, however, nor did his blade meet Broderick's. It could not—for the sword, the Crimson Frost, was through Sir Fredrick Esmund—hilt full against his chest, blade jutting from his back.

Monet gasped as Sir Fredrick Esmund looked to the Crimson Knight, who held the hilt at his chest—the Crimson Knight, who had run him through.

Clutching the dying man's throat in his free

hand, Broderick drew near to Sir Fredrick's face. "I told you . . . I am weary of playing at swords," the Crimson Knight said.

Pushing at Sir Fredrick's shoulder, the Crimson Knight drew his sword from the body of his enemy. Sir Fredrick Esmund crumpled to the ground.

"You will leave him!" Broderick shouted to the Rothbainian soldiers standing silent in astonished awe. "You will leave this blackguard thus . . . till his blood is wholly frozen and a crimson frost upon him!"

"Broderick!" Monet cried. She started toward him, but King James held tight to her arm.

"You will remain here," James growled, "or I will order him killed."

"Would your soldiers yet follow such a cowardly king?" Monet whispered.

King James looked to her. His eyes narrowed, yet she knew she had kept doubt in his mind.

"And now, King James," Broderick said, "for my price as victor in this battle."

"You fell Princess Monet's captor, Crimson Knight," King James said. "I have allowed this. I will allow no more."

"I fell the man who took my wife," Broderick growled. "I have yet to fell her captor."

King James's eyes narrowed. "What is this price you think you may demand of me?"

"I wish you to prove your worth to the people

of Rothbain," Broderick said. "I wish you to prove to your men that you are a king who owns honor . . . a king worth the sacrifice of their lives on the battlefield of greed and vexation."

Monet looked to the soldiers standing near. Their brows furrowed with thoughtful interest.

"I am their king! They are bound to me because I am their king!" James shouted.

"You gave your word . . . before all these men of Rothbain who battle for your purpose," Broderick shouted. "Not for theirs. Not because they are threatened. But for your purpose alone. Then I would have you show them. I would have you prove that you deserve to command them."

"I do not need to prove myself," King James said. "I am their king!"

Monet stepped back from James. He was distracted and had released her arm. She looked at the faces of the soldiers—saw their doubt growing.

"I have your word . . . here . . . before your men. You agreed to my price before I battled Sir Fredrick," Broderick said. "Did not you hear your king agree?"

King James looked to his men. "You will hang for treason! Everyone will hang if you do not abide by my commands!"

"Who will hang them, James?" Broderick asked. "Will they hang one another?"

James glanced back to Monet. "Take her! Do not let her away!"

Monet paused, yet no guard laid hand to her. The soldiers of Rothbain were in doubt of their monarch.

King James straightened broad shoulders. Monet could see he was pensive—desperate, but pensive.

"Perhaps you are right, Sir Broderick," King James said. "Perhaps I should display my worth to my men. I have asked them to battle with and for me. I must show them I am their king. What is your price?"

"A pledge of individual battle," Broderick said.

"You wish me to battle you as Sir Fredrick has only just so pitifully done?"

"I do not challenge you, King James," Broderick said, "though it would serve me well to see you run through. No . . . the challenge comes from another."

"Who?" James growled. "Dacian?"

"No."

Monet watched as Broderick pointed to the Exemplar Knights on the crest of the hill. As Broderick raised one hand, one Exemplar rode down the hill toward the encampment. Armor glinting, the knight riding carried an emerald banner with the symbol of a white armored arm—the symbol of strength, of a great leader.

The horse bearing the great Knight Exemplar

reared, stomping the ground before King James.

He lifted his helmet shield, and Monet gasped in a whisper, "Bronson!"

King James sneered as he said, "Ackley Carrington! Defiler of princesses!"

"James of Rothbain," Bronson growled. "Coward!"

"My helmet! At once," James shouted. He was full armored, save his helmet. A small squire stepped forward, handing King James his helmet. King James put on his helmet, drawing its shield over his face. "Men of Rothbain! Now you shall see how worthy your king is of your loyalty . . . and your lives!"

Bronson dismounted and drew his sword. Holding the blade before his face as Broderick had done, he tipped his head to one side and light kissed the glinting steel. Bronson dropped his helmet shield and attacked.

James shouted and Bronson roared as steel clashed! King James was known as a fierce king—a battle-ready beast. Yet Bronson fought strong and sure. All eyes were upon the battle before them—the battle of king against banished knight. And though she was fearful for Bronson—though tears moistened her cheeks at realizing then that Sarah was indeed King Dacian's sister and her own aunt—still, she slowly crept aside. She would not linger within reach of any Rothbainian.

Blade met armor, blade met blade, and the battle between King James and the great Exemplar Knight Sir Ackley Carrington raged on.

Monet drew near to Anais. She took hold of her arm, capturing her attention—for even Anais was overcome with the battle. Slowly, she led Anais to the margin of King James's encampment.

"Anais, you must run!" Monet said. "Run to the wood . . . there . . . near the crest of the hill! There stand the Exemplars . . . and your father."

Anais started to run, yet paused.

"What of you?" Anais asked.

"I will not leave without my husband," Monet said.

Anais nodded and started toward the wood.

Monet looked to the encampment—the place where Bronson battled King James—as, of a sudden, there was no noise upon the air. The battle had ceased—but who was champion?

"Broderick!" Monet breathed. If James was victor, he would sure order his men to murder Broderick. She owned no thought of herself then—only Broderick. Thus, she hastened to the place where soldiers stood in silence.

Monet slowed as she approached. Broderick was there, well and unharmed. No archers readied to let fly arrows; no soldiers drew swords. She moved closer still—glanced to see the great Knights Exemplar riding down the hill toward her.

King James lay upon the ground, the tip of Bronson's sword pressed to his throat above his breastplate. King James reached up, removing his helmet.

"You have bested me, Ackley," James panted. "Once again . . . it would seem."

"I should run my blade through your coward's throat!" Bronson growled.

"Perhaps," King James said.

"You will cease this battle, James," Bronson said.

Broderick looked up, catching sight of Monet. She started toward him, but he held up a hand to stay her. All was not safe as yet.

"The white flag!" someone shouted. "Dacian approaches!"

Monet felt tears leave her eyes to moisten her cheeks as her father approached, mounted on his white charger. Next to him rode Sarah. As understanding washed over her, Monet gazed at the lost Princess Eden—Bronson's Sarah.

"Father!" Monet whispered as he neared.

Channing was there too, mounted behind Wallace. The castle guards were heavily armed and surrounded the royal party. The great Knights Exemplar also surrounded the king and the Princess Eden.

"Sir Ackley Carrington," King Dacian said.

Bronson straightened his posture. "My king!" Sir Ackley answered.

"You have bested King James?" Dacian asked.

"I have."

"Then the war is ended." Dacian said.

"Ended?" King James said, struggling to his feet. "Ended?" Turning to his soldiers, King James shouted, "I have proven my honor! I have proven myself a king! You would turn so quickly on the king who only endeavors to ensure your prosperity? Have I not led you to valiance? Many times to victory?"

Monet could see the Rothbainian soldiers' countenances. Their doubt in their king was fast fading.

"Would you have a knight humble you? Would you see a knight of Karvana slay your own first knight—the First Knight of Rothbain—without consequence? Would you see your king threatened? I ask you . . . would you see a Karvanian sit on the throne of Rothbain?"

The soldiers' hearts were turned back to their king, but Broderick's wit was quick!

"Knights of Karvana—attack!" he shouted.

At once, there was the clash of steel as the Exemplar Knights rode toward the place where Sir Ackley and the Crimson Knight stood, backs together, fighting Rothbainian soldiers.

"Monet!" King Dacian shouted.

Monet looked to her father as he rode to her.

"Up the hill! At once!" he told her as he drew his sword and rode toward the battle.

Of a sudden, Tripp was at her side—as if Broderick had sent the horse to her. She clung to his mane and mounted—rode up the hill with Sarah and Channing and Wallace at her side.

A great roar commenced, and she looked to see not only villagers from Ballain but also Alvarian soldiers charging down the hill toward the battlefield. Anais stood on the hill's crest—with her father.

As Monet and the others reached them, King Rudolph said, "King James will not live to threaten Karvana . . . or Pershtera! He will die for taking Anais!"

Monet turned Tripp, searching the battle below for Broderick. He was there, his raven hair a beacon to her heart.

"He is not armored!" Monet cried.

"He is the Crimson Knight," Sarah said. "And he has Sir Ackley Carrington at his back."

"Aunt!" Monet whispered as Sarah reached forth and clasped her hand. "And Channing." She wept for joy at seeing them safe, yet she wept for fear as the battle raged below. "Broderick . . . my love!" she breathed.

The Crimson Knight felt steel graze his arm. He turned, plunging the Crimson Frost into a Rothbainian who endeavored to kill him. He fell another enemy—another. Yet he was not armored, and there were twenty men to his one—

to Bronson's one—to each Knight Exemplar's one! He could hear the pounding hooves. He hoped it was approach of the villagers Stroud led. Still, they were villagers, and these were Rothbainian soldiers.

He looked to Bronson—turned to see his friend catch hold of his arm, blood flowing from a deep wound. They would not survive long at twenty to one. He defended a blow and glanced about.

He looked up and saw King Dacian mounted on his white charger and slaying the enemy to his left and right. This was a good king before him! This was his king—the king who had chosen him, Sir Broderick Dougray, as his successor! This king could not fall!

"Where is James?" he shouted to Bronson.

"There! Just there!" Bronson pointed through the battle to King James, standing behind a line of soldiers shouting orders.

He looked to Bronson. "I would not leave you," he said.

"Go!" Bronson shouted. "Sever the head of the serpent, and it dies! Go!"

He went then—the Crimson Knight of Karvana advanced upon Rothbain's king. Three men he fell—four more. A vision of the bloody fields of Ballist was upon him—a vision of the Reaper and the crimson frost. He pressed one hand to his belly as he fell another soldier with the blade of the Crimson Frost. He felt it there—against his body—the leather pouch with his treasured token it in.

"Monet!" he breathed as he ran the soldier through. He advanced, the token at his chest burning—spurring him on with consummate power!

"James of Rothbain!" he shouted. James looked up, anger pure on his face—and Broderick charged forth. There were but three men between him and the wicked king who endeavored to crush Karvana—three men between him and the man who had taken Monet from him—three men who fell by the Crimson Frost wielded well in the hand of the Crimson Knight.

"She is my wife!" Broderick shouted as he stood before James. "And this is my kingdom!"

"Knights are not meant to have princesses! And this kingdom shall be mine!" James shouted as he attacked. Broderick blocked the blow—and another. Near mad with fury, roaring his strength, the Crimson Knight of Karvana wielded the Crimson Frost wide and strong—severed the head of the serpent.

Sir Broderick Dougray stood over the beheaded King of Rothbain. The Reaper was reaping at his feet, yet the sound of battle began to hush at his back. King James was dead.

"Broderick!"

It was Dacian's voice.

Broderick turned. His king was there—and eight great Knights Exemplar.

"Behold, Sir Broderick Dougray!" King Dacian shouted. "Son of Kendrick Nathair! First Knight of Karvana! Favored Warrior of King Dacian! Commander of the First Legion! Commander of the Second Legion! Slayer of a Thousand Enemies! Blood Warrior of Ballist! Protector of the Kingdom! Guardian and husband of the Scarlet Princess! The Crimson Knight . . . Karvana's successor king!"

Such a roar Broderick had never before heard. The Rothbainians began to retreat as Ballainians, Ballistians, and Karvanians from the nearby village cheered. Broderick looked to see Alvarian soldiers as well. All hailed the Crimson Knight, heralded of the king—he who had severed the serpent's head and ended the war with Rothbain!

Still, for all the glory that they would heap upon him—king and subject alike—Broderick thought not of it. In that moment his heart was glad with living—living for one purpose.

"Monet?" the Crimson Knight whispered as he looked to the hill crest beyond. There stood Tripp—the Scarlet Princess on his back.

"Broderick!" Monet breathed. She saw his raven hair—saw her father, the King of Karvana, dismount—saw Broderick take his place on the white charger—saw the great Crimson Knight of Karvana spur the charger toward her.

As tears streamed over her cheeks—as her heart beat so wild and mad as to cause her pain—Monet whispered, "On, Tripp! Carry me to your master. Carry me to my love."

It seemed an eternity! Though Tripp was as swift as the wind—though it was mere moments—it seemed an eternity before Monet felt the strength of Broderick's arms about her, the moist heat of his mouth crushed to hers. She cared not that the multitude of peasants, soldiers, knights, and royalty looked on. She only cared for him—for her Broderick—her beloved.

"Forgive me, Monet," Broderick breathed when he had kissed her long. "I should never have let you leave the smithy without—"

His words were silenced by her fingers pressed to his lips.

"Hush," she breathed. She reached up, combing trembling fingers through his hair, gazing into the pure sapphire of his eyes. "It was no fault of yours," she whispered. "No fault of yours. Yet look what you have done."

Broderick frowned. "I . . . I killed the warring king?" he mumbled. Monet smiled, for his humility was only further proof of his greatness.

"You preserved me in exile," she said. "You hailed forth the great Exemplar Knights from their hiding . . . and you gathered the people of the kingdom in unity."

He pressed a bloodied hand to her cheek, yet she did not draw back from it.

"I care only that I have you, Monet," he said. "All I did . . . I did to hold you . . . to taste your kiss . . . to hear your voice." He smiled, though she saw the excess moisture lingering in his sapphire eyes. "All I did . . . I did for the champion's prize."

Monet smiled. "Then claim it, my pretty knight," she whispered, weeping with joy. "Claim your prize. Claim me as your token of favour . . . for I have ever been yours, Broderick." She trailed soft fingers over his handsome brow, whispering, "Thus, ever can Karvana trust . . . no enemy will ever thrust . . . his blood or bones of flesh to dust . . . for my pretty knight is strong and just . . . and no crimson frost will bind him."

There he kissed her. As all Karvana cheered, the Scarlet Princess Monet bathed in the bliss of the Crimson Knight's kiss.

After

The herald stepped to the stage. Dressed in the sapphire tunic with black shield and fisted gauntlet of his lord, he raised one hand.

"Good people!" the herald began. The crowd hushed—waited. "It is honored I am to herald my lord to the final joust of King Broderick's great tournament of knights!" A deafening roar burst forth as the people of Karvana and all others attending King Broderick's tournament cheered the young herald. The herald raised a hand, and the crowd settled once more.

"It is well you know my lord . . . and well you know he bears the favour of the Sapphire Princess of Karvana, Princess Afton, in this, her father's tournament!" The crowd roared their approval, and the herald again waited for the noise to settle.

"Thus, I herald to my King Broderick, to my Queen Monet . . . to all kings, queens, knights, and nobles who here attend . . . and to you good people of the Kingdom of Karvana . . . to those of all other realms," the herald began, "I offer my lord for your approval! Sir Channing Snow . . . Son of Drake Elmar . . . First Knight of Karvana . . . Favored Warrior of the Crimson King . . . Commander of the Fourth Legion . . . Vanquisher of Enemies . . . Beloved of the Scarlet Queen . . . Protector of the Kingdom!"

Queen Monet rose from her seat, cheering as Channing's charger entered the jousting arena. The white charger, robed in mail and sapphire robes, reared once—twice—thrice. The gathering of subjects, nobles, and royals cheered as Sir Channing Snow—First Knight of Karvana—raised his lance in honor of his king and queen. Tears brimmed in the queen's eyes as she looked at the brave young knight—to the man who had once been a boy—a boy who had saved the kingdom for his infinite courage and loyalty. Channing's shield of black with white-fisted gauntlet shone bright, as did his armor.

"He will unhorse this Sir Fulton of Avaron," King Broderick said aside to Lord Ackley Carrington.

Lord Ackley laughed. "Even Stroud could not unhorse Sir Fulton," he said. "Nor Wallace, nor Kenley. If my sons cannot unhorse this knight, then your Sir Channing will not . . . even at three lances."

Monet smiled at her Aunt Eden. Eden smiled as well.

"Our Stroud did not hope to win the hand of Karvana's princess," Eden said to her husband.

"Will you grant Channing the hand of Afton if

he triumphs as champion, Broderick?" Ackley asked.

"Yes," Broderick said, "though I will grant Afton's hand to Channing whether or not he wins the tournament. However, I do not know if Channing full believes my assurance of this."

Broderick chuckled, and Monet smiled at her husband—the Crimson King of Karvana. Gazing lovingly at him, she thought it did not seem so many years before that he had reared his own charger in King Ivan's arena—that he had triumphed and won the great champion's prize. He was as handsome as ever he had been; Monet fancied he was more handsome. She smiled, thinking the white at his temples well served to embellish his comely countenance—only accented the smoldering sapphire of his eyes. How Afton did resemble him! Monet glanced to her children, seated in the stands nearby. As her sons, the Princes Bronson, Marius, and Dacian, owned Monet's amethyst eyes and ebony hair, so Princess Afton owned her father's raven locks and eyes of flaming sapphire. Monet smiled as she watched Afton's gaze affixed to Channing, her countenance beaming with admiration and immeasurable love.

Ackley laughed, saying, "Then I will not wager! For if the hand of Afton is Sir Channing's inducement to unhorse Sir Fulton . . . only a fool would wager against him!" The familiar, beloved, and boisterous laughter of Lord Ackley Carrington echoed through the roaring of the crowd.

"Age is sore upon my love," Eden said, gazing at her husband, one of only three Exemplar Knights still living. "Yet his laughter is still strong . . . and warms my heart as ever it has."

"As it warms mine," Monet said. She was, of a sudden, somewhat saddened at the thought of only three Knights Exemplar still owning breath. After the long-passed battle that found King James beheaded at the hand of the Crimson Knight, Monet's father, King Dacian, had bestowed great wealth, title, and honor on those brave and loyal once-banished knights who rode to Karvana's aid. All the long-lost Exemplars had returned to Karvana. Each Exemplar was honored to sit at Dacian's table round of conferring, and each remained at the table until he was heralded to paradise or was stricken too aged or ill to rise and confer. One by one the great aged Knights Exemplar faded to heaven, till only three remained. Lord Ackley was one—and Lord Alum. Lord Aldrich yet lived, though too weak to attend the conferring table or tournament. Thus he lingered in Karvana Far with the aged King Dacian, who had abdicated his throne to his daughter, the Scarlet Princess, and her successor king husband near ten years before.

The crowd fell silent of a sudden. Monet looked

to the arena as the banner bearer dropped the starting banner. Sir Channing's mount reared; the First Knight of Karvana leveled his lance. The thunder of hooves beat the ground as the two knights bore down. Monet did not draw breath. Sir Channing's lance was leveled and steady, as was the lance of his challenger. A brutal crash echoed then as Sir Channing's lance struck armor—shattered—unhorsing Sir Fulton.

The cheering roar of the crowd was deafening! Monet clapped, calling out her delight at Sir Channing's well-won victory. Broderick turned to her, smiling. He took her face between powerful hands and kissed her firm on the mouth. Blissful in his kiss, Monet pressed her hand to his chest—felt the leather pouch yet hidden beneath his kingly robes.

Breaking the seal of their lips, Broderick smiled and said, "Our Channing has triumphed!" Yet his smile faded, and Monet's eyes filled with tears at the sight of the moisture full in her husband's. "Still, I have lost my daughter this day," he whispered.

Monet tenderly caressed his strong jaw with the back of her soft hand. "No," she said. "You have only gained another son."

Broderick nodded and coughed once as Lord Ackley pounded him hard on the back with approval.

"I have not seen such strength in jousting since

the Crimson Knight of Karvana endeavored to win the champion's prize at Avaron many years ago," Lord Ackley chuckled.

"I would yet face any challenge or enemy for hope of winning that prize again," Broderick said, and Monet could not resist. Taking hold of the front of Broderick's kingly robe, she raised herself to press lips with his. As the king's arms bound his queen against his body as he endeavored to drink nectar from her lips, the crowd cheered once more—for never was there a kingdom so happy in the love of their king and queen as was the Kingdom of Karvana.

"Father!"

Broderick sighed as he ended their kiss, and Monet giggled at the excitement in her daughter's voice.

"Father! Sir Channing has won your tournament! He has won!" Afton cried with delight.

Broderick yet lingered in gazing at Monet.

"How I love you, my pretty knight," Monet said.

"And I love you, my Scarlet Princess," he mumbled.

"Father!" Afton whispered, tugging at her father's ermine-trimmed crimson cloak.

Inhaling deep, King Broderick turned as Sir Channing Snow approached the stands yet mounted on his charger. Sir Channing stepped down from his horse, stepped onto the heralding stage, and took a knee before the Crimson King of Karvana.

"My honor is for you, my king," Sir Channing said. He raised his shattered lance and offered it to the king. Broderick chuckled and accepted the lance.

Tossing it into the arena, however, King Broderick heralded, "Behold the tournament champion . . . Sir Channing Snow! Rise, Sir Channing, and claim your champion's prize . . . the hand of the Sapphire Princess Afton!"

The crowd roared near to thundering all the earth! Monet laughed as Broderick then lifted Afton in strong arms. Afton giggled as her father lowered her into the waiting arms of Sir Channing Snow.

"Are you in earnest, my king?" Sir Channing asked, yet cradling Afton in strong arms.

"I am!" King Broderick said.

"My queen?" Sir Channing asked, looking to Monet.

Again Monet's eyes filled with tears. Could this gallant knight standing before her—this champion, this man with such broad shoulders and comely countenance—could this truly be the brave young page who once stood so brave in defense of his princess and kingdom?

"Your king is most earnest, Sir Channing," she said, "as is your queen."

"Thus, kiss him well, daughter!" Broderick

chuckled. "For he well deserves the champion's prize!"

All of Karvana cheered! Laugher and merriment were heavy on the air—joy and hope and all things good and happy.

Long was the day in celebration of the betrothal of the Sapphire Princess Afton to Sir Channing Snow. Feasting at banquet, honor bestowed, dancing, and all manner of friendly conversation ensued. Many royals were there—King Martin of Avaron and his queen, Lenore. Lord Terrence Langford was there—Lord Terrence Langford, who had won the hand of his lady, the Princess Portia of Norvola. It was even the Queen of Alvar was there—Queen Anais, who had taken the Alvarian throne upon her father's death and never married. The young princes of Karvana reveled in the banquet—in talking of the tournament and the honors earned. Still, it was Sir Channing Snow and his betrothed, the Sapphire Princess Afton, who knew most their zenith, for they loved as deep and as true as the Crimson Knight and the Scarlet Princess had loved—and still loved.

And when the cheering had ceased—when the stands of King Broderick's arena had emptied and the banquet hall of Karvana Castle was quiet—there lingered near the royal mausoleum a man and a woman—a husband and wife—a horseman and peasant girl.

"Do you remember when we came here, after you fell King James," Monet began, "when Father insisted we take the secreted instructions from the place in my mother's tomb and break the seal?"

Broderick placed powerful hands at his wife's waist, pressing her back against the outer wall of the mausoleum. Monet felt gooseflesh prickling her limbs as the smoldering sapphires of his eyes flamed love as he gazed at her.

"I do," he said. His voice was low and alluring, and Monet smiled. "King Dacian bade me break the seal myself—read what he had penned upon the parchments full four years before."

"That I would marry only Sir Broderick Dougray," Monet whispered as Broderick pressed his strong body against her own. "That my true betrothed had ever been Sir Broderick, the Crimson Knight of Karvana—that it was he who was charged with one day ruling Karvana with me."

"I yet cannot fathom he would entrust me with his kingdom. I cannot fathom he would entrust me with his daughter," Broderick said. He bent, placing a lingering kiss on Monet's neck.

"He knew who best would rule the kingdom," Monet said. She reached up, combing her fingers through the raven hair of his head—the snow at his temples. "He knew the people of Karvana loved their great Crimson Knight . . . that you

474

were, and are, the greatest ruler they could know. And he knew I loved you."

"He knew *I* loved *you,*" Broderick said. He kissed her light once—twice—thrice.

In the distance, Monet could hear music. She knew Marius lingered atop the keep as he often did, plucking his lute and singing ballads to cheer or soothe any who may hear him. She smiled as she heard—ever light on the air—the ballad of the Scarlet Princess and the Crimson Knight.

"It is yet ever his favorite," Monet said, warming in her lover's embrace.

"As it is Reynard's," Broderick chuckled. "You would think the people would grow weary of it."

"I never grow weary of it," she said.

"Would you grow weary of me, Monet?" he asked.

Monet giggled. "I only grow weary that you endeavor to tease me . . . instead of kissing me as I desire my pretty knight should."

Lips pressed then—blended in passion—in promise and love eternal. As the Crimson King of Karvana and his Scarlet Queen lingered in loving, the voice of the Minstrel Marius floated soft on the air . . .

Oh, he holds her still in his power—safe
in love—boundless-embraced.
As the fragrant wind whispers to them,
they blend kisses, sweet nectar-laced.

And she knows he will hold her
always . . . that he loved before ever
she knew,
For he carries her braid at his bosom,
He yet carries her braid at his bosom,
Still he carries her braid at his bosom . . .
o'er his heart . . . his love ever in
view.

The Crimson King Broderick and the
Scarlet Queen Monet of Karvana . . .
begat the Sapphire Princess Afton.

The Sapphire Princess Afton wed
Sir Channing Snow . . .
who did inherit the taken Kingdom of Rothbain
upon the death of his wife's brother.
King Channing and the Sapphire Queen Afton
of Rothbain . . .
begat the Princess Vanya.

The Princess Vanya wed Prince Hillton
of Avaron.
King Hillton and Queen Vanya of Avaron
begat the Princess Felice.

The Princess Felice of Avaron wed
Prince Michael of the Kingdom of Graces.
King Michael and Queen Felice of the Kingdom
of Graces thus begat the princess . . .
Saphyre Snow.

About the Author

Marcia Lynn McClure's intoxicating succession of novels, novellas, and e-books—including *The Visions of Ransom Lake, A Crimson Frost, The Pirate Ruse,* and most recently *The Chimney Sweep Charm*—has established her as one of the most favored and engaging authors of true romance. Her unprecedented forte in weaving captivating stories of western, medieval, regency, and contemporary amour void of brusque intimacy has earned her the title "The Queen of Kissing."

Marcia, who was born in Albuquerque, New Mexico, has spent her life intrigued with people, history, love, and romance. A wife, mother, grandmother, family historian, poet, and author, Marcia Lynn McClure spins her tales of splendor for the sake of offering respite through the beauty, mirth, and delight of a worthwhile and wonderful story.

Books are produced in the United States using U.S.-based materials	Books are printed using a revolutionary new process called THINKtech™ that lowers energy usage by 70% and increases overall quality	Books are durable and flexible because of Smyth-sewing	Paper is sourced using environmentally responsible foresting methods and the paper is acid-free

Center Point Large Print
600 Brooks Road / PO Box 1
Thorndike, ME 04986-0001 USA

(207) 568-3717

US & Canada:
1 800 929-9108
www.centerpointlargeprint.com